FIRE AND THUNDER ON THE PLAIN

When a summer storm struck two nights later, so did the renegades.

They waited until the thunder and lightning became intense enough to stampede the herd. With the long-horns running toward the south, and the riders trying to head them, the band of outlaws rode in from the north. Slipping in behind the hard-riding cowboys, they began shooting.

When Ten first heard the shots, he thought it was his own riders trying to head the herd. He changed his mind when a slug burned its way across his thigh, and another ripped off his hat.

Ten reined up, drew his Henry, and began firing at muzzle flashes mixed in with the stampeding herd . . . .

THE CHISHOLM TRAIL

Ralph
Compton

St. Martin's Paperbacks

This is a work of fiction, based on actual trail drives of the Old West. Many of the characters appearing in the Trail Drive Series were very real, and some of the trail drives actually took place. But the reader should be aware that, in the developing of characters and events, some fictional literary license has been employed. While some of the characters and events herein are purely the creation of the author, every effort has been made to portray them with accuracy. However, the inherent dangers of the trail are real, sufficient unto themselves, and seldom has it been necessary to enhance their reality.

THE CHISHOLM TRAIL

Copyright © 1993 by Ralph Compton.

Map on p. ix by David Lindroth, based upon material supplied by the author.

All rights reserved.

For information address St. Martin's Press, 175 Fifth Avenue, New York, NY 10010.

EAN: 978-0-312-92953-4

Printed in the United States of America

St. Martin's Paperbacks edition / April 1993

20   19   18   17   16   15   14

Respectfully dedicated to the working cowboy. His is a saga sparked by the turmoil following the Civil War, and the passing of more than a century has not diminished the flame. While the old days and the old ways are gone, and the trails have grown dim, the working cowboy—from south Texas to the high plains—is alive and well. Our hats are off to you, pardner, wherever you are.

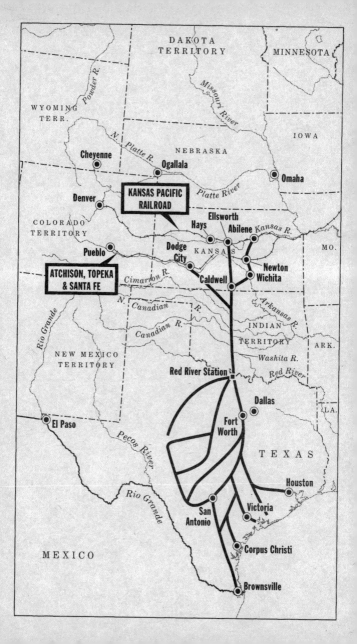

AUTHOR'S FOREWORD

*J*esse Chisholm was born in Tennessee, the son of a Scottish father and a Cherokee mother. He spoke fourteen Indian languages and was trusted by whites and Indians alike. Many captive white and Indian children were returned to their families through his efforts. He was a frontiersman and scout who "got things done." In 1832 he helped lay out a wagon road from Fort Smith, Arkansas, to Fort Towson, in Indian Territory. In 1836 he guided a group of gold seekers up the Arkansas River to the mouth of the Little Arkansas. Their destination was the site where Wichita, Kansas, would stand more than thirty years later. The gold mine didn't exist, but Chisholm liked the area. He returned and built a trading post on the Canadian River.

Chisholm often supplied Indian cattle to the military at Fort Scott, close to the Missouri border. For ten years, from 1843 to 1853, he drove herds along a military road that followed the border of eastern Kansas, taking cattle north to Westport and Kansas City. When Congress created Kansas Territory (Kansas and Nebraska Act—May 30, 1854), the route Chisholm took was called the "Kansas Road."

But there was trouble ahead for those who drove Texas longhorns to the northern markets. In 1855 there was an epidemic of "Texas fever" in Missouri, the result of a tick carried by Texas longhorns. While the longhorns were themselves immune, the tick was fatal to other cattle. Missouri took the issue to court and passed a law forbidding Texas cattle to enter the state. The controversy continued until 1861, when the rumblings of war became reality. The Civil War closed all the trails.

By war's end there were five million wild longhorns in the Texas brakes, but they were just as unwelcome as ever in Missouri. Texas needed a miracle, but it didn't come until February 1867, when the Kansas Pacific Railroad reached Abilene. At that time, Jesse Chisholm's soon-to-be-famous trail stretched from Red River to within a few miles of the Kansas town. Strangely enough, this most celebrated of all cattle trails was established in 1865 for a totally different reason. The government had decided to move three thousand Wichita Indians to a reservation in the southern part of Indian Territory.

Major Henry Shanklin, in charge of moving the Indians, arranged for Jesse Chisholm to open a trail and establish supply points along the way through Indian Territory to the banks of the Red River. The proposed trail would cross the Salt Fork, Cimarron, and North and South Canadian rivers. These were treacherous waters, fraught with ever-shifting quicksand, where a safe crossing today might become a death trap tomorrow. With this in mind, Chisholm started from the Arkansas River with a large train of teams, driving before him a herd of one hundred horses. The animals were driven back and forth across each river until it was safe for crossing.

The Wichita Indians followed, with thousands of ponies, accompanied by many mounted soldiers and guards. This group, passing over the trail blazed by Chisholm, formed a solid, beaten road. The area from which the Wichitas were moved later became the site of Wichita, Kansas. Once the railroad reached Abilene, it became the nearest point from which Texas longhorns could be shipped to eastern markets.

The original Chisholm Trail led only from Wichita to

the Red River, but as the rails moved west, Chisholm's wagon road became the most direct route to northern markets. By 1870 every Texas trail from Austin to the Gulf Coast was tied to Chisholm's trail on the banks of the Red, and as the rails moved west, so did the trail. When the railroad reached Dodge in 1872, it became the queen of all cattle towns.

As a frontier scout and ambassador to the plains tribes, Jesse Chisholm had no peer, but he is remembered for the blazing of a trail that became western history. Ironically, Chisholm never knew of the glory days of his namesake. He died in Indian Territory in the spring of 1868.

PROLOGUE

$\mathcal{J}$esse Chisholm enjoyed an occasional trip to St. Louis, but not this one. He was there in response to a letter from Josiah Buckner, headmaster at the St. Louis Academy for Young Men. Buckner hadn't gone into detail, but he hadn't needed to. The problem would be Tenatse, now seventeen, the illegitimate result of Chisholm's affair with a young Cherokee woman.

The American Civil War had erupted when Tenatse had been thirteen, and it had seemed like the sensible thing to do, sending the boy away to school. There had been problems enough for Jesse Chisholm. Thanks to the war, he was torn between loyalties. Born and reared among the Cherokees, he had owned slaves and had embraced the southern culture. On the other hand, he had long been in close association with the Office of Indian Affairs, in the nation's capital. He counted among his friends the personnel at many of the frontier forts. Thus he had been forced to walk a thin line between the Union and the Confederacy. Now the war was over and the nation was in mourning over the assassinated Abraham Lincoln, shot down by a southern sympathizer. The South had been beaten to its knees, but nobody had won. God alone knew what lay ahead. Chisholm left the street and made his way across the well-kept, shaded grounds of the academy. It was a sprawling complex of red brick, its wooden parts painted an ugly mud-gray. It had always reminded Chisholm of a prison. Perhaps it had that same effect on young Tenatse.

The elderly woman at the desk in the reception parlor personally led Chisholm to Buckner's office. Jesse put his feet down carefully, lest his boots make some unwelcome noise. People passed them in the hall without a sound. It was eerie. He wondered what the penalty was for violating that profound silence. His escort knocked on Buckner's door and was given permission to enter. Instead, she opened the door and stepped aside. Chisholm entered, and she closed the door behind him. Buckner stood up behind his mahogany desk.

"Good morning, Mr. Chisholm. Please be seated."

Chisholm took the chair to the left of Buckner's desk. The headmaster sat down in his leather-upholstered swivel chair. He was bald, wore steel-rimmed spectacles, and had low-hanging jowls. He reminded Chisholm of a bulldog owned by one of the officers at Fort Gibson.

"I presume," said Buckner, "you know why I've asked you here."

"I have a fair-to-middling idea," said Chisholm. "But let's not beat around the bush, Mr. Buckner. What's he done this time, and what do you aim to do with him?"

"To answer your first question," said Buckner, "it would be simpler to tell you what he *hasn't* done. Curfew means nothing to him. He comes and goes as he pleases. He has been forbidden to play cards anywhere on this campus, at any time. He is indifferent to punishment. He counters all our efforts with the stoicism of . . . of . . ."

"An Indian," finished Chisholm. "What else?"

"Have you any idea where and how he spends his time?"

Chisholm said nothing, waiting. It was a question needing no answer. It was what Buckner was building up to.

He wiped his brow and continued. "He's been hanging around the dives along the waterfront, gambling with the undesirable element that frequents such places. His favorite seems to be a den of iniquity called the Emerald Dragon. His last visit there ended in a brawl in which he injured seven men, several of them seriously. One of them almost bled to death from being thrown through a window. The police finally subdued him and came after me."

"And?"

"They refused to release him unless I paid his fine and took responsibility for him. Naturally I did not."

"Naturally," said Chisholm, "so he's still in jail."

"He's still in jail."

Clearly, he would have liked to add, "where he belongs," but resisted the temptation. He opened his desk drawer and took out an envelope.

"As for what I intend to do with this unruly, incorrigible young man, I believe this will adequately answer your second question. Although it is now mid-June, I am refunding your tuition from the first of the month through the end of this year. You will find the boy's belongings packed and in the hall, near the door where you came in."

Buckner looked at him with an almost smile, as though expecting him to protest. Silently vowing to deny him further satisfaction, Chisholm got to his feet and put on his hat. He took the envelope from Buckner's desk and walked out without a word. He yanked the door shut behind him with a satisfying crash, stalking through the reception area and down the hall. There was only a worn duffel bag awaiting him, and it wasn't quite full. Did it contain all Tenatse's belongings? He didn't care. He wanted only to be shut of this formal, dreary place. Shouldering the bag, he stepped out of the gloom and into the welcome sunshine.

"Seventy-five dollars," said police sergeant McDaniel, "and he's all yours. Two-thirds of that's his fine for disorderly conduct and inciting a riot, and the rest is for damage to the saloon. The barman knocked him sense-less, so he didn't kill nobody, but there was some sore heads, includin' his. Here, let me get you his stuff, an' then I'll get him."

He opened a desk drawer and brought out a canvas sack. From it, he removed three items. There was a worn deck of cards secured with a length of string, a Navy Colt revolver, and a throwing knife.

"No money," said Chisholm.

"None that we could find. Some of them likely rolled him 'fore we got there. It's that kind of place."

Chisholm dropped the deck of cards into his coat pocket. The Colt looked well-used, and he picked it up carefully. He made sure it held only five shells and that the firing pin rested on an empty chamber. He then slipped it under his belt, muzzle down. The throwing knife was half a foot long, a flat piece of steel, both edges of its blade honed razor-keen. It had a narrow, flat handle and was blade-heavy. In skilled hands it could be deadly. Wrapping a bandanna around the le-thal blade, he put the weapon in his coat pocket with the deck of cards. If Sergeant McDaniel expected a re-action, he was disappointed. Chisholm said nothing. The sergeant took a ring of keys from a desk drawer and got to his feet.

"I'll get him," he said.

Tenatse wore his hair short. The jet black of it, his high cheekbones, and the bronze of his skin were a star-tling contrast to his eyes. They were pale blue. Chisholm hadn't seen him in a year, and he was shaken at the change in him. Physically, Tenatse was as much a man as he'd ever be. He stood more than six feet tall, and weighed at least 180. He wore drab-gray shirt and trou-sers, with sleeves and legs ridiculously short. He seemed to have grown from a boy to a man so rapidly that the transition hadn't allowed him time to change clothes. He looked at Chisholm with a twinkle in his eyes.

"Howdy, Jess. Sorry I ain't wearin' my Sunday go-tomeetin' suit. This outfit's on loan from the jail. I reckoned old man Buckner would be so glad to be rid of me that he'd let you in long enough to get my clothes, anyhow. Did he?"

"There's your bag," said Chisholm. "It's all they gave me. Take it back yonder and dig out something that fits you decent."

Tenatse slung the bag over his shoulder and turned back down the hall.

"That bunch at the Dragon give him the full treatment," said McDaniel. "When we got there, 'cept for the gun, knife, and cards, they'd picked him clean as a skint coyote. His duds was in rags."

Tenatse emerged wearing Levi's, a faded blue shirt, and run-over boots. "I need a hat," he said.

He balanced the duffel bag on his shoulder, and when they left the jail, they walked in silence until they reached a park. They found a wrought-iron bench beneath an oak, and Tenatse stretched out his long legs, resting his feet on the duffel bag.

"I reckoned old Buckner would kick me out," said Tenatse.

"I've never seen anything pleasure a man more," said Chisholm.

"Well, hell, Jess, I can read and write. What more do you expect from a no-account Injun?"

"The truth. You aimed for Buckner to boot you out, didn't you?"

"What if I did? I'd have been out in six months, anyhow. All they want is your money. If I'd run off, he'd have just had the law drag me back. I'm underage, and the only way I could escape for good was for you to come and take me off their hands. Buckner had to *want* to be rid of me."

"So you started a fight."

"This big rooster called me a damn slick-dealin', no-account, half-breed Injun, three generations lower than a yellow-bellied coyote. Then he got a mite insulting. I only hit him once, and the clumsy bastard fell through a window."

"Twenty-five dollars worth of window," said Chisholm. *"Were* you slick-dealing?"

"They couldn't prove it. Besides that, after somebody slugged me, they got all their money back. With interest."

"You were cheating, then."

"No more'n I had to. Look, Jess, I'm straight as folks will let me be. I don't cheat unless I'm bein' cheated. A man's got the right to defend himself, whether it's with cards, knives, guns or fists. That bunch was bruisin' for a fight, so I accommodated 'em. I used 'em to get me out of Buckner's clutches. I admit it. You wanted the truth, so here it is. I'm fed up to the gills with town living, neckties, boiled shirts, and Sunday afternoon tea parties. These ain't my kind of people and I want to go home, to the frontier. If I'm that much of a disappointment to you, if you've had a bellyful of me, then I'll go on my own. But I *am* going."

Nothing Tenatse had said had impressed Chisholm until now. Suddenly the years fell away and he saw himself in Ten's place. Caught up in the confines of civilization, the young man's words could well have been his own. Chisholm recalled the days before the war, when the Cherokees had occasionally sold him a herd of Texas cattle. Not being a cattleman himself, he put one of his trusted men in charge of Indian riders and they resold the cattle to forts in Indian Territory. Young Ten had grown up among Indian riders, and in the years before he'd been sent away to school, had held his own as a cowboy on these trail drives into Indian Territory. Chisholm got to his feet, a grin on his weathered face.

"Come on, Ten, we're going home to Indian Territory. It's a wild, violent land, and with the coming of the railroads and the conquering of the hostile tribes, the western frontier will come into its own. It's a time and a place where a man can make some big tracks. Time is *your* friend, but once you've ridden as many trails as I have, it will turn on you, becoming your enemy. Let us not waste any more of it. Let's go home."

Time *was* short, and it was just as well that neither of them knew what lay ahead. In a few short months Ten would be riding the long trails alone. Jesse Chisholm's star was growing dim.

1

Jesse Chisholm and Tenatse took a steamboat south along the Mississippi to its confluence with the Arkansas. At Mound Bayou, Mississippi, they boarded a westbound stern-wheeler, traveling the Arkansas as far as Fort Smith. Once the unpleasant episode in St. Louis was behind them, Jesse Chisholm found that young Tenatse possessed some surprisingly mature ambitions.

"Despite what old man Buckner likely told you," said Ten, "I didn't spend *all* my time playing poker. Sure, I hung around the saloons, but I listened, and I learned. There's millions of wild longhorn cows roaming the rivers and plains of Texas. They're there for a man with enough sand to go in and take them. That's what I aim to do; build a herd and trail-drive it north."

Chisholm, well-known at all the frontier outposts, was assigned a small officer's cabin at Fort Smith. He had left his horse there, and tomorrow he would borrow a horse and saddle for Tenatse. After supper they went to the post store.

"We might as well have left that bag of town clothes in St. Louis," said Chisholm. "Go ahead and outfit yourself for the frontier. There's a new Henry repeater in the gun case. Have them throw that in, along with a thousand rounds of shells."

They returned to their cabin laden with purchases, and the first thing Tenatse did was clean the Henry and load it to capacity. It was the mark of a western man, a frontiersman, and Chisholm watched approvingly.

"You'll be seeing a lot of Fort Smith, Ten. The horses and mules I take in trade are driven here as often as need be. Our other goods, like pelts and hides, are rafted down the Canadian, then shipped from here by steamboat to the port of New Orleans. One of us— maybe you—will need to travel with the next load and meet with our buyers. From what I hear, there'll be Union soldiers occupying all the South, and I don't know how—or if—that's going to affect our moving our trade goods to New Orleans."

"There'll be soldiers in Texas, then. But I'm not a Texan. How's that going to affect my trail drive? Or will it?"

"I'm not sure," said Chisholm. "Federal occupation may hinder the moving of *everything,* including cattle. That's why I want you to take this next load of goods to New Orleans. Don't go running off to Texas just yet. Give it a while, and let's see what the presence of soldiers is going to mean to us."

"I heard talk in St. Louis, after Booth shot the president, that the Union aims to give the South hell. Some Yankee congressmen are blaming all the Rebs for what one man did."

"I'm expecting that," said Chisholm. "Never underestimate the evil of which men are capable in the name of justice. Congress is concerning itself with a vindictive occupation of the South, when those soldiers could be of more benefit to the Union on the frontier. I've devoted—maybe wasted—a good part of my life trying to get some workable peace treaty with the Comanches. The West, especially Texas, won't have any peace until they're beaten. God only knows how many years we are from that, with most of the Union army on a spite mission to the South."

"You stayed out of the war," said Ten, "and you kept me out of it. Now we're both going to feel the aftereffects of it."

"Should you need it, I can help you with the military. I have considerable influence there, because of my work with Indian Affairs. But that won't help you against the Comanches in the Texas brakes. There may be a better way. I'm by no means poor, Ten. I can send you to Texas with enough gold to *buy* a herd."

"Whoa, Jess! What's the use in a man forkin' his own broncs if he ain't man enough to gamble on gettin' throwed and stomped? You'd send me to Texas to *buy* a herd, when the brakes are full of cows for the takin'?"

"No," chuckled Chisholm, "if I was your age, I'd do exactly what you aim to do. I'd get me an outfit, ride to Texas, and commence draggin' them free cows out of the chaparral. I'd take along my Henry rifle, a saddlebag full of shells, and the everlasting hope that I could get in there and out without the Comanches liftin' my hair."

"It's not that I'm ungrateful, Jess, but I want to ride my own trails, stomp my own snakes. You could send a banker from New Orleans or St. Louis to *buy* a herd, but it'll take a *muy bueno hombre* with sand to rope them out of the brush. But I'd be obliged, if you'd loan me enough to buy horses, guns, shells, and supplies. I'll repay you. With interest."

"I'll stake you," said Chisholm, "but wait until the first of the year. Take a couple of trips to New Orleans and see what you can learn about this Federal occupation and how it may affect us. You'll need some time to build yourself an outfit. If you like, you can take your pick of the horses and mules we'll be buying from the Indians. More important, when you ride into those Comanche-infested Texas brakes, take some fighting men with you. When you meet them, you'll recognize them. They'll be the survivors of four years of war, and they've already been to Hell and back."

June 28, 1865, they set out for Indian Territory, Chisholm riding his bay, while Ten rode a borrowed roan. They covered forty-five miles and made camp beside a willow-lined creek. Something had been bothering Jesse Chisholm. He had some questions that needed answers. For all Ten's bold talk, he was still only seventeen and untried. Brawling in a saloon was one thing; facing hostile Indians and outlaws was another. When they'd had their bacon, beans, and coffee, he went to his saddlebags, taking out the Colt, the throwing knife, and the deck of cards.

"Here," he said, handing them to Ten. "The police gave me these."

"Thanks," said Ten. "I'm surprised that bunch at the Dragon didn't grab these, along with all my money. Decent of them."

He dropped the cards into his shirt pocket, slid the Colt under his belt and the throwing knife into a sheath sewn into the inside of his right boot. There was no easy way, so Chisholm took the bull by the horns.

"Where did you get the weapons, Ten?"

"Bought 'em off of some hard-up hombres in the saloons."

Now came the touchy part. It was a question that a prideful man quick with knife and gun might consider an insult. He risked it.

"Have you had a chance to work . . . practice . . . with these weapons?"

Ten caught the hesitation, realized Chisholm was uncomfortable with the question, and he laughed.

"I'm not the fastest gun around, I reckon, but I have some talent for it. And I hit what I'm shootin' at. Watch."

He whipped out the Colt, cocking the hammer as he drew. He fired five times, a continuous drumroll of sound that seemed the prolonged echo of a single shot. From a branch of the tree under which they stood, five pinecones fell, almost at Chisholm's feet. Only one had been hit dead center. The other four had been clipped off neatly, where they had joined the branch.

"There was a border outlaw taught me how to draw and shoot," said Ten. "He was pretty good with a throwin' knife too. He showed me how to pull and throw this one."

He took the deck of cards from his shirt pocket, fanning them out until he found the ace of hearts. Head high on the trunk of the pine, a bubble of resin had seeped out. Ten pressed the back of the card against the gum until it stuck.

"Now stand away from the tree," he said.

Taking ten paces from the pine, he paused, crouched, turned. He held the thin haft of the knife with the thumb and the first two fingers of his right hand, and the act was unbelievably swift. The blade went true, burying itself in the center of the card. Chisholm walked back to the tree. The blade had pierced the red heart, cutting it neatly in half. Ten withdrew the knife, ran it into the ground, and wiped the blade on the leg of his Levi's. He then returned the lethal weapon to its boot sheath.

"There's another question," he said, "likely the most important of all. It's just as well you didn't ask it, because I can't answer it. This tree can't throw its own knife or fire its own gun. When I'm facin' a man, can I shoot as straight or throw as true? I don't know. I believe I can. Have you ever wanted to know somethin', but feared the learnin' of it could be the death of you?"

"More times than I like to remember," said Chisholm, "but it's something a man has to face, else he's not much of a man. Now you'd better reload that Colt. That shooting could bring unwelcome visitors."

"I don't have any more shells. I came off like a tenderfoot, didn't I, emptying the gun at a tree?"

"For a fact," said Chisholm. "That's overkill. If your enemy's dead after one shot, four or five more won't kill him any deader. Never empty your gun at a single opponent, if you can help it. Any Comanche worth his salt can scalp you in considerably less time than it takes to reload. Look in my saddlebags and you'll find a tin of shells for the Colt. I got them last night at Fort Smith. I'm satisfied you can handle knife and Colt, but I want you to get the feel of that Henry and get in the habit of carrying it with you wherever you go. The Colt's good at close range, but the first time your horse is shot from under you at three hundred yards, you'll bless the Henry."

Chisholm's trading post and ranch was on the north bank of the Canadian River, 140 miles west of Fort Smith. Ten hadn't seen the place in four years, and much had changed. The slave quarters were still there, but they were now occupied by entire families of Cherokees. Chisholm needed many hands. There were two barns. An adjoining corral beside the first contained only horses. A similar corral next to the second seemed devoted entirely to mules. Roosters crowed, dogs barked, mules brayed, and from somewhere came the steady thunking of an axe. There were four wagons, all with hay racks, loaded high.

"You've built a town," said Ten.

"There's a dock down by the Canadian, beyond the barns. Built so's we can back the wagons right up to the boats."

"What's that building this side of the first barn?"

"Warehouse for pelts and hides," said Chisholm. "We still have to build a flatboat for the next trip. Three men will be going with you as far as Fort Smith. Once your goods are loaded on a steamboat, you're on your own. When our buyer in New Orleans has approved the bills of lading, you're given a check. Then you can leave."

"You don't need me for this," said Ten. "You must have a dozen men you could trust to represent you."

"I like to think so," said Chisholm, "but I have my reasons for sending you. By the time you reach New Orleans, Washington should have lifted the blockades from southern ports, and it may be possible to get cattle to market by boat. Before the war, trail drivers had a problem in Missouri, and nothing's been done to resolve it. Texas cows carry some kind of disease that doesn't bother them, but it kills other cattle. Missouri has a law that says Texas cows can't enter the state. Violation can get the herd and the riders shot. The railroad is still eighteen months away. I want you to talk to Roberts and Company. Find out how expensive it's going to be, shipping cattle by water to northern markets."

"Trail drives to New Orleans?"

"Do you have a better idea? What good is a herd without a buyer? You can't carry those cows across Missouri in your pocket."

Ten was disappointed. He wanted to lead a trail drive across the western frontier, not to some swampy place in Louisiana where folks sat under magnolia trees, swatting flies and mosquitoes. At best, he expected New Orleans to be as dull and uninspiring as St. Louis. But he was to learn that death was not restricted to the untamed western frontier. It could—and did—prowl the cobblestone streets of New Orleans.

July 5, 1865, Ten and his crew of three poled the flatboat out into the swirling brown current of the Canadian river. Time after time, just when Ten was convinced the crude craft would capsize and drown them all, somehow it righted itself and continued on its way. He took heart in the knowledge that his "crew" had done this before and survived. He quickly wore blisters on his hands, helping pole the heavy barge loose from sandbars on which it was constantly marooning itself. Worse, they hit occasional shallow water, where the flatboat dragged bottom. There, they got into the water to lighten the load, using their poles to pry the clumsy craft along an inch at a time, until it reached a depth where it could float.

For three days they fought the river, tying up to a convenient tree only when darkness overtook them. Ten gave silent thanks they only had to pole this cumbersome thing to Fort Smith. None of them would ever live enough years to get it to New Orleans. But he couldn't complain. The ill-concealed grins of his three-man crew strengthened his resolve. He caught them looking slanch-eyed at him, expecting him to whine. He vowed he would die first, and before the second day ended, he thought he was going to. He was forced to face the brutal, unpleasant truth. Four years of town living had ruined him! He was a damn tenderfoot Injun, and this was just the lesson he had needed. Roping wild cattle, fighting Comanches, and a trail drive from Texas, demanded more than a fast hand with knife and gun. Despite his misery, he almost laughed. He was admitting to himself what Jesse Chisholm had probably known since the day they'd left St. Louis. After a few sixteen-hour days in the Texas brakes, he'd have been sent back to Indian Territory, belly-down over his saddle. He would be forced to pole this miserable log raft down the Canadian and lay his hands to some hard ranch work before he even considered going into the Texas brakes. Chisholm had been right: he *did* need some time.

Since Fort Smith was the jumping-off place, with only Indian Territory for three hundred miles westward, there was a steamboat only twice a week, on Monday and Thursday. After unloading freight and passengers, it returned to New Orleans. The layover was seldom more than two hours, or as long as it took to replenish the vessel's supply of wood and load the outbound passengers and freight. Ten had reached Fort Smith on Sunday, July 9, and he welcomed the night of rest before departing for New Orleans. He was accorded the same accommodations and courtesy as Jesse Chisholm. At the post store he bought a round-trip passage to New Orleans, and found he still had more than a hundred dollars of the expense money Jesse had insisted he take.

He wandered through the store until he found the guns and ammunition. He selected and bought a belt and holster, a silver-mounted rig, solid black, with tie-down thongs. He had begun to feel self-conscious, carrying his Colt stuck under the waistband of his Levi's. His three Cherokee boatmen had been amused with the way he carried the pistol, and he'd heard them speculating as to how long it might take him to accidentally shoot off his privates while drawing the Colt. Illegitimate or not, Chisholm had accepted him as his son, and nobody could change that. The Cherokees living on or near the ranch had been nice enough, but he felt he was a constant source of amusement to them. They simply weren't impressed. On the frontier nobody cared a fig what you thought or said, or who your daddy was. The measure of a man was what he did or failed to do.

Ten was part of a small crowd at the dock the following morning when the steamboat whistled for the landing. She was a handsome twin-stacked vessel, with an upper and lower deck, and was a gaudy red and white, with gold trim. Gilt letters a foot high spelled out her name: THE NEW ORLEANS. There was always cargo, most of it government-related, but nobody seemed interested in that. The four passengers got all the attention. Two of them, with their heavy leather cases, had to be drummers bound for the post store. The other two had no baggage, and once off the boat, seemed to have no real purpose in being there. Ten judged the younger man to be maybe twenty-five. He wore town clothes, with nothing particular calling attention to him. The older man, in his fifties, was far more eloquently dressed. He wore a flat-crowned white hat, white linen suit, frilled shirt, and a flowing black string tie. His black boots were highly polished, and might have been handmade. The deckhands were unloading the freight, and one of them dropped a load near Ten.

"Who's he?" Ten asked. "The man in the white suit?"

"That's Colonel LeBeau," said the sweating deckhand. "That old devil's got it all. Big, fancy house, handsome wife, beautiful daughter, and likely more money than anybody else in New Orleans."

Ten waited until the Chisholm freight had been taken aboard, and then made his way back to the fort. He wondered what a visitor would do for the three days until there was another boat to New Orleans. He expected the two drummers to conclude their business in time to depart this same afternoon, but what of the

other two men? They didn't seem to be together. Le-
Beau looked to be everything the deckhand had said he
was. For lack of anything better to do, Ten wandered
back to the dock long before *The New Orleans* was to
depart. To his surprise, LeBeau and the other man returned, and the gangplank was lowered for them to go
aboard. The pair of drummers returned after maybe an
hour and a half. When the plank was again lowered, Ten
followed them aboard.

Ten was directed to the lower deck, to a room that
wasn't too much larger than his closet at the academy
had been. He dropped his saddlebags on the floor, took
off his hat, and stretched out on the bunk. His head
touched a wall at one end, and his feet a wall at the
other. He heard voices in the next room, and held his
breath, listening. He couldn't quite make out the words,
but he doubted these men were the drummers. The
loudest voice was bullfrog deep, and it was angry. It was
exactly the kind of voice he would have expected Le-
Beau to have. With a blast of its whistle, *The New Orleans* backed away from the dock. Ten got up and put on
his hat. He would go to the upper deck. He stepped out
into the narrow corridor just as LeBeau's companion
swung open the door to the adjoining cabin. For a fleet-
ing moment Ten saw LeBeau seated on one of the
bunks. Spread out before him was a deck of cards.

Hastily the man closed the door, and Ten followed
him up a narrow set of steps to the upper deck. He
waited until the other man went to the rail before he
walked to the opposite end of the deck. LeBeau's companion had seemed upset when Ten had glimpsed Le-
Beau with the cards. Why? These two were up to something, and having seen the cards, Ten had a pretty good
idea what it was. He had a little over eighty dollars. Old
LeBeau looked flush enough to maybe double or triple
that stake. Of course, Jesse wouldn't have approved, but
Jesse wouldn't know.

2

*T*ired of the cramped cabin, Ten decided to explore the steamboat. Having spent some time on the St. Louis waterfront, he knew western boats were smaller, and mostly all stern-wheelers, as was *The New Orleans*. When a stern-wheeler encountered a sandbar, the pilot just turned the boat around and let the big wooden wheel dig a channel through the sand. If that wasn't possible, they'd resort to "grasshoppering," which allowed the steamboat to "walk" across the sandbar. Near the bow, one on each side, were long, heavy spars mounted vertically on derricks. When the boat became stuck on a sandbar, the ends of the spars were driven to the bottom of the river, their tops slanting forward. With the paddle wheel churning, in combination with block, tackle, cable, and capstan, the spars performed like huge crutches, moving the boat forward a few feet. After each "grasshopper" leap, the spars had to be reset and the procedure had to be repeated until the sandbar was cleared. One of the deckhands paused near the rail, tossing the butt of a cigarette into the murky brown water below.

"Just five paying passengers," said Ten. "How can this boat go all the way to Fort Smith twice a week with so few passengers?"

"Government freight mostly. But we'll have as many folks as we can board once we get to Natchez. Always do. Some feller built a quarter-mile track alongside the river, and there's hoss races ever' Saturday. We'll dock there next Sunday mornin', a full day ahead of the next boat from St. Louis. We'll lay over to take on fuel and freight, and when we pull out, we'll be loaded. Them high rollers from New Orleans that's been to the races will be goin' home. Ever' poker table in the saloon will be full. There'll be enough booze sold to profit the boat for the run to Fort Smith and back."

Ten's interest quickened. People who could afford the fare to Natchez to bet on the horses ought to have money to lose at the poker tables. Ten had known gamblers from the St. Louis waterfront who regularly bought passage to New Orleans and back to St. Louis for the express purpose of gambling in the boat's saloon. But these smaller "working" boats, traveling to Fort Smith and other frontier outposts, offered the professionals few opportunities to ply their questionable trade. So this bunch that would be boarding at Natchez, bound for New Orleans, might be "gentlemen gamblers" who could well afford to while away the time at the poker tables. While Ten had but eighty dollars, he had made do with less.

Ten decided *The New Orleans* was larger than it looked, once you got aboard. Coming up the gangplank, stepping onto the main deck, you were at the open end of what might have been a long shed. Forward, in the center, was the housing for boilers and engines. Hatches opened to holds below deck for every conceivable kind of freight. Here were the many stacks of cordwood that fed the insatiable fireboxes under the boilers. Many immigrants bought "deck passage" and slept on the planks. There was nothing cheaper, except walking. The roof of this catchall deck was the cabin deck, and here were the fancy, first-class accommodations. There was a central lounge, and clustered about it were the individual cabins. The lounge was divided into thirds. The front portion was for male passengers only, the center was the dining room, while the extreme back part was reserved

for females. The men's lounge was large enough to include a saloon, complete with bar, polished brass cuspi-
dors, and a dozen poker tables.

Ten climbed the steps to the very top of the vessel. It
was the roof of the cabin deck, and was uncovered. It
was called the hurricane deck, and in the central portion, forward, were quarters for the boat's crew and
deckhands. Finally, sitting atop this small cluster of cabins, was the pilothouse. It was octagonal, encircled with
glass windows that offered a panoramic view. Immediately in front of the pilothouse two lofty stacks belched
twin columns of wood smoke. At the rear of the pilothouse was a long bench. On it sat a gray-haired, gray-
bearded man smoking a pipe.

"You can't go in the pilothouse," he said.

"Are you one of the crew?"

"One of the pilots. Most boats carry two. We're working four hours on and four hours off."

"How fast are we traveling?"

"Eight to ten knots an hour. Sometimes, on a good
stretch, we might get twelve. But that's daytime. Come
dark, we drop to five or less."

Two deckhands entered the pilothouse and brought
out a pair of big lanterns, each of them standing maybe
three feet tall. One globe was red, the other green. Ten
watched the men clean the big globes. Finally, they
filled the lamp reservoirs with coal oil.

"That's our passing lights," said the pilot. "Before
dark, they're lit and hoisted to the tops of the stacks.
The green one goes on the river side, and the red one
on the bank side. When we meet another boat in the
dark, he knows which side of the river we're on and
where our near bank is."

Even at a slower speed, and with the lessened motion
of the boat, Ten slept very little. He was up with the first
gray of dawn, ready for breakfast, long before the ap-
pointed time. Afterward, he returned to the cramped
cabin and remained there as long as he could stand it.

Finally he went into the central portion of the cabin deck, to the lounge area. Early as it was, the saloon was already in business. LeBeau, his companion, and the two drummers sat at one of the tables, engrossed in a poker game. The barman lifted his eyebrows questioningly, but Ten shook his head. He wandered to the table where the game was in progress, and was ignored. When it became obvious he wasn't going to leave, LeBeau spoke in that bullfrog voice.

"Draw poker, boy. Dollar a game, if you feel lucky."

Whatever LeBeau had in mind, it wouldn't be for table stakes, with limited betting. Ten dragged up a chair and bought in. He received five cards, a perfectly lousy hand, nothing to draw to. Each of the drummers drew three new cards, discarding three of their original five. LeBeau looked at Ten.

"I fold," said Ten.

LeBeau dealt himself three new cards, and the fourth man folded. LeBeau took the pot with three of a kind. He lost the next pot to one of the drummers, and took the one following with a king-high full house. Ten had gotten their attention. Three times he'd drawn a poor hand, and three times he'd folded, losing a dollar each time. The drummers, he was sure, had drawn equally poor hands, but had each taken three new cards on a second draw. It was poor odds, poor poker. One of them lucked out, with three of a kind. Ten hadn't drawn a face card in three hands, so it came as a surprise when he drew two jacks on the fourth. He discarded three cards, took three new ones on the second draw, and threw another dollar in the pot. He won the pot with three jacks. LeBeau ordered a round of drinks. Ten shook his head.

"Ain't you man enough to drink with us, kid?" asked LeBeau's companion.

"Man enough that I don't have to prove it," said Ten mildly.

LeBeau and the drummers laughed. The fourth man, still nameless, didn't see the humor. His thin lips were hard-set, his gray eyes cold. LeBeau might be the bull of the woods, but his companion was the man to watch. His coat bulged on the left side, poorly concealing the shoulder holster. Ten played three more hands, leaving the game two dollars poorer. The game had been boring. He decided he'd as soon stand on the deck, watching the big paddle wheel thrash through the muddy water of the Arkansas. Late that afternoon, they met and passed another steamboat scheduled to arrive at Fort Smith on Thursday. It was *The Talequah,* named for the capital of the Cherokee nation. Its pilot acknowledged them with a blast of his whistle, and the pilot of *The New Orleans* returned the greeting.

After supper, although it wasn't good dark, Ten returned to the tiny cabin. He listened for voices in the next room, but heard nothing. LeBeau and his cohort were probably still in the saloon, playing their low stakes game. He didn't know how well he'd fare with the well-to-do gamblers from New Orleans, but he determined to risk a few hands. It might be worth it, if he could force his way in at LeBeau's table and observe the old reprobate's style. Those four years in St. Louis hadn't been a total loss, he decided. It was hard to imagine there being any sleight-of-hand or slick-dealing he hadn't witnessed in the riverfront saloons. Finally, done in by the lack of sleep the night before, he slept.

By Thursday morning they were steaming down the broad Mississippi, but it seemed to Ten they traveled more slowly than ever. While the mighty river was wider and deeper, in other ways it was more treacherous. No sooner were they out of one hairpin turn then there was another. The poker game in the saloon continued, but Ten steered clear of it. He took out a whetstone and honed his throwing knife until he could have shaved with it. Satisfied with that, he turned to his Colt. He owed a lot to that old ex-outlaw in St. Louis, whom some said had ridden with Bloody Bill Anderson; others claimed he'd been with Quantrill; but none of them said it to his face. The old-timer had taken an interest in Ten, showing him how to reduce the trigger pressure required to ear back the hammer. It required taking a file to the sear, the catch or lock in a Colt that held the hammer back until released by the trigger mechanism. The "doctored" Colt had always been sensitive to Ten's touch, and now, with the file he kept for that purpose, he set about to even further reduce the pull. With his file he set to work on the sear, until the pull was so light he could draw and shoot without fear that the cocking of the weapon would pull the muzzle off target. Speed without accuracy could be the death of a man. His accuracy assured, he could further increase the speed of his draw, and with the Colt unloaded, he spent hour after hour in the small cabin, practicing his draw. He hadn't lied to Jesse. Until he actually faced a man who could and would return his fire, he'd never be sure he could measure up. But when the time came, he would be ready.

Natchez was like all other river towns of the time. Everybody took an active interest in the river and the steamboats that traveled it. While there appeared to be no freight on the dock, there were passengers in plenty, male and female. They were impatient to come aboard, jostling one another as deckhands hauled loads of cordwood below the cabin deck. For the first time since leaving Fort Smith, the captain made an appearance, welcoming the new passengers aboard. They *looked* wealthy, most of them dressing as well or better than LeBeau. There was a scramble for the cabins, and considerable grumbling, as men had to share cabins with other men. Ten was glad his cramped cabin had but a single bunk. He headed back to it, in case some disgruntled newcomer tried to claim squatter's rights. LeBeau and his companion seemed to have the same idea. One of the newcomers, a big man in a blue pin-stripe suit and bowler hat, stood watching them. Suddenly aware that Ten was watching him, he turned quickly away.

What was his interest in LeBeau? Was he friend or enemy? It would be interesting to see where Bowler Hat fitted in once the gambling started. Ten waited what he judged to be an hour before leaving his cabin. LeBeau and his partner had long since departed, and chatter in the narrow corridor had ceased.

The saloon was filled to overflowing. Not only was every table fully occupied, but folding card tables had been set up in the adjoining dining room. There were now two barmen on duty, and three stewards hustling drinks to the tables. Men sat on every stool along the bar, most of them waiting for a chance at one of the poker games. A table could comfortably accommodate only four players, but some of them, including LeBeau's, had as many as six. To LeBeau's left sat his gun-toting companion, and to his right, the man in the bowler hat. He was a big, grim-faced man, with the red, bulbous nose of a heavy drinker. He chewed on an unlighted cigar and didn't seem all that interested in the game. The other three men also had boarded at Natchez, and played with an abandon only the wealthy could afford. Ten wore range clothes, his fanciest piece of attire being a new gray Stetson. Some of the men nursing drinks at the bar looked curiously at him, their eyes dropping inevitably to the tied-down Colt he wore.

Ten made his way to LeBeau's table and found they were playing draw poker. There appeared to be no set limit, but they'd begun with five dollars. Ten had about given up getting into the game when one of the men kicked back his chair and got up.

"I'm out," he said.

"I'm buying in," said Ten. He wanted to find out where LeBeau fitted in.

LeBeau cast him an unfathomable look but said nothing. He turned to his pistol-toting companion.

"Sneed, flag down somebody and order us another round of drinks."

So his name was Sneed. The familiar manner in which LeBeau spoke to him changed Ten's mind about their relationship. A typical "cold-deck" scheme would have depended on LeBeau and Sneed not knowing one another. LeBeau, appearing to lose like everybody else, would be feeding Sneed the winning hands. But if Sneed wasn't part of a cold-deck team, what *was* he? A bodyguard? One of the men who'd boarded at Natchez was shuffling and dealing. Ten put his five dollars in the pot. His five cards were unworthy of a second bet, so he folded, losing his five dollars. Without at least a pair to draw to, the odds against bettering his hand with three more cards were poor. He watched the others, especially LeBeau and Sneed, but saw nothing to arouse his suspicion. He even won a pot. Down twenty dollars, he got two queens on the first draw. He put another five dollars in the pot, discarded three of his original cards, and drew three more. One of them was a third queen, and at the showdown, the sixty-dollar pot was his.

They seesawed along, each man winning an occasional pot. Ten was expecting the size of the bets to increase dramatically at some point, and when the proposal came, he was thirty dollars ahead.

"Gentlemen," said LeBeau, "why don't we elevate this to a man's game, and increase our bets to twenty dollars?"

Nobody objected. Ten's first hand offered him nothing to draw to, so he folded, losing his money. One of the men who'd boarded at Natchez took one pot, the big man in the bowler hat a second, and Sneed a third. It was LeBeau's turn to shuffle and deal. Ten's stake was dwindling fast, and he'd be forced to withdraw from the game if LeBeau didn't make his move soon. But on the next draw, two of his five cards were kings. It could be the start of a bottom deal. Jacks, kings, and queens were dealt—scattered—so that nobody stood a chance of drawing more than three of a kind, making four aces an unbeatable hand. Was that what LeBeau had in mind? It would cost Ten another double eagle to find out. He put his money in the pot, calling for three more cards. LeBeau dealt them, and one was a third king. LeBeau dealt three cards to Sneed and was about to deal three more to himself when Ten made his move.

"Put the cards on the table, Mr. LeBeau. Facedown."

Everybody froze except Sneed. He got his hand on the butt of his pistol, only to find himself looking into the rock-steady muzzle of Ten's Colt. His thin face paled, and he slowly withdrew his hand. Without a word, LeBeau placed the deck facedown on the table.

"Now," said Ten, "deal yourself three cards. Off the top. Slow."

LeBeau dealt them.

"Now deal me three cards. Off the top."

LeBeau dealt them. Then he glared at Ten, his face livid.

"I'll have you horsewhipped for this, you young fool!"

"You'll have it to do," said Ten. "But let's wait until after the showdown before we decide who gets the whipping. Show your hand, LeBeau."

With hands not quite steady, LeBeau faced up the two cards from his original hand, revealing a pair of aces.

"Now," said Ten, "show the three cards you just dealt yourself. I'll bet my horsewhipping against yours, one of them will be an ace, and one of the other two a king."

LeBeau turned over the cards, revealing an ace, a king, and a ten. There was a moment of shocked silence. Then one of the men across the table kicked back his chair and got to his feet.

"I've got three queens," he said, "and I have the feeling I could sit here all day and never get the fourth."

"I've got two jacks," said another. "Where's the other two?"

"Mr. Sneed has the queen and two jacks," said Ten.

LeBeau jumped up, kicking back his chair, and there was a yelp of pain as it struck somebody at another table.

"Hold it," said Ten. He still gripped the Colt, and shifted it quickly to cover the furious LeBeau.

"We haven't finished the game," said Ten. "Show your hand, Sneed."

Reluctantly, the little man turned his cards faceup. Among them was the missing queen and two jacks.

"This is an outrage!" shouted LeBeau. "You can't prove a thing!"

"I reckon I can prove this pot belongs to me," said Ten. "The rest of you, show your hands."

Nobody had anything close to a winning hand. The big man in the bowler hat glared at LeBeau with something akin to murder in his hard eyes. The shouting and chair-kicking had brought everything else in the saloon to a standstill. Ten had an audience that hung on his every word.

"There's not a winning hand on this table," he said, "except LeBeau's. While my three kings would have beaten three jacks or three queens, none of us stood a chance against four aces. That's the hand Mr. LeBeau would have held at the showdown, had he been allowed to deal as planned. He'd have dealt himself two cards from the top of the deck. One of them would have been an ace and the other the king I needed. He would then have dealt himself a fourth ace—the ace of diamonds—from the bottom of the deck."

The angry man who had held the three queens took the remainder of the deck, slowly peeling off the bottom card. It was indeed the ace of diamonds. There was pandemonium in the saloon. Amid the thud of fists, men shouted and cursed, chairs crashed, glasses and bottles shattered. LeBeau and Sneed were wrestled to the floor, lost in a sea of thrashing arms and legs.

"That's enough!" bawled a voice. "This is the captain! Stop it or I'll have the lot of you jailed when we dock. What's the meaning of this?"

"Cheating," somebody shouted. "That old bastard in the white suit was caught slick-dealing!"

They yielded to the captain's authority. He ordered LeBeau brought to the captain's quarters. Bruised and disheveled, LeBeau and Sneed left the saloon amid grumbling and cursing. The big man in the bowler hat remained where he was. Ten holstered his Colt. Somebody handed him the $240 pot. He now had nearly three hundred dollars. He had shown up LeBeau for the cheat he was, but had it been worth it? He hadn't even reached New Orleans, and he already had two enemies there. Standing on deck, watching the big paddle wheel churn the muddy water of the Mississippi, he sensed somebody behind him. He spun and dropped to one knee, the Colt cocked and steady in his hand. He found himself facing the man who had held the three queens.

"You're mighty sudden with that iron, my friend. When we reach New Orleans, I'd like to talk to you in private. Here's my card."

Without another word the man turned away and Ten looked at the card. The stranger's name was John Mathewson, head of the New Orleans division of United States Customs. Ten dropped the card into his shirt pocket and started back to his cabin, unaware that Sneed had seen the brief encounter with Mathewson. The little gunman stepped out into the narrow corridor and Ten halted, thumbs hooked in his pistol belt. Sneed spoke.

"That was slick, kid, but not very smart. Mr. LeBeau ain't thinkin' kind thoughts of you. The captain raked us over from here to yonder, and we won't be allowed to gamble on the boats anymore."

"My heart bleeds for Mr. LeBeau," said Ten, "and your concern is touching. Who are you, his daddy?"

"I'm just deliverin' a message, kid. Whatever business you got in New Orleans, tend to it and get out. I kind of admire your nerve, and I don't really want to kill you."

"Only one way you could do it, Sneed, and I don't aim to turn my back."

He said no more. Sneed stepped back into the cabin he shared with LeBeau. Ten entered his own cabin, and for the first time since coming aboard, bolted the door. Suddenly he was very tired. He removed his hat, dragged off his boots, and stretched out on the bunk.

He was awakened by a knock that he at first thought was on his door. Then LeBeau's door opened and there was a rumble of voices. Ten got up and eased his own door open just a little. He was in time to see Sneed emerge from LeBeau's cabin and wander down the narrow corridor.

3

When Sneed answered the knock on the door, he found himself facing the big man with the unlit cigar and bowler hat. The stranger didn't beat around the bush.

"I'm here to talk to LeBeau," he said. "In private."

Sneed turned to LeBeau, but the man in the corridor didn't wait. He stepped into the room and closed the door.

"Get out of here!" snapped LeBeau. "I don't have any business with you."

"Oh, but you do," said the big man with a grim smile. "Some past-due business. You don't know me, but you know who sent me, and you know why." He turned to Sneed. "Take a walk, friend. This doesn't concern you."

Sneed looked uncertainly at LeBeau, and LeBeau nodded. Sneed went out, closing the door behind him.

"You have no right to follow me, to spy on me!" snarled LeBeau.

"Wrong, LeBeau. I have *every* right. A man that owes us twenty-five thousand dollars and loves the cards like you do, he gets our undivided attention. You *do* have the money in a safe place, do you not?"

There was no humor in his faint smile, and the chill in his hard eyes touched LeBeau's spine with icy fingers.

"I . . . yes, but—how do I . . . Who *are* you?" stammered LeBeau.

"Bradley Montaigne. Remember that. It's me you'll be dealing with, until your account has been settled. One way or another."

"What happened to . . . ?"

"Hardesty? He made mistakes, LeBeau. Big mistakes. Just as we were about to teach him the error of his ways, he went mad. Blew his brains out."

The grim warning wasn't lost on André LeBeau. He shuddered.

"There's another matter we must discuss, LeBeau. Your gambling. The customs people are aware there is —and has been—a considerable amount of black marketing and smuggling going on, but the government's been involved in a war. Now the war's over and they're looking for weak links in the chain. Like you, LeBeau. High rollers, men who spend beyond their means. We approached you because of your position, your credibility. But you've become flamboyant and careless, drawing attention to yourself. Like that episode at the poker table a while ago. A man should never gamble, LeBeau, if he can't afford to lose. When a man's in as deep as you are, I get nervous, seeing him cheat on a twenty-dollar bet. John Mathewson, the chief of U.S. Customs in New Orleans, was at your table, LeBeau. He was later seen talking to the young man who exposed you as a cheat."

"Our . . . business arrangement is just that," said LeBeau. "It doesn't entitle you to dictate my every move, to intrude in my personal life. Now that the war's over, the blockades will come down and normal commerce will resume. You'll be out of business, and I'm getting out, Montaigne. I'm gone."

"In more ways than you know," said Montaigne, with an evil half smile. "The customs people would love to know who masterminded this despicable scheme that took advantage of a nation at war. There's more than enough evidence to convince them it was all your idea, LeBeau. You could be sent to Federal prison for more years than you've got left."

"You bastard!" shrieked LeBeau. "You cheap, double-crossing bastard!"

"Don't bother looking for me, LeBeau. I'll find you exactly thirty days from today. Remember, it's as much for the sake of your wife and daughter as for you. No scrip, no checks, no excuses. Just gold."

He paused, his hand on the doorknob. When he spoke again, his voice was low, deadly, almost a hiss.

"Today, LeBeau, before the elite of New Orleans, you became far less valuable to us. You made a total, irrevocable ass of yourself. Don't let it happen again."

He closed the door and was gone. LeBeau gave in to his trembling legs and dropped onto one of the bunks. He could feel the sweat soaking the armpits of his shirt, and he wiped his sticky palms on the legs of his trousers. Where—how—could he possibly raise $25,000 in gold in just thirty days? Or for that matter, in thirty *years*? There was Emily's trust fund, and the lawyer who had set it up was a personal friend. Why couldn't he use that money to get Montaigne off his back, and replace it before Emily was the wiser? Given time, he could win that much, and more.

While Ten had heard the angry exchange between Le-Beau and Montaigne, he hadn't been able to distinguish their words. He was at his own door when Montaigne departed. Ten wasn't surprised to find Sneed eating supper alone. He felt a momentary twinge of pity for Le-Beau, but the old fool had gotten off easy. Men had been shot dead or hung for similar offense. Ten saw John Mathewson occasionally and was tempted to talk to him. But he had the impression Mathewson didn't want them seen together, so he would wait until they reached New Orleans. On one wall of the saloon there was a display board on which businessmen and drummers were invited to post their cards. Ten was looking at the board when a man of maybe thirty stopped to post his card. Ten's eyes went to the card, finding the man's name was Maynard Herndon, that he dealt in livestock, and that his was a New Orleans address. Herndon left the saloon, walking out on the cabin deck. He was leaning on the rail, watching water roll off the paddle wheel, when Ten approached him.

"Your card says you buy and sell livestock. I'm going to New Orleans with a load of trade goods, but was planning to talk to some stock buyers while I'm there. I'm going to Texas and trail wild longhorns to market. Is there a chance for a drive to New Orleans? Would it be worth it?"

"I doubt it," said Herndon, "unless you could ship them by boat to the northern markets. I call myself a livestock dealer, because it's easier than admitting I'm unemployed. Louisiana folks like beef, but we're broke, like the rest of the South. During the war, we've lived on fish and whatever else we could catch in the bayous, rivers, and creeks. Only the rich can afford things like coffee, tea, sugar, and beef."

"And steamboat trips to Natchez."

"My uncle Drago, an old mountain man, owns the horse track at Natchez. Sometimes I go there and help him with the horses, and he pays the steamboat fare. You didn't see *me* at the poker tables. Best I could manage was a couple of beers at the bar."

"Got any idea how much per head it might cost to ship cows by boat?"

"No," said Herndon, "not until the blockade comes down. But I expect it'll be expensive. An occasional herd won't be enough to justify regular service, and you'd probably have to charter a boat. Remember, our big crop was cotton, and there hasn't been a crop in five years. Our land's grown up in field pines. God knows when we'll have cotton again. Or, for that matter, even a decent mess of turnip greens or roasting ears. Some of our men never came back from the war, and those who have are too sick and shot up to do much of anything. I was lucky. I got lung fever and they kicked me out after a year."

Ten liked the gray-eyed young man, and promised to

talk to him later. Despite Herndon's negative information, he would still do as Jesse Chisholm had suggested, and talk to Roberts and Company. Chisholm had dealt with them for years, and trusted them. But Herndon had made sense, and his words had the ring of truth.

Ten found New Orleans strung out mostly along the north bank of the river. His first duty was to see Jesse's freight off the boat and safely into a warehouse. When deckhands had removed and stored the goods, he went to the cubbyhole of an office to determine what he should do next.

"Go to the Roberts office at four o'clock," he was told. "By then, the freight will have been checked against the bills of lading."

He reviewed what he needed to do while in New Orleans. He still had to talk to Roberts about the possibility of shipping cattle by boat, but he could do that when he went to their office at four. He had more than two hours to wait. He took out the card John Mathewson had given him. The address was in the Vieux Carré, at the corner of Barracks and Royal. There were no numbers on the buildings, but thankfully, the names of the streets and avenues were posted on each corner. Eventually he came to Barracks, turned north and followed it two blocks until he reached Royal. The building he sought was on the corner. It was an old two-story office building with an iron railing across the entire front of the second story. Once it had been a mission; there was an open bell tower on the roof. The office he wanted was on the first floor, identified only by a small sign. Mounted above the door, it read: U.S. CUSTOMS.

The huge oak door, oval at the top, yielded grudgingly when Ten turned the brass knob and pushed. At the desk, the elderly secretary looked up from her ledger. But before Ten could announce himself, Mathewson stepped out of his office and beckoned. He closed the door behind them, motioning Ten to a plush chair upholstered in red velvet.

"Now," said Mathewson, "perhaps you'd better tell me your name. You already know mine."

"Tenatse Chisholm. Half-breed Injun. Call me Ten."

"Ten it is. Are you related to Jesse, the frontiersman and scout?"

"He's my father. I'm here to deliver and collect for trade goods."

Mathewson whistled. "You come well-recommended, young man. I suppose it's time I told you why I asked you here."

"I think so," said Ten. "I can't think of one good reason why you'd want to talk to me. I reckon I'm here because my Injun curiosity got the best of me."

"First," said Mathewson, "I'd like to know what you know—if anything—about André LeBeau."

"Nothing, except what I learned on the boat."

"Which is?"

"He's a man who likes to gamble," said Ten, "but he's not very good at it. He can't leave it alone. He's likely hurting for money, and that's why he cheats. The big man with the cigar and bowler hat knew LeBeau, and they had some hard words there in LeBeau's room, after that fuss in the saloon."

"Got any idea what they might have argued about?"

"No," said Ten. "They sent Sneed out of the room. I saw him leave."

"Know anything about Sneed?"

"Not much," said Ten. "I thought at first he was LeBeau's pardner in a cold-deck scheme. He did stop me in the corridor and tell me LeBeau was a mite upset with me. Threatened to shoot me if I linger in New Orleans."

"Do you intend to heed the warning?"

"No," said Ten, "I'll go when I'm ready."

"I wouldn't want you to remain in the face of such a threat, unless by your own choice. Ten, your father has always gone to great lengths to help his country, and I'm wondering if I can ask the same of you."

"That depends," said Ten, "on what you want me to do, and why."

"I'd like you to help us gather some evidence linking André LeBeau to the smuggling and black marketing that has taken over and run rampant during the war."

"Why me? I'm just a troublesome Injun that got himself booted out of school six months ahead of graduation."

"Because you're just the right age," said Mathewson, "and because you have the sheer nerve to make it work."

"If you want somebody gunned down, I got to admit I never shot a man."

"Nothing as crude as that," said Mathewson. "I want you to attend a birthday party for a young lady who's going to be seventeen this Saturday. She's Priscilla Le-Beau, and I want someone close to her that I can trust."

"You've been grazing on loco weed. I wouldn't get past the front door. LeBeau would shoot me—or have me shot—on sight."

"He won't be there," said Mathewson. "This is the doing of Emily, his wife. You'll be invited as the friend of a friend of hers. I want you to become friends with the girl. You'll bless me when you meet her. My God, she's a beauty, the very image of her mother."

"You expect me to trick her into betraying LeBeau. He's a scoundrel, but he's still her daddy. I won't do it."

"You're not going to trick her into anything," said Mathewson. "It's for her safety and that of her mother. We doubt they're aware of LeBeau's activities, and they may be in some danger."

"You expect me to move in on Priscilla and her mother without telling them *anything* of what you're tellin' me?"

"I'm asking only that you become friends with Priscilla. If she knows or suspects anything, insofar as Le-Beau's concerned, she'll be upset and worried. Is it trickery if she trusts and confides in you as a friend?"

"I reckon not, but why would she confide in me instead of her mama?"

"Because her mother and LeBeau are totally estranged," said Mathewson. "Emily lives in a world all her own, and as far as she's concerned, LeBeau might as well not exist. That's what I'm trying to tell you. Poor Priscilla needs someone she can trust, someone to confide in."

"Your interest in LeBeau I can understand, but what's your interest in Priscilla and her mother? You seem to know them mighty well."

"I've known Emily since before she married LeBeau, and I've known Priscilla since the day she was born. Emily is—was—more than just a friend, and while I'm forced to go after LeBeau, I don't want Emily or Priscilla hurt."

"How long is LeBeau goin' to be gone?"

"The weekend. LeBeau won't allow Priscilla out at night. The available men in town aren't even allowed to speak to the poor girl on the street. Given the chance, and if you do your part, she'll trust and confide in you."

"You don't want much, do you, Mathewson? While I'm performing miracles, you want me to change the Gulf of Mexico into forty-rod whiskey?"

Mathewson continued as though Ten hadn't spoken. "There's an old brick, two-story hotel—the Magnolia— at the corner of Bourbon Street and St. Louis. Anytime after five o'clock this evening there'll be a room in your name. For as long as you need it. I can arrange for your meals, if need be."

"No," said Ten, "I can manage that. But what in tarnation do I *wear*? I've never been to any social doings like this, and I don't have a blessed thing any fancier than what I'm wearing."

"Sometime between now and Saturday there'll be a package brought to you at the hotel. It will contain proper clothes. There'll be a carriage to pick you up at four o'clock Saturday afternoon. LeBeau owns the old Logan house, in the Garden District, just off St.

Charles. I'd like to talk to you again on Monday afternoon. Good luck, Ten, and thanks."

There was a wall clock in the outer office, and Ten was surprised to find it already past four o'clock. He hurried back to the offices of Roberts and Company. He asked to speak to Harvey Roberts, and was ushered into a plush office. Roberts was a fat man, mostly bald, wearing a dark suit and red-striped tie.

"Pleased to meet you, Ten. Shook me, when Jesse didn't show. Was afraid he'd broke a leg and had to be shot." He chuckled at his own macabre humor.

"He wants me to have the experience," said Ten. "He wants your advice about maybe trail-driving Texas cattle here and shipping them north, by boat. Do you think it's possible, and is it something we can afford?"

"Possible, yes," said Roberts, "but affordable, no. The war sapped our economy, and we're maybe five years away from producing anything to be sent anywhere. We have Union troops in the state, and we have yet to discover how Federal occupation is going to affect us."

"What about the pelts, hides, and such, that I brought this time?"

"The southern states will be under some kind of restriction," Roberts said. "For instance, a Texan may need permission to take a herd across the state line, but I can't see any of this affecting Jesse, since he's there in Indian Territory. Besides, the government will be forever indebted to him for his scouting and treaty-making with the plains tribes."

"I aim to gather a herd in Texas," said Ten.

"You shouldn't have any trouble bringing them out," said Roberts, "but your least expensive and most dependable means of getting them to northern markets is to trail them northeast, to the nearest end-of-track. When things return to normal here, if they ever do, herds can be shipped by boat."

"Well, thanks," said Ten. He stepped out, closing the door behind him.

Finding St. Louis, Ten followed it north three blocks

to Bourbon Street. He was still able to read "Magnolia
Hotel" on the sign above the door, even though the
letters had long since faded from black to washed-out
gray. The inside, however, was far more impressive than
the outside. When he told the desk clerk his name, he
was immediately given a key, and found he was in Room
12 at the head of the stairs. At the other end of the hall
there was a back door, and on the wall beside it, a
bracket lamp burned. But even with the lamp, the far
end of the hall was in shadow, and the breath of air he
felt would have been too late. The door eased open so
slowly, he wasn't aware of the movement, but with the
sudden guttering of the lamp's flame, he threw himself
belly-down in the hall, his Colt roaring before he hit the
floor. Two slugs slammed into the door frame, chest
high, where he'd stood just seconds before.

Doors opened along the hall, and were just as quickly
closed. He waited, offering as little target as possible,
should there be more shots. Cautiously, he got to his
knees, and then to his feet. He'd ejected the three spent
shells from his Colt and was reloading when a big man,
gone to fat, came panting up the stairs. By the time he
had caught his breath enough to speak, Ten had holstered the Colt.

"Mister, I'm the manager here, and we don't allow
the firing of weapons. What's your room number and
for how many nights are you registered?"

"Room twelve," said Ten. "I don't know how many
nights I'll be here. Why don't you ask the gent that registered me?"

His words had the desired effect. Mathewson had
some influence.

"I'm sorry," said the manager, "but the shooting—"

"See that splintered door frame? Somebody threw
some lead at me from that back door, and when I'm
shot at, I shoot back. Even in your hotel. But if you want
me to leave, I will."

"No, sir," said the manager. "Your room has been

guaranteed for an indefinite stay. Forget what I said. Should I report this to the police?"

"No," said Ten. "If anybody gets curious about the shooting, just tell them a half-breed Injun had too much to drink."

4

*T*en locked the door and cleaned his Colt. It was still early, not yet six o'clock, and he was hungry. But he had some thinking to do. He held out his hands, and they were steady, and despite the narrow escape, he was neither nervous or afraid. In fact, he felt better, more sure of himself than at any time since leaving the Chisholm ranch. Then, without any awareness of *how* he knew, it came to him, and he understood the change in himself. Without time to think or plan, his reflexes had taken over and he'd survived under fire! Being honest, he realized the experience could have had exactly the opposite effect, leaving him skulking about like a scared coyote, jumping at shadows. Instead, he now had the strength of his convictions. From the tin in his saddle-bags he took a handful of extra cartridges, stuffing them into the pocket of his Levi's.

After leaving the hotel, he paused for a moment on the street corner. He wasn't more than three or four blocks from the riverfront, and somewhere among all the saloons there had to be a place to eat. As he walked down Bourbon Street toward the river, a question dogged his mind. While he had no doubt LeBeau hated his guts, he didn't believe the attempted ambush was the result of his having shown the man up for a cheat. There had to be some other reason why he had become enough of a threat to justify being shot at. He reviewed everything that had happened following LeBeau's disgrace in the saloon. Finally it hit him, and so startling was the impact, he just stopped cold, considering the implications. Sneed had witnessed Ten's brief meeting with John Mathewson. If Mathewson's suspicion of LeBeau was well-founded, and LeBeau *was* involved in smuggling, then Sneed and LeBeau would certainly know who Mathewson was. What they *didn't* know was where Tenatse Chisholm fitted into the picture, and that would account for them trailing him to Mathewson's office. Even with LeBeau away for the weekend, Sneed could still trail him to the LeBeau house for his meeting with Priscilla. Under these circumstances, Ten wondered if his involvement with Priscilla might not do more harm than good, and he wished he could talk to John Mathewson again. But suppose Mathewson still wanted him to fulfill his promise?

He decided he wouldn't risk a second visit to Mathewson's office. Mathewson had been right. He could protect the girl only by her being unaware of his real reason for being there. If Priscilla didn't know anything, she couldn't be made to tell anything. They would have to come after him. He paused, looking around him, and went on. Near the end of Bourbon Street, facing the river, he found a hole-in-the-wall eatery called the Blind Goose. Instead of tables, there was just a row of backless hard stools strung out along the counter. He took a stool near the end, as far from the door and windows as he could get. The cook poured a cup of hot black coffee and slid it sloshing down the counter toward him.

"Roast pork, potatoes, bread, butter, pie, an' coffee," the cook said. "Ten cents, an' you pay in advance."

"You took a chance, trusting me with the coffee," said Ten.

He slid two bits along the counter in the trail of spilled coffee. The food was leftovers from dinner, and the coffee likely from breakfast, but Ten finished it all. Stepping out the door, he closed it quickly, for the light made him an excellent target. Rather than return the way he had come, he took a different route along the river. If he was being trailed, then he wouldn't make it easy for them. He passed a dimly lit rooming house, its ROOMS FOR RENT sign illuminated by a bracket lamp beside the door. Behind the house there was a narrow alley, its interior black as the ace of spades.

Ten paused. Somewhere down the dark corridor there was a scuffing, not unlike the sound of leather against stone. In an instant the Colt was in his hand. He waited, straining his ears, but the sound wasn't repeated. He was about to proceed when he heard a low moan that trailed off into a whimper. Somebody was hurt, or doing a mighty convincing imitation. His back against a rough brick wall, he inched sideways into the darkness, relying on his peripheral vision. Slowly his eyes adjusted to the intense darkness. His boot touched something, and he froze. There was a groan that ended in a sigh. Perhaps it was just a drunk, suffering the aftereffects of his folly, but he doubted it. He'd seen his share of them, heard them whine piteously for some hair of the dog. But this seemed more a genuine cry of physical pain. When he heard it again, he was near enough to see the dim outline of a man, lying on his back.

Still suspicious, he inched his way past until he was able to see the end of the dark passage. What had at first seemed an alley was only a gap between two buildings. Farther down, the next structures were back to back. Ahead, the narrow passage came to a dead end, like a box canyon. A perfect trap. He paused, looking back toward the dim entrance, half expecting to see the gray outlines of men coming for him. But there was only darkness. Cautiously he knelt, extending his free hand until he felt the man's hair. It seemed stiff, sticky, bloody. Touching the face, he could feel the swelling around the eyes and the lips. The man's shirt seemed wet, but the dew hadn't yet fallen and the ground was dry. Blood.

He hurried back to the street, rounded the corner and found a saloon he had passed earlier. It was a nondescript place called the Blue Anchor, and for fifty cents he bought a quart of rotgut whiskey. He returned to the dark corridor and again made his way to the injured man. Regretfully, he holstered the Colt. He would need both hands. He soaked his bandanna with the whiskey, gagging at the vile fumes. It seemed potent enough to revive a dead Comanche. He set the bottle down and spread the bandanna over the man's face. The man's breathing was ragged, irregular, but he began to cough and wheeze almost immediately. Ten removed the bandanna.

"Sorry, pardner. I had to bring you out of it somehow. I don't know how bad you're busted up, but you can't stay here. See if you can move."

He tried to rise, but lay back, gasping.

"I'll take hold of your shoulders," said Ten. "If you can sit up, edge your back up against the wall, and I'll give you as much of the firewater as you can stand."

Slowly he lifted the man to a sitting position, the man's teeth grinding as he resisted crying out. By the time his back was to the wall, his breathing was more ragged than ever. Ten fumbled around until he found the whiskey, and pulled the cork from the bottle. The wounded man's head sagged and again he seemed unconscious.

"Raise your head some," said Ten, "if you're still with me. I can't get you out of here without your help. Here's the whiskey."

Slowly the head came up. Ten couldn't see well enough to position the bottle so he could drink. Uncertainly, the right hand came up and guided the bottle. He took only a little, gagging it all out. Finally he swallowed some, coughing and choking. Either he wasn't a drinking man or he was accustomed to better whiskey. He took one more swallow, then pushed the bottle away. His breathing became more regular, less labored. Finally the man spoke.

"Who . . . are you?"

"A friend. Do you feel any broken bones?"

"I . . . don't think so."

Speaking through swollen lips his voice was a raspy rumble that Ten could hardly understand.

"I'll help you to your feet," said Ten. "Let's see if you can stand."

The man got to his knees on his own. After a few seconds of rest, and with Ten's help, he stumbled to his feet. He staggered against the brick wall, and Ten steadied him.

"Dizzy," he mumbled. "Head . . . hurts."

"You need a doc to look at you. Where can I take you?"

"Texas," he said. "Crockett . . . Texas." Between a bitter laugh and a sob, his voice broke. "No," he said. "No more. Nowhere . . ."

"Then I'll get you a room. We're behind a rooming house."

"No," he said. "No . . . no money."

"Pardner, you're in no shape to be prideful. I'll stake you to a room. Now, let's find out if you can walk."

His left leg wouldn't support him, and he almost fell.

"Get your left arm over my shoulder," said Ten. "Lean on me."

Slowly, and in that manner, they reached the front door of the rooming house. The wounded man was breathing hard. Ten turned the knob and booted the door open. The parlor was shabbily furnished, with a rocker, two cane-bottom ladderbacks, and a horsehair sofa. Two men sat on the sofa, and a tall, gray-haired woman stood in the dining room door, glaring at them.

"I'm Velda Kendrick, and I own this place. I don't cater to drunks, so turn him around, boy, and walk him right out of here."

"He's not drunk," said Ten. "He's been beaten. He's bad hurt, needin' a room and a doctor."

As though in mute appeal, the wounded man lifted his bloodied face, and the woman gasped. Blood from his head wounds had crusted, reddish-brown, from his hairline to where the collar had been ripped from his shirt. The rest of it hung in tatters. His trousers had been ripped to above the knees, and he was barely decent. But for his heels-out socks, his feet were bare.

"The upstairs rooms are cheaper," she said.

"He's in no shape to climb stairs," said Ten. "If you'll trust me until I get him in bed, I'll pay you."

She flushed, and without a word led them out of the parlor and down the hall. She opened a door, and Ten got the wounded man to the bed. When he turned to Velda Kendrick, the hostility had left her.

"See to him," she said, and closed the door.

With a sigh, the man stretched out gratefully on the bed. He didn't resist when Ten peeled off his socks, what was left of the shredded shirt, and the ruined trousers. He was left only his drawers. He was tall, well over six feet, and should have weighed close to 200. But he was gaunt. In places where his hair wasn't bloodied brown, it was corn-silk white, and his eyes were just a bit darker blue than Ten's. From knee to ankle his left leg was little more than bone. The little flesh that remained was a mass of scars. What passed for a grin on his smashed, swollen lips was ghastly.

"Left the rest of it . . . somewhere in Virginia," he said. "Knee hurts. They kicked me . . . when I . . . was down."

"I'll find a doc for you," said Ten.

Velda Kendrick and her pair of male boarders waited in the parlor.

"He needs a doctor," said Ten. "Who can I get, and where do I find him?"

"Doc McConnel," said one of the men. "He'll be in one of th' saloons."

"Oh, not *that* old sot," sniffed Velda.

"I'm not bothered by his personal habits," said Ten, "long as they don't get in the way of his doctorin'. Has he got a favorite hangout?"

"One of th' saloons near th' docks," said the man who'd recommended him. "He'll be in th' Amsterdam,

Mother Burke's Den, or th' Baltimore. He'll be all right. He gen'rally don't git petrified until aroun' midnight."

Ten turned to Velda. "How much for the room?"

"Dollar a night. Meals is extra."

He dropped a gold eagle on a table next to the chair in which she sat. "He'll be needin' some food. I'll be back with the doc."

He found McConnel in the Amsterdam. The doctor was a mild little man, bald except for a gray fringe, wearing steel-rimmed spectacles. He seemed accustomed to unusual hours, perhaps preferring them, for he had his satchel with him. He seemed unconcerned with what the town in general, and Velda Kendrick in particular, might think of him. He stalked through the parlor without a word to anybody. He studied his bloodied patient for a moment, and turned to Ten.

"Hot water, soap, and towels," he said.

When Ten returned with the requested items, he washed his hands and set to work. Once he had washed off the dried blood, it appeared most of it had come from severe lacerations of the scalp. McConnel took a razor from his bag, shaved off enough hair to get to the wounds, and deftly sewed the torn skin together. The rest of the cuts seemed minor. His chest, shoulders, and arms were yellowed and purpled with bruises, and there was a particularly livid bruise on the side of his left knee, just above the mutilated calf.

"Stay off your feet," said the doctor, "until you can move that knee without it hurting."

Given the two dollars he asked for, the doctor departed, promising to return on Friday. Ten turned to the man on the bed.

"I reckon you'll be all right here, unless somebody's got a grudge. Will they be looking for you?"

"No," he said. "I'd never seen them before. I'd stopped in a diner for a bowl of stew, and they . . . trailed me when I left. They wanted my money, my pistol, and my boots. There was four of 'em, but I . . .

didn't give up without a fight. They got hurt, and they got even."

"You asked me who I am," said Ten. "I'm Tenatse Chisholm, from Indian Territory. My friends call me Ten."

"I'm . . . from Texas, but I . . . told you that. My name is Martin Brand, and my friends, when I got any, call me Marty."

"We'll talk when you've rested and healed some. I'll see you tomorrow."

"I'll count on it," said Brand. *"Mucho gracias."*

Ten returned to the Magnolia Hotel, utilizing shadows and side streets, making it impossible for a potential bushwhacker to get a clean shot at him. The same darkness in which his enemies stalked him allowed him to elude them, and the time would come when it would be Tenatse Chisholm's turn to deal the cards. Before he was done, Ten vowed the hunters were going to become the hunted. His room was on the second floor, but he latched the window, bolted the door, and put a ladderback chair under the knob. He put the Colt under his pillow. But he wasn't disturbed, and he awoke feeling a bit foolish for all his precautions. When he reached the rooming house, he found Brand sitting on the edge of his bed. Despite the beating, Brand had already begun to heal. Much of the swelling around his eyes had diminished, and his battered lips had healed enough for him to talk without mumbling. Ten decided there was more to the man than met the eye. On a bedside table there was a pot that had soup stains and a glass still faintly colored with milk.

"Well," said Ten, "at least she fed you. That woman's got a disposition like a cactus patch."

"Can't say I blame her. When I come in, I didn't have much goin' for me. She's been nice enough. Last night I wasn't sure I'd ever eat again, but I just finished a pot of soup and a big hunk of corn bread."

The silence between them grew uncomfortable.

Brand seemed to be mustering up his courage. Finally he spoke.

"I'm beholden to you, but I got a confession to make. Even before I was robbed, I was lower'n a man can go and still think of himself as a man. I barely managed to keep myself in grub. Since Lee put down the sword, I've been half starved, afoot, and I've slept everywhere 'cept in a bed."

"I'd hate to have to keep myself alive in this town," said Ten. "Likely, I'd end up loading and unloading steamboats."

"I did that, but with this bad leg, I couldn't keep up the pace. They said I was too slow."

"You're a Texan," said Ten. "If you know cows, you oughta be working from a saddle, a good horse under you."

"I'd count it a miracle from God if I could. But nobody in Texas has a plugged peso. I don't even own a horse, and got no hope of ever ownin' one. I joined the Confederate army when I was eighteen. Ma tried to talk me out of it. She said they'd never see me again, and she was right. While I was gone, the Comanches killed her and Pa, and burned our place to the ground. I hitched rides when I could, but mostly I walked from Virginia. I got home to find only the chimney standing, young cottonwoods growin' where the house used to be. Down by the creek, where me and Pa fished, there was a pair of graves. No horses, no cows, nothin'. Took me 'most a week just to find out what happened to my folks. I had nothin' to hold me, so I come back to New Orleans. God knows why. I was so down and out, I didn't have any shells for my Colt, or them four lobos that jumped me would of been left dead in the street."

Ten recalled the words of Jesse Chisholm.

". . . when you ride into those Comanche-infested brakes, take some fighting men with you. Texas men. You'll know them when you meet them. They'll be the survivors of four years of war. They've already been to Hell and back."

"Suppose," said Ten, "you had a chance to be part of an outfit trailing Texas cows to Indian Territory, and later to the railroad? Could you fancy ridin' for and with an Injun like me?"

"Pardner, I'd fight the devil with a single tree for the chance to set a Texas saddle, on a good hoss, and ride with an honest-to-God cow outfit. Why, I'd paint my face, put feathers in my hair, and ride for your grandma."

"We'll be goin' into the brakes after the cattle," said Ten. "There'll be Comanches, maybe outlaws, and then the long trail north."

"Injun, you got yourself a Texas cowboy. When do we ride?"

5

On Friday, Ten visited different stores and shops, until he found Levi's, shirts, and boots for Marty Brand.

"You had to have these before you could go out," he told Brand, "but a man ought to choose his own hat and six-shooter. When you're up to it, we'll see to that."

Ten had taken a room for Marty at the Magnolia Hotel, and Marty left the rooming house on Saturday morning. Before going to the hotel, they made the rounds, until Brand found a black Stetson he liked. He completed his outfit with a new Colt, belt, and tie-down holster.

"I never reckoned I'd live long enough to be dressed as fine as this," he said.

Ten found it necessary to take Brand into his confidence regarding his visit to the LeBeau house.

"Pardner," said Marty, "I don't know whether to call you a brave man or cuss you for a fool. Takin' on them smugglers and black market gents might be interestin'. Even goin' after Comanches I can understand. But cozyin' up to a lonesome gal without any friends? Whooee!"

Ten grinned, pretending a calmness he didn't feel. The butterflies in his stomach felt as big as turkey buzzards and seemed to be having a violent disagreement among themselves. Just after four o'clock he knocked on Marty's door and was told to enter.

"Marty, I'm going to leave most of my money with you."

"You expectin' her to pick your pockets?"

"I don't know what to expect," said Ten. "Wolves around here seem to run in packs."

"Want me to tag along? Between the two of us, we could gut-shoot a pile of the varmints."

"I reckon not. I'll likely have enough trouble explaining why I'm there. Gettin' shot might not be as tough as what I'm about to do."

He returned to his room and dressed in the clothes Mathewson had sent. There was a white shirt with ruffled front and cuffs, a black string tie, and a fancy black suit with a square-tailed coat. The shoes were matching black, highly polished, and they cramped his feet. He wore them only because his boots were pretty well used up.

Marty grinned. "My God, you look like somethin' between a circuit-ridin' preacher and a hundred and eighty pound buzzard. I never seen so much black all at once. If you get in trouble, just hide out till dark and you'll disappear. Wanta wear my black hat?"

"No thanks," said Ten. "This is about all the finery I can stand."

The clock in the lobby said 4:25, and when he stepped out the door, the carriage was waiting. He got in, the liveryman clucked to the team, and they were off. The carriage was black, the horses were a team of matched blacks, and the liveryman wore black. Ten felt like he was on his way to a funeral. Perhaps his own.

The Logan house, built in the mid-nineteenth century, could only be described as elegant. It was two stories, white, with a porch across the entire front. Huge white columns supported a second-floor balcony encircled with white wrought iron. A white wrought-iron gate opened to a stone walk, while an iron picket fence set the house apart from the street. The fence extended as far as he could see, and appeared to surround the property. To the left, palms hung their graceful heads over the second-floor balcony, while on the right, the granddaddy of all magnolias shaded the lower porch, the east end of the balcony, and brushed waxy green leaves against the second-story windows.

"Your name, sir?"

Ten told him, and the butler finally found it on the second page of the guest list. He expected the man to lead him—or at least point him—where he was expected to go, but he was left on his own. He felt as out of place as a range bull in a sheep pen. He started down the hall. The first door he came to was wide enough and high enough to accommodate a Conestoga wagon and a six-mule team. He walked into what obviously was a parlor. The deep wine floral carpet looked as though nobody had ever set foot on it. The love seat and many chairs were richly upholstered in a plush velvet that matched the carpet. Paintings hung at perfect intervals along the walls, and magnificent burgundy drapes graced the windows from floor to ceiling. Strangely enough, on the far side of the room another door led to a second parlor as elaborate as the first. Except for the butler, he hadn't seen a soul.

Ten was in the second parlor when he heard a door close. He started toward the sound of it. The door on the far side of the second parlor was closed. He had his hand on the knob when it suddenly opened and a dark-haired, dark-eyed girl ran headlong into him. What he did next, he never fully understood the why of it. He kissed her full on the lips, and for just a heart-stopping second she responded. Then she backed away, took a deep breath, and slapped him so hard his ears rang.

Off balance, he stumbled into a spindly-legged glass-top table, and it toppled with a tinkling crash. He lay there amid the wreckage, afraid to open his eyes.

"Oh, you're hurt!" she cried.

He opened his eyes. The oval top of the table had been a frame for the glass, and some shards remained.

On one of these he had gashed the top of his left hand, and if appearance meant anything, the wound was mortal. His entire hand was bloody, and it dripped grotesquely off the tips of his fingers.

"What on earth . . . ?"

The woman was an older twin of the girl. It had to be Emily LeBeau.

"Come on!" cried the girl, taking his uninjured right hand. "We have to stop the bleeding!"

She led him into an enormous kitchen, filled a pan with cold water, and he put his bleeding hand into it. She left on the run, returning with a towel and a medicine kit. By the time she had the bleeding stopped and the cut bandaged, they had a considerable audience, including Emily LeBeau.

"Ma'am," he said, "I'm sorry about your table. I'm as clumsy as a cow on loco weed."

"Do I know you?"

"I doubt it," said Ten, "but I'm sure you know *of* me. I'm Tenatse Chisholm. My father is a frontiersman and scout. Jesse Chisholm is quite well-known in Washington. I'm sure you've heard Mr. LeBeau speak of him."

"I . . . ah, I'm sure that I have," she stammered.

"Mother," said the girl, "why don't you take our guests back to the summer house? Tenatse and I need to talk."

"Very well," said Emily, obviously relieved. "But don't neglect your other guests. Dinner is at six."

Ten viewed the "guests" with a critical eye. He doubted a one of them was under twenty-five, and every last one was female. John Mathewson pretty well had his facts straight. The girl pulled out a chair and sat down at the table. He straddled another, folding his arms across its back, and resting his chin on them. He simply stared at her. She had big gray eyes and hair as raven-black as his own. She had a pert nose, even teeth, and skin without blemish. When he didn't speak, she did.

"Why didn't you tell her the truth? You wouldn't have fallen if I hadn't slapped you."

"It would have served no good purpose," he said. "It would only have embarrassed you, and made me look like the fool I likely am. Besides, I had no right to do . . . what I did."

"Then why did you do it?"

"Because you're the most beautiful girl I've ever seen in my life, and I wanted to," he said. "If I had it to do over, I'd do it again, even if you pulled out a pistol and shot me between the eyes."

There was no doubting the truth of his words. She leaned forward, kissed him on his left cheek and again on the right. There was just a hint of moisture in the big gray eyes.

"Once for your honesty," she said, "and once more, because I wanted to."

It was suddenly unbearably hot. He stood and took off his coat, forgetting the Colt against his belly, under the waist of his trousers.

"A pistol!" she gasped. "Is it . . . loaded?"

"Yes, ma'am."

"Isn't that dangerous? You might shoot off some . . ."

"Parts I'd purely hate to lose," he finished.

He laughed, and she covered her crimson face with her hands. She spread her fingers and peeked at him with one big gray eye.

"You must think me a terrible, forward woman."

"I told you what I thought of you," he said. "That hasn't changed, and it never will."

"You totally flustered Mother. She never heard of you."

"But your daddy has."

"They never— They . . . oh, damn it," she cried, "I'm so *tired* of covering up for them! They each lead separate lives, and I . . . I'm alone. I don't have either of them. Mother flutters about, trying to impress people I simply can't stand. He—Father—goes off for days at a time, to horse races, card games, and . . . and God only knows what else. I have no friends. You *saw* my guests! Dear God, some of them are so old they—their female parts have—have grown up in weeds!"

He laughed, and again she blushed, hiding her face with her hands.

"I'm sorry," he said. "I wasn't laughing at what you said, but the way you said it. You talk honest, without put-on, like a western woman."

"Why haven't I seen you before, if you're a friend of . . . my father?"

"I've never been here before. This is my first time in New Orleans."

"You have an Indian name, but you speak English as well as I do."

"Jesse Chisholm, my father, is one-half Cherokee. My mother was a full-blooded Cherokee. Whatever that makes me, that's what I am. Jess sent me to school in St. Louis, and I stayed there three and a half years."

"Then you can't be much older than me."

"I won't be eighteen until the fourth of next April."

"I thought you were older. You seem . . . so mature, so sure of yourself."

"On the frontier, it's shoot or be shot. It ages a man. I never knew my mother. Sometimes, I think an Indian is born old, with a Bowie knife in his hand and raising hell his only option."

"What a profound thing to say." She giggled. "If Mother finds out you're Indian, she'll simply die. If Father were here, if he knew—"

"Then I'd die," said Ten.

"So would I, when he was through beating me."

The light had gone out of her eyes. She bowed her head, and a single tear slipped down her cheek.

"Priscilla."

When she finally looked at him, she tried to speak, but could not. She swallowed hard, and when the words came, they were almost a whisper. Ten leaned closer to hear.

"I have so enjoyed this little while with you. I'm not used to being treated like I . . . I'm a person with feelings of my own. When I think of how it's been, how it is, and how it's going to be, it's . . . it's the contrast that's hurting me."

He took both her hands in his, and she didn't resist.

"Priscilla, in another year you'll be eighteen. Your life will be your own, to live as you please. You can choose your own friends."

"No," she said, and her voice broke. "I'm to marry old Jason Brawn."

"What?" He gripped her hands so tightly she winced.

"He's . . . dear God, he's older than my father. But he's got money. He's the wealthiest man in New Orleans. He controls gambling in nearly all the saloons, and on some of the riverboats. Daddy says it's—it's in my best interests."

Like hell it was! Ten made a silent vow that he'd gutshoot this pair of conniving old bastards, if that's what it took. He turned his attention back to Priscilla.

"If you don't want him, then I swear he'll never have you!"

"I'll kill myself first," she exclaimed. "God help me, I will!"

"It won't come to that," he said. "You're not alone anymore."

She smiled, and chills broke into a fast gallop up his spine.

"Thank you," she said. "It's wonderful of you to want to help me, but what can you do?"

"I can take you so far into Indian Territory they'll never find you," he said grimly, "and I can kill anybody that tries to stop me."

"You're serious, aren't you?"

"Dead serious."

He still held both her hands, and she was looking at him in frank amazement, when the butler appeared in the doorway.

"Dinner is about to be served," he said.

Ten waited until he had gone before speaking to her again.

"Think of some excuse to get away from these people, and we'll talk again before I have to leave."

To his dismay, there were place cards at the dining tables, and the card with his name was far from Priscilla's. With her on his mind, he ate almost nothing. Finished, they retired to the parlors. There was an hour of foolish conversation, of which he later remembered nothing. He caught Priscilla's eye once, and she shrugged helplessly. There simply was no way they could escape together, without the reason being obvious. When the grandfather clock struck nine, the others began excusing themselves and leaving. Each of them paused for a parting word with Emily LeBeau and then with Priscilla. Ten waited until last. He mumbled something to Emily. Priscilla waited at the door, disappointment in her eyes. He spoke as softly to her as he could.

"Where's your room?"

"Upstairs," she said.

"Near the balcony?"

"Yes," she said. "At the end where the magnolia tree is."

"When the house is dark, I'll meet you on the balcony in the shadow of the tree."

She started to say something, but he was already in the hall, on his way to the front door. He was relieved to find that Mathewson didn't have the carriage waiting. He walked far enough from the house that he could see without being seen, and waited in the shadow of a tall hedge. He froze, thinking he'd heard a stealthy footstep, but it wasn't repeated. The wait was making him jumpy, he decided. First, it had been the endless socializing in the parlor, and now the wait until Priscilla reached her room. His heart leaped when a lamp was lighted in the room she'd said was hers, but every downstairs window was still ablaze with light. The big magnolia tree on which he depended stood between two of those lighted windows. The upstairs lamp went out after a few minutes, and he waited impatiently for those downstairs to be extinguished. Finally, one by one, they were. By the stars, it was no later than ten o'clock, but it seemed he had waited half the night. He delayed a little longer after the last lamp went out, then returned to the house. The gate creaked like something out of a bad dream, and he held his breath. But there was no sound except the crickets, and he went on.

Once he was in the massive shadow of the magnolia tree, he felt safe. The tree was old and gnarled. Its lower branches were within easy reach, and worthy of ten times his weight. Two-thirds of the way up, he came to an enormous branch that reached out over the balcony. Directly above it was a lesser limb to which he could cling for balance. Once over the balcony, he let himself down as quietly as he could. She had changed her pale blue gown for a thin, white dressing gown. She came to him with a sob, clung to him, and he could feel her slender body trembling. She had spread a quilt up against the wall, and although the balcony was roofless, the friendly big magnolia concealed them with its shadow.

"I was so afraid you wouldn't come," she whispered. "Mother would never have left us alone as long as she did if she hadn't had all those people in the house."

"Can't you talk to her, tell her how you feel?"

"No," she said. "Do you think she asked *me* if I wanted this so-called birthday party, with a bunch of silly females simpering over me? She just used me, like my father intends to use me, buying favor at Brawn's gambling tables. I'm so sorry I'm burdening you with all this, but I have nobody else. I'm ashamed of myself for being so selfish. It's not your problem."

He drew her close to him, so that he could speak into her ear.

"I'm making it my problem. I want you, Priscilla Le-Beau, if you'll have me. Say that you want me, and I'll take you west, to the frontier. I'll swear by the stars that *nobody*—your daddy or anyone else—will ever use you or abuse you again."

He felt her tears on his cheek, and it was a moment before she found her voice. Even then, it trembled with emotion.

"Tenatse Chisholm, I've known you just five hours, but I trust you. I believe in you. If you really and truly want me, I'll go with you."

"Not just because there's nobody else?"

The tone of his voice took the sting out of his words, and her response took his breath away. The night was cool, but when she let go of him, sweat ran into his eyes and dripped off his chin. Somehow, the flimsy gown had gotten above her waist, and she wore nothing else. Reluctantly he withdrew until she had it back in place. She then turned to him with a whisper.

"Now do you believe me?"

"I believe you," he said. "There's never been anyone else, Priscilla, and now there never will be."

"Tenatse—"

"Call me Ten."

"Ten, let's not . . . run away just yet. Neither of us will be of age for another year, and if I try to leave now, there'll be a fight with my father. When I go, I want nothing to stand in my way. When I'm eighteen, you will be too, and—and sure that you . . . want me."

"I *am* sure I want you, damn it. What must I say? What must I do? If I want you and you want me, what *else* do we need?"

Weeping silently, she tried to turn away, but he caught her. He said nothing, waiting until she quieted. Finally she spoke.

"Ten, I'm sorry. I didn't say that like I . . . meant to. I wish, oh Lord, how I wish I could go with you tonight. I'm asking you to wait because we would never even get out of New Orleans. Until I'm of age, the law will force me to answer to my father. Jason Brawn controls the law, Ten, and you would be killed. You'd be accused of kidnapping me, and shot on sight. I don't doubt your courage, Tenatse Chisholm, but the odds are just too great. I believe we'd be safe on your frontier, but I want us to go legally, not like frightened mice, with the cat in hot pursuit. Damn it, Ten, I want you, but I want you *alive,* not shot dead before my eyes. Can't you understand that?"

"I reckon I do. I'm just . . . well, disappointed. It's like I won you and lost you all in the same night. But you're right. More right than you know. I wasn't going to tell you, but your daddy hates my guts. I'd rather have you hear it from me than to learn of it later and believe I hadn't been honest with you."

"What did you ever do to him?"

"Caught him dealing from the bottom of the deck on *The New Orleans,* and he was banned from the poker tables. Maybe on other steamboats too."

"Oh, dear God! He'll have you killed!"

"I don't think so. Not for that, anyway. That saloon was full of prominent men from New Orleans. If I end up dead, he'll be suspected."

"Ten, you don't *know* him. He has a vicious temper. I'm afraid for you, and I want you to get out of town as quickly as you can, although I'll miss you terribly. When will you be coming back?"

"October, if Jess has another load of trade goods for Roberts and Company. You're afraid for me, and I'm more afraid for you. Suppose something goes wrong? How am I going to know?"

"There's a little bit of good news I haven't told you. If things get too bad, I can always go to Louisville and stay with my grandmother. She's my mother's mother, and she never has liked or trusted my father. He hates for me to go there, but he doesn't try to stop me. That's one of the few ways Mother stands up for me. If I go, I'll write to you from there, and you can write to me. Where do I send my letter to you?"

"Send it in care of Jesse Chisholm, Fort Smith, Arkansas. We only get the mail twice a month. You can use the telegraph too. Somehow, get me a letter before I come back to New Orleans. Tell me how I can see you while I'm here. Things being the way they are, I just hate to leave you here."

"You have no choice. Perhaps when you return, you can arrive quietly, without my father knowing you're here. God knows *what* he'll be like by then. There's something eating at him, threatening him. There's one thing you haven't told me, Ten. How and why did you get yourself invited to that foolish party tonight?"

"That's the one thing I can't tell you without violating a confidence. Let's just say it was done through a friend you and your mother aren't aware of, a friend who thinks you need somebody to stand by you. But after tonight, after finding you, I feel like all the chips are on my side of the table. Someday, when all this is behind us, maybe I'll tell you the whole story. Until then, will you trust me?"

"I'd trust you with my very life. It's going to hurt me terribly, but you'd better go. You just don't know how I'm tempted to keep you here, or to just go with you. Go, and come back to me when it's safe for you."

Fearfully, she watched him depart, relieved that he was safely away from the house, but uncertain of his safety until he left New Orleans. Something bothered her, and she stood there watching, listening, long after he had vanished into the night. Suddenly she was cold, and the thin gown offered little protection. She would have been sorely tempted had he tried to take her, but he had not. She trusted him all the more, for his concern for her had overcome everything else. While he was young in years, he was a man.

With Ten on her mind, Priscilla tried in vain to sleep, unaware that but a few hundred yards away other eyes had watched Tenatse Chisholm fade into the darkness; brutal men who had lain in wait, then beaten Ten until he lay unconscious, soaked in his own blood.

6

When the steamboat had docked in New Orleans, LeBeau and Sneed were the first ashore. They had positioned themselves behind some freight wagons, where they could see without being seen.

"I want you to follow him," said LeBeau, "for as long as he's here, and at six Friday evening, meet me in the lobby of the St. Charles with a report."

"I'll tail him," said Sneed, "but suppose he leaves before Friday? You want me to come to th' house and tell you?"

"Under no circumstances are you to come to the house. Whatever you have to tell me, save it for Friday."

By five-thirty Friday evening LeBeau was pacing the lobby of the St. Charles Hotel. He had planned a weekend at one of Jason Brawn's gambling houses. It was remote enough that Brawn provided carriages for his patrons from New Orleans. The carriages departed promptly at seven, and if LeBeau wasn't ready, he'd have to provide his own transportation. Six o'clock came and went without a sign of Sneed. It was half past the hour when he finally arrived, and LeBeau was furious.

"You're late," he snapped. "Whatever you have to say, say it. I have something for you to do tomorrow night."

They seated themselves as far from the desk as possible, and Sneed began his report. LeBeau listened indifferently until Sneed came to Ten's visit to the U.S. Customs office. At that point he bounded out of his chair as though prodded with a hot iron.

"So *that's* what he's up to!" he all but shouted.

Several people, including Sneed, looked at LeBeau in surprise. He forced himself to sit down, but his teeth were clenched, and he gripped the arms of the chair so fiercely, his knuckles were white.

"When he left there," continued Sneed, "he—"

"I don't care a damn about the rest of it," interrupted LeBeau.

Sneed said no more, waiting. Finally LeBeau got back to him.

"What name is he using?"

"Tenatse Chisholm."

LeBeau rested his elbows on his knees and covered his face with his hands. He spoke without looking at Sneed.

"This . . . Chisholm has gotten himself invited to my daughter's birthday party tomorrow night. He'll be there until maybe ten o'clock. I want you to hire half a dozen men. You know the kind. When he leaves the house, follow him. When he's far enough away, in some dark, deserted place, give him a beating he won't forget. I want him out of this town, and I want him to leave with some strong reasons against coming back."

"Why don't I just shoot the troublesome bastard?"

"My God, Sneed, use your head! Too many people saw him make a fool of me on the boat. If he ends up dead, who do you think will be suspected? I want a report from you Sunday evening. Be here at five, and don't fail me."

It was nearly midnight when Ten left Priscilla, and she so occupied his mind, he could think of little else. It had all begun with his feeling sorry for Priscilla, but now, having known her for just a few hours, he was awed by the depth of his feeling for her. He forced his thoughts away from Priscilla and considered what she had told him about Jason Brawn. If LeBeau had underworld connections, and this Jason Brawn controlled the law, then their escape would be far more complicated than just getting her out of the LeBeau house. Engrossed in his thoughts, he found himself in a section of the Garden District where every window was dark. The moon had set, and there was only the starlight. Suddenly there were footsteps, and he could see the dim outline of a man approaching him. Wary, he continued, allowing the stranger plenty of room. Coming even with him, the man's brawny arm shot out and a hand grabbed the front of Ten's coat. Ten had caught the movement from the corner of his eye, but not soon enough. He fought, the coat ripped, but before he could free himself, a massive arm was around his throat.

His wind had been shut off, and it seemed he was drowning in a dark sea, with the roar of the pounding surf in his ears. Suddenly the pressure let up, but he was surrounded by men. Blows rained on him, and from the numbing pain, he knew some of them were from brass knucks. He could feel blood welling from his smashed nose and lips. Somebody dug a knee into his groin, and waves of nausea swept over him. Something came crashing down on his head, and he felt himself falling . . . falling. If it would free him from the pain, he welcomed unconsciousness, but he was denied even that. When he was down, they began kicking him. Only when a boot heel smashed against the side of his head did welcome oblivion take him.

With the clop-clop-clop of hoofs and the rattle of a carriage, the brutal, one-sided affair ended. The attackers faded into the darkness, leaving the young man from Indian Territory where he had fallen, breathing raggedly, unconscious.

Marty Brand was uneasy, and he had come by the emotion naturally. His mother had been like that. She would get a feeling in her bones that something awful was about to happen, and would fidget about like a worm in hot ashes until she knew what it was. By eleven o'clock he *knew* something had gone wrong, and he wasn't going to camp in that hotel any longer. While he had agreed not to accompany Ten, he hadn't promised he wouldn't follow later. He checked his Colt, stuffed extra shells into his pocket, and went down to the street. It was late, but it was Saturday night, so he found a livery open. By lantern light the hostler and two other men were playing poker.

"I need a carriage for a while."

"Nothin' left but a couple of buckboards," said the hostler, irritated by the interruption.

"I'll take one," said Marty, "and I'll hitch up the team, unless you got rules against it."

The man said nothing, and Marty took that for approval. He didn't care diddly about a matched team, so he took the two handiest horses, a roan and a black. He could have taken a saddle horse, but was less likely to draw attention to himself in a buckboard. Besides, he might need a buckboard. He had confidence his young Injun partner could take care of himself in a fair fight, but from his own experience, who could say the fight would be fair? While a man might be hell on little red wheels with a pistol, he died just like anybody else when he was shot in the back.

Marty was a cautious and observant man, and while he didn't know the town well, he knew where St. Charles was, and the nearest cross street to the LeBeau house. There were markers on the street corners, but they were less than useless in pitch-dark. Departing the LeBeau house, a man on foot didn't have that many options as to direction. Marty judged it was near midnight when he reached the heart of the Garden District. The LeBeau house was near the middle of the block, a respectable distance off St. Charles.

Keeping to cross streets, Marty paralleled the house to the east and west. Not a house on the block showed a lighted window, and he had no way of knowing where

Ten might be. Had he somehow gotten the girl out of the house, or was he somewhere within it? Coming to St. Charles on the east side, he reined up, undecided as to what direction next to take. Then, somewhere to his left, he heard something, and it reminded him of a sickening sound he'd heard before. Once, fighting for his life with no chance to reload, he had killed a Union soldier with the butt of his rifle. He had never forgotten the sound of the death blow to the man's head.

He wheeled the team to the east and set off down St. Charles. In the shadows ahead he thought he saw movement, but in the darkness he'd have missed Ten if the horses hadn't shied at the smell of blood. Looping the reins over the brake handle, Marty drew his Colt and stepped down. Satisfied the attackers were gone, he found Ten's wrist and sought a pulse. It was there, but weak. It would be risky, moving him without knowing the extent of his injuries. Movement might worsen some internal hurt of which he was unaware, or a broken rib might puncture a lung. But he had no choice. He was scarcely healed from his own beating, and his weakened left leg threatened to give out as he struggled to get Ten into the buckboard. Reaching the Magnolia Hotel, he searched the street in vain for someone who might help him. Finally he went into the lobby. The night man had his feet on the counter and was leaning back in his chair, snoring. Marty whacked the bell as hard as he could, and the clerk was jolted awake.

"Sorry," said Marty, "but I have a friend who's been hurt, and I need help getting him to his room. There's nobody else around, so it's up to you."

The man was disgruntled and wanted to argue. "Where is he? *Who* is he?"

"Outside in a buckboard," said Marty. "The man from room twelve."

"Oh, him!"

He had been on the desk the night Ten had returned the ambusher's fire. Wordlessly, he followed Marty outside. The twin lamps at the hotel entrance cast some light into the street, and for the first time, Marty could see just how brutally Ten had been beaten.

"My God," cried the clerk, "is he alive?"

"He won't be," said Marty grimly, "if we don't get him to his room and find a doctor."

Ten was heavier than he looked, and it wasn't easy, getting him up the stairs. Marty was more fearful than ever of the damage all this movement might be doing internally. They eased Ten down on the hall floor, while the clerk unlocked the door. By the time they had the wounded man stretched out on the bed, they were exhausted.

"Much obliged," said Marty. "I'd never have got him up here without you. Where can I find a doctor this time of night?"

"Maybe Doc Lowell. He's got no family, and he lives at the St. Charles Hotel. If he ain't there, he might've left word at the desk."

Marty drove as fast as he dared, along the dark, narrow streets. He'd considered going to the riverfront saloons in search of old Doc McConnel, since he wouldn't have as far to go. But he drove on to the St. Charles. Doc McConnel, even if he found him, would be totally "petrified" by now.

"Doc's down the hall," said the night man. "Room four. But he's likely dead on his feet. Was up all night last night, all day today, and he ain't been in more'n two hours."

Dr. Lowell could sleep tomorrow. Tenatse Chisholm might be dead by then. Marty pounded on the door a dozen times before he got a sleepy response. Lowell proved to be a young man, sandy-haired, so thin he mightn't have had a square meal in his life. He also looked sorely in need of the sleep from which he'd been awakened.

"Sorry, Doc," said Marty. "My friend's been beaten almost to death. He's at the Magnolia Hotel. I have a buckboard. I'll take you there and bring you back."

"Give me five minutes," said the sleepy doctor.

Marty, thinking of Ten's bloody, battered body, begrudged every minute. Despite the cool night air and the added chill from the river, the horses were lathered by the time they reached the Magnolia. Marty vowed they'd be rubbed down when they were returned to the livery, if he had to do it himself. This time the desk clerk was wide-awake.

"We'll need some towels, soap, and plenty of hot water," said Marty.

Marty took the stairs two at a time, the doctor right behind him. Ten still lay on his back, and if appearance counted for anything, he could have been dead. Dr. Lowell looked at Ten and shook his head.

"Let's get him out of those clothes. What's left of them."

Marty answered a knock on the door and found the night man there, with towels, soap, a tin wash pan, and a bucket of hot water.

"Thanks," said Marty. "You've been mighty helpful."

The doctor carefully removed the Colt from beneath Ten's belt, placing it on the table beside the bed. Once they had the ruined, bloody clothes off, he looked even more brutally beaten than before.

"He's had a severe blow to the head," said Lowell. "If he doesn't have a fracture, it'll be a miracle. He was slugged, and then kicked while he was down. His ribs are a mess; maybe some of them broken or dislocated."

"Punctured lung?"

"Probably not," said Lowell, "but I won't know for sure until I wash away the blood from his nose and mouth. Then we'll see if he's breathing without the bloody foam. I see no evidence of it, and that's a good sign."

Most of the wounds on Ten's head and face needed stitches. The gash on the back of his head was the worst. There was another above his left eye, and a lesser one over his right ear. The jagged cut on his right cheek had barely missed his eye. His coat had partially protected his upper body, and while he was black and blue with bruises, there were no serious wounds.

"Now," said the doctor, "you'll have to help me. I'm going to bind his ribs, and you'll have to lift him enough for me to pass the bandage around him."

When at last they were finished, the doctor took a small bottle from his bag.

"Laudanum," he said. "I'm going to get a dose of this down him now, and leave the rest. He's scarcely going to be able to move for the next three or four days. I'll see him again tomorrow afternoon."

Marty drove the doctor back to his hotel. When he returned to the livery, the poker game was still in progress, a fourth man sitting in. Marty unhitched the team, rubbed them down, and paid his bill. Back in the Magnolia, Ten lay as they'd left him. Marty took his wrist and felt for the pulse. It was there, but still weak. Suddenly the battered lips moved.

"Pardner," said Marty, "it's your turn to rest. Don't do anything but breathe and sleep."

He went to his room, returned with his blankets, and spread them on the floor next to Ten's bed. He kept his Colt within reach, in case there was a need for it.

André LeBeau returned home Sunday evening in a foul mood. He had some good reasons. He had just come from the meeting with Sneed, and had learned of Ten's visit to the balcony and, from what he'd heard, Priscilla's bedroom. Besides that, he had lost heavily at Brawn's gambling tables. He had no idea how deep was the hole he'd dug for himself, and he was afraid to find out. He salved his conscience as usual, by vowing to win big next time, and free himself once and for all. While Jason Brawn never mentioned money, he never failed to inquire about "the beautiful Priscilla." The implication was clear: LeBeau's gambling debts would be forgiven when Brawn took Priscilla. LeBeau shuddered. It was enough to sicken even him.

He had to vent his anger and frustration on somebody, so he went looking for Emily. He found her in the dining room, going through the latest edition of the weekly newspaper. Priscilla was there too. So much the better, because he had a bone to pick with them both.

"I want to know why this Tenatse Chisholm, Indian scum that he is, was allowed in this house while I was away."

"Since when have you taken any interest in anything that goes on in this house?" snapped Emily. "He's new in town. A friend of mine, who's a friend of his family, asked that he be invited. Why is it of any concern to you?"

"Because your daughter—our daughter—threw herself at him like a riverfront whore, and he practically spent the night in her bedroom."

"That's a lie!" shouted Priscilla. "He never set foot in my bedroom."

"You can't accuse her of anything," said Emily. "You weren't here."

"I have a witness," bawled LeBeau. "Chisholm used your stupid party to get into this house. He left when the others did, then climbed up to the balcony . . ."

"So what?!" shouted Priscilla defiantly.

"So you've disgraced yourself and me," snarled Le-Beau. "How can I face my friends? You'll be the gossip of the town. Jason won't—"

"Now that I'm used goods," interrupted Priscilla, "Jason won't have me. That's what's bothering you, isn't it? You'd trade my body to that lecherous old pig for the privilege of getting in over your head at his poker tables. Well, I have some news for you. I'd rather be dead and in Hell than married to Jason Brawn, and if there's no other way of escaping it, I'll kill myself!"

She was leaning across the dining table toward him, the fury in her eyes such as he'd never beheld. A blind rage came over him, and he hit her much harder than he'd intended to. She stumbled backward, hit her head against the wall and went to her knees. Emily LeBeau stood in open-mouthed amazement, coming to her senses only when he'd hit Priscilla. Then Emily turned on LeBeau, in a fury all her own.

"I don't care *what* she's done, André LeBeau. If she finds favor with this young man, or any man of her choosing, she's entitled to it."

"All right," snarled LeBeau, "so it doesn't bother you that she's disgraced the LeBeau name. Must she consort with the very scum that's out to destroy me? Do either of you know *why* this young scoundrel weaseled his way into my house? Certainly not to romance you, Miss High-and-Mighty. He came here looking for evidence that my enemies can use against me."

Priscilla laughed. "Now I know what your problem is," she said. "You don't care a damn about me *or* my reputation. You just hate *him,* and you're using me as an excuse to cut him down. The truth of it is, he caught you cheating at cards, exposed you before half the town, and got you banned from the poker tables on the steamboats. *That's* why you hate him, isn't it?"

LeBeau's face flamed, not with embarrassment, but with fury. The real issue—the true cause of his hatred for Tenatse Chisholm—was his belief that the customs people were using Ten to get to him, through Priscilla, to expose his suspected smuggling and black-marketing activities. It was a truth LeBeau dared not reveal to Priscilla or Emily. Let them believe what they wished. Now that Emily had turned on him, he wouldn't have to feel so guilty when he robbed her trust fund. The money would buy his freedom from Brawn, Montaigne, and their bunch of cutthroats. LeBeau was jolted rudely back into the present by Emily's words.

"I believe," she said, "this is a case of the pot calling the kettle black. If Priscilla disgraced us with this young man—which I doubt—at least she did so in private. You managed to make a fool of yourself on a steamboat loaded with the very people you're afraid of. So don't talk to me about disgrace. Priscilla can't hold a candle to you."

"It's hereditary," said Priscilla.

Without another word, LeBeau stomped out into the hall. He could hear them laughing, in their newly discovered camaraderie.

That afternoon, without a word to her husband, Emily LeBeau saw Priscilla off on a visit to Louisville.

When Dr. Lowell returned on Sunday afternoon, he pronounced Ten's condition much improved.

"His temperature's near normal," said the doctor. "If he'd been hurt internally, there would be infection by now, and that's what causes fever. When he comes around, lay off the laudanum, unless he needs it for pain."

Monday morning, just before daylight, Marty was leaning back in a chair, dozing. Unexpectedly, Ten spoke.

"When—What . . . day is it?"

"Monday morning," said Marty. "I reckon this will sound foolish, but how do you feel?"

"Like I—I'd put my head . . . on an anvil, and . . . somebody took a . . . nine-pound sledge . . . to it."

"Anything I can get for you?"

"Water. I'm . . . almighty dry. Starved too. Go somewhere . . . get me . . . some soup. Maybe a gallon. Any kind."

Even with smashed and swollen lips, Ten had eaten most of the soup, when a knock on the door caused Marty to draw his Colt.

"Who is it?" he asked.

"John Mathewson."

"Let him in," said Ten. "He's the man who sent me to see Priscilla."

7

Mathewson was visibly shocked at Ten's condition. He looked questioningly at Marty Brand, then back to Ten.

"Perhaps I'd better come back another time."

"No," said Ten. "This is Marty Brand. He knows all about this. It was him that hauled me in, after they jumped me Saturday night. I can talk. I don't feel any worse'n if I'd been trampled in a buffalo stampede."

"I'm sorry I got you into this," said Mathewson. "LeBeau must have had you followed, and when you came to my office, he got scared. You took a bad beating for nothing."

"I didn't enjoy it," said Ten, "but it wasn't for nothing. I found the girl I'm going to marry. My God, Mathewson, you didn't do her justice. When Priscilla turns eighteen, I'm taking her away."

"So *that's* what put sand in her craw and fire in her eye," said Mathewson. "LeBeau came home last night, and using you for an excuse, jumped on both Emily and Priscilla. The girl stood up to him, and her mother sided with her. This afternoon, Emily will put Priscilla on a boat for Louisville. The word I have is that when Priscilla is eighteen, Emily will leave LeBeau for good."

"I'm obliged to you for telling me," said Ten. "I hated to leave her there, but she's not of age, and neither am

I. We decided we'd have to wait a year. How did you learn all this?"

"I suppose I can tell you now. I have a contact in the house. Even so, I didn't know until last night, there's some kind of arrangement that would have Priscilla marry old Jason Brawn after she turns eighteen. You brought it to a head, by giving Priscilla hope. Not only did she shoot down this so-called arranged marriage, she seems to have gotten her mother on her side."

"I've seen some wild Saturday nights myself," said Marty, "but nothin' like this. When these Injuns come to town, they sure know how to cut loose a sackful of bobcats."

"In a roundabout way," said Ten, "this may yet lead you to whoever's at the head of the smuggling and black-marketing bunch. If this Jason Brawn controls the gambling *and* the law, why can't he also be the tall dog in the brass collar in other crooked affairs? Maybe he's used LeBeau's weakness for gambling to rope him into smuggling and black-marketing."

"You're practically handing me back my own thoughts," said Mathewson. "The more I learn of Le-Beau's connection with Brawn, the more convinced I am that it goes deeper than LeBeau's interest in Brawn's gambling tables. I suspect you're right—Le-Beau's insatiable lust for gambling is at the bottom of it. A man spending as much time at the tables as LeBeau does is always needing money, and lots of it. If Brawn *were* seeking prominent men to front for him, he need look no further than his own gambling tables. For perpetual losers like André LeBeau."

"Keep your eyes on LeBeau," said Ten. "When Brawn gets the word that Priscilla won't have him, I'd give heavy odds he'll start to burn LeBeau's tail feathers. Let a pair of thieves rub each other the wrong way for long enough, and there'll be big smoke. Then some fire."

"Excellent thinking," said Mathewson. "I can get you

an appointment as a U.S. Customs agent, if you're interested."

"Thanks," said Ten, "but I've had about all I can stand of New Orleans. But I aim to come back in October, if for no other reason than to spend some time with Priscilla. Since she's legally tied to old LeBeau for another year, before I see her, I'd like to talk to you. If he does anything that's harmful to her, I'd take it as a favor if you'd write or telegraph me at Fort Smith."

"That I will," said Mathewson. "I plan to establish contact with Emily LeBeau. That woman has courage, and I'm as concerned for her safety as I am for Priscilla's. I'm told LeBeau has a violent temper."

When Mathewson had gone, there was a long silence. It was Marty who finally spoke.

"Give old LeBeau a year, and he won't have a wife *or* a daughter. You ought to introduce me to this Emily, before Mathewson gets too set on her."

"She's old enough to be your mother," said Ten. "Besides, she's a town woman, used to rich living."

"You reckon her daughter ain't? Injun lad, you're goin' to need some *pesos*. We'd better head for Texas and start draggin' them longhorns out of the brush. Got any idea when we'll be leavin' here?"

"Friday," said Ten. "I need to see Doc Lowell again. Then I can heal on the boat as well as I can here, and we'll be on our way that much quicker."

On August 1, 1865, Jesse Chisholm rode to Fort Smith for a meeting with Major Henry Shanklin. It was at Shanklin's request.

"I suppose," said Shanklin, "you're aware it's the government's wish that the plains tribes, as many as are willing, move to assigned lands in Indian Territory?"

Chisholm nodded.

"We have reached an agreement with Chief Tusaquach," said Shanklin, "and he has agreed to relocate his village of some three thousand Wichitas. As you know, they're presently a few miles south of Abilene, at the joining of the Arkansas and the Little Arkansas."

Again Chisholm nodded.

"I have several reasons for meeting with you," said Shanklin. "First, and most important, your position of trust among the plains tribes is unparalleled. Our agreement with Tusaquach hinges on your assisting with the move. Second, and of utmost importance from a military standpoint, we understand that a few months ago you blazed a wagon road from your ranch on the Arkansas, in Kansas, to your trading post on the Canadian, in Indian Territory. Is that correct?"

"It is," said Chisholm. "Close to two hundred and twenty miles, by my calculation."

"Good," said Shanklin. "That was my understanding. So you see, your road leads from the present Wichita camp to within a few miles of the lands assigned in Indian Territory, on the Canadian River. On behalf of Indian Affairs, I wish to enlist your help."

"I'll help in any way I can," said Chisholm. "What you're referring to is a trade route. It's recently been extended south as far as Red River Station, to the mouth of Salt Creek, at the western edge of Cross Timbers. The Cherokees have found it useful, driving a few small herds of Texas cattle into Indian Territory."

"How far is it from your trading post on the Canadian to Red River?"

"I'd say a hundred and twenty miles."

"Interesting," said Shanklin. "I'll see that Washington is aware of this. With an adequate wagon road from the Red to the Canadian, it might be to our advantage to ship military supplies by boat to Red River Station, and freight them into Indian Territory by wagon."

Chisholm said nothing. Shanklin continued.

"Getting back to my original proposal, how much time do you need to prepare for moving the Wichitas from eastern Kansas to Indian Territory?"

"I'll have to take some of the wagons and teams from the trading post on the Canadian," said Chisholm. "Figure three weeks from there to the Wichita camp. Will I be furnishing provisions, or will you?"

"Why don't you just contract for it all?" said Shanklin. "Besides the three thousand Wichitas, make allowances for several companies of soldiers. Could we expect to make the trip to Indian Territory in another three weeks?"

"Maybe," said Chisholm. "That's allowing for only ten miles a day. My teams, teamsters, extra horses, and mules will be an advance party. We'll be crossing the Arkansas, the Cimarron, the North Canadian, and Canadian rivers. There's a problem of quicksand. It's constantly shifting. Where you crossed safely yesterday, you could be sucked under today. We'll need to stay far enough ahead of the party so that we'll have time to beat down the riverbeds, for safe crossing."

"I'm responsible for this move," said Shanklin, "but you'll be in charge. It's important that it go smoothly. Washington is hopeful that the success of this venture will induce other tribes to follow. I'll inform my superiors that you'll be prepared to depart the Wichita camp on the Arkansas by the first of September."

Ten and Marty left New Orleans as planned. Ten's face still bore the evidence of his beating, but he could walk with hardly a limp. He had seen Dr. Lowell on Friday morning, before leaving.

"Too soon to remove the stitches," Lowell had said, "but they'll have to come out."

There would be a doctor at Fort Smith. Besides Ten and Marty, there were three passengers. One man was an officer, the other two were drummers. There was no shortage of room, but Ten and Marty shared a cabin. The journey soon grew tedious and boring.

"If you aim to go back to New Orleans in October," said Marty, "you won't much more'n get home 'fore you have to leave again. I swear, I'd as soon get me a good hoss and light out across country."

"The boats seem almighty slow," said Ten, "but that's

how Jess gets his pelts and hides to New Orleans. I just
hope there'll *be* another load ready by October, and that
he'll let me take it. I should have been back long ago."

"That's a powerful long ways to go a-courtin'," said
Marty. "I just hope this little gal gets word to you about
where she is. It could get to a man, forkin' this slowpoke
contraption all the way to New Orleans, just to find out
she ain't there."

"She'll be there," said Ten. "She knows that's when
I'll be there."

"There's all them cows in Texas, and there's just you
and me. I'd say we're a mite short-handed."

"I'd have to agree with you," said Ten. "When we
leave New Orleans the next time, we'll be looking for
riders, and we won't be on a steamboat. Jess has promised to stake me until we can gather and sell a herd. I'm
thinking we'll buy horses in New Orleans and ride for
Texas. Since you're *from* East Texas, maybe we can build
an outfit with some of the folks you know."

"Maybe," said Marty, "but so many of us rode off to
war, and so many won't be comin' back . . ."

Ten understood, and they left it there.

Reaching Fort Smith, Ten had a pair of surprises
awaiting him. One was a brief telegram from Priscilla,
telling him her address in Louisville and requesting a
letter. The other was a single, handwritten page from
Jesse Chisholm.

"Not bad news, I hope," said Marty.

"No," said Ten. "Not the telegram, anyway. It's from
Priscilla. This other is a note from Jess. Read it."

Marty read it and handed it back.

"He figures three weeks there and three weeks back,"
said Ten. "If he starts back September first, that means I
won't be seeing him until almost the time I need to start
back to New Orleans."

"You just come from there, and got yourself considerably busted up whilst you *was* there. You reckon he'll
want you just turnin' around and goin' again?"

"You mean," said Ten, "when he finds out *why* I'm wantin' to go back."

Marty grinned. "I didn't like to say it that way, but yeah, that's what I'm gettin' at. It's a mighty long ways to go, just to see a gal."

"I promised Priscilla I'd be there, and I aim to. I might not see her again until she's eighteen. Maybe not even then, dependin' on how these trail drives work out. Jess promised me a stake, so's I could go to Texas and build a herd. But he wants me to wait until after the first of the year, when the blockades come down. It won't matter to us whether they *ever* come down or not, because we can't afford to ship cattle by boat. So I don't aim to wait another three months to start buildin' a herd. What's to stop us from going back to New Orleans, and from there to Texas?"

"Nothin' I can think of," said Marty, "if you're hell-bent on goin' back before goin' to Texas. Makes sense to me. In the time it takes this boat to get back to Fort Smith, we can *be* in Texas, with a gather started."

"Exactly what I'm gettin' at," said Ten.

"Since shipping from New Orleans is out of the question, where do you aim for us to trail this herd, once we wrassle it out of the brush?"

"I aim to trail 'em right into Indian Territory," said Ten. "Jess has gone after a tribe of Wichitas, moving them to assigned lands. There'll be other tribes, as soon as the government can get 'em to move. They expect these Injuns to farm, and maybe they will, but a man's got to have meat. Reservation Indians can't follow the buffalo, and that means beef. Besides that, there's five forts in the territory, every one with soldiers to feed."

"I can see that," said Marty, "but what're these Injuns and garrisoned soldiers eatin' *now*?"

"Texas beef," said Ten, "when they can get it. Texas Cherokees run in small herds from time to time, but nothin' regular, like I aim to."

"Texas Cherokees don't raise cows. They didn't in my neck of the woods, anyway. They stole 'em."

Ten chuckled. "Still do. Horses and mules too. Jess offered me the pick of what he buys off the plains Indians, but I got some serious doubts about ridin' horses to Texas that just come from there."

Marty grinned. "You *do* look ahead. I like that. Trailin' a herd north, we could follow that wagon road—Chisholm's trail—from Red River to the Canadian, or even into Kansas."

"Not Kansas," said Ten. "There's problems with tick fever. But Jess says that'll be settled one day. From what I found out in New Orleans, there'll be a railroad into eastern Kansas in less than two years. Know what that means? We could trail us a thousand longhorns into Indian Territory, graze 'em along the Canadian or North Canadian until the rails get there, and we'd have us a *real* herd to ship east."

"I like the sound of that," said Marty. "We'll be reapin' our natural increase. Sounds more like an honest-to-God cow ranch than just drivin' a few cows here and a few cows there."

"I know," said Ten, "but I want to start *now,* not wait for the rails. We'll sell what we can, to the forts in the territory. Before we leave, I'll talk to the quartermaster. Might sell some here at Fort Smith."

Ten was allowed to talk to Sergeant Higgins about the possibility of supplying beef to Fort Smith.

"I can't imagine the son of Jesse Chisholm dealing in stolen cattle," said Higgins dryly, "but I'm required to ask. You *will* be going to Texas and gathering this herd —not buying from questionable sources?"

"I aim to drag 'em out of the brush and burn my brand on 'em," said Ten. "I'll sign your bill of sale myself."

"I can get authorization to accept two hundred head at a time," said Higgins, "but I'm allowed to pay only sixteen dollars a head. You could get nearly twice that in Omaha or Chicago."

"Too far," said Ten. "Omaha and Chicago will have to

wait for the rails. You'll have your beef come spring, no
later than mid-April."

They rode out of Fort Smith the next morning on
borrowed horses, bound for the Chisholm trading post
on the Canadian. Ten had left a letter at Fort Smith, to
be sent to Priscilla.

"I reckon," said Marty, "you've made a pretty good
case for us gettin' started to Texas. Two hundred head,
that's thirty-two hundred dollars. I ain't never *seen* that
much in my whole life, all at once."

"If that's *all* we bring out the first time," said Ten
happily, "it's a start. Anyhow, it'll keep Jess from holding off any longer on this trail drive from Texas. If I'm to
keep my word to Higgins, we'll have to be there chasin'
longhorns, by November first."

"You *are* a sneaky little Injun," said Marty, "but we
got five weeks before your pa returns with them Indians.
What do you aim for us to do until then? I'm tired of
loafin', and ridin' steamboats."

"I aim for us to ride to the other forts," said Ten,
"and set up some more beef sales. Fort Cobb and Fort
Arbuckle are closest, so we'll go there first. Fort Washita
and Fort Towson are practically in Texas, at the north-
eastern border of Indian Territory, just across the Red.
Fort Gibson's to the northeast, where the Neosho flows
into the Arkansas."

"We could've got some supplies at Fort Smith and
gone to these other forts first. If your pa ain't there,
we're in no big hurry to get to the trading post, are we?"

"Not as far as he's concerned," said Ten, "but I want
to see if there'll be another load of pelts and hides ready
for New Orleans by October. Besides, we can get us
some better mounts, and a pack mule."

"I feel better," said Marty, "now that this cow hunt
and trail drive is shapin' up. I just wish that next visit to
New Orleans was behind us."

"We'll only be goin' there on the steamboat," said

Ten. "From there to Texas it'll be bacon, beans, hard saddles, and harder ground."

"Ten, I look for trouble in New Orleans. Gun trouble."

"Nobody's going to know I'm in town," said Ten, "except Priscilla and maybe Mathewson. Besides, LeBeau won't have me killed, for the same reason he hasn't already."

"It ain't LeBeau you got to worry about. You think this Jason Brawn don't know about Priscilla's blow-up, and the reason for it?"

"I want him to," said Ten, "so he'll leave Priscilla alone. Just because she's put him down don't mean he has to know of my plans for her."

"He'll know," said Marty, "and he won't stand for it. He'll be the kind that if he can't have her, he'll see that you don't either. Laugh if you want, but I got my ma's uneasy nature, which kind of prods me when there's trouble comin'. That's what told me to get a buckboard and go lookin' for you that Saturday night in New Orleans."

Tenatse Chisholm didn't laugh.

Jason Brawn surveyed the papers on his desk with a satisfied smile. He paid for information, and he paid well. He had been rewarded with a veritable network of informants from all walks of life, and he reveled in the sense of power that was his. The first sheaf of papers, handwritten, provided him with as much information on Tenatse Chisholm as could be had, from the revelation of LeBeau's cheating aboard *The New Orleans,* to Tenatse's departure from New Orleans.

The second pile of handwritten pages had actually been part of the first report, but he had separated them for a reason. They dealt entirely with what was known of Tenatse Chisholm's relationship with Priscilla LeBeau.

Finally he turned to the third sheaf of papers. They were promissory notes, totaling almost fifty thousand dollars, signed by André LeBeau.

8

For the tenth time in as many minutes, André Le-Beau looked at his watch. He hardly knew which was worse: waiting in an agony of suspense, or the actual confrontation with Jason Brawn. Because he was vulnerable on so many fronts, he found it impossible to rehearse what he might say in defense of himself. He expected to catch hell over Priscilla's rebellion or his delinquent gambling debt. Or maybe both, he thought gloomily, since his foolish promise of Priscilla was all that had held Brawn at bay on the staggering debt. If that wasn't bad enough, there might now be a third crisis, more formidable than either or both the other two. Suppose Brawn had somehow learned of Tenatse Chisholm's visit to the U.S. Customs office? This fear was fueled by the fact that Sneed had seen Mathewson with Chisholm, following his own disgrace at the poker table. No doubt others had witnessed that brief meeting on the deck of *The New Orleans*. Mathewson had given Chisholm something. What? How much did Brawn know or suspect?

"Come in, LeBeau."

LeBeau swallowed hard and got up, feeling like a condemned man. Brawn had sent his secretary on an errand. When Brawn was in an especially bad mood, he didn't want an audience. LeBeau knew it was going to be even worse than he had expected. To the left of

Brawn's mahogany desk there was a plush armchair. With a sigh of resignation, LeBeau slumped down in it.

"Did I ask you to sit?" shouted Brawn.

The chair overturned as LeBeau stumbled to his feet. In his frantic eagerness to right the chair, the tail of his coat snagged a whiskey decanter, dragging it off Brawn's desk with a resounding crash. LeBeau got the chair upright and stood gripping its back so his hands didn't tremble.

"Now," snapped Brawn, "sit down!"

LeBeau sat, mentally cursing Brawn for his cruel intimidation, and himself for yielding to it. For a long moment Brawn sat without a word, looking for the world like a harried, prosperous banker. He had thinning gray hair, cold blue eyes, and a mouth that seemed to turn down at the corners. Soft living had given him jowls and a ponderous belly, over which was draped a heavy gold watch chain. In fact, his ample person was testimony to his fondness for gold. He wore a gold tie pin, gold cuff links, and, on the third finger of his left hand, a gold ring with an enormous diamond. His gray pin-stripe suit was accented by a flaming red tie over a white ruffle-front shirt. LeBeau glared at him in defiance, torn between hate and envy. When Brawn finally spoke, his voice was deceptively calm.

"I'm hearing talk, LeBeau. Disturbing talk. I am told the fair Priscilla has repudiated me, refusing to honor our . . . ah, agreement."

"It—It's a year, yet," stammered LeBeau. "She's gone—been sent—to Louisville . . . for a rest. She's . . . distraught, upset. . . ."

"Her reason for being distraught and upset," said Brawn, "is a troublesome young man from the West. Tenatse Chisholm."

"He—He's gone," said LeBeau, licking his dry lips. "I . . . took care of him."

"He's gone," said Brawn contemptuously, "but your clumsy attempt to scare him had nothing to do with it. He'll be back."

"You don't *know* that! How—How do you know?"

"How I know doesn't matter," snapped Brawn. "What *does* matter is his disgraceful conduct with Priscilla, and his apparent ties with U.S. Customs. They're trying to get to me through you, LeBeau. As my chances diminish with Priscilla, so does your usefulness to me. When Chisholm returns, I want him dead. *Dead!*"

He pounded the desk with his beefy fist, and LeBeau jumped. From then on Brawn seemed to dismiss LeBeau from his thoughts. He sat there leafing through papers that LeBeau recognized as his own promissory notes. Brawn hadn't mentioned them, but he hadn't needed to. He simply wanted LeBeau to see them; reminding him, damning him, accusing him. Long after LeBeau had stumbled from his office, Brawn sat there fondly thumbing through the notes. Fifty thousand dollars! It was a lot of money to pay for a woman, but young Priscilla LeBeau would be worth it.

Ten and Marty didn't waste any time at the Chisholm trading post. The second day after their arrival, they set out with two good horses and a pack mule for Fort Cobb on the Washita.

"I doubt there'll be enough trade goods to justify another trip to New Orleans anytime soon," said Ten. "When Jess is off scouting, or negotiating with the tribes, not much tradin' takes place. Him bein' gone for six weeks will cut pretty deep."

"Plains Indians don't exactly trust the Cherokee help, I reckon."

"That's what it amounts to," said Ten. "One Indian will beat another, if he can. It's their way. They expect that, and they'd rather trade with a trusted white man than another Indian."

"So if we're goin' back through New Orleans," said Marty, "it'll be without the trade goods. You reckon he'll agree to that?"

"I hope so," said Ten, "because I *am* going."

In five days they had visited Fort Cobb, Fort

Arbuckle, and had further committed themselves for two hundred head of cattle to each fort.

"I can't believe Jess won't be impressed," said Ten exuberantly. "He's a trader; how can he not be excited? Me, a no-account, secondhand Injun, kicked out of school because he ain't worth a damn, and I've already got commitments for six hundred head!"

"Don't flap your wings and crow too quick, you young rooster. We got to catch them six hundred brutes and trail-drive 'em eight hundred miles."

They followed the Washita until it joined the Red. At Fort Washita they struck a deal for another two hundred head. Proceeding east along the Red to Fort Towson, they brought their commitment to a full thousand head.

"Five forts, a thousand head!" shouted Ten as they rode away. *"Bueno!"*

"If you'll pardon the expression," said Marty, "a feather in your hat. But give credit where credit's due. Your bein' Jesse Chisholm's *hijo* sure didn't hurt our cause."

"Oh, I don't aim to steal any of Jess's thunder. He's a *bueno hombre* among the Injuns, and on speaking terms with the Great White Father in Washington. All I'll ever be is a cowboy, if I'm lucky. We're a long ways from Fort Gibson, but I reckon we ought to ride up there. We don't, and they'll wonder why I didn't make them the offer I made the others."

"Come on, then," said Marty. "Let's ride. Let's don't quit while we're rollin' sevens."

They had no trouble making a similar deal at Fort Gibson. Even taking their time, it was only mid-August, still two weeks away from Jesse Chisholm's return.

"A couple of days down the Arkansas," said Ten, "and we'll be at Fort Smith. Why don't we spend a day or two there, instead of ridin' on back to the Canadian? We're waitin' for Jess now."

"On to Fort Smith," said Marty. "There may be a letter from Priscilla."

Their visit to Fort Smith accomplished nothing. Ten

was half hoping for a letter from Priscilla, but it wasn't there. Despite his faith in her, he needed to know that she would be in New Orleans when he arrived. That it would be difficult for him to see her, he had no doubt. He feared she would be under constant pressure from LeBeau.

"We'd as well head for home," said Ten after the second day.

Their return to Chisholm's trading post was uneventful. They found a secluded area by the river and took turns firing Ten's new Henry rifle.

"It's a sweet-shootin' gun," said Marty. "If this trail drive works out, maybe I can afford one."

"You won't have to wait for that," said Ten. "I aim for you to have one before we ride into Comanche country."

Jesse Chisholm returned three days earlier than expected. He looked at Marty Brand approvingly and put out his hand. Ten told him of the negative responses to his inquiries about shipping cattle by boat. He mentioned the coming of the rails to Kansas, a year and a half away.

"Well," said Chisholm, "if that's how it is, I don't suppose there's any hurry in trailing a herd from Texas."

"Oh yes there is," said Ten. "I've already sold twelve hundred head, and promised delivery by spring."

With considerable relish, he detailed their activities of the past three weeks and the commitments he had made to the various forts.

"While I admire your ambition," said Chisholm, "I'll have to question your judgment. You don't know what difficulties you may encounter in Texas. The cattle are wild. You could spend sixteen hours in the saddle, and catch maybe two or three cows. You'll need half a dozen good men besides yourself, and you have only one."

"You don't believe I can do it, do you?"

"I didn't *say* that," said Chisholm. "Now that you've given your word, you'll have it to do, whatever the difficulty. I'm just telling you that you're allowing yourself no slack, and before you're done, you'll see the need for it. On the frontier, nothing is ever cut and dried, dead certain. What you plan to do in one day may take two or three. Or a week. Once you have some cows, Comanches may stampede the herd, and then ambush you when you go looking for it. Now that the war's over, there'll be deserters and renegades from both sides to contend with."

Ten looked from Chisholm to Marty and back to Chisholm. When neither of them spoke, he did. Angrily.

"I reckon I'm just an ignorant damn Injun. What do I know about catchin' wild cows, or anything else?"

He stomped out of the barn and headed for the river. Marty got up to follow, but Chisholm bade him stay.

"He's got the bit in his teeth," said Chisholm. "Just let him run till he's winded. Then we'll talk business. I notice he's picked up some battle scars. Fight?"

"I reckon it's his place to answer to that," said Marty uncomfortably.

"You're right," said Chisholm. "Sorry. How do you feel about this wild cow hunt and trail drive?"

"I favor it," said Marty, "and I got my reasons. The Yanks beat us to a finish, and I left Virginia afoot. Got back to Texas and found my family all dead. Our place was gone to hell. I was walkin' the streets of New Orleans, half starved, when a bunch of *pelados* bashed in my head and robbed me of the little I had. Even my boots. This no-account, hotheaded Injun found me, got me to a doc, got me a room so's I could heal, and I been with him ever since. He don't always look before he jumps, I can see that. But give him time, and he'll make some almighty big tracks. If he decides to tackle Hell with a bucket of water, I reckon I'll grab a bucket and go along."

Chisholm laughed and slapped the young Texan on the back. "Once in his life, every man deserves a friend he feels that strong about. You'll do, Marty Brand. I only wish he had some more like you. Let's go get some coffee. He'll be along pretty soon, ready to pull in his horns and make some sensible plans."

Marty sighed. The cow hunt and trail drive seemed definite, but Ten still had some rocky ground to plow. He hadn't so much as mentioned the situation in New Orleans and his determination to return there.

When Jesse Chisholm and Tenatse eventually got together, Marty Brand made himself scarce, not wishing to get caught in the cross fire. While he was loyal to Ten, and sympathetic toward his strange relationship with Priscilla LeBeau, he couldn't help admiring Jesse Chisholm. While the man was mild-mannered and slow to anger, there was nothing weak or irresolute about him. He hadn't disagreed with what Ten proposed to do, only the way in which he was going about it. Ten was enough like Jesse that he wouldn't allow this standoff to go unresolved. Marty finished his coffee, excusing himself just in time. Ten was returning for the showdown. While he didn't speak, he flashed Marty a lopsided grin. He understood Marty's reasoning and his hasty departure. Only a fool got himself gunned down in somebody else's fight.

Ten seemed repentant for his angry outburst, but not to the extent that Jesse Chisholm had expected.

"Sorry, Jess. I reckon there's times when I'm not near as much a man as I'd like to be. It's just . . . well, I want to make something of myself, and this trail drive means a lot. When you— I felt . . . like I'd been stomped by the bronc before I ever got in the saddle."

"Like I told you," said Chisholm, "I have nothing but admiration for you, in the way you've ridden to the forts and set this up. But I fail to see the necessity of rushing into it ill-prepared. I've been a trader most of my life, and I'm not penniless. I never suggested that you give up the cow hunt and trail drive, only that you wait until after the first of the year. Now just tell me why you can't —or won't—and we'll go from there."

It was precisely the opening Ten needed, but dreaded. He took a deep breath and plunged in.

"I want to be more than just a half-Injun, leaning on you. I want to be a man who can stand on his own feet, make his own way. I reckon that sounds vain, but it's not for me. It's for the girl I aim to marry. I won't have her livin' in a mud hut, cooking rabbit stew over an open fire."

After a lifetime on the frontier, Jesse Chisholm was rarely caught off his guard, but this was an exception. Ten, apprehensive as he was, laughed at the incredulous expression on Chisholm's face. It was a while before the old plainsman trusted himself to speak.

"You spent an almighty lot of time in New Orleans. I reckon you'd best start at the front, and don't leave anything out."

Ten began with his exposure of LeBeau's cheating aboard *The New Orleans* and dwelt extensively on his meeting with John Mathewson. While he revealed none of the intimate details of the hours he'd spent with Priscilla LeBeau, he did explain her wretched predicament and the arranged marriage LeBeau sought. He was careful not to mention the possibility that Jason Brawn was the head of a smuggling and black-market ring. He concluded with his proposal to Priscilla, her acceptance, and his determination to return to New Orleans.

"I see," said Chisholm. "You're going to save the young lady from an arranged marriage to a man she despises. Her daddy is in the clutches of this Jason Brawn, probably as a result of his gambling debts. To save his own hide, he's about to sacrifice her to a man who may well be responsible for smuggling and black-marketing. The girl's being used, and she knows it. How sure are you of *her*?"

"You make it sound like she's just . . . using me to save herself, like old LeBeau's trying to use her!"

"Now that you mention it," said Chisholm mildly, "how do you know she's not?"

It was a possibility Ten had already privately considered, so it didn't shock or further anger him. Instead, it had the opposite effect, and he grew calm. He had already reached a decision in his own mind, and he just gave Jesse Chisholm the result of his own conclusion.

"I won't fault her if she *is* using me. I want her, Jess, and if that's the price I have to pay, then I'll pay it."

"From the scars," said Chisholm, "I'd say you've already paid some of it. Am I out of line if I ask how you aim to see her again without getting yourself killed?"

"I'm not sure," said Ten, "until I hear from her. There'll be a letter by the time I get to Fort Smith. Whatever the risk, she's worth it. I'll take my chances."

"If you plan to go to Texas by way of New Orleans," said Chisholm, "you'd best plan on taking the next boat out of Fort Smith. If you're to meet the beef deadline you've set, you'll have to be roping cows by the first of November."

Ten looked at Chisholm as though he couldn't believe what he was hearing. He swallowed hard, and it was a moment before he trusted himself to speak.

"You mean you'd . . . *still* be willin' to stake me, after . . . this?"

"I've never broken my word to any man," said Chisholm, "whether I agreed with him or not. When you're ready, I'll advance you a thousand dollars. I expect you to build yourself a decent outfit. You've made a start, but you need more men the caliber of this Marty Brand. But you want to straddle your own broncs, and I respect that. Better to be pitched off and stomped than to not have the sand to mount up."

Ten and Marty reached Fort Smith on Sunday. Monday, October 2, they would depart for New Orleans. Ten had a rough map Chisholm had drawn for him. It included the major rivers in Texas, landmarks, and towns with which Jesse Chisholm was familiar. Marty breathed a sigh of relief when Ten found that all-important letter from Priscilla waiting for him. There was another letter without a return address. Ten read Priscilla's letter first, and his delight quickly became disappointment. Marty saw it in his eyes.

"She ain't goin' to be there, is she?"

"No," said Ten. "Something's wrong at home. Her mother's told her to stay in Louisville. Here, read it."

There was but a single page, and he read it quickly. The girl's distress came through in every line. The last sentence was a frantic appeal, every word underlined:

Please, please don't go back to New Orleans now!

Marty returned the letter, and Ten handed him the second one. It was brief, signed by John Mathewson. It said:

Come to my office as soon as you can. Of vital importance. It concerns Priscilla.

Marty returned the letter and waited for Ten to speak. He knew what was coming.

"I'll have to go," said Ten. "I asked him to send me word if anything happened involving Priscilla. But I won't force this boat ride on you. Go on back to the trading post and wait for me there. Texas will have to wait."

"No," said Marty, "I'll stay. I don't hanker to explain to Jesse Chisholm how come I let you go by your lonesome to get shot dead or stomped into doll rags. You'll need somebody with a gun, to watch your back."

So they boarded *The Talequah* and began the monotonous journey down the Arkansas. Ten read and reread the two letters, trying to get something more from them than the few words revealed.

9

Following his disastrous meeting with Jason Brawn, LeBeau stopped at a saloon to salve his mangled pride. When he left, he took a quart of bourbon with him. Emily wasn't at the house, but he didn't care. He kicked off his shoes, stretched out on his bed, and did the one thing at which he had always been successful. He got stinking drunk, and it was sometime the following morning before he awoke. He was sick, sick! Somewhere, somebody was striking an anvil, and every blow kept time to the throbbing of his head. Then came the dull realization that the anvil *was* his head. He groaned and sat up. In his fogged mind, he picked up the remnants of the previous day, going over his ultimatum from Jason Brawn. He had to find Sneed.

It was noon before he was presentable enough to leave the house. He still hadn't seen Emily. He wondered if she had returned home and had left again, or had simply been gone all night. He decided he didn't care, after she'd hustled Priscilla off to Louisville without a word to him. That again brought to mind Priscilla's angry repudiation of Jason Brawn, and the haunting stack of IOUs that Brawn held. Somehow he had to force the girl back into the cruel shackles he had forged for her. He went to the rooming house where Sneed lived, pounding on the door until he awoke the grouchy little man. LeBeau entered the dingy room, closing the door behind him.

"Until I tell you different," said LeBeau, "I want you there when the boats come in from Fort Smith. When this Tenatse Chisholm shows up, follow him. Find out what hotel he goes to."

"That all? You don't want me tailin' him ever'where, like before? What if he don't go to a hotel?"

"Don't be stupid," said LeBeau. "He can't leave until the next boat."

Twice a week, for a month, Sneed met the boats from Fort Smith. Just as he had decided it was a useless vigil, and was about to give it up, he sighted Tenatse Chisholm on the deck of *The Talequah*.

As the boat neared New Orleans, Ten and Marty had a final talk.

"We can't afford to be seen together," said Ten. "Do you know where the St. Charles Hotel is?"

"Yeah," said Marty. "Is that where we're goin'?"

"That's where *you're* going. When we dock, you leave ahead of me and go rent us a room in your name. Wait in the lobby, and when I come in, signal me the floor. I'll go up, and once you're sure nobody's trailing me, you can follow."

"Good plan," said Marty. "When will you go to the customs office?"

"Early in the morning. There's no way to avoid havin' them trail me once I leave the hotel, but that's where you come in. I want you at a great enough distance behind me that you're behind anybody that's trailin' me."

"You're countin' mighty strong on bein' followed from the hotel," said Marty. "If they know you're here, all they got to do is stake out Mathewson's office until you show up there."

"All the more reason for you not to be close enough to get sucked in. If nothing else, I can always hole up in

Mathewson's office. I don't think they'll gun me down right at the customs office. You'll have the Henry; watch for snipers at the windows, and on the roofs of other buildings."

"This office you're goin' to, what kind of place is it?"

"Mathewson's office takes up half the bottom floor of the building," said Ten. "The stairs to the second floor are outside, leading to a railed balcony that runs across the front of the second story. I reckon the place used to be a Spanish mission. It's got an open bell tower that reaches from the first floor to above the roof."

"Sounds like a perfect trap. A box canyon."

The steamboat whistled for the landing. Ten got up off his bunk, and Marty took the Henry rifle. *The Talequah* nosed in to the dock, and they waited until they heard the creaking of the gangplank being lowered.

"Time for you to go," said Ten. "I'll be in the lobby of the St. Charles in half an hour."

Ten waited, going on deck only after he was certain that Marty would be ashore and out of sight. He paused on deck, but saw nobody on or near the dock that he recognized or that might recognize him. He took his time, so that Marty could arrive at the St. Charles well ahead of him. When he did enter the lobby, Marty was seated near the desk, apparently absorbed in a newspaper. Using the paper as a shield, he quickly held up three fingers. Without pausing, Ten walked through the lobby and up the stairs to the third floor. Marty followed a few minutes later, hurriedly unlocking the door to Room 31. They entered, and he locked the door behind them.

"I'd forgot about this place havin' first-floor entrances on all four sides," said Marty. "I'd say that's goin' to make it almighty hard for them to stake out this place without attractin' attention. I reckon you'd best look close for trouble once you reach Mathewson's office."

"I aim to," said Ten, "but I *still* want you stayin' as far behind me as you can. However and whenever they come at me, stay far enough behind me that we don't both walk into the same trap."

"If I'm too far behind, I won't be much help, if they hit you close up."

"But if we're both pinned down behind the same rock," said Ten, "you'll be no help at all."

The St. Charles had its own dining room. For locals and travelers alike, it was one of the most fashionable places in New Orleans to eat. Marty went to the dining room first, and Ten remained in their room until he had returned. Despite what the morning might bring, they slept. They arose well before daylight and began preparing for whatever might lie ahead.

"Go on down and have your breakfast," said Ten. "When you're done, wait in the lobby. I'll give you half an hour before I go to the dining room. When I'm finished there, I'll leave the hotel and go to Mathewson's office."

"We goin' to keep this room?"

"No," said Ten. "If we walk into a trap of Jason Brawn's making, we won't be safe anywhere in this town. He'll have us hunted from here to yonder. Remember—trail me at a distance, don't risk gettin' trapped with me."

"If you need help," said Marty, "I'll be within rifle range."

He stepped into the hall, closed and locked the door, and Ten began counting the minutes.

Ten finished his breakfast, walked through the hotel lobby and out the front door. He walked around the block and then crossed the street, pausing at various shop windows. He used his peripheral vision, looking right and left. He saw nobody; not even Marty. The big clock in the hotel lobby had struck eight as he was leaving. He had no idea what time Mathewson arrived at his office, but the town seemed to have already begun the day. He paused at the corner, a block away from his destination. His eyes searched the rooftops and windows of other buildings. The morning sun winking off a windowpane or rifle barrel might appear much the same. The lead would make the difference.

Although Ten saw nothing alarming, an eerie sense of unease hung over him like a pall. Were they going to allow him to enter the building, and trap him there? John Mathewson was a Federal agent, and he found it hard to believe that LeBeau—and especially Jason Brawn—would have him gunned down on Mathewson's doorstep. It was the one advantage he'd believed he'd have. Now he wasn't sure. Reaching the door to the customs office, he looked up and down an apparently deserted street. He lifted his eyes to the balcony, and even to the bell tower. Seeing nothing, he took a deep breath and tried the heavy oak door. He thought at first it was locked, but it grudgingly gave as he put his weight to it. The outer office was empty, so he shoved the door, closing it as noisily as he could. Mathewson's office door opened, and Ten found himself looking into the inquiring eyes of Mathewson's secretary.

"Ma'am," said Ten, "I need to see Mr. Mathewson."

She removed her spectacles, wiping her eyes before she spoke.

"I'm afraid that won't be possible, young man."

"He asked me to come. I have his letter."

"Let me see that," she said.

Biting her lip, she returned the letter to him. Then she pointed to several sheets of official stationery and envelopes on her desk. They were engraved with the name of the agency, its address, and the great seal of the United States.

"That's what Mr. Mathewson used. Never just plain paper. Besides, that isn't his handwriting. When did you receive this letter?"

"The first of October," said Ten.

"I'm sorry to say that John Mathewson was ambushed near the docks on the second of September, and his body was lost in the river. I'm keeping the office open until Washington sends an agent to replace Mr. Mathewson."

Ten stared dumbly at her. Recalling that last sentence in Priscilla's letter, he could almost hear her pleading voice.

Please, please don't go back to New Orleans now!

Then, sounding faint and far away, there was the distinctive bark of a Henry rifle.

The big door had barely closed behind Ten when Marty saw the start of it. He stood in a doorway near the north end of the block and watched a man step out of a door across the street from the customs office. The morning sun flashed off a pistol, and Marty cut him down with a slug from the Henry. The shot might be Ten's only warning.

Ten didn't know if he'd have to face one man or a dozen, but he knew full well he had walked into a trap. They were coming for him, and they hadn't gone to all this trouble for it to end with a beating. He ran past the startled secretary, to the window in Mathewson's office. The drapes were drawn. He thrust them aside, and a slug shattered the upper pane just above his head.

Marty leaned out of the doorway and drew immediate fire. Two rifles cut loose, lead slapping into the door frame, showering him with splinters. From the sound of the earlier shot, he knew there was at least one man behind the customs-office building, and maybe more. In a matter of minutes one of them could sprint down an alley to the north of him and catch him in a deadly cross fire from the other end of the street. It was exactly what Ten had feared. Gripping the Henry, he lit out in a zig-zag run, as lead from the hidden rifles pursued him. He had to get Ten out of there, but where could they go? They were afoot in a hostile town. Then he heard the clopping of hoofs and the rattle of a wagon somewhere ahead. His hat in one hand, and the Henry in the other, he turned west on the next street, running toward the sound.

* * *

In frightened silence, the woman stared at the glass littering the carpet in John Mathewson's office.

"Ma'am," said Ten, "how can I get to the upper floor from here?"

"You . . . can't," she stammered. "Outside. The stairs are outside. . . ."

Desperately, he tried to recall what the exterior of the building was like. A wrought-iron railing encircled a second-floor balcony, with stairs leading to the balcony at each end of the building. Every office door opened directly to the outside, and from the shooting, he knew at least two riflemen covered the front of the building. For that reason, the last place they'd expect to see him was on the second-floor balcony, or the roof. From there, with Marty's help, he might shoot his way out. But how was he to *get* there? He had but one chance: the old bell tower! On the inner wall separating the secretary's office from the floor-to-roof bell tower, there was a door. But it had no knob, no lock. It had simply been nailed shut. He threw all his weight against it, but it held. Three more times he put his shoulder to it. He stood there panting, sweat dripping off his chin. There was a veritable fusillade of gunfire from outside, and he redoubled his efforts. The door finally splintered down one side, and he kicked enough of it away to crawl into the very center of the building. The bell tower above him was open to the roof. The old brass bell had blackened with age and was big as a wash pot. From it dangled a rope!

Having finished his route, the milkman was half asleep, depending on the horse to find its way to the barn. The wagon was a box affair, like a hearse, with a flat roof and hinged doors at the rear. The front of its wooden roof overhung the seat, with the interior in back of it open. Marty was on the wagon's seat before the sleepy driver was aware of him. Marty snatched the reins, giving the startled milkman a shove. He lay in the street and watched his wagon careening away, cans clanking and bottles rattling. Reaching the street he'd just left under fire, Marty sent the milk wagon clattering down it. *If* that bunch of *buzardos* didn't shoot the horse, *if* Ten somehow escaped that old mission, and *if* neither of them came down with lead poisoning, they had a chance.

Ten grabbed the rope, and the bell let go with an awesome clamor, seeming to grow in volume with every stroke of the clapper. Since the tower was open to the elements, he expected the rope to snap under his weight, but it held. If they got him, he thought grimly, there'd be plenty of witnesses. The clanging of that fool bell could be heard for miles. Slowly, painfully, he hoisted himself toward the roof. Reaching the upper third of the tower, where the sides were open, he stopped to suck air into his starved lungs. He struggled on. No sooner had he dragged himself out onto the balcony than the riflemen discovered him. Slugs began whanging off the iron railing, and he went belly-down, returning their fire. He had the satisfaction of seeing two of his antagonists leap for the safety of an open door. A third lay motionless in the street.

"Heeeeeeyah," bawled Marty. "Heeeeeeyah!"

He was hunched over the wagon seat, the reins in his left hand, his Colt in his right. Yet another gunman stepped around the corner of a building, and Marty fired, sending him diving for cover. Ten stepped over the balcony railing, clinging to it, as Marty and the clattering milk wagon drew closer. Timing the speed of the wagon, Ten dropped onto the flat roof. Two rifles cut loose, and there was the breaking of glass within the wagon, as lead tore through its thin wooden sides. There was a low iron railing around the edge of the wagon's roof. His boots against the front railing, Ten lay flat, facing the rear. He returned fire from the roof of the jouncing wagon as long as he was in range. Finally he holstered his Colt, grasped the railing at the front of the wagon's roof, and swung down to the seat beside Marty.

"Bad news," said Ten. "John Mathewson's dead."

"No deader than we're goin' to be," said Marty grimly, "if we don't get the hell out of this crazy town."

10

Marty slowed the horse to a trot and kept to the side streets. In their situation, a galloping horse hitched to a milk wagon could only attract unwelcome attention.

"Much as I hate bein' afoot," said Ten, "we have to rid ourselves of this wagon. Head for the river; that's likely what they'll expect."

Marty pulled the wagon in behind a boarded-up warehouse, and they found themselves in a weed-infested lot shaded by a fair stand of young field pines.

"There's a coil of rope under the seat," said Marty. "Bring it along. We might fall down a well, the kind of day we've had so far."

They stepped down from the wagon box, and the bay horse looked around at them reproachfully. He wasn't used to galloping wildly through the streets at the end of his route.

"With or without the wagon," said Marty, "he'll make tracks for the barn. Let's unhitch him, and they may not find this wagon for a week. With the horse loose, by the time somebody allows it was him pullin' our wagon, they won't know for sure which way we went."

"Once they decide we didn't take to the river," said Ten, "there's only two ways we can go: north or west. East or south, and we're in the Gulf."

They ducked from one building to the next, traveling

east along the river. Once they were far enough from the wagon, they stopped to rest.

Marty groaned. "I know we had to leave the wagon, but I'm startin' to think we should of kept the horse. My feet are killin' me already. Bein' Injun, you'd ought to have at least a pair of moccasins handy."

"If I did, I'd be wearin' 'em myself."

"With nothin' but the Gulf ahead of us, how far do you aim to follow the river?"

"Until we reach the edge of town," said Ten. "Then we'll turn north."

They froze at the sound of horses' hoofs. Peering from behind what had once been a cotton warehouse, they saw three mounted policemen riding down the river toward them.

"The law's huntin' us," said Marty, "when it was us them ambushin' coyotes was out to kill. All we done was return the favor to some of 'em."

"That won't be the story the law and the newspapers are told," said Ten. "Priscilla says Brawn controls the law, and I reckon this is proof enough."

"Brawn knows there's nothin' but water east and south, and he's got to know we're from the West. Why are the lawmen ridin' east?"

"He's not sure we won't travel east," said Ten, "in the hope of boarding a sailing ship bound for Texas ports by way of the Gulf."

"Might save our hides, if we could do that."

"We dare not," said Ten. "With the blockade down, ships will be docking at New Orleans. The law can search any ship or steamboat."

"Well, if we got to walk, we'd ought to be walkin' west."

"They'll expect that," said Ten. "If there's three mounted lawmen looking for us here, there may be a hundred of 'em west of town."

"So we're goin' north."

"Far as we have to," said Ten, "to get out of Louisiana. We ought to be safe in Mississippi, if we can dodge the law. We'll keep to small towns, so they can't send word ahead by telegraph. Once we're able to buy some horses, we'll ride cross-country through northern Louisiana to Texas."

"My God," groaned Marty, "my feet are already cryin' surrender. Without hosses, we'll never make it."

"We'll have horses, and soon. Those lawmen won't ride far. Once they head back this way, we're goin' to appeal to their better natures and ask to borrow their horses for a while."

Marty looked at him pityingly for a moment before he spoke.

"I reckon you got enough Injun in you so's it don't bother you, grabbin' somebody's hoss, but my God, man, not from the very law that's already after your scalp! You—We—are purely goin' to wind up on the business end of a rope, with the other end slung over a limb. I'd as soon face a charge of murder as hoss stealin'. If we're goin' to steal mounts, then let's grab 'em somewhere else, not from the law!"

"Sorry," said Ten, "but we don't have time to be particular. You just lay back out of sight. It's me they want, and if I'm caught, they can't hang me but once. Besides, when we're beyond Brawn's reach, we'll free the horses. Come on. I want to find a place with some cover, before those hombres give up and head back to town."

They waited in a wooded bend of the river. Marty was silent, mulling over his misgivings. Ten looked at the sun and judged it wasn't much after ten o'clock. He felt like it had been days since his escape from Mathewson's office. Bothering him most was the more than seven hours before nightfall. They must somehow elude their pursuers until darkness gave them an edge. Then they must ride all night across streams, through unfamiliar woods and bayous. Ten hadn't needed Marty to remind him of the penalty for horse stealing. He suffered pangs of guilt as he wondered what Jesse Chisholm would think of his decision. Did the end really justify the means, even when your life was at stake?

"Here they come," said Marty. "Sorry 'bout what I said. I worry like an ol' granny. I'll side you."

"No," said Ten, "keep out of sight. I'd as soon they don't know how many of us there are. I'll get the drop and disarm them. When they're dismounted and belly down, you can tie their hands and feet. Whack that rope into the right lengths and tie 'em tight. That's all the edge we'll have, just until they manage to get loose."

The three mounted policemen rode clumsily, as though it was something they did only when absolutely necessary. When they were barely past, Ten stepped out from behind a tree.

"Rein up," he said. "You're covered."

The command, deliberately accentuated by the ominous cocking of the Henry, shocked them into instant obedience.

"Now," said Ten, "with thumb and forefinger, lift your pistols and drop them to the ground. Do it slow."

In silence they obeyed.

"Now," said Ten, "step down easy, and you won't be hurt."

"You won't live till sundown," snarled one of the lawmen.

"My problem," said Ten. "Move!" They dismounted.

"Belly down," said Ten, "hands behind your backs."

Marty had cut the rope into convenient lengths. Once they were facedown, he swiftly bound their wrists and ankles.

"Now," said Ten, "it's into the brush and out of sight."

He took one of the lawmen by the ankles and began dragging him toward the woods that lined the river.

"Hey!" bawled the captive.

"Heap sorry," said Ten. "Close your eyes and keep your head up."

Mounted on two of the horses, with Marty leading the third, they headed downriver at a fast lope. Once, hearing the whistle of an approaching steamboat, they paused in the brush until the boat had passed. Soon they were clear of the town.

"Time for the big gamble," said Ten. "We have to skirt the town to the east, and get into the open country to the north without being seen."

"I know a little about what's north of here," said Marty. "After Lee give up, I come through Mobile on my way back to Texas. North of New Orleans there's a lake so big it looks like part of the gulf. Lake Ponchartrain. Just barely west of that, there's a smaller one, Lake Maurepas, and there's just a little strip of ground between 'em. Maybe enough for a wagon road. We got to get around both them lakes before we can turn north. We're purely doin' this the hard way, ridin' around New Orleans to the east and then doublin' back."

"I know," said Ten, "I know. But I believe they're layin' for us to the west, so we have no choice. I ought to have my Injun license revoked for not gaggin' them three jaybirds we left by the river. They'll squawk their heads off every time a boat passes."

"We purely got to get around the town and north of them lakes before a posse takes our trail. Even then, losin' 'em won't be easy. They'll be lookin' for the tracks of three hosses. Should we let this third one go?"

"No," said Ten. "Set this one free, and he'll light out for home. When they meet him, or backtrack him, they'll know they're on our trail. We'll turn them all loose at the same time."

They paused only to rest and water the horses. More than once, what had appeared to be a floating log suddenly became an enormous reptile with protruding eyes, whose powerful jaws were studded with teeth. The horses shied away in fear, refusing to drink.

"I flat don't trust a place," said Marty, "where the lizards grow this big and have teeth. Be mighty easy to stumble over one of them varmints in the dark."

"Come dark," said Ten, "we'll have to slow down some, but we have to keep moving. We got to stay far enough ahead, so that when we turn the horses loose, that posse can't catch up and ride us down."

Soon they were riding along the south shore of Lake Ponchartrain. When its shoreline began to curve northward, they could see the shimmering waters of Lake Maurepas to the west.

"If we were sure there was solid ground separating them all the way," said Ten, "we could be away into the open country to the north that much quicker."

"I only seen 'em from the north side, and they looked from there about the same as they do from here. But I can't help thinkin' we'd get maybe halfway through and find open water ahead of us."

"And the posse behind us," said Ten. "We'll ride around this other lake, just to be safe. I've already drawn one busted flush today."

Rounding the smaller lake wasn't as time-consuming. By three o'clock they were beyond the lake and into marshy, open country. Each time they stopped to rest and water the horses, Ten looked at the westering sun. He also listened. He had heard of southern lawmen using dogs on the trail, and he half expected to hear an ominous baying to the south of them. But there was no alien sound, just the cawing of a distant crow, and the chatter of birds in the cypress and live oak trees towering above them. The sun lost its battle with dusk and dipped below the western horizon, leaving only a crimson afterglow. There was the distant, distinctive cry of a whippoorwill.

Spanish moss hung from the trees like ghostly silver wraiths in the shadowy world through which they rode. The gathering darkness seemed all the more intense because of the lush vegetation and moss-shrouded trees. Each time they forded a stream or crossed a marsh, Ten held his breath, fearful of those reptile jaws whose teeth could snap a horse's foreleg like a twig. The moon finally rose, making the going easier, allowing them to pick up the pace. Moonset slowed them down again, and the sky was starting to gray with approaching dawn when they smelled wood smoke.

"It's ahead of us," said Marty, "so it can't be the posse. Do we ride in, or circle 'em and ride on?"

"It's too soon for word to have come this far. Sooner or later we'll have to test our luck. Why not try it here? Keep your Colt handy."

They rode a little closer and reined up.

"Hello the camp," said Marty. "All right if we ride in?"

"Depends," said a voice. "Who are you?"

"Friends," said Ten. "Western frontier."

"Raise your hands an' ride in. Slow."

Too late, Ten recalled Jesse Chisholm's warning of renegades and deserters from both armies. This had all the earmarks of just such a gathering. There were five men, each dressed in the remnants of Confederate gray. Each had pieced together his outfit as best he could. One wore a gray shirt with trousers of Union blue. It was he who had issued the command. They were a grim lot. Several of them grinned. Like wolves, lips skinned back over yellowed teeth, anticipating a kill. Having made a bad play, Ten tried to bluff it out.

"We're low on grub; wonder if you could spare us some breakfast?"

"Matter of fact, we can't. We're on short rations ourselves. You with th' rifle, let it down slow, butt first. Then th' both of you pull an' drop yer pistols. Slow an' easy. You with th' extry hoss, drop th' reins."

"Who are you," demanded Ten, "to take our horses and guns?"

"Captain Tremaine. We're takin' yer hosses an' guns in th' name of th' Confed'racy. Fer th' cause."

"The cause is lost," said Marty. "I was with Lee when he surrendered at Appomattox."

"He surrendered. We ain't. Drop th' guns an' dismount, or I'll order you shot out'n th' saddle."

Three of the five had their weapons drawn.

"Do what you're told," said another of the band,

speaking for the first time. "We need your guns and horses. Give 'em up, and you won't be hurt."

It was a lie. Ten saw it in their eyes. With his left hand he took the Henry by its muzzle and slowly, butt first, lowered it to the ground. Every eye was on the weapon. The instant Ten let go of it, he rolled out of his saddle on the off side, palming his Colt as he fell. He thumbed two shots under the belly of the startled horse, and Tremaine died with his hand on the butt of his half-drawn pistol. Expecting the move, Marty had quit his saddle shooting, and a second man went down. The three with their guns drawn got off a shot apiece, and seeing their comrades down, vanished into the brush like frightened quail. Freed of their riders and spooked by the gunfire, the three horses had turned tail and lit out back the way they'd come. Any sound, any movement, might invite a bullet. Silent, unmoving, Ten and Marty lay there until the sound of the running horses had faded to silence. Ten snaked his way over to the fallen Henry and cocked it. Only then did he break his Colt and replace the spent shells.

"We can't stay here," said Marty. "I'd say they're gone, since we cut down two of 'em. Why don't I trot out a ways and look around?"

"No," said Ten, "we can't waste any time. We're afoot, and we'd best move out. They may yet double back and try to ambush us."

Warily and wearily they went on their way, resting only when exhaustion and their booted feet demanded it. By noon their shirts were soaked with sweat and their feet were a mass of blisters.

"I purely hate losin' the hosses," said Marty, "and while my feet don't agree, it's likely the best thing that could of happened to us. I'm just a mite surprised them three didn't circle and try to waylay us."

"We cut down two," said Ten, "when they had the drop on us. Even poorly mounted, they must have had horses, and they had a chance to pick up three more. I'd say they weighed the odds and settled for the horses."

"Bad choice. I got me an idea that bunch was headed for New Orleans, and them that's left is goin' to run headlong into the posse that's trailin' us. That was almighty smart, us keepin' that third hoss. That posse's been trackin' three men, and they can't be far away from findin' 'em."

The sun was two hours from the western horizon when they dropped beside a shaded creek to rest.

Marty sighed. "I'd give my share of every cow in Texas if I could drag off these boots and soak my feet in that cold water for about three days. I'm so all-fired hungry, I could eat a saddle blanket, and my belly's startin' to cry louder than my feet."

They trudged on, their only consolation being that they apparently were no longer pursued.

"Can't be much farther," panted Marty, "until we're in Mississippi. But how are we goin' to know?"

"First folks we meet that don't try to rob and kill us, we'll ask."

It was desolate country. They followed a deep, clear creek that flowed from the north. Humans, especially farmers and ranchers, settled along such streams. The shack, when they came upon it, was slab-sided, with a shake roof. It had weathered to a pewter gray, and seemed deserted. There was a pitiful excuse for a barn. It was as gray and weather-beaten as the shack, and a gable end of its shake roof had fallen in. They paused, listening. There was the scrape of a shovel on rock. Somebody was digging. Following the sound, they came upon a little ridge behind the shack. Beneath an old poplar tree was a grassed-over mound that could only be a grave. Beside it was a growing mountain of dirt. A second grave was being dug.

"Hello," said Ten. "We're friendly."

A head appeared. Shaggy brown hair; sweaty, freckled face; Ten judged him barely out of his teens, if that. He hoisted himself out of the hole and sat on the edge of it, his feet dangling. He had deep brown eyes, and he rubbed sweat from them with the backs of his hands. He wore no shirt, and his patched trousers had once been Confederate gray.

"If you ain't friends," he said, "you a couple of days late. I got nothin' left. It's been took in the name of the Confederacy. For the cause."

His laugh was bitter.

"We're not here to rob you," said Ten. "We lost our horses to the same cause. But they paid. We left a couple of 'em for buzzard bait. You fixin' to plant one of 'em in that hole?"

"No," he sighed. "I wisht that's all I had to do. This is for my mama. She died early this mornin', and I'm makin' a place for her beside Daddy."

"Sorry," said Ten. "We showed up at a bad time. Before we move on, can you tell us where we are? Are we still in Louisiana?"

"Mississippi. Barely across the line, maybe six or seven mile south of a little place called McComb. I ain't got much to offer, but you're welcome to stay and eat. After I do what's . . . got to be done."

"We're obliged," said Ten. "Why don't you let us finish here?"

"It's deep enough," the boy said.

"We've come a long way," said Ten, "mostly afoot. I reckon we'll go to the creek for a spell."

He knew they were leaving him alone with his grief. They could do no more. Without a word he turned and went into the shack. The sun was down and the water was cold, but they stripped off their dusty, sweaty clothes and waded in. It was still light enough for them to see him step out the door with his blanket-wrapped burden and vanish around the corner of the old shack. Finally they got out and stood shivering, waiting for some of the water to dry before getting back into their clothes. They sat on the steps at the front of the shack until their host returned, carrying the shovel. With a sigh, he leaned against the rickety porch. Ten got up.

"I'm Tenatse Chisholm. Ten to my friends. My pardner is Marty Brand."

"John Wesley Fedavo," he said, shaking their hands. "Mama named me that, hopin' I'd make somethin' of myself. You can see it didn't work. Just call me Wes."

"You said you was robbed," said Marty. "Sounds like the same renegades we tangled with. Five of 'em?"

"That's all I saw," said Wes. "They wanted horses, guns, and grub. Told 'em I had no gun. I got a Navy Colt, but no shells. They took the mule I rode back from the war. I kept 'em out of the house by tellin' 'em Mama was down with the smallpox. She wasn't. Just old and tired. Come on in."

The squalid little shack had but three rooms. Only one, obviously the bedroom, had a door, and it was closed. The furniture, little as there was, had been homemade. In one corner was a bundle of blankets, probably their host's bed. From the third room, the kitchen, came the torturous aroma of something cooking.

"Bring a pair of chairs with you," said Wes, "and have a seat at the table. We was down to one old rooster, so I put him out of his misery yesterday. Boiled him all night, just to make Mama some chicken soup. She died without ever tastin' it."

He paused, swallowing hard. He took the big pot off the stove and set it on the not-too-sturdy table. From a shelf he took a big porcelain bowl with chipped edges, a blue granite pan with much of the granite flaked off, and an iron skillet.

"Ya'll take the bowls," he said, "and I'll make do with the skillet. I ain't too well fixed for comp'ny. Pitch in; that ol' bird's tender as he'll ever be. Ain't no coffee. Not a damn thing to drink but creek water, but there's a plenty of that."

Wes ate very little, watching them. Ten and Marty ate every morsel, and then drank the broth.

"If I live to be a hundred," said Marty, "I reckon I'll never enjoy anything as much as I did that old rooster. I ain't much of a drinkin' man, but if I could get my hands on a bottle right now, I'd drink to his memory."

Ten and Wes laughed, easing the tension and lifting the gloom. Then Ten realized they had told the young man nothing about themselves, and etiquette didn't allow him to question them. Briefly, Ten told him of their intention to raise a herd in Texas and trail it to Indian Territory. He concluded on a light note.

"Truth is, the girl I aim to marry is in New Orleans. We took the steamboat from Fort Smith, aimin' to buy horses in Texas, plannin' to go to Texas from there. The girl's daddy purely hates my guts. He lined up half a dozen coyotes to gun us down, and we shot a couple of 'em. We left town with a posse on our trail."

"Then run into a bunch of renegade Rebs," said Wes, "and was left afoot."

"That's it," said Ten. "All we hoped to do was get out of Louisiana, buy some horses, and head for Texas. This little town of McComb, do they have the telegraph?"

"Lord, no. Didn't have it 'fore the war. I doubt there's a workin' telegraph or uncut wire anywhere in Mississippi. Men are still limpin' back from the battlefields. Nobody knows what's goin' to happen. While Mama was alive and sick, I couldn't even think of leavin' here. But now . . ."

"If you can shoot, rope, and ride," said Ten, "there's a place for you in our outfit. I'll stake you to a horse, a saddle, a gun, and grub. When we sell the herd, I'll pay you forty dollars a month, startin' now."

"I can shoot and ride," said Wes, "but I'll have to be honest with you. I've been a farmer, not a cowboy. I'll need some work with a rope."

"By the time you get to Texas," said Ten, "you'll have the feel of it."

"Then let's go to Texas," said Wes. "The sooner the better."

❦

11

*W*ith a blanket apiece, they slept on the floor of the poor shack. They were awake at first light, with nothing for breakfast but creek water.

"We need horses and grub," said Ten. "I know it's hard times, right on the heels of the war. What's likely to happen if we show up in this little town, trying to buy what we need? Any Union soldiers there?"

"Not yet," said Wes, "but there's talk there will be. What we're able to buy is goin' to depend on what folks is willin' to sell, what they can spare, and I doubt it'll be much. This is farmin' country, and that's all anybody knows. I doubt there's a horse for sale anywhere in Mississippi. Probably no mules either. Them that's got livestock ain't likely to sell. They'll be hopin' to get somethin' planted, so's they can eat."

"We'll be headin' west," said Marty. "What's the nearest town in that direction, and how far is it?"

"I'd say Natchez. Seventy-five mile, at least, and nothin' in between."

"We might as well see what McComb has to offer," said Ten. "Wes, since we're strangers, I reckon you'd better go in without us. Take this gold, and if nothing else, get us some grub. Whatever there is. When you ask about horses or mules, be sure to mention that renegades took your mule."

Wes looked at the five double eagles in his hand, and he looked at Ten.

"I doubt there's this much cash money in all of Mississippi. How much do you want me to spend?"

"All of it," said Ten, "if there's horses or mules to be had. Otherwise, as much as it takes for grub. We can hoof it from here to Natchez if we have to, but not on empty bellies."

Ten and Marty sat on the edge of the porch and watched him out of sight.

"I reckon that's the most money he's seen at one time in his life," said Marty. "Suppose he don't come back?"

"He will," said Ten, "unless somebody kills him. If he starts asking around for horses and mules, somebody's likely to wonder what he aims to use for money. We should have let him take a loaded Colt with him."

"You're right," said Marty. "That old Navy Colt he's wearin' won't be much help, him without shells."

The sun was noon-high when Wes returned. He was afoot, with a gunnysack over his shoulder. He was without the Colt, holster, and belt. He returned the five double eagles to Ten.

"No horses and no mules," he said. "Got us a side of bacon and a sack of cornmeal. It was the best I could do. I traded the Navy Colt. I knew nobody had any money to make change, and no way was I goin' to pay twenty dollars for this little bit of grub. Besides, there's some in town I'd not want knowin' I had money, or knew anybody that did."

"Here," said Ten. "Use this Henry until we're able to replace the Colt."

There was little in the shack worth taking. They each took a blanket, and Wes an old daguerreotype of his parents.

"I know it's heavy," said Marty, "but let's take the iron skillet. We got meal, and with bacon grease we can have corn pone."

"Be handy for fryin' fish too," said Wes. "I got hooks and lines."

"Let's go," said Ten.

"Go ahead," said Wes, "and I'll catch up. I may never come this way again, and I—I got some good-byes to say."

Ten and Marty started toward the westering sun. Wes soon caught up, and they continued until the sun was about to dip out of sight. When they came to a willow-lined creek, Ten called a halt.

"Likely there's nobody in these woods but us," he said, "but we can't gamble on it. We'll take supper early and douse the fire before dark."

"I believe I could put away that side of bacon by myself," said Wes. "Why don't I see if there's fish in this creek?"

"Great idea," said Marty. "What do you aim to use for bait?"

"Bacon rind. Come on; I got a bunch of hooks and plenty of line."

Wes cut a pair of slender hickory saplings for poles, trimmed away a few limbs and cut off the tops. From his pocket he took a little leather bag, and from the bag several little wooden spools. The line was wrapped around the spool like sewing thread and was held tight by the barb of the hook that bit into one end of the wooden spool.

"Bought me a bunch of hooks before the war," said Wes, "and hid 'em away. When I got home, these hooks an' lines was all I had left."

They found a portion of the creek that was so deep they couldn't see the bottom. Sunlight crept through the overhanging willows to dapple the water with freckles of gold. There they dropped their hooks, and Marty caught the first trout, a wriggling beauty as large as his hand. Seconds later Wes hooked another, and he grinned at Marty as he spoke.

"These ol' boys ain't never had bacon rind before, I reckon."

"I've had rank bacon," said Marty, "but never a rank

trout. Maybe we'd oughta just chunk the bacon and keep the rind."

Ten already had a small fire going. He joined them at the creek and began cleaning the fish they'd caught.

"Call it quits with a dozen," Ten said. "That's all we'll have time to fry before dark."

Once the trout had been caught and cleaned, Wes dunked them in the creek, one at a time. On a trio of stones Ten balanced the old iron skillet over the coals. Wes hacked off some bacon fat, and as it sizzled in the skillet, he began dunking the raw fish into the sack of cornmeal. The skillet would take only three trout at a time, and while a second panful was frying, the three hungry travelers ate the first batch.

"Southern style," said Wes through a mouthful of fish. "Give a Reb a little bacon, some cornmeal, a line and a hook, and he'll eat like a king."

Ten and Marty could only agree. They put out the fire, rolled in their blankets and slept. For breakfast they broiled strips of bacon over the fire, carefully saving the rind for bait.

"If I ain't bein' too nosy," said Wes, "I got a question."

"Go ahead," said Ten. "I hope I have an answer."

"Once we get to Natchez, we'll still be in Mississippi. Suppose we can't find horses or mules there? It must be near two hundred miles across southern Louisiana to the nearest town in Texas."

"I'm counting on finding mounts in Natchez," said Ten. "There's an old ex-mountain man who's built a racetrack there, and while I don't know him, I know Maynard Herndon, a horse-tradin' nephew of his. I'm gambling that Herndon's uncle will either sell us some horses or send us to somebody who can. This nephew of his lives in New Orleans, but sometimes takes a boat to Natchez to help with the horses during the Saturday race."

Weary and footsore, they reached Natchez on Friday, October 13. They found a rooming house where nobody looked at them twice and no questions were asked. In a café near the river, not far from the steamboat landing, they had steak, onions, fried potatoes, dried apple pie, and coffee.

"Lord," said Wes reverently, "this is the first coffee I've had in five years. I'd forgot what it was like."

"There's boats out of St. Louis all the time," said Ten, "and we ought to find a general store or trading post with some of the things we need. Like Levi's pants, shirts, socks, and a Colt for Wes."

While they were able to find the clothes, they found no weapons and no ammunition. There were newspapers from St. Louis and New Orleans. Ten got a New Orleans paper, almost a week old.

"Let's get back to our room," said Ten. "In the morning we'll go looking for this racetrack, and the old-timer it belongs to."

In the privacy of their room Ten stretched out on the bed, and on page two of the paper found what he was looking for. The headline, which ran across two columns, read: JOHN MATHEWSON'S KILLER BELIEVED SLAIN. Quickly he read the story, and passed the paper to Wes and Marty.

"No wonder that posse was so eager," said Marty. "It wasn't a posse, but a mob, and there was a thousand-dollar price on you, dead or alive. It says your two companions was unidentified, but the grateful folks in New Orleans raised another five hundred dollars apiece for them."

"None of that surprises me," said Ten. "What does surprise me is that I'm accused of shotgunning John Mathewson on September second. I was in Indian Territory then, and can prove it."

"My God," said Marty, "it's lucky for us we're both dead, with all the charges they've laid on you. They're sayin' that even after you'd killed Mathewson, you was breakin' into his office to get the evidence he supposedly had against you. You're gettin' the blame for all the smuggling and black-marketing that took place during the war."

"I've been a busy little Injun," said Ten. "Been smuggling and black-marketing since I was twelve, using the St. Louis Academy for a hideout. But what really burns my hide is the way they've accused me of going back to Mathewson's office to steal the evidence against me, offering not a shred of proof. Somebody's put words into this newspaper writer's mouth, and I'm almighty sure I know who."

"Somethin' else they don't explain," said Marty. "They say your robbery was foiled by six 'concerned citizens,' two of whom were killed. They ain't sayin' how them six coyotes just happened to be there waitin' for you at eight o'clock in the morning, or why they all just happened to be armed with repeatin' rifles."

"I'm lost," said Wes. "I thought this was over a girl, that her daddy—"

"My God!" cried Ten, coming off the bed. "Priscilla will have a copy of this. Old LeBeau, that no-account, yellow coyote—"

With that, he was out the door.

"By now," said Marty, "the girl likely thinks Ten's dead, thanks to her crazy old daddy. I reckon Ten's gone to send her a telegram, if it ain't too late."

"Where is she?"

"For all Ten knows, at her grandma's in Louisville."

Marty explained the complicated situation as best he could.

"The last part makes sense," said Wes. "The three renegades that took your horses done you a favor. They was taken for you, gunned down, and the bunch that was after your hides is countin' you dead."

"That's how it looks," said Marty, "but this ain't over. This stubborn damn Injun ain't even eighteen, but let him make up his mind, and you don't change him. It's like tryin' to head a buffalo stampede. Sooner or later, this little gal's got to go home, and I ain't all that sure ol' Ten can survive another trip to New Orleans. But I'm sure of one thing: if she's there, then our Injun pard will be goin'. I never seen one so young fall so hard."

The subject of their conversation returned, only slightly less agitated.

"I sent her a telegram," he said, "and asked for an answer. I'll call for it tomorrow, after we see about the horses."

Neither of his friends said anything, but their thoughts and misgivings were identical. Suppose the girl didn't answer?

The following morning they went in search of the racetrack, and had no trouble finding it. A quarter-mile stretch had been cleared off along the west bank of the Mississippi. There was a barn, a corral, and a shack. A bay and a roan picked at some hay at one end of the corral, while a nicker from the barn attested to the presence of other horses. While the track had been cleared of bushes and trees, it hosted a waist-high crop of ragweed and yellow-crowned goldenrod.

"I purely don't believe there'll be a race here today," said Marty.

"Something must've gone wrong," said Ten.

They went to the shack, and Ten pounded on the door. It opened, and he found himself looking into the surprised face of Maynard Herndon, the young man he'd met on the boat.

"Come in," said Herndon. "I wondered what had become of you."

Ten introduced Marty and Wes. Then, without mentioning the trouble in New Orleans, he told Herndon of the planned cow hunt, the trail drive, and their need for horses.

"Like I told you on the boat," said Herndon, "I dabble in livestock, so I don't have to admit I'm unemployed. Uncle Drago's the only kin I got left, on my pa's side. He closed the track at the end of August and went to Omaha. Him and Bill Cody aim to shoot buffalo for the Union Pacific Railroad. He bought enough grub for the winter, and left me here to look after things."

"The horses," said Ten, "are they yours or his?"

"Mine," said Herndon. "I bought the bay and the roan. In the barn there's four wild horses, broomtails, Uncle Herndon got from the Crow Indians in Montana Territory. He had the idea he could groom these ponies to run the quarter mile. Then he got word Bill Cody wanted him in Omaha, so I kind of inherited the broncs. Mighty expensive, just feedin' 'em. Feed has to come from St. Louis, by boat."

"I reckon we can cut down on your feed bill," said Ten. "I'd like to see those wild broncs."

"They're stalled," said Herndon, "because they're still skittish. Uncle Drago said they've been Indian gentled, and likely carried nothing heavier than a blanket. You'd need to work with them a few days to gain their trust, before trying to use a saddle."

The broncs were stocky animals, their hindquarters powerful, their chests deep, their withers low. They had short necks and broad, short heads. One was sorrel, one was buckskin, and two were blacks.

"They got the makings of cow horses," said Marty. "Every one of 'em."

"There's the bay and the roan," said Ten. "What about them?"

"Good, average horses," said Herndon. "As for cow savvy, I don't know."

"Since they belong to you," said Ten, "I'd be willing to take them all. Good horses don't seem too plentiful. How much for all six?"

"When you've gathered, trailed, and sold your herd, two hundred dollars. With one condition."

"We'll be selling the herd in Indian Territory," said Ten. "That's an almighty long ways from here. How do you aim to track me down and collect?"

"That," said Herndon, "is the condition. I want to join your outfit, to be a part of the hunt and the trail drive. I want to be there at the end."

"But you came from the war with lung fever," said Ten. "How—"

"So the army doctors said. But I'd rather stand on my hind legs like a man for a year than linger for ten years, lettin' it take me slow. Besides, if I cash in before the finish, you don't owe me a thing but a decent burial. The horses are yours."

Ten looked into those level gray eyes and liked what he saw. This was a man to ride the river with. He put out his hand and Herndon took it.

"Sixteen-hour days," said Ten. "Shootin' Comanches, riding, and roping. That's the easy part. We got to ford four of the meanest rivers in the West, startin' with the Red."

"I'm countin' on all that," said Herndon.

"What about this place? Your uncle left you in charge of it."

"Only because I had nothin' better to do, no way to support myself, and these four broncs needed to be fed or sold. We'll be takin' them with us. I can't leave this grub, though. We'll take it too. Uncle Drago bought it in St. Louis, so there's stuff you can't buy here or in New Orleans. Like good coffee, tinned goods, sugar, and salt."

"Lord," said Wes, "how many years since I've seen such foodstuffs."

"I'm purely ashamed to ask," said Marty, "but you got any way of findin' us some saddles, guns, and extra shells?"

"No saddles," said Herndon. "We'll need double-rigged Texas saddles, and even if we hadn't just come out of a war, you wouldn't find 'em around here. Anyhow, these four broomtails ain't saddle-broke. Best to bareback it from here to Texas, until they get used to the weight of a rider. For guns and shells, I can wire St. Louis in Uncle Drago's name, if you want to wait."

"This uncle of yours must've made some big tracks," said Marty.

"He has," said Herndon. "He's followed the same

trails as Kit Carson and Jim Bridger. He stands tall enough as a government scout to get about anything he wants, within reason. Now he's shootin' buffalo with Bill Cody, to feed Union Pacific grading and track-laying crews. The government will do whatever it has to just to get the Union Pacific built. Make me a list of the guns and shells you need, and I'll telegraph St. Louis today."

"You'll have to get them the money," said Ten.

"Later," said Herndon. "I'll get them on open account, and you can pay when the herd's sold. I'll square it with Uncle Drago. I'll leave word here and in town so he'll know where I've gone. He'll be pleased."

"We're bunking in a rooming house," said Ten, "and since we'll be here a few days, I'd like to get out of there. Care if we spread our blankets on your floor?"

"Make yourselves at home," said Herndon. "Sorry I don't have enough bunks, but I do have extra blankets. I'd better get into town and send that telegram."

"I'll go with you," said Ten.

Marty and Wes remained at Herndon's place, going to the barn and beginning what they hoped would be a long and rewarding friendship with a pair of the broomtails.

Ten and Herndon reached the telegraph office, and Ten was alarmed when there was no answer to his telegram to Priscilla. Why hadn't she responded? He was jolted out of his reverie when Herndon spoke to him.

"I have a Colt and rig of my own, but I want a rifle too."

"Send for one .44 caliber Colt six-shooter," said Ten, "along with a belt and right-hand holster. That's for Wes. Order three Henrys; one for Marty, one for Wes, and one for you. Then get us four thousand rounds of shells for the Colts, and four thousand for the Henrys."

"We'll be here a few days," said Herndon, "and I'll have time to find us a couple of pack saddles. We'll use the bay and the roan for packhorses."

Ten turned in early Saturday night. He spent all day Sunday shuffling and reshuffling a deck of cards. Marty explained to Herndon Ten's silence insofar as Priscilla was concerned. Him and Herndon then spent most of the day teaching Wes to build and throw a loop. He had a talent for it. Marty predicted by the time they reached Texas, he'd be ready. On Monday, Herndon received a confirming telegram from St. Louis.

"Our guns and shells will be here October twenty-second," he said, "on the *Robert E. Lee.*"

They would be in Natchez another week. There still had been no answer from Priscilla, and Ten tried in vain to put her out of his mind. He heard the lonesome sound of a steamboat whistle as it drew away from the Natchez landing, and watched it out of sight as it churned down the river toward New Orleans.

Aboard the steamboat, Priscilla LeBeau sat on her bunk in a tiny cabin. The boat's whistle sounded so lonesome, so haunting. Only the beating of her heart assured her of its presence. Otherwise, it felt cold, dead. She dabbed at her eyes with a much-used, wadded handkerchief. Why had he returned to New Orleans, after she had begged him, specifically warned him, against doing so? Despite what the newspapers had printed, she didn't believe a word of it. It had the smell of something André LeBeau and Jason Brawn had cooked up. While she had no idea how or why John Mathewson figured into it, charging Tenatse Chisholm with his murder and the attempted theft from his office just didn't make sense. It all seemed false, contrived. While Priscilla fully appreciated her mother's good intentions in sending her away, she had made up her mind to return to New Orleans and fight! For herself, and for Ten, even if he was dead. She would begin by learning the truth of his relationship with John Mathewson, the reason for his visit to Mathewson's office. She would reveal that truth, even if it destroyed her father. If Ten was dead, then whatever happened to her wouldn't matter. If she went to hell for her efforts, she vowed to destroy them for what they'd done to the young man who had tried to save her. She thought of him as she'd last seen him, and lay back on her bed. There she wept for Ten, for herself, and most of all, for a future that now seemed hopelessly cold and uninviting.

12

*A*ndré LeBeau was jubilant. True, his poorly con-
ceived ambush had cost the lives of two men, but
Brawn's influence with the newspaper had used even
that to further discredit Chisholm. It had been a stroke
of genius on the part of Brawn to implicate the young
fool in Mathewson's murder. If that hadn't been
enough, Chisholm had been named the possible head of
the wartime black-market and smuggling ring. Despite
LeBeau's unsuccessful ambush, a mob had run down
Chisholm and killed him. It was far more satisfactory
than gunning him down on the street, perhaps raising
questions. While LeBeau knew he must still somehow
force Priscilla to accept Jason Brawn, at least this troublesome Chisholm wouldn't be around to inspire her to
future rebellion.

While Ten found it impossible to free his mind of
Priscilla, he blunted his misery by throwing himself into
the task of becoming friends with one of the newly ac-
quired wild horses. Marty and Wes had wasted no time
in winning the trust of two of the animals, and soon
staged a race on the weed-grown track. Herndon and
Ten watched, their respect for the wild horses growing.

"They're going to be fine cutting horses," said Ten.
"Watch how they make the turn without givin' up their
speed. I've seen Injun-broke horses work cows before,

but these broncs are purely goin' to be the best. When you have a chance to talk to your uncle Drago, express my admiration for his horse savvy. It'd be worth a ride to Montana just to round up a herd of these broncs."

Herndon found a pair of old pack saddles that were usable, once the old leather had been greased. When the *Robert E. Lee* arrived the following Monday, they were at the landing with their pack animals. They returned to Herndon's shack before unpacking their weapons and ammunition. Herndon, Wes, and Marty each took one of the Henrys, and Wes belted on his new Colt.

"It's a mite late in the day to start," said Ten. "Let's get everything ready and move out in the morning, at first light."

When Priscilla reached the house, she found only LeBeau there. He was sprawled in the front parlor, nursing a half-full bottle of bourbon. He'd drunk just enough to become surly and mean.

"Where's Mother?" the girl asked.

"I don't know, and I don't give a damn. It's about time you came to your senses. Jason's been asking about you."

"The old fool's wasting his time asking about me," snapped Priscilla, "because I have come to my senses."

She took the envelope with the newspaper clippings he'd sent and threw them to the floor at his feet.

"Lies!" she cried. "You framed him, didn't you? You and Jason Brawn. Well, I'm going to learn the truth. Will you hire a mob of killers to shut me up?"

"Go ahead," said LeBeau, unperturbed. "Learn the truth. You'll find this young fool was no more than a spy, a pawn of Mathewson's. Mathewson tried to get to Jason Brawn through me, and that's the only reason for young Chisholm's interest in you. Nobody but an impressionable idiot like you would have believed otherwise."

"It might have started that way," she cried, "but he

was honest with me. If he was using me, he had a reason, and I intend to learn what that reason was. John Mathewson was head of U.S. Customs. If he was after Jason Brawn, that means Brawn's into something crooked, something criminal. So if John Mathewson tried to get to Brawn through you, that means you're mixed up in it. You're in it so deep, you planned to have Tenatse Chisholm murdered to save yourself, didn't you?"

"He had his warning," snarled LeBeau. "Now you'd just as well put him out of your mind, because he's dead."

"He's not dead," she cried, "and someday, when I'm of age, he'll come for me. When he does, I'm going with him, and you won't stop me!"

"Let's get one thing straight," said Herndon. "Call me 'Hern,' or just 'Herndon,' but not 'Maynard.' Damn it, I sound like a dude, a tenderfoot. My ma read too many dime novels."

They laughed, but they took him seriously. Given names meant little on the frontier. Many a cowboy, when his grave was marked at all, was remembered simply as Slim, High Pockets, or Lefty.

Their cross-country journey was uneventful. The only Louisiana town along the way was Alexandria, and they passed to the north of it. They were covering at least forty miles a day, by Ten's estimate. Taking their time, they rode into San Augustine, Texas, on October 31, 1865.

"San Augustine was a town before Texas was a state," said Marty. "There was a fine college, the University of San Augustine, started here in 1837. The Methodists started another college in 1844. The two schools got on the outs with one another, started fightin', and both of 'em shut down in 1847."

"Marty," said Ten, "Texas is your stompin' ground. Before we do anything else, we'll need saddles. When you lived here, before the war, who made your roping saddles?"

"Old man John Bowdrie," said Marty. "Had a shop in Nacogdoches. That's maybe thirty miles east of here. With everybody gone to war these four years, I doubt he's had any call for ropin' saddles."

"We'll try him first," said Ten, "and gamble that he has some on hand. We don't have time to wait for them. From what Jesse told me, we ought to start our gather on the Trinity or the Brazos. How far are we from the Trinity?"

"Not more'n a hundred miles," said Marty, "but nearly twice that, to the nearest point on the Brazos."

"I've heard Uncle Drago speak of the Trinity," said Herndon. "There's two or three forks that join somewhere south of Dallas, and it flows into the Gulf."

"We'll set our sights on the Trinity," said Ten. "Like Hern says, it runs all the way to the Gulf. If we're goin' to follow a river, let's make it one that's long enough, deep enough, and wild enough for these longhorns to feel at home."

"That'll be the Trinity," said Marty. "We could head for Crockett. My old home place is, or was, seven miles south of there, on the Trinity. We can set up a camp there, I reckon, without anybody botherin' us, 'cept maybe the Comanches."

"You must know somebody there," said Wes, "if you lived there. We need some cow wrasslers."

"While I was with the Confederacy," said Marty, "the Comanches murdered my ma and pa. When I got back to Crockett, I had the devil's own time just findin' somebody that could tell me what happened. There was nothin', nobody, for me to come home to, so I went to New Orleans. That's where I met Ten. I can't say for sure, but I'm lookin' for most of the men to have left these parts, them that was able. Them that's been through the war and got home alive, I expect they'll be too sick and shot up to be of any help to us."

"Sorry," said Wes. "I wasn't thinking. I was in the war myself. That was a fool thing for me to say."

"Not really," said Ten. "That's kind of how I was thinking. I reckon I've been countin' mighty heavy on us findin' Texans home from the war and needin' work. Marty's just shot some holes in my plan to hunt longhorns. With just the four of us, we're almighty short-handed."

"I don't know that we won't find some riders," said Marty, "but even if we do, there's a chance they won't throw in with us. What's to stop them from gatherin' their own herd?"

"They likely won't have money for an outfit or grub," said Herndon. "Not only do we have that, but the herd's already sold."

"But it's a herd we don't have," said Ten. "Without enough riders, we may not have time to gather, brand, and deliver it."

"This is your drive, Ten," said Marty, "but I'm goin' to throw this out for you to think on. Texans ain't the kind to let grass grow under their feet. I'm bettin' we'll find somebody that's already got the start of a herd. You might dicker with them for the longhorns they've already caught. When the herd's sold, they get paid for what they've gathered, calculated on what you can afford to pay."

"Good thinking," said Ten. "Half a loaf's better'n none. These riders would have to make the drive with us, so's they'd get paid when the herd's sold. It might be the only way I can deliver the longhorns I've promised. I reckon we'd best wait until we reach the Trinity, and see what we're up against. Suppose nobody else is gatherin' wild longhorns? Then I'll really have my tail in a crack."

They rode into Nacogdoches, and were immediately halted by a pair of Union soldiers. The privates eyed their loaded packhorses and the belted Colts they wore, and didn't seem to hear Ten when he explained their reason for being in Texas. The four of them were escorted to the courthouse, above which flew the stars and stripes. One of the privates dismounted and returned with his superior.

"I'm Captain Thomas," he said. "I am in charge of the occupation of Nacogdoches. Who are you, and why are you here?"

Briefly, Ten explained.

"While your purpose for being here is acceptable," said Thomas, "your possession of arms is not. Under Federal law, I'm required to confiscate them."

Ten dismounted and stalked over to confront the officer.

"I didn't grant you permission to dismount," snapped Thomas.

"Captain," said Ten, "I don't need permission to dismount. I'm not a Texan. I'm from Indian Territory, and I'm not about to surrender my weapons or those of my men. Taking any man's guns and leaving him at the mercy of the Comanches is an unconscionable thing to do."

"Are you finished, *Mister* Chisholm?"

"No, sir," said Ten. "I'll take responsibility for the men in my outfit. I want you to satisfy yourself as to who I am. You have the telegraph, and I want you to telegraph the commanding officer at Fort Smith and ask him about me. While you're at it, you're welcome to telegraph Fort Cobb, Fort Arbuckle, Fort Washita, Fort Towson, and Fort Gibson. Send your telegrams to the post quartermasters; they've contracted to buy the longhorns we've come here to gather. This is beef for the frontier outposts in Indian Territory."

For a moment Captain Thomas said nothing. When he finally spoke, the grim set of his jaw had relaxed a little.

"You have permission to go about your business," he said, "and in view of the Indian threat, you'll be permitted to keep your weapons. But only on the condition that you'll sign an oath not to take up arms against the Union."

They signed the necessary papers, and went in search of John Bowdrie's saddle shop. Once they were safely out of the captain's hearing, Marty spoke.

"Injun, that took sand. You reckon he'll telegraph them forts?"

"No," said Ten. "He knew I wasn't bluffing."

Bowdrie's place, when they found it, was closed. A written notice on the door directed them to Bowdrie's house. He was a stooped, gray-haired old man who walked with a cane.

"I got no new rigs," he told them. "Some of th' men that went to war wanted new saddles, an' they traded in their old ones. I ain't made a new kak since 'sixty-two. Rheumatism in my hands just ruint 'em."

He led them to the barn, to the tack room. Across one end there were poles upon which rested six well-worn, double-rigged Texas saddles.

"They sold new for ten dollars," he said, "and I can let you have 'em for four dollars apiece. Nothin' wrong with 'em a little grease won't cure, and I'll provide th' grease."

They spent most of the afternoon greasing and working the old leather into shape. Bowdrie seemed to enjoy the diversion, telling them of the old days and of the hard times in Texas during the war. They rode quietly out of Nacogdoches just before sundown, without seeing Captain Thomas or any of the Union soldiers.

November 4, 1865, they reached the little town of Crockett, Texas. It crouched in a bend of the Trinity River, and consisted of a saloon, a blacksmith shop, and a general store.

"Ma and Ed Satterly own the store," said Marty. "Have from as far back as I can remember. Ma's in charge of the post office, such as it is, and if there's anything worth knowin', she always finds out."

"Since they know you," said Ten, "you do the talking for us. We need to know if there's riders in these parts needin' work, and if there's anybody gatherin' wild long-horns."

Ma Satterly was a slight, gray-haired woman who dipped snuff and wore wire-rimmed spectacles. She was maybe sixty-five, and would have been hard put to weigh ninety pounds, soaking wet. She sat in an old oak rocker that creaked with her every move. Most of the store's shelves were bare, mute evidence of hard times and four long years of war. Ma seemed more than a little re-served, and not at all friendly, Ten thought. Her old eyes frosted when she looked at him, and he suspected the Indian was showing through. He recalled what Jesse Chisholm had told him. The Comanches had raised so much hell in Texas, every Indian was suspect. Marty introduced the outfit, and then asked about the possibility of finding riders to help with their gather.

"They ain't many folks left in these parts," said Ma, "except them that's too old an' tired to git up an' leave. Most of our young men that went off to war ain't come back, and they ain't comin' back. Heard th' blue bellies has already took over Waco."

Marty tried again.

"Ma, have you heard of anybody else that's gatherin' these wild longhorns down in the brakes?"

"Charles Goodnight's outfit," she said. "They're on th' Brazos, somewheres south of Waco. Nobody else I know of, 'cept them Ward boys. I hear they're ropin' an' brandin' some wild critters. God only knows why. Nothin' to be done with 'em. Their daddy's a sorry old scutter that don't know th' meanin' of honest work, an' he's livin' with some Jezebel that belongs in a saloon or worse. Th' lot of 'em lives in a shack downriver, eight or nine mile south of your old place."

"Thanks, Ma," said Marty. "How's Ed, and where is he?"

"Not too good," said Ma, without a trace of a smile. "Been dead an' buried near six weeks."

They departed the store with as much grace as they could.

"She's changed some," said Marty. "Still tore up over Ed, I reckon."

They mounted, and Marty led out downriver.

"We learned two things, anyway," said Herndon. "There's wild longhorns on the Trinity for the taking, and there's at least two riders that might throw in with us. Is that where we're going? To talk to this pair of young cow wrasslers?"

"That's what I have in mind," said Ten. "We were on our way to Marty's old home place anyway, and it's downriver, same as the Wards'."

Marty's old home place had a forlorn beauty all its own. All that remained of the house was the chimney and a few blackened logs, scattered in a head-high stand of young cottonwoods. Angling in from the northwest was a creek that emptied into the Trinity. There was a natural ford, where the river ran little more than hock deep over a sandy bottom. Cow tracks were abundant on both banks of the Trinity and along the banks of the creek. From somewhere beyond where the house had stood, a cow bawled.

"We'll leave the horses here," said Ten. "Somebody's got some longhorns penned. Let's take it slow."

"I just about know where they are," said Marty. "The creek runs through a canyon, and with the ends fenced off, it'd make a good holding pen. I was thinkin' we could use it."

They followed the creek and were within sight of the six-rail fence at the south end of the canyon when a voice halted them.

"That's far enough. I got you covered."

They waited, unmoving, until their challenger stepped out from behind a jumble of rocks on the far bank of the creek. He wore Levi's pants, a faded blue flannel shirt, run-over boots, and an old black hat whose crown had a hole in it. Shaggy black hair was down to his collar and over his ears. The most impressive item of his attire was a .52 caliber Spencer, cocked and pointed at them. He paused.

"Lou," he bawled, "get over here. We got company."

Lou, carrying another Spencer .52, came trotting down the canyon. He drew up at the rail fence, poking the Spencer over one of the rails. This was the younger of the two, similarly dressed, but with unkempt curly red hair.

"Now," said the older, "who are you, and what do you want? Why are you sneaking around through the woods?"

Before Ten could speak, Marty held up his hand for silence.

"I'm Marty Brand, and I'm talkin' for the outfit, because this is my old home place. I was born here, so I got a right to be here now. I lived here until I joined the Confederacy in 'sixty-one. Tenatse Chisholm is from Indian Territory, and this is his outfit. Our two pards is Wes Fedavo and Maynard Herndon."

"We're here to gather wild longhorns," said Ten. "Are you the Wards?"

"Suppose we are," replied Black Hair. "What's it to you?"

"We need cows and we need riders," said Ten. "We thought you might join our gather."

"We have the start of a herd; why do we need you?"

"The Union army's going to occupy Texas," said Ten. "On your own, you can't get a herd out of the state."

"But you can?"

"I can," said Ten. "I'm known at all the forts in Indian Territory, and they've agreed to buy the herd we'll gather. Besides that, I've just gotten permission from Captain Thomas, the Union commander at Nacogdoches."

"Just what we needed in these parts," snorted Lou. "A damn Yankee Injun that feeds at the same trough with blue bellies and carpetbaggers. Now git, all of you. If Chris won't shoot, I will."

"Then you'd best start shootin'," said Marty angrily. "Down the creek a ways, there's two graves. That's where my ma and pa is buried, and that gives me every

right to be here. Now why don't the two of you just lope
your high hosses on out of here? And take your cows
with you. This is my land."

"Back off, Lou," said Chris. "He's right. If he was
lying, he wouldn't know of those graves."

Chris took the Spencer off cock, lowered its muzzle
and turned back to Marty.

"We've put a mighty lot of work into that holding pen.
We didn't know this land belonged to anybody. I reckon
I'm asking a lot, but would you let us go on using this
holding pen?"

"I'd be inclined to," said Marty, "if you was workin'
with us."

"Damn it," shouted Lou, "we won't beg!"

"Lou, just shut up," said Chris, turning back to Marty.

"We can't join your gather because we have . . .
other commitments. Downriver about fifteen miles
there's a crook in the Trinity where the water backs up
into a bigger canyon than this."

"And you're wantin' us to go there," said Ten.
"Why?"

"Because our daddy, Brady Ward, ain't a sociable or
neighborly man. Get too close, and he'll give you hell.
It's the way he is."

Ten looked at Marty. Marty shrugged.

"We'll ride downriver," said Ten, "and have a look at
this canyon. If it's a bigger one, it'll better suit our purpose."

They reached the horses before anybody spoke.

"Thank God one of 'em had some sense," said Marty.
"I reckon that young hellion would of just shot us, no
questions asked. He must be a lot like his unsociable old
daddy."

"I've always been suspicious of folks like these," said
Herndon. "They live back in the woods, and get nasty if
anybody comes around. Makes me wonder if there's
something crooked goin' on."

"I believe Chris was bein' honest with us," said Wes.

"Them words had the sound of truth. Anyhow, we're still up against it for riders."

"Short-handed or not," said Ten, "we'll dig in and start ropin' longhorns. Later on, we'll mosey upriver when they're away from that holdin' pen. I'd like to know how many longhorns they have. There's somethin' uneasy about that pair. Before we're done, they'll be wantin' to join our gather."

They passed the Ward cabin, and it looked forbidding and silent. Less than a mile south, they found tracks where seven shod horses had forded the river to the east bank. Wes said what they all were thinking.

"For a man that don't like visitors, he has a mighty lot of them."

They continued downriver until they found the canyon.

"It's lots bigger than the one the Wards are usin'," said Marty, "and that's good. But if there's lots of rain, that may not be so good. The Trinity could flood and scatter our fence from here to yonder."

"We'll risk it," said Ten. "We'll have to move out in March, and that ought to be too early for spring rains."

"Before we worry about the fence bein' washed away," said Herndon, "we have to figure a way to build it. We need a pick, a shovel, and an axe."

"The Wards ought to have them tools," said Marty. "They're squattin' on my old place, so they owe us. Why don't we ride back up there and just borrow their tools?"

"Why not?" said Ten. "Wes, you go with him. If the Wards get ornery, don't push it. Just ride on to Satterly's store. Ma buried Ed, so she's got to have some diggin' tools. If she won't make us the loan of them, then buy 'em. Here's twenty dollars."

The double eagle winked in the sun. Marty palmed the coin and grinned. "With this," he said, "I could likely buy the whole damn store, plus bed privileges with Ma."

"Just bring us the diggin' tools," said Ten, "and keep Ma for yourself."

Marty and Wes reined up almost a mile south of the Wards' holding pen.

"We'll leave the horses here," said Marty, "and hoof it the rest of the way. That pair's too damn handy with them rifles to suit me."

They reached the creek without seeing or hearing anything. Following the stream, they came to a willow thicket a few yards below the south end of the holding pen. There was a splashing of water and the sound of voices.

"We come at a good time," whispered Marty. "They're takin' a swim."

"In November?"

"Folks get dirty in November just like in July," said Marty. "Besides, it's plenty warm enough. We're sweatin', ain't we? Come on, let's surprise 'em."

They crept along the creek bank, dodging low-hanging limbs and long, snaky, green briars. Finally free of the tangle, they stepped out and came face-to-face with the Wards. And as it turned out, the Wards weren't the only ones surprised. They stood in the knee-deep water staring at Marty and Wes. Marty and Wes stared back, awestruck, petrified. Before them stood two shapely, stark-naked females!

13

Chris and Lou recovered first, dropping into the water and concealing themselves as best they could. Once the shock had worn off, Marty saw the humor in the situation and laughed.

"You sneakin' coyotes," shouted Lou, "just you wait'll I get out of here and get my rifle!"

"That bein' the case," said Marty, "you'll be in there till dark. If I'm gonna be shot when you get out, then I aim to keep you in there as long as I can. I reckon I'll just stand right here. When the sun goes down, that water's gonna get plumb cold."

"It already is," said Chris, her teeth chattering. "Please, go somewhere so we can get out of here. Then we'll talk."

"You quit beggin' them bastards!" said the redheaded Lou.

"Lou, just hush!" snapped Chris. "What's done is done."

Marty and Wes made their way back through the thicket, forgetting the low-hanging limbs and briars. Breaking free, they sleeved the sweat from their eyes and looked at one another.

"Hell's bells on a tomcat," breathed Marty. "Did you ever see the like?"

"Never," said Wes. "I wouldn't mind knowin' that little woodpecker some better, if she could get that Spencer off her mind. You reckon they'll come out shootin'?"

"No," said Marty. "I don't think it shook the oldest one all that much. She wanted to talk to us before we left this mornin', but she was afraid to. Now, I expect we'll find out what their trouble is."

When they finally emerged, dressed, Lou blushed from her hairline to her shirt collar. It was a while before she could look at them.

"Honest to God," said Marty, "we didn't come here with anything in mind except to maybe borrow some diggin' tools and an axe. We got to fence both ends of that canyon."

"I believe you," said Chris. "Lou and I . . . we've had some . . . bad experiences with men. Daddy makes us cut our hair and dress this way. . . ."

"If you're goin' to tell them anything," said Lou, overcoming her embarrassment, "tell them the truth. Our daddy lives with a whore he met in a saloon. It's her that makes us dress like men. She looks like purgatory with the lid off, and she can't bear havin' us around."

"So you're draggin' wild cows out of the brush," said Marty, "just to stay out of the house."

"That's kind of how it started," said Chris. "Then we thought—somehow—we might build us a little herd and sell them. For enough to . . . to get away."

"Now," said Lou bitterly, "that—that woman has convinced Daddy he ought to drive the herd to Louisiana once we have five hundred head. She wants money to take a boat to St. Louis. She don't aim for us to go, but Daddy's such a fool, he can't see that."

"That's why we need to keep our cows where they are," said Chris. "They don't know of the hundred and fifty head we have here in your canyon. There's a smaller gather—about thirty head—on a creek four or five miles east of the house."

"I reckon that's why you didn't want us goin' near the house," said Wes. "Or did it have somethin' to do with them seven riders that crossed the river just south of your place?"

"We don't know—" began Chris.

"Yes, we do," interrupted Lou. "You started this, so they might as well hear the rest of it. Those men are thieves and killers who rode with William Quantrill. He was run out of Texas last spring, but these cutthroats didn't go with him. They're livin' in a shack back in the woods, and from there they raid as far away as Louisiana. Afterward, this is where they hide out. Once a month our dear daddy takes a pair of packhorses to Beaumont. They pay him to bring in their grub, whiskey, and ammunition."

Chris sighed. "Now you know the whole rotten story. We're trapped here, gathering a herd for someone else."

"Maybe not," said Marty. "Let me talk to Ten about this. Suppose we could add your herd to our gather and take you on our trail drive into Indian Territory? Would you go?"

"My God, yes!" cried Lou. "But the Quantrill bunch would be on your trail. Bertha, Daddy's woman, is in awful thick with those thieves and killers. It's them that'll be driving the herd to Louisiana, pretending to be honest cowboys. If you tried to take us and our cows with you, they'd never let you out of here alive."

"We're goin' to talk to Ten," said Marty. "He's a gambler, and he wins more often than he loses. Now, if you'll loan us them fence-buildin' tools, we'll ride back and see what he's got to say about this situation."

"Just keep the tools," said Chris. "We'll ride downriver in a few days and get them. Then the rest of your outfit can meet Christabel and Louise."

Once Marty and Wes had ridden away, Lou collapsed on the ground in a fit of giggles.

"Why, you little hypocrite," said Chris. "All that fuss was just an act."

"And wasn't it a *good* one?" cackled Lou. "Did you

see their eyes? They got big as pie tins when they saw us standing in the creek."

"You ought to be ashamed of yourself," said Chris. "They didn't mean for that to happen, and now they think we're mad at them."

"Come on, Christabel," said Lou, drying her eyes. "Act your age. You let me down, going all meek and mealy-mouthed. After they'd seen us naked as a pair of plucked pullets, they *expected* us to raise hell. Now they'll respect us, and want to see more of us."

"How can they possibly see *more* of us than they have already?"

"Don't be silly," said Lou. "You know what I mean. I like the youngest one, the one with freckles and brown hair. He talks like he's from somewhere south of the Sewanee River. You can have the other one; he can't be much older than you. I reckon he can't be anything but a fiddle-foot Texan with ragged drawers and holes in his socks."

Returning to their proposed camp, Marty and Wes rode for a while in silence. It was Wes who finally spoke.

"You reckon they're tellin' us the truth?"

"I believe they are," said Marty. "What would they gain by lying? Lou—Louise—didn't have to tell us all that. Besides, when I was here back in the summer, after Lee surrendered, I heard that Quantrill and some of his bunch was in East Texas somewhere."

"I reckon Brady Ward's in a mess of trouble," said Wes, "between them Quantrill renegades and that high-handed saloon woman."

"So much that I look for it to spill over on us," said Marty. "If Ward's woman aims to take the cows Lou and Chris are gatherin', what's to stop her and them Quantrill riders from comin' after *our* herd?"

Priscilla LeBeau opened the big door to the U.S. Customs office and stepped inside. From behind her desk, the elderly secretary looked at her inquiringly.

"I'm Priscilla LeBeau, and I . . . I need some help."

"I'm Emma Muldaur," said the secretary. "What kind of help?"

Priscilla told her as much as she knew about Tenatse Chisholm's visit to the office, which was actually no more than the newspaper had printed.

"I know him," said Priscilla, "and I don't believe he came here to do what he's been accused of. Were you here? Can you tell me anything about why he would have come here?"

"My dear," said the kindly secretary, "I can't tell you the nature of his business with Mr. Mathewson. However, I can tell you that he was here the first time—in July, I believe—at Mr. Mathewson's request. The second and last time he was here—when all the shooting started—he had a letter asking him to come. It had John Mathewson's name signed to it, but it wasn't his signature, nor had it been written by him. I didn't read it, but I remember the last line, above the signature, 'It concerns Priscilla.' Your young man seemed shocked when I told him of Mr. Mathewson's death. Our conversation ended there, when the shooting started. But you're right; he was here only because he thought Mr. Mathewson had asked him to come."

Priscilla controlled herself until she was out of the office. With her heart pounding and her knees trembling, she leaned against the big oval door. Now she knew why Ten had come back to New Orleans, despite her pleas. Whatever his business with Mathewson had been, it had somehow concerned her.

Ten and Herndon listened in amazement as Marty and Wes explained that the Wards were females and that Brady Ward was harboring a band of thieves and killers.

"Tarnation," said Ten, when Marty and Wes had recounted what they had learned. "All we need now is the damn Comanches on our trail. We got everybody else."

"It ain't the fault of the Ward girls," said Marty.

"You got a powerful lot of confidence in them females," said Ten.

"He's seen more of 'em than you have," said Herndon.

His chuckle died when he saw the anger in Marty's eyes.

"Sorry, Marty," Ten said. "You're right. The Ward girls are caught in a trap that's not of their making. If we're sucked into it, at least we've been warned. We're obliged to them for that."

"They're ridin' down here in a few days," said Wes.

"Good," said Ten, "because I need to talk to them. I want them to continue what they're doing. Brady Ward and that bunch of renegades will find out we're here, but they don't have to know the Ward girls are planning to join our drive. We won't get out of here without a showdown, but maybe we can delay it until we finish our gather. We can't hunt longhorns if we're spending all our time fighting for our lives."

For the next two days, Ten, Herndon, Wes, and Marty worked from first light until dark, digging post holes, cutting posts and rails. Two of the posts at each end of the canyon were placed in the riverbed. While the water was shallow, the bed was sandy, offering little or no support.

"This ain't gonna work," said Marty. "Them posts will be so weak, Ma Satterly could push 'em down with one hand."

"No they won't," Ten said, "because we're goin' to fill the holes around the posts with stones, and pack 'em tight with the pick handle."

They set up their camp in the canyon against the west wall, under a slight overhang. It offered protection against rain, but little else.

"It won't help us against the Comanches," said Marty. "If we had the time, we could dig into the back wall, fort up, and stand off an army."

"The Comanches may be more interested in our

horses than our scalps," said Herndon, "but I reckon we can't afford to gamble on that. Fact is, we don't have anything we can afford to lose."

"Amen to that," said Ten. "We'll picket the horses close by and take turns standing watch. There's four of us, the Ward girls seem handy with rifles, and there's the remnant of Quantrill's bunch. That might be enough to give the Comanches second thoughts. Marty, did the Wards say anything about the Comanches being a threat?"

"No," said Marty, "let's remember to ask them when they get here."

The first several days of their hunt for longhorns was a learning experience for both horses and riders. Maynard Herndon summed it up.

"Ropin' a cow is one thing, but ropin' a wild Texas longhorn is somethin' else. There ain't nothin' else in the world like it."

The horses they'd brought with them from Natchez were fast on their feet, but they too had to learn. Riders worked in pairs, and it required coordinated efforts to safely rope, throw, and hog-tie a wild longhorn. The first rider got his loop over the animal's horns, while his partner roped the hind legs. Once the longhorn was down, the safety of both horse and rider depended upon the horse. A good cow horse kept the rope taut, while the rider scrambled from the saddle, piggin' string in his teeth, to bind the longhorn's legs. The first rider tied the front legs, while the second rider secured the hind legs. They then removed their catch ropes and began beating the brush for another longhorn. Several hours later, when a hog-tied animal was exhausted from thrashing about, they loosed its feet and led it to their fenced canyon. Herndon worked with Ten, and Wes with Marty. After three days they had exactly six longhorns in their canyon holding pen.

"At this rate," said Wes tiredly, "we'll be two years gatherin' this herd. Them Ward girls will laugh at us."

"We've had to take it slow," said Ten, "because we

couldn't be sure our horses had the hang of it. Give us a week, and we'll double or triple what we're doin' now. Once our horses learn it's their duty to keep these wild cows on the ground, we'll move faster. The Cherokees taught me to rope and ride. I always thought I throwed a pretty good loop, but I'm having to do some learnin' myself. Like Hern says, this is entirely different. Nothin' you've ever done in your life prepares you for the roping, throwing, and hog-tying of these wild Texas longhorns."

"I've never been on a trail drive," said Wes, "so maybe this is a fool question. After we've trapped these longhorns and bunched 'em in this canyon for a while, will that make 'em any easier to handle on the drive?"

"No," said Ten. "They've been caught, not tamed."

"You can't teach a cow nothin'," said Marty. "Pen up these brutes for ten years, and they'd still be wild as Texas jacks once they hit the trail. When we start the drive, it'll take a week of swattin' their behinds with doubled lariats before they finally get the notion they're a herd."

The fifth day after their meeting with Marty and Wes, Chris and Lou were until after dark returning to the Ward cabin. They only slept there, on a straw tick in the loft. When Bertha wasn't around, they slipped food out, cached it, and did their cooking over an open fire. One of the shack's three rooms was a kitchen. Brady Ward, Bertha, and Bodie Tomlin sat at the table drinking coffee. A gallon jug before them on the table suggested the coffee had been laced with something stronger. Chris and Lou climbed the ladder to the loft as quietly as they could. Removing only their boots, they lay down on their straw tick and listened to the loud voices from below. Brady Ward was speaking.

". . . fifteen miles downriver. They fenced both ends of that canyon, where th' river runs shallow. They're ropin' wild cows an' buildin' a herd. What d'you aim t' do about it?"

"Nothin'," laughed Tomlin, "till they git a good bunch. Then we'll add it to ours."

With that, Tomlin left the shack. Chris and Lou heard no more, but it was enough. Next morning, at first light, they rode downriver to Tenatse Chisholm's cow camp.

"Step down," said Ten, "and join us for breakfast."

"Thank you," said Chris. "We will. But we have some bad news. Do you want it before or after breakfast?"

"Knowin' it's bad news, and not knowin' what it is, would plumb kill my appetite," said Marty. "Why don't you tell us what it is while we get the grub ready?"

There was little enough to tell, but the content was explosive.

"You invited us to join your gather," said Chris, "and now you know why we couldn't. I didn't want you having to fight that bunch of killers on our account. Now it looks like you'll have to, with or without us."

"Consider yourselves part of the outfit," said Ten, "but let's leave things as they are as long as we can. There'll be trouble enough, soon enough. Besides, as long as you can stay in the house without suspicion, there's a chance we can stay a jump ahead of whatever they have planned for us. Sooner or later, they'll discover the herd of longhorns upriver on Marty's old place. This is the larger herd you've gathered, the one we came upon when we first saw you. When they discover that herd, tell them it's ours. I reckon we're goin' to need all the longhorns the lot of us can catch. I've promised delivery of fourteen hundred head by next April, in Indian Territory. So I can guarantee you four dollars a head when the herd's sold. Besides that, you'll each get forty dollars a month. Fair enough?"

"My stars!" cried Chris. "Five hundred longhorns would bring us two thousand dollars! We wouldn't expect more than that, and the chance to get away from here."

"You'll earn the forty dollars a month," said Ten. "It's no more than I planned to pay if we'd been able to hire riders. After we've gathered the herd and faced up to this fight with Tomlin, we've still got the trail drive ahead of us. How're you fixed for grub and ammunition?"

"We slip food out of the house," said Chris, "and as long as Daddy and Bertha think we're increasing our gather, we'll have ammunition."

"Try to get some extra ammunition, and hold it back," said Ten. "All we have is for our Henrys and Colts. You're welcome to share our grub, if need be. Are we likely to have trouble with the Comanches?"

"Not unless they come after your horses," said Chris. "The only Indian camp we've heard of is four days' ride, downriver. Somebody's making moonshine and trading it to the Indians for horses. The Comanches ride as far south as Houston and Victoria, stealing horses."

"We need horses," said Ten. "Each of us need three, and we have one. We need at least eight more."

"We need four more, then," said Lou. "One horse can't take more than a few hours of this punishment. That's why we have so few cows. We started this last spring."

"Twelve hosses!" exclaimed Marty. "Where in thunder are we goin' to find even *one* that's gentled enough to learn cow savvy? We ain't got the time for hoss breakin', even if we had 'em to break."

"Bodie Tomlin and his bunch bought some Indian-gentled horses somewhere downriver," said Chris. "That's how we learned where the Comanche camp is. Just a few miles north of it, a half-breed has a horse ranch."

"Even if we make it through the gather," said Ten, "we'll need a remuda—extra horses—for the trail drive. We'd better take the time to call on this Injun and see if he's got a dozen gentled mounts that are fast learners."

"We can't *all* go," said Herndon, "without packin' up everything and taking the packhorses. It'll take four of us to lead a dozen broncs, if we can get that many."

"Since you're getting extra horses for us," said Chris, "we can help."

"Send Marty and Wes," said Lou innocently, "and there'll be four of us."

"You're lookin' at maybe four days there and four back," said Ten. "How can you be gone for a week without your daddy knowin' where you are?"

"I'll tell him where we're going," said Chris. "I just won't tell him we're going with some of you. I've already told him we need more horses, or we'll never get a decent herd. When mama died, she left us a little jewelry that Bertha don't know about. I'll tell him we're swapping that for some horses. Even if he don't want us to go, Bertha will talk him into it."

"She'd be tickled silly if the Comanches got us," said Lou.

"One more thing," said Ten. "This Bodie Tomlin and his bunch. How much do they know? Do they know you're—"

"Females? My God, no!" said Chris.

"Your daddy's idea?"

"Bertha's," said Chris.

"She wants to be the only woman in sight," said Lou, "if there's one man or fifty. That's why we have to get away. She's just waiting for the right time to get rid of us."

Marty, Wes, Chris, and Lou rode out the following morning at first light. They packed enough food for ten days, and Marty carried two hundred dollars in gold double eagles.

"Marty and Wes," sighed Herndon. "I'm torn between being glad for 'em and envious of 'em."

"I reckon they could do worse," said Ten.

His mind was on other things. As Chris had ridden away, her long, black hair had reminded him of Priscilla.

Wes and Lou dropped behind, while Chris kept pace with Marty. Covertly, she studied him. His hair was the white of new corn silk, his eyes a deep blue. Their eyes met once, but he turned away without speaking. She decided there was no pretense in him. He was a Texan, a cowboy, and probably, as Lou had suggested, had ragged drawers and holey socks. But he was a man, a strong man, and Christabel Ward decided she liked him.

14

$\mathcal{W}$es kept his eyes straight ahead, aware of the red-headed girl at his side but saying nothing. She stood the silence as long as she could.

"You don't say much, do you?"

"No, ma'am."

"Are you like this with everybody, or just me?"

"Mostly just you. What would I have to say to a woman that's threatened to shoot me?"

"Do you take everything a woman says as gospel?"

"Yes, ma'am, when she backs it up with a loaded gun."

"I'm sorry. I wouldn't have shot you."

"I didn't know that, ma'am."

"Damn it," she flared, "stop calling me ma'am! You're talking to me like I was your grandma! Call me Lou, or Louise."

For the first time he looked her full in the face. The quick burst of anger had left her cheeks rosy, and green fire in her eyes. He decided he liked her best that way.

"Lou," he said, "I never had much chance or much reason to talk to a woman, 'cept for 'Yes, ma'am,' or 'No, ma'am.' The teacher at our one-room school was old enough to be my ma. The girls, what few there was, just looked at me and laughed. I was tall and gawky, with big feet and a face full of freckles. I just tried to stay out of everybody's way. I left school when I was twelve, lied about my age, and joined the Confederate army when I was fifteen. Pa died while I was gone. Ma lasted until I got home. After I buried her, I throwed in with Ten and Marty."

"How old are you, Wes?"

"I'll be nineteen the tenth of this December."

"I'll be seventeen the fourth of next April," said Lou. So long was he silent, she became irritated.

"You've been to war," she said, "and made your way in the world. I just wish I was as much a woman as you are a man."

He looked her over carefully, a mischievous light in his brown eyes, and he almost smiled. He edged his horse closer to hers, until they were stirrup to stirrup. He grasped her saddle horn, leaning over until he was looking her full in the face. She felt herself blushing furiously.

"Lou," he said, "you're about the *most* woman I ever laid eyes on. If you was any *more* of one, God only knows what you'd do with it."

He'd fairly taken her breath away. She became so flustered, it was a while before she trusted herself to speak.

"For a man that . . . don't know how to . . . talk to a woman, you . . . learn awful fast."

"It's a mite easier when she ain't hollerin', cussin', and wavin' a rifle at me. I'd like to see less of you like that, and more of you like this."

"Thank you," she said, pleased. "I'll try to remember that."

Just after sundown they came upon a creek that angled into the Trinity. They pitched their camp a hundred yards east of the river, among the willows that lined the creek. They finished their supper, dousing the fire before dark.

"Are we goin' to stand watch?" Wes asked.

"No," said Marty. "I'm a light sleeper. We'll picket the horses close by, and they'll warn us."

For the lack of anything better to do, they rolled in their blankets and tried to sleep. After a while, as quietly as he could, Wes got up and headed down the creek. He had gone only a few yards when he stopped, drawing and cocking his Colt as he turned.

"Wes, it's me!" hissed Lou.

"Go back," he hissed in reply. "I got somethin' private to do."

"So have I, but it's dark. Let me go with you."

They continued, but their departure hadn't gone unnoticed.

"They're about as quiet as a pair of likkered Indians," said Marty.

"Where are they going, in pitch-dark?"

"I reckon they got business in the bushes," said Marty, "and not the kind you're thinkin'."

"How do you know what I'm thinking?" asked Chris.

"I ain't spent the day with you for nothin', Miss Christabel Ward. Lou puts on a big show, cussin' and yellin', but you don't. It didn't bother you a bit, us catchin' you jaybird naked, did it?"

"Of course not," said Chris. "We didn't plan it. What harm did it do? With all your apologies, you're not *really* sorry you caught us, are you?"

Marty chuckled. "I'd by lyin' if I said I was. I'll be as honest with you as you was with me. I thought I'd died and gone to heaven. The best most Texas cowboys can expect is a once-in-a-while look at somethin' like your daddy's shacked up with."

It was an insensitive remark better left unsaid. Her response to his careless words was a muffled sob. Despite her callous attitude toward Brady Ward, he was still her father, and she was hurt. What kind of man would forsake his daughters for a saloon whore? Marty rolled out of his blankets and went to her, half expecting her to slap his face. But she didn't. She only buried her face in his flannel shirt and wept. Finally, but for an occasional sniffle, she was silent.

"I'm sorry," he said. "I'll never say anything like that again."

"There's no denying the truth of it," she said, "but it still hurts. Thank you for understanding. For months I've needed to do that—to just let go and cry—but I had nobody to cry to, except Louise. I . . . I've tried to hold back for her sake. I'm the oldest and—"

"How old are you, Chris?"

"I'll be eighteen the fifteenth of January. Sometimes I feel so old, like I've always been old, and that my life will never be any better, whatever I do. When—If—we do gather a herd and reach Indian Territory, what's going to happen to me . . . and to Lou?"

"I can promise you one thing," said Marty. "Unless me and Wes is killed stone dead, you and Lou will get to Indian Territory. Where you go from there, I reckon, is up to you."

"Will it matter to you where I go . . . from there?"

"It will," he said. "When the time comes, I'll have somethin' to ask you."

"You've had a look at both of us," she said, her mood changing. "Are you sure you'd take me over Lou? She's a year younger."

"I like older women. Besides, I'd have to shoot Wes, and that'd leave us short-handed."

"What do you plan to do once we reach Indian Territory and the herd is sold? Where will you go from there?"

"Eventually we'll come back for a bigger herd. But before we do, I expect Ten will be goin' back to New Orleans, and he may need me to side him. We barely got out alive last time."

"Then why go back? What's the reason?"

"Her name's Priscilla LeBeau," said Marty. "She's about Lou's age, and she lives in New Orleans. Her daddy's mixed up in black-marketing, smuggling, and gambling. He's tryin' to force Priscilla to marry some bastard that's old enough to be her daddy. He's the big pelican that controls the law and most of the gambling in New Orleans. It had to be him and Priscilla's daddy that set up the ambush me and Ten walked into."

"You'd go *back* there with him, after being ambushed and barely getting out alive?"

"He picked me up off a New Orleans street, after I'd been stomped and robbed and couldn't help myself. He's no older than Lou, he's half Injun, but by God, he's a man! When he goes back to New Orleans, if he needs me, I'll go. Does it bother you, me standin' by him?"

"It would bother me if you *didn't,*" she said. "I've always wanted to see New Orleans."

By noon of the fourth day, they had reached what had to be the Indian's horse ranch. Until now the banks of the Trinity had been devoid of human habitation. The "ranch" consisted of an ugly adobe hut and a barn with an adjoining corral. There were a few horses wandering about, staring at them over the six-rail fence.

"I reckon this is it," said Marty.

They reined up before the barn. It was unlikely they had approached unseen and unheard, so Marty paused before hailing the house. A cow hide covered the entrance, and it was shouldered aside by a man who held a Spencer rifle. He had high cheekbones and shoulder-length black hair streaked with gray. His old high-crowned black hat had an eagle feather in the band. His face was gaunt and most of his front teeth were missing. He wore moccasins, dirty overalls, and an equally dirty red flannel shirt with the elbows out. He said nothing, waiting for them to speak. They dismounted.

"Horses," said Marty. *"Caballos."*

"Oro," said the Indian. *"Twenty dolla' oro, uno caballo."*

"Oro," repeated Marty, spreading ten fingers, countering the offer.

The Indian refused, shaking his head.

"Oro," said Marty, showing ten fingers, then five.

The Indian said nothing.

"Caballos," said Marty, showing ten fingers, then two. *"Caballos, oro."*

"Caballos," repeated the Indian, extending all ten fingers, then two.

"Fi'teen dolla', uno caballo."

Marty nodded his head in agreement. The Indian would sell them twelve horses at fifteen dollars each.

"Donde?" inquired Marty.

The Indian shifted the Spencer to a comfortable position under his arm and nodded for them to follow. He led them around the adobe and half a mile into the woods. It was a typical holding pen, created by fencing both ends of a small canyon. A stream ran the length of it, created by a seep at the upper end. Marty counted twenty-five horses. They were broomtails, but they had the same stocky bodies and broad heads as Maynard Herndon's broncs.

"I like them all!" cried Lou. "How can we ever choose?"

"Color won't matter," said Marty. "Any one of 'em will make a good cow horse. Take your pick."

Chris chose a black and a gray, Lou a bay and a sorrel. They pointed out their choices to the Indian, and he climbed through the six-rail fence, carrying only a blanket.

"Watch how he handles them," said Marty. "We'll have to approach them the same way, until they get to know us."

The Indian approached the black, and at first the horse seemed nervous. His ears went up, and they realized the Indian was speaking to the horse. He gestured with his hands, as though conversing with a friend. Carefully, he placed his hand on the horse's withers, and the animal didn't flinch. Finally he spread the blanket across the broad back, and still the horse remained calm. He stretched his arms across the animal's back, then lifted his feet off the ground, putting all his weight on the horse. When the black accepted his weight, he draped one arm casually around the horse's neck, as

Marty and Wes dropped the rails to let them out. Chris approached the black slowly, talking to it as the Indian had. The horse held steady, allowing her hand on the broad shoulder.

Marty and Wes chose an assortment of blacks, bays, grays, sorrels, and chestnuts. The Indian patiently repeated the procedure until they had their twelve horses. Slowly, carefully, they made friends with the animals, as the Indian had. Marty counted out nine gold double eagles, $180, into the Indian's hand. He followed them as they led their new horses back to the barn, where they'd tied their mounts. The Indian pointed downriver, shaking his head.

"Indios," he said. *"Malo Indios."*

Marty shook his head, pointing upriver, the way they had come. They rode out, their new mounts following on lead ropes.

"He warned us of bad Indians downriver," said Chris. "That's bound to be the Comanche camp Bodie Tomlin mentioned. Have we been warned not to ride downriver or to look out for our horses because of the Comanche camp?"

"Likely both," said Marty. "I reckon he's got some agreement with them, so they don't steal him blind, but it won't help us. It's the kind of thing that would just tickle hell out of the Comanches—let us pay for the horses, and then steal them from us."

"So we'd better stand watch," said Wes.

"We're going to," said Marty. "You and Lou will take one watch, me and Chris the other. We're goin' to cover as many miles as we can before dark, and just hope that Comanche camp has laid in a good supply of moonshine to keep 'em occupied."

Chris and Marty took the second watch. They sat close together and talked quietly, their eyes roaming the moonlit clearing where the picketed horses grazed.

"Lou's been awfully quiet," said Chris. "That's not like her."

"I expect that's for Wes's benefit," said Marty. "He

thought the minute she got out of that creek and got her britches on, she'd start shootin'. She come on mighty strong."

"I called her down," said Chris, "and for once, I think she listened."

"You said your pa brings back ammunition for Bodie Tomlin and his bunch. Where does he get it? We had to send to St. Louis for guns and shells, and was able to do that only because Herndon used his uncle's name."

"I hate to tell you," she said. "All you hear from me and Louise is the things Daddy's done, none of them good. We lived in Galveston for a while. Me and Lou was alone a lot, because Daddy took goods from incoming ships and hauled them to other towns, by pack mule or in wagons. The town he mostly hauled to was Beaumont. The ships were unloaded at night, because their load was black-market and smuggled goods. That was last year, long before the war ended and the blockades came down. One night when a ship docked, the law was there. Some of the crew was killed, and Daddy escaped only by leaving his pack mules and running for it. He sneaked out of town, me and Louise with him, and we went to Beaumont. That's where he took up with Bertha, and our lives just went to hell."

"So when Bodie Tomlin sends him to Beaumont, he's buying ammunition from the same place where he once delivered illegal goods."

"I think so," said Chris.

"Ten needs to know about this," said Marty. "The U.S. Customs people in New Orleans believe Priscilla LeBeau's daddy is involved in this. I think he is too, and I think this old bastard who LeBeau's tryin' to force Priscilla to marry is the head of it. The customs man in New Orleans, before he was gunned down, got Ten involved, and that's why old LeBeau wants our young Injun's head in a gunnysack."

"Dear God in heaven," sighed Chris. "Why can't he just take Priscilla away and leave all of this mess behind?"

"He'd like to," said Marty, "but he's underage, and so is Priscilla. God knows what'll happen before Priscilla's eighteen. She likely thinks Ten's dead, thanks to her sneaking old daddy. Ten's not even sure where she is, but I'd bet she's back in New Orleans. She seems like a real wampus kitty, not the kind to hide out, hopin' everything will be all right."

"So that's where Ten will be going once this trail drive is done?"

"Damn right," said Marty, "and there'll be the biggest fight since 1814, when Andy Jackson stomped some British butts."

"Pair of riders comin'," said Herndon.

Ten had been at the breakfast fire, pouring himself a last cup of coffee. He put down his cup and got to his feet. He and Herndon stood together as their visitors reined up a dozen yards away. The man wore town clothes, was graying at the temples, and looked to be about fifty. His female companion might have been forty, but she looked older. She was plump, big-bosomed, her divided skirt was too tight, and her hair was jet-black. She wore enough makeup to have put a tribe of hostile Indians on the warpath. Were she to smile—however unlikely the possibility—Ten thought her face might just shatter like a looking glass.

"I'm Brady Ward," said her companion, "and this is Bertha."

"I'm Tenatse Chisholm," said Ten, "and my pardner is Maynard Herndon."

He said nothing more, allowing the silence to grow long and painful. Whatever the purpose of their visit, he wouldn't make it easy for them.

"Gatherin' a herd, I see," said Ward.

Ten nodded, saying nothing.

"They's a right smart of a herd upriver, maybe fifteen mile," said Ward. "Them yours?"

"They are," said Ten.

"You ain't bin here much more'n a week. That's a heap of cows."

"We work nights and Sundays," said Ten.

"Long ways from there t' here," said Ward. "Riders could make off with them cows, 'fore you knowed it."

"Mister," said Ten grimly, "you do them riders a *big* favor. You tell 'em if *any* man takes just one cow out of that herd, he'd better be wearin' his burying clothes. I'm an Injun from the Cherokee nation, and I can track a lizard over solid rock. You pass the word along to any rustler or group of rustlers. Tenatse Chisholm will stretch their necks from here to yonder, and leave 'em hanging for buzzard bait."

"How dare you threaten us!" snarled Bertha, in a low, venomous voice.

"I don't make threats," said Ten, equally venomous. "When I tell you something, you can damn well count it as a promise. Now ride out of here!"

Without a word or backward look, they rode out.

"I never heard it put any straighter or any plainer," said Herndon.

"We know what their plans are," said Ten, "so we have nothing to lose. They came here to intimidate us, to soften us for the kill."

"Ward don't seem like much of a threat," said Herndon. "I have an idea it's that she-buffalo ridin' with him that'll cause trouble."

"I'll hang her from the same limb as Bodie Tomlin," said Ten, "if that's what it takes. I don't cut any slack for female rattlers."

15

❦

Marty, Wes, Chris, and Lou reached Ten's camp without difficulty. They listened solemnly while Ten told them of the visit by Brady Ward and Bertha. Chris was the first to respond.

"If you mean what you've said—about us being part of your trail drive—take the longhorns from our holding pen and drive them here."

"We haven't been here long enough to gather that many longhorns," said Ten. "They're going to *know* you've thrown in with us."

"I don't care," said Lou. "It's about time for Bodie Tomlin's bunch to ride out again. Suppose they take our herd? What can we do? Let's bring them here, where we'll at least have a chance of keeping them."

"I reckon you're right," said Ten. "They *could* just grab your herd to keep us from gettin' it. Besides, I think we'd be fools to try and protect two herds, fifteen miles apart."

"There'll likely be trouble at the house," said Herndon. "Ward's doin' the talking, but the words are comin' from that woman of his."

"You're so right," said Chris. "I don't know how much longer we can stay there, or if we can stay at all."

"I don't *want* to stay there," said Lou. "Why don't we just move out into the brush and be done with it?"

"Ten," said Marty, "let's have them move into our

camp. Once we bring their herd down here, Ward and Tomlin will know they're with us. We'll have them gunning for us whether Chris and Lou are here or not. Bringing us all together will cut the odds, and give us two more guns."

Ten sighed. "I'll have to agree with you. I had some hope we could gather most of our herd before we had to fight, but now I doubt it. If it's goin' to be that way, then we'll just lay all the cards on the table. Chris, tell Brady Ward the two of you are leaving, that you are no longer gathering a herd for him to sell. I've already told him the cows in your holding pen are ours. I don't believe the two of you will be welcome or safe in the same house with Bertha. Do you want a couple of us to ride there with you?"

"No," said Chris. "I want a chance to get our belongings and the few things mother left us. Bertha would stop us from taking anything if she knows we're leaving. She's just that mean."

Once they'd ridden out, Marty shook his head.

"I don't like them goin' there alone."

"Me neither," said Wes.

"They're not going alone," said Ten. "Marty, you and Wes trail them, but don't go near enough to the house to be seen."

When Marty and Wes had headed upriver, Herndon spoke.

"The Wards have sand, but I'd bet a horse and saddle neither of them is eighteen. You reckon that'll be a problem?"

"No," said Ten. "There's no law closer than Nacogdoches, but it's not the law we have to worry about. Eighteen or not, I believe Chris and Lou have the right to make up their own minds. The next move is Ward's. Or Bertha's."

"Or Tomlin's," said Herndon. "They sound like the kind that would bushwhack us while we're huntin' longhorns."

"If they do," said Ten, "we'll be ready. But I'm not

sure old Bertha won't hold them off until we have a larger gather. If you aim to steal a herd, why settle for a hundred or two?"

Chris and Lou rode in at sundown, followed by Marty and Wes. Chris was pale and shaken, Lou still flushed with anger.

"Daddy begged us not to leave," said Chris.

"Sure he did," snapped Lou, "and you saw how quick he shut up when that woman lit into us. She told us to get out and not to come back."

By first light they were prepared to ride upriver for the 150 longhorns Chris and Lou had gathered. Much against their wishes, the girls were being left to secure the camp.

"Remember," said Ten, "I told Brady Ward this is our herd. Besides, we must protect the camp. Keep your rifles handy while we're gone."

In a little more than two hours they reached the holding pen. Warily, they scouted the area, but saw nobody. Marty had some last minute advice.

"Once we loose these critters, everybody's goin' to get a taste of trail driving. Remember, this is just about a tenth of the herd we'll drive north, so you'll have some idea as to what we're in for. I can promise you this bunch will scatter from hell to breakfast if we ain't careful. Wes, you lower the rails, get behind then, and get 'em moving. Hern, when they come out, you ride flank on the far side, and I'll flank 'em on this side. We'll head 'em for the river. Ten, you'll be ahead of 'em, and when they reach the river, it'll be up to you to turn 'em south. As they turn, I'll be right behind you. Hern, you'll have to ride the outside flank by your lonesome. Double your lariat and swat the hell out of any bunch-quitters. Wes, push 'em hard from the drag. Keep 'em bunched so's they don't scatter."

The freed longhorns exceeded Marty's prediction. Prepared to run, they needed little urging. The leaders

headed for the river. Marty and Herndon rode hard,
swatting potential deserters back into line. Ten reined
up fifty yards from the Trinity. He began waving his hat
and shouting at the approaching herd. Just when it
seemed the charging longhorns would trample him and
run into the river, the leaders began to turn. Marty
turned with them, swatting their flanks and yelling like a
Comanche. Herndon had managed to hold the other
flank, and Wes kept them bunched at drag. Except for
an occasional bunch-quitter, the herd seemed content to
follow the river. It was a controlled stampede, and as
the longhorns began to tire, they slowed to a trot. Soon
Wes was popping the behinds of the stragglers to keep
them moving. The river became shallow where it flowed
through their fenced canyon. Marty and Ten crossed to
the west bank, while Herndon forced the lead longhorns
into the river. Chris and Lou had removed the rails,
allowing the herd to enter the canyon.

"That wasn't so bad," said Wes when they had dismounted.

"We won't always have a river for them to follow,"
said Ten, "or a chance to get ahead of them."

"Not much predictable about a cow," said Marty.
"We was lucky with this bunch, gettin' 'em headed the
way we wanted 'em to go."

"We had a visitor while you were gone," said Chris.
"Bodie Tomlin."

"So he knows you're with us," said Ten. "Did he say
or do anything?"

"He just looked at us," said Lou, "and rode away. I
can't stand him."

"He's taking our measure," said Marty. "He wanted
to see how much of an outfit we have."

"That's why two of us will be staying in camp from
now on," said Ten. "It'll slow down our gather some, but
not as much as losin' our horses and grub."

"I hope you're not leading up to what I think you
are," said Lou. "Well, I don't aim to spend all my time
in camp, fetching wood for the fire and cooking."

"There's six of us," said Ten. "That means you'll be here every third day. You and Chris will never be here alone. Wes will be with you, and Marty with Chris. I reckon Herndon and me are stuck with each other. Now, that don't mean you get to rest every third day. These longhorns have to be trail-branded, and besides keepin' an eye on the camp, that's what two of us will be doing every day. We'll build the branding fire right here and keep our rifles handy."

"What brand?" Lou asked.

"The X Diamond," said Ten. "I had it made in Natchez."

"A curious brand," said Chris. "What does it mean?"

"The X is 'Ten' in Roman numbers. The diamond covering it means that some hombre with a running iron won't have much luck turning the X into something else."

After breakfast they cut the cards. Ten drew a card, Marty another, and Wes a third. Wes drew the low card, Marty the highest.

"Wes and Lou will spend today in camp and start the branding," said Ten. "Tomorrow, it's Herndon and me, and the day after, Marty and Chris. After that, we start over with Wes and Lou."

Twice a day the four riders hunting wild longhorns changed horses. The first week they added sixty cows to their gather, and the second week, seventy-five.

"This is too good to last," said Marty.

He was right. Ten and Herndon had just left one hog-tied, struggling longhorn and were in search of another when they saw the seven riders. Unobserved, from a stand of cottonwoods, Ten and Herndon watched the men ride across the river and along the west bank, heading south.

"Bodie Tomlin and his bunch," said Herndon. "We're rid of them for a few days, but somebody in the settlements will catch hell."

"All the hell-raising may not be in the settlements,"

said Ten. "You can bet your horse and saddle the Comanches will know there's seven *less* whites up here in the brakes."

It happened the fourth day after Tomlin's gang had ridden out. Marty and Chris had been left to defend the camp and brand captured longhorns. The rest of the outfit had ridden downriver at first light, in pursuit of more wild cows. They were no more than an hour from camp when they reined up, reading a grim message on the river's sandy banks. The water was shallow, and eleven riders had crossed. They rode unshod horses.

"Comanches!" said Lou.

"But they're riding east," said Wes. "Maybe they'll keep going."

"We can't risk that," said Ten. "They crossed here about the time we rode out. We may already be too late. Let's ride!"

They kicked their horses into a gallop, and almost immediately they heard the distant thunder of rifles.

"They'll expect us from downriver," shouted Ten. "We'll ride east and double back."

They tied their horses almost a mile from the besieged camp.

"On foot from here," said Ten. "Some of them will be on the east wall of the canyon, overlooking our camp. Don't shoot until I do. Make every shot count."

As they ran through the woods, one of the rifles in the canyon camp went silent. They were halfway through a scrub oak thicket when somewhere to their left a horse nickered.

"Spread out and belly-down," said Ten. "They know we're here."

He went down just as an arrow thudded into an oak, chest high. Leaves long since fallen, the scrub oak was bare, offering little cover for the attacked or the attackers. The Comanches couldn't advance, and their only retreat was along the sparsely wooded banks of the river. So they turned and fought. Ten cut loose with his

Henry, and rifles roared on either side of him. There was no time to aim, to select a target. The Comanches were coming too fast, moving from tree to tree, utilizing what little cover there was. While they'd lost the element of surprise, they were laying down a deadly fire. Ten began raking the woods with .44 slugs as fast as he could cock and fire the Henry. Within his field of vision two Comanches fell, one of them victim to his Henry. Suddenly there was no movement, nothing to shoot at. The firing from the camp had ceased. Nobody moved, nobody spoke.

"Ten?" shouted Marty. "We got a couple of the bastards, but Chris is hurt."

Cautiously, Ten got to his knees. When his movement drew no fire, he looked around him, seeking his companions. He found Herndon and Lou waiting for him to make a move, and Wes with the left sleeve of his shirt bloody.

"We're here, Marty," he called. "They nicked Wes, but we got some of them." He turned to the others. "Be careful getting back to the horses. I aim to be sure they've gone, and to see how many we took out of the fight."

Ten knew his force had accounted for three Comanches, and Marty was claiming two more. Having half their number shot down should have convinced this bunch their medicine was bad. It was a superstition common to most tribes, and a war party whose luck had gone sour might simply withdraw from a fight. Ten found where the Comanches had fallen, but the dead had been taken away. Only patches of dried blood on the ground attested to the accuracy of their fire. Ten followed the sign of their retreat to a thicket where their horses had been concealed. They had ridden away, making no effort to conceal their tracks. Ten hurried back to his own horse. His concern was for Wes and Chris. The worry in Marty's voice had told him the girl's wound was serious. He found Wes with his shirt off, and Lou tying a bandage around his upper arm. The fire had been stirred to life, and water was starting to boil. Chris lay on her back, her head on a saddle. From the inside of her right thigh protruded the ugly shaft of a Comanche arrow. Marty was kneeling beside her. When Ten reined up, she opened her eyes.

"Sorry," she said. "I'm not much good in a fight."

"You did your best," said Ten. "There was just the two of you, against eleven of them. Not very good odds for us, but we killed five and wounded another. If there's any fault, it's mine. I didn't take the Comanche threat serious enough. Marty, one of us will have to drive that arrow on through."

Chris looked at Ten, then at Marty.

"Sorry, Chris," said Marty. "There's a barb. It'll have to be driven out, pushed on through."

The girl's face paled, but when she looked at Ten, she blushed. It was an awkward place for a wound, especially an arrow wound. Her Levi's would have to be cut away. Marty came to the embarrassed girl's rescue.

"I've done this before, Ten. You and Hern will have to drift off down the canyon a ways. Lou can stay, if she wants."

"No," said Lou. "I'll take a walk with Ten and Hern."

"Chris is goin' to be the first to sample that jug of whiskey we brought from Natchez," said Herndon.

"Ugh!" said Chris. "Do I have to?"

"No," said Marty, "if you can stand having that arrow driven the rest of the way through your leg. The whiskey will put you under for a while. It's all we got."

"Get the whiskey, then," said Chris.

Herndon brought the jug.

"Give me an hour," said Marty, "but don't go *too* far. This kind of thing is hell on a man's nerves, and I can't think about anything else. I don't hanker to have an arrow in my back while I'm drivin' this one out of her leg."

"They won't be back," said Ten, "but we'll be close enough to see the east rim and the fence at the head of the canyon."

When the others had gone, Marty stirred the coals under the boiling water. Chris sat there holding the jug of whiskey. She looked up at him.

"You've never done this before, have you?"

"No," he said, "but it was me or Ten."

"How much of this stuff do I have to swallow?"

"Enough to put you out cold. Even then, this is goin' to be hard on me."

"I know," she said, "and I know why. Thank you."

She choked and gagged on the whiskey, losing as much as she swallowed.

"I'm afraid I'm . . . going to . . . be sick," she gasped.

"Try to keep it down," he said, "else you'll have to do it again."

She forced down as much as she could, then lay back gasping. Marty took the blankets from her bedroll and, with her help, managed to get them under her. When the ordeal was over, he would cover her with his blankets.

"I'll have to cut your Levi's," he said.

"I—I only have one other pair. Is there no way to . . . take them off?"

"Not with that arrow in your leg. I'll have to leave most of the shaft in place, so there's enough length to push it on through."

"Drive the arrow on through, out of the way," she said. "Then just take them down as far . . . as you need to."

Wrapping his bandanna around his hand, he turned to the fire for the pan of boiling water.

"Marty."

She spoke so softly, he barely heard her. He left the water to boil and knelt beside her. She reached her arms for him, and he leaned to meet them. For a long moment she held him close, and he could feel the fever in her flushed face. He could feel her arms trembling. He held her until he felt her going limp, then gently drew away. Her eyes were closed. The time had come.

He removed the shells from his Colt. With his knife he weakened the feathered end of the arrow's shaft until he could break it. Finally there was nothing left but to drive the rest of it on through. He had seen it done only once, and had never done it himself. He had to get on with it, before he lost his nerve. He began the grisly chore, and each time the butt of the Colt struck the shaft of the arrow, Chris groaned. He clenched his teeth in response to her pain, and the pistol barrel became slippery in his sweating hands. He paused just long enough to wipe them on his Levi's. Her painful responses became more intense, and he feared the effects of the whiskey might wear off before he was finished. Finally he was able to feel the barbed tip, and he drove it out with a final blow from the butt of his Colt. Emotionally and physically drained, his shaking hands could barely draw the arrow's shaft through the cruel channel he had prepared for it. His shirt was soaked with sweat, and he sleeved more of it from his burning eyes.

Now he must cauterize and bandage the wound. He felt a moment of guilt as he unbuttoned the unconscious girl's Levi's. She wore nothing under them. But once he saw the wound, and the swollen, purple flesh, his concern for her overcame everything else. Infection was the killer they had to contend with.

He tore one of his undershirts in half, making two bandages. The first he soaked with whiskey, using it to cover the torn flesh where the arrow's barb had been driven out. Then he tipped the jug, pouring whiskey into the wound where the arrow had gone in. Over this wound he placed the second bandage, soaking it with the whiskey. Finally he bound the bandages in place, so that the restless girl's movements wouldn't loosen them. He took the blankets from his bedroll, covered her, and tucked them in around her. She was feverish, and would have to swallow some more of the detested whiskey. He folded her torn, bloody Levi's and put them under her saddle. Somehow, he didn't want the others knowing she was naked beneath the blankets.

* * *

The outfit spent the rest of the day in camp. Chris had developed a raging fever. Until her condition improved, nobody was of a mind to ride out. Marty forced her to swallow more of the whiskey, until only a little remained. Supper was a silent, cheerless affair. Marty left the girl's side only to go for more cold water. Time after time he bathed her fevered brow. Sometime after midnight her fever broke. In the dim light from the fire, they could see the sweat on her face. She opened her eyes, and when she spoke, they held their breath.

"I don't *ever* want any more whiskey."

Lou was the first to laugh, and the others joined in.

Two days after the Comanche attack, Ten made some decisions and some changes.

"Marty, you and Chris will stay here until her wound heals. Forget the branding for a while. So we don't lose any time with the gather, the rest of us will ride the brakes as usual. But we'll do one thing we haven't been doing. When we ride out every morning, we'll scout the area to the south, for Indian sign. If trouble comes from another direction—from Brady Ward and the Tomlin gang—grab your rifle and fire three shots. We'll come on the run."

Chris was out of the saddle for two weeks, but insisted on hobbling about the camp, doing all the cooking. By December 15, 1865, their gather had grown to six hundred head. A week before Christmas the weather turned chill and wet. Rain, a steady drizzle, hounded them for seven straight days. A continual west wind added to their misery, making the chill seem more intense than it actually was. All they had in their favor was a dry camp. The west wall of the canyon jutted out over the river, the overhang protecting them from wind and rain.

"If I could have one wish," said Lou, "it would be for a whole day of just being dry, next to a big, warm fire."

"You're going to get that wish," said Ten. "Tomorrow's Christmas. We're going to spend it eating, sleeping, and staying dry."

Just the prospect of a single day's respite from the miserable weather cheered them, but Ten's mood remained somber. He found himself envying Wes and Marty. They had Lou and Chris to share their feelings, their worries, their troubles. Wes and Lou, Marty and Chris. They were always together, while he spent all his time with Herndon. He was unable to talk to Herndon, because it was his concern for Herndon that troubled him. The man was sick. He needed a warm, dry climate, and the winter months in Texas were anything but that. Ten was constantly recalling his first conversation with Herndon, aboard *The New Orleans*. Herndon had spoken lightly of his release from the Confederate army, and Ten recalled his exact words:

". . . I was lucky. I got lung fever, and they kicked me out after a year."

Ten had witnessed some of Herndon's agonized coughing fits. They had become more frequent in the chill, rainy weather. They spared him while he rested, troubling him most during the brutal days in the saddle. Herndon would cough until his breath came in short, painful gasps. His face had the pallor of death, and his hands shook. On the ground, following the seizures, was a sprinkling of blood.

Tenatse Chisholm and Maynard Herndon shared an uncomfortable secret. They both knew Herndon was dying.

16

Despite André LeBeau's questionable conduct, the LeBeau name still had some social clout. While Priscilla LeBeau detested social climbers and their pretensions, she wasn't above using them when the need arose. She started by learning the names of the men who claimed to have ridden down and killed Tenatse Chisholm. While custom forbade her going directly to these men, their wives were fair game. The truth, at least some of it, began to emerge. The so-called "posse" didn't know *who* they had killed. The dead men had been ex-Confederates, not one of them young enough to be Tenatse Chisholm! Somehow, somewhere, he was alive, and she had to get word to him that she was in New Orleans. She toyed with the idea of writing to Jesse Chisholm, but something Ten had told her came to mind. She doubted Ten would be coming back to New Orleans with Chisholm's trade goods, and if he didn't, then who would? Perhaps Chisholm himself. The day after Christmas, she prowled through the commercial buildings and warehouses until she found the offices of Roberts and Company.

André LeBeau had spent a cheerless Christmas day, his only companion a bottle of bourbon whiskey. Now, the day after Christmas, he waited outside Jason Brawn's office. Hung over, he was in dire need of a drink, but he dared not face Brawn while drinking or drunk. He sensed—in fact, knew—he was about to be handed an ultimatum, insofar as Priscilla was concerned. If the girl failed to live up to the promises he had made, then he would be held accountable for that formidable collection of IOUs Jason Brawn held. So deep had LeBeau sunk in his morbid thoughts, Brawn's secretary had trouble getting his attention.

"Mr. LeBeau," she said impatiently, "you may go in now."

LeBeau stepped into the office, closed the door, and waited. Brawn looked up, nodded to a chair, and LeBeau sat down. Brawn continued to move papers about on his desk, letting LeBeau wait. But LeBeau didn't care. He staggered under a burden far greater than anything Jason Brawn might lay on him. He had sacked Emily's trust fund to get Bradley Montaigne off his back. Now he was faced with the fearful task of replacing the money he had taken from the trust. Years ago, Emily's father had set up the trust. While he'd believed in LeBeau, trusted him, Emily's mother never had. LeBeau was fearful the old woman would discover his treachery and crucify him. She would get a copy of the annual statement that went out on September 30, allowing him less than nine months to raise $25,000! He was startled back to reality when Brawn slammed his fist down on the desk.

"Damn it, LeBeau, pay attention when I'm speaking to you!"

LeBeau swallowed hard and said nothing, knowing the tirade was coming.

"I've been patient and discreet, LeBeau. Too patient, and too discreet. I'm going to be blunt enough, so even you can understand. I'm prepared to trade you fifty-five thousand dollars in gambling debts for Priscilla's hand. October first, 1866, LeBeau. That's the day you play out your string, one way or the other. But I'm a generous man; you have several options. The first, and the one I prefer, is that Priscilla and I announce our engagement, the marriage to take place on Christmas Day. Your other option is to simply pay your gambling debts. No more IOUs, LeBeau."

"Thank God you're a generous man," said LeBeau bitterly. "Suppose I don't deliver Priscilla *or* the money?"

"LeBeau," said Brawn, with an evil smile, "you underestimate my resourcefulness. I too have a pair of options, and you aren't going to like them. One of them is to send the committee around to teach you the error of your ways. Then—if you're still alive—I'll see that your disgraceful activities during the recent war are exposed. Given that much information, it won't be too difficult for the Federals to figure out who shotgunned John Mathewson."

Livid with rage, it was a moment before LeBeau could speak at all, and then in almost a whisper.

"I paid," hissed LeBeau. "Montaigne said I owed twenty-five thousand, and I paid in full. That was to free me from your devilish scheme. As for killing Mathewson, I had nothing to do with that, and you know it."

"It seems Mr. Montaigne made a mistake in the accounts," said Brawn. "The twenty-five thousand you've paid is only about half what you owe. I might overlook that, LeBeau, as a favor to my father-in-law. Of course, I know you didn't kill Mathewson, but he *was* investigating the illegal activities in which you've been involved. Who would have had a better motive than you, the scoundrel who masterminded the smuggling scheme?"

"You double-crossing son of a bitch," shouted LeBeau, "before I'd force Priscilla to marry you, I'd as soon be dead and in Hell."

"That," said Brawn, "can be arranged."

Priscilla was shown into Harvey Roberts's office. She found the big man kindly, sympathetic, and a good listener. She told him everything she knew, much that she suspected, and concluded with her investigation. Finally she came to the purpose of her visit.

"Mr. Roberts, I believe Ten's father, Jesse Chisholm, may be here soon. Could you—would you—arrange for me to . . . talk to him?"

"I can and will arrange it, Priscilla. From what you've told me of the impact Ten's had on you, I believe Jesse will welcome a meeting with you. I have known Jesse Chisholm for many years. While I don't know your young man that well, I was impressed with him. I thought enough of him that I couldn't allow this ugly incident to pass without Jesse being aware of it. So I wrote him a letter, sending a copy of the newspaper account, along with the posse's sworn statement that Ten had been killed. I have received an answer to my letter, and have been asked to keep in confidence the information sent me. But knowing Chisholm as I do, and knowing your feelings for Ten, I believe Jesse would want you to read that letter. Would you like to?"

"Oh, yes," she cried. "Please!"

The letter was brief, and Priscilla read it through tears.

Dear Harvey:
    I'm obliged to you. I know nothing about this. Ten will have to explain it. He left here bound for Texas, to gather a herd of wild longhorns. When I received your letter, I telegraphed Washington and had them wire the field officers in charge of occupational forces in Texas. Ten was in Nacogdoches in early November. He is alive, and for his sake, I ask you to keep this in strictest confidence. I won't have another shipment for you until the middle of January. We'll talk then. Again, on Ten's behalf, much obliged.

                                              Jesse

"Thank God," said Priscilla. "He's gathering a herd, and that means he'll be driving them somewhere, instead of coming back here. Please, when Mr. Chisholm gets here, arrange for me to talk to him."

"That I will," said Roberts. "January fifteenth is on

Sunday; come here the next morning. If he's not on that steamboat, he'll make the next one."

Once Chris was able to ride, they redoubled their efforts. Beginning the third week in January, they had more than a thousand longhorns in their holding pen.

"Let's build a herd of fifteen hundred," said Ten. "We'll lose some on the drive. From now on the pair of us securing the camp and doing the branding will have to be especially watchful. The herd's gettin' big enough to arouse the interest of Tomlin and his bunch."

The next morning, while Wes and Lou were branding longhorns, Bodie Tomlin rode in. He ignored Wes, looking directly at Lou.

"I brought you a message from your daddy," he said.

"He can ride," said Lou. "If he's got anything to say to me, let him say it himself. I want nothing to do with you."

"Time's comin' when you won't have a choice, girlie," said Tomlin, with an evil laugh. "Your daddy's some concerned, you an' your sister layin' out with four men. He wants the both of you back at the house."

"He told you our secret," said Lou, "and it's *you* that wants us back at the house. You and that scruffy bunch of coyotes you ride with. Me and Chris, we like it here."

"You've delivered your message, Tomlin," said Wes. "Now ride."

"Kid," said Tomlin, "you'd best get whatever good out of her you can, 'cause you ain't got much time. Me an' the boys, we got plans for the two of 'em."

Wes froze, his hand on the butt of his Colt. Tomlin had him covered, the pistol cocked. Tomlin laughed.

"You're slow, boy. My old granny could outdraw you, left-handed. I could of shot you dead twice. Next time, I will."

He holstered the Colt, contemptuously turned his back and rode out. Wes stood there, his head down, his face flaming red. Lou had her rifle cocked and was aiming for Tomlin's broad back when Wes snatched the weapon away.

"No," he said. "You can't shoot a man in the back."

"He walks on his hind legs like a man," snapped Lou, "but he's a lowdown, sneaking coyote. You're goin' to be sorry you didn't let me shoot him."

They spent a miserable day trying to ignore each other. When the rest of the outfit rode in, Lou told them what Tomlin had said. She didn't tell them Tomlin had drawn on Wes, and Wes said nothing. After supper Ten caught Lou away from the others and spoke to her.

"You didn't tell us everything, did you?"

"I told you what Tomlin told me," she said, refusing to look at him.

"Wes is cowering like a whipped dog. What took place between him and Bodie Tomlin?"

"Why don't you ask him?"

"I will," said Ten. "With Tomlin's bunch after us, this is no time to have differences among ourselves."

He found Wes, his back to a cottonwood, staring into the river.

"Lou didn't tell it all," said Ten. "Why don't you tell me the rest of it?"

"Why not?" said Wes. "It can't get any worse. Lou looked up to me like I was a man. This mornin' she saw me for what I am. A still wet-behind-the-ears kid, tryin' to be somethin' I'm not, an' likely can never be."

"Lou didn't say that. Those are your words, and you won't be worth a damn to anybody, not even yourself, until you shuck that notion. With Tomlin threatening us, we can't afford to lose you. Now talk!"

Eyes averted, his head down, Wes began to talk. When he had finished, he looked up, and Ten was touched by the misery in his eyes.

"You came out of Mississippi not knowin' how to use a rope," said Ten, "and now you can build and throw a loop as well as any of us. How fast you can draw and fire a Colt depends on you. On your reflexes, and your willingness to practice. I can get you started, but you're going to have to want it bad enough to work at it. Do you?"

"Help me," said Wes, getting to his feet, "and I'll show you how bad I want it. I'm ready to start now."

"Unload the Colt," said Ten. "Every day, every spare minute, practice gettin' your iron out and on the target. When you throw it on your target, do it like pointin' your finger. When you're slick enough at gettin' your Colt out an' ready, I'll show you a trick an old-time outlaw taught me, and you'll be ready to burn some powder."

Night after night, long after the others had rolled in their blankets, Wes worked with his Colt. He wore the holster on his left hip, his Colt butt forward for a cross-hand draw. Ten watched approvingly as Wes became more and more skillful at getting the Colt into action lightning fast.

"You're fast enough and slick enough at gettin' the iron in action," Ten said, "but that can only get you killed if you don't hit what you're shootin' at. We'll start with these."

In his hand there were six large brown acorns. He held his gun hand out palm down and placed one of the acorns on the back of the hand. Slowly, he raised the gun hand shoulder high, then tilted it enough for the acorn to roll off. His hand a blur of motion, he drew and blasted the acorn to bits before it hit the ground.

"Good God!" Wes gasped, in awe.

"You might want to practice some dry shootin'," Ten said, "until you're comfortable with the trick."

Wes kept at it for two weeks, using so much ammunition that Ten was about to call a halt to the practice, when Wes finally shattered one of the acorns.

"Once you're able to hit what you're shootin' at," Ten said, "you need to practice shootin' from different positions. You should be able to shoot belly-down or flat on your back, and to draw on a man who's got the drop on you. A man who has you covered won't expect you to draw, and that gives you a slight edge. Never throw yourself backward or belly-down, because he has only to drop the muzzle of his iron. Always fall to right or left, drawing as you go. That forces the other man to shift his weapon, gainin' you maybe half a second."

Finally the time came for a test. From a deck of cards Ten took the ace of hearts, and with a bit of rosin, positioned it chest high on a pine.

"Load five shells," said Ten, "and back off fifty paces."

Ten watched with pride as Wes drew with blinding speed, emptying the Colt with a drumroll of sound. All five slugs had centered the card, leaving a jagged hole that could be covered with a two-bit piece. . . .

February was unusually mild, the wind balmy, the sun warm. In camp, Wes and Lou had been branding long-horns all morning.

"I'm so sweaty and dirty," said Lou, "I'm tempted to get in the water for a few minutes. In that bunch of willows down yonder, nobody could see me."

"No," said Wes, "it's too risky."

Even as he spoke, a covey of birds dipped down beyond the willows and were immediately up and away.

"Somebody's down there," said Wes. "Stay here, and keep your rifle handy."

Wes drew his Colt and ran along the riverbank, using low-hanging underbrush and willows for cover. He wanted to reach the heavy growth of willows ahead of the intruder, but discovered he was too late. A slug sang through the willows just inches above his head, and so thick was the underbrush, Wes still had no target. He drew up, hunkered down, and waited. He would force the other man to make a move. A light wind rustled the leaves, but there was no other sound. Wes was sure the stranger had left his horse beyond their fence, so that left him afoot, and he couldn't retreat without making some sound. When it came, it was the snapping of a twig. Finally, on the farthest bank of the river, Wes caught what might have been the crown of a man's hat.

His adversary was crawling along the bank, using underbrush for cover, trying to get back to his horse. Wes fired three times into the brush, and a dirty gray hat skittered down the bank and into the water. There was a rustling sound behind him, and Wes threw himself to the right, away from the river. He ended up on his belly, his cocked Colt practically in Lou's frightened face.

"By God," he hissed, "I told you to stay in camp. I almost shot you!"

She said nothing, and he turned away in disgust. He worked his way upriver, back the way he had come, until the water was shallow enough for him to cross. Keeping his head down and using the underbrush for cover, he crept along the bank until he was near the point where the shooting had taken place. Finally he could see the sole and heel of a boot, and he found his man facedown, but Wes moved on. When he had traveled a hundred yards without seeing or hearing anybody, he then concluded the man had been alone. He made his way back upriver to the man he'd shot. Lou stood on the opposite bank of the river, looking doubtfully at him.

"Come on across," said Wes, "and take a look at this hombre."

"That was a foolish thing," she said when she reached him, "and I feel terrible."

"Not near as terrible as I'd feel if I'd shot you," said Wes. He rolled the dead man over so they could see his face. "Do you know him?"

"I don't know his name," said Lou, "but I've seen him. He's one of the Tomlin gang. What are we going to do with him?"

"For now," said Wes, "we leave him where he is. His horse too. We're not sure he was alone, although I saw nobody else. He just about had to be here on Tomlin's orders, and that means they'll come looking for him. We'd best leave off branding and keep a close watch. When Ten and the others get here, we'll decide what to do. I reckon I've just kicked over the beehive and we're goin' to have to fight."

* * *

On a good day, the X-Diamond riders roped, hog-tied, and penned sixteen wild longhorns. Even after the brutes had struggled for half a day, thrashing themselves to exhaustion, it was no easy task getting them behind a fence. Since they were never sure how ornery a long-horn was going to be, or how long it might take to pen the animal, they stopped their gather at noon. Starting with the longhorns that had been hog-tied the longest, they began the arduous drive to the holding pen. Some days it took them most of the afternoon to get the morning's gather penned. Following the shooting, Wes and Lou had less than an hour to wait for the rest of the outfit to ride in with their first longhorns. Ten's reaction to the shooting surprised them all.

"Good shootin', Wes," he said. "Now they'll have to come after us, instead of back-shootin' us one or two at a time, and we'll be ready for them. Since we've opened the ball, we'll make them dance to our fiddler. Wes, you and Lou ride back with Marty and Chris, and bring in the other four longhorns. Hern, you and me are goin' to find this dead man's horse, rope him across the saddle, and send him back to Tomlin."

"That'll blow things to hell an' gone," said Marty.

"I aim for it to," said Ten. "Once we bring in the last of today's gather, we won't ride out again. Not until Tomlin's finished. With two of us in camp, and the rest scattered through the brakes, they can back-shoot us one at a time. They're one man down, so now it's six of us and six of them. Our only chance is to force them to come after us while we're all together."

Marty, Chris, Wes, and Lou rode out. Ten and Herndon started downriver. Curious, they stopped in the willows for a look at the dead man.

"Look at that," said Herndon. "Wes put two slugs in this hombre and didn't get a scratch."

"Prime shooting," said Ten. "Wes has been through the fire."

They found the horse—a roan—and led it to the willows. The nervous animal shied at the smell of death, and it was all Herndon could do to hold him. Ten slung the body across the saddle, and using the dead man's lariat, roped his hands and feet together, under the belly of the horse. Ten let down the rails at the upper end of the canyon, and Herndon slapped the roan on the flank. Already skittish, the animal lit out in a gallop.

"Let's hope," said Herndon, "our outfit gets back before that horse reaches Tomlin. How do you reckon Brady Ward's goin' to fit into this, once the shootin' starts? It's goin' to be some awkward, Chris and Lou shootin' at their own daddy."

"I doubt they'll have to," said Ten. "The way he lets Bertha gee and haw him around, I don't believe he's got the sand to fight."

Sundown came and went, and still there was no sign of the Tomlin gang.

"They're the kind to ambush us," said Ten, "cutting us down while we sleep. We're going to give them every reason to think we *are* sleeping, by spreading our bedrolls beneath the west wall's overhang, just like we've been doing. Use leaves, stones, willow branches, anything to hump your blankets. There won't be a moon, and in the starlight we can convince them we're in those bedrolls. Once they open fire, we'll use their muzzle flashes for targets and cut them down."

"They won't be in one bunch," said Marty. "They'll split up."

"I'm counting on that," said Ten. "I'm expecting some of them to slip in at the upper end of the canyon and the rest at the lower end. They'll try to box us in a cross fire, but we're going to be waiting for *them*. We'll set up an ambush and cross fire of our own. Marty, you'll take Chris and Hern to the lower end of the canyon, and I'll take Wes and Lou to the upper end. I want all of us on the east bank of the river, close to the canyon wall. I look for them all to be on the west bank, since that's where our camp is. We'll be facing each other, but firing *across* the river, so none of us gets caught in our own cross fire. Keep your Colts out of it; use your rifles."

"It sounds perfect," said Chris, "but suppose they *don't* split up, coming at us from opposite ends of the canyon? They *could* all do their firing from the east wall of the canyon, like the Comanches did."

"There was just you and Marty against eleven Comanches," said Ten, "and it was daylight. They could see you. Tomlin's bunch would lose the advantage of a cross fire, because the west wall's overhang would protect us. I can promise you, they won't risk shooting from the east wall. There'll be enough starlight to skyline them, making them better targets. Besides, they'd be shooting from a lighter position into a darker one. If your night vision's going to adjust to the dark, you've got to be *in* that dark."

It was an impressive argument. There was another question Ten had been half expecting, and Marty came up with it.

"Ten, when they come, Brady Ward may be ridin' with them. Chris an' Lou, he's their daddy—"

"He's not my daddy," shouted Lou.

"I'm afraid he is," said Ten, "whatever wrong he's done. I won't fault either of you if you don't shoot. The odds are in our favor, and I reckon four of us can take six of them."

"No," said Chris. "You're being partial to us because we're women. If we're going to be part of this trail drive, then we'll take the good with the bad. If he rides in here with Tomlin, knowing what's going to happen to us, then he deserves what Tomlin gets. I'll fire with the rest of you."

"So will I," said Lou. "I even hope old Bertha's with them. I'd like to shoot her corset strings off."

It was a long, uncomfortable wait. The west wind caressed them with its chill fingers, making them long for their protected camp. Ten watched the big dipper as hour after slow hour dragged on. He thought of Priscilla, of her promise to him. That night now seemed so long ago, and so far away.

So long had he waited, it took a moment for Ten to identify the first sound of their coming. First light was an hour away, the time when a man's slumber is deepest, when the faintest sound is audible to a listening ear. Somewhere close, there was the chink of a horse's hoof against stone.

"They're coming," whispered Ten.

They waited, watching three silent shadows climb through the fence, their rough clothing whispering against the cottonwood rails. Just as Ten expected, they crept along the west bank of the Trinity. Quickly they faded into the shadows of the canyon, and on the opposite bank of the river, Ten, Wes, and Lou followed. Once Ten was within rifle range of the deserted camp, he halted. He knelt, his Henry ready. Wes and Lou took their positions on either side of him. Across the river they heard the snick of a hammer being eared back. The outlaws were ready.

"Now," bawled one of the men they had followed. "Fire!"

There was the roar of rifles as the outlaws fired into the silent camp. Downriver, on the west bank, came the thunder and muzzle flashes of three more rifles. The rest of Tomlin's bunch were firing into the deserted camp. Beyond the farthest trio of outlaws, from the Trinity's east bank, Marty, Chris, and Herndon had begun firing.

"They're across the river!" shouted a frantic voice.

Slugs thudded into tree trunks near Ten's position as the outlaws fought back. There were cries of pain, and their defense was short-lived. Their firing ceased and there were sounds of hasty retreat. There was sporadic firing toward Marty's downriver position, and the rest of the outlaw rifles went silent. They too were retreating the way they had come. It was over for now. After the initial burst, there had been few shots from Marty's position. First light was only minutes away, and there was no movement on the opposite bank of the river. Behind them the east bank was clear. Ten took a chance.

"Marty?"

"Here," said Marty. "We got at least one of 'em, but we're hurt. Come a-runnin'."

Coming abreast of their camp on the other side of the river, Ten could see the bodies of two of the outlaws. But from the tone of Marty's voice, he feared they had paid too great a price. They were almost to the willows when they saw Marty and Chris kneeling. Slowly they got to their feet, and Ten saw the tragedy in their faces. Chris clung to Marty, silent tears on her cheeks. Maynard Herndon lay on his back, eyes closed, his teeth clenched against the pain. The front of his old denim shirt was soaked with blood.

17

*T*en fell to his knees beside the wounded man and began unbuttoning the bloody shirt. Herndon groaned and opened his eyes.

"No," he said. "No . . . use. I . . . I'm done."

His eyes were open, but the soul, preparing to depart, had taken his sight. Blindly, his right hand moved, and Ten understood. He gripped it hard.

"Ten . . . where are . . . you?"

"Hern, pard, I'm here."

He could feel Herndon's nails biting into his palm. Herndon's lips moved but the words wouldn't come. As his strength ebbed, his voice had weakened to a whisper. Ten leaned closer to hear his last words.

"You . . . it . . . it's been an outfit . . . to ride the . . . river with," Herndon gasped. "Glad . . . I was part . . . of it. Uncle Drago . . . tell him . . . I cashed in . . . like a . . . man. . . ."

Maynard Herndon would never see Indian Territory, but neither would he spend his last days in a sickbed. Ten felt the hand gripping his own relax, and he knew Herndon was gone. Blindly he got to his feet. He sleeved tears from his eyes, and it was a while before he could swallow the lump in his throat and turn to face the others. Their anguish was as great as his own. Tough-talking Lou was taking it the hardest of all. When Ten spoke, his voice was soft.

"Just beyond the head of the canyon there's a little rise overlooking the river. Wes, will you and Marty make a place for him there? Under the big cypress tree."

When the grave was ready, they wrapped Maynard Herndon in his blankets and carried him to it. Chris handed Ten a worn Bible.

"It was our mother's," she said. "There's no preacher, but someone must read the word over him. We owe him that."

It was all Herndon had asked, that and the chance to die with his boots on. But it was the most difficult thing Tenatse Chisholm had ever been called upon to do. How could he speak to God on behalf of Maynard Herndon, when he was himself unworthy? Not knowing how to choose a text, he opened the Bible and began to read the shortest chapter on the page.

"The Lord is my shepherd, I shall not want . . ."

His voice trembled at first, but as he read, he found himself drawing strength from the words. The eastern horizon was aglow with the rising sun. When he had finished reading, they stood there a moment in silence. Finally he closed the Bible and returned it to Chris.

"Thank you," he said.

Wordlessly, Marty and Wes began filling the grave. When they returned to their camp, they still had two dead men to contend with.

"I reckon we'll have to plant these coyotes," said Ten. "It's more than they deserve, but if we don't, they'll stink up the canyon. While we're taking care of that, I'd be obliged, Chris, if you and Lou would put on some coffee to boil and see to breakfast."

It was a grim task, the sooner finished the better. They buried the two outlaws in a single grave and returned to camp. None of them were very hungry, but they needed the coffee, finishing it in silence. They all knew what had to be done; they were waiting for Ten to give the word. He did.

"Saddle up," he said. "Bring your rifles and plenty of shells. We're going to finish this Tomlin bunch before we rope another longhorn. Chris, you and Lou lead out. Take us to Brady Ward's place. Since he wasn't with Tomlin's gang, I expect he's in trouble. Tomlin's the kind to use him and the woman against us. I look to find them holed up at Ward's cabin."

"We've cut into their ranks pretty deep," said Wes. "Maybe they just rode out."

"No," said Ten, "they'll be there. They're on the defensive, but Tomlin won't run. You gunned down that pard of his yesterday morning, and you saw how quick he came after us. We cut down two more of his boys this morning, and he's not sure they even nicked any of us. I hope they *are* still here. I don't aim for a man of them to leave Texas alive, and it'll save us the trouble of trackin' the bastards down."

They approached the Ward cabin cautiously, reining up just short of rifle range. There was no sign of life.

"There's a poor excuse for a barn behind the house," said Lou. "Not much more than shelter for the horses."

"Ward," shouted Ten, "if you're in there, come out. We need to talk."

"Ward ain't feelin' good. He ain't goin' nowhere."

"That's Bodie Tomlin," said Lou.

"Tomlin," shouted Ten, "You *know* why we're here. We've got no fight with Ward or the woman. Let them go."

"Ward stays where he is," bawled Tomlin.

"No," cried Brady Ward in a quavering voice. "No!"

The door was flung open and he stumbled down the rickety steps, falling to hands and knees. He staggered to his feet.

"Come on," said Ten. "Move in close enough to cover him!"

In range, they cut loose with their rifles, careful to shoot over Ward's head. He came toward them in a shambling run, close enough until they could see the sweat of fear and desperation on his face. There was a single rifle shot from the cabin, and Ward seemed to pause, suspended in midair. Then he fell facedown, a growing circle of crimson on the back of his shirt. With a broken cry, Chris was out of her saddle, but Marty caught her before she could run to the fallen Ward. Slugs were whipping the air above their heads now.

"Fall back," shouted Ten.

"You murdering bastards!" shouted Lou.

Once they were out of rifle range, the firing ceased.

"Wes," said Ten, "take Lou, and the two of you cover the back of the house. Let none of them escape. When I figure a way to smoke the coyotes out, I'll find you. Take shelter in the barn, if you can, and loose all their horses."

Marty had calmed Chris, and Ten turned to her.

"Is there anything at the rear of the house, besides a back door? Any windows?"

"No windows," said Chris, "but there's cutouts along the back wall for rifles, in case of Indian attacks."

"Damn it," said Marty, "they can stand us off all day, and then sneak out after dark. By the time it's dark enough for us to set fire to the place without gettin' shot, it'll be too late to do any good."

"There's a way out of the house," said Chris. "It's a tunnel that comes out in the barn. There's just room enough to get through it, and that's on your hands and knees."

"If it's a way *out* of the house," said Ten, "it's also a way in. But it could also be a death trap, if Tomlin knows of it. Where does it come out in the house?

"Tomlin won't know about it," said Chris. "The shack was here when we came, and so was the tunnel. It was me and Lou that found it. When Daddy brought that woman here, we were so . . . so disgusted, we never told him about it. There's just a big, hollowed-out place under the house. The kitchen is kind of long, and there's a sack curtain across one end, making a pantry. Lou and me took our baths there. Part of the floor lifts out, and we spread a blanket over it. We thought whoever built the cabin must have been pretty scared of the Comanches."

"He had every right to be," said Ten. "Chris, you've just told me how we're goin' to salt down this bunch of coyotes. Marty, Wes, and me are going into that house, through the tunnel. We'll have to depend on you and Lou to cover the front and back doors. Leave your horse here, and move up close enough to throw some occasional lead against that front door. We'll have Lou doin' the same thing at the back door. Make all the noise you can, so they can't hear anything else."

Chris swallowed hard, looking at Marty. Ten knew what she was thinking. They were going against four outlaws, and even with the element of surprise in their favor, they might be seriously hurt or killed. Ten turned away as Marty held the girl close and spoke to her.

Ten and Marty circled wide, well out of sight of the cabin. Leaving their horses in the woods, behind the barn, they walked the rest of the way. Lou seemed shaken, following the death of her father, and was as reluctant as Chris to have them enter the house.

"Please, please, be careful," she urged. "We've lost so . . . much today, and I . . . I just can't bear any more."

They left Lou with the same instructions Ten had given Chris. When they were ready, Ten turned to Marty and Wes.

"We'll leave our rifles. This is Colt work."

Lou took them to the tunnel exit, and Chris had been right. There was barely room for a man to crawl, and if there was a cave-in, they were in big trouble. They tied bandannas over their mouths and noses, lest they suck up the dust of their movement. The air in the tunnel was oppressive and stifling hot. Sweat dripped off Ten's nose and soaked his shirt. There were places where dirt had fallen into the tunnel. They were forced to their bellies, snakelike, until the obstruction was past. Just when Ten was becoming light-headed for the lack of good air, he all but fell into the hollowed-out area under the house. For long minutes they sat there, taking long gulps of the blessed, fresh air. They could hear the firing of distant rifles. Chris and Lou were doing their part. Then, to their surprise, they heard a woman's voice.

"Bodie, why'n hell didn't we just ride out of here? For God's sake, there's Shreveport, Beaumont, Houston—"

"*Nobody* makes a fool out of Bodie Tomlin. *Nobody*, you hear?"

There was a metallic clang as a slug struck something in the kitchen. Bertha cursed, and started whining to Tomlin.

"Git back there in the other room," shouted Tomlin. "Slide your fat carcass under the bed and stay there!"

There was a scraping of chairs. Their vision had adjusted to the half dark, and they saw a makeshift, five-rung ladder. Ten took the lead, pausing when his head touched the floor of the pantry. It was a dangerous move. If he was discovered, with Marty and Wes trapped behind him, he was a dead man. Taking a deep breath, he put his shoulders to the wooden floor. When it moved, dust sifted down into his face and he fought back a sneeze. He lifted the panel enough to get a grip on two sides of it. It snagged on the blanket that had covered it, and as he raised the wooden panel, the blanket descended on him like a shroud. He shoved the whole mess forward, praying he wouldn't dislodge something breakable. Then his head was free and he found himself facing a bare wall. The sack curtain was behind him, as was the rest of the kitchen. Gently, he leaned the wooden panel against the wall, stepping into the pantry, making way for Marty and Wes.

When they were ready, Ten shoved aside the sack curtain and they were in the narrow kitchen. There was only an open doorway to the front room and what had served as a bedroom, and it was their misfortune to have Bertha spot them before they could fire a shot. The big woman screeched like a gut-shot bobcat, rolling off the bed onto the floor. Although taken by surprise, the outlaws reacted quickly. A slug slammed into the wall above Ten's head, and he killed the man who had fired. A second outlaw was down, but so was Marty, the left side of his face and head bloody. Next to the fireplace Bodie Tomlin fired from behind a pile of wood. One of his shots struck Wes's Colt, sending it clattering to the floor. Ten's Colt clicked on empty, and Tomlin got to his feet with a wolfish grin. His shot dug a fiery path across Ten's ribs, under his left arm. Beneath the waistband of his Levi's, Ten carried Maynard Herndon's Colt. He drew the weapon and shot Bodie Tomlin twice, just above his belt buckle.

Ten turned just in time to find Bertha in the bedroom door, leveling a shotgun at him. He shot her twice, and as she went down, the shotgun tore a hat-sized hole in the loft above. Marty was sitting up, his bandanna against his bloodied head. Wes was looking ruefully at his mangled Colt.

"Here," said Ten. "This was Herndon's Colt. It's yours now."

Once the shooting had stopped, there was the sound of galloping horses. Chris and Lou could no longer bear the suspense.

"Marty, you and Wes take them away from here. Tell them I'm all right but for some hide off my ribs. See if there's any digging tools out there in the barn. We still have to bury Brady Ward."

"Then we got all this bunch," said Wes.

"No," said Ten, "I have other plans for them. Go head off the girls, and I'll be with you in a few minutes."

Marty and Wes were digging a grave for Brady Ward when they saw Ten riding toward them. Chris and Lou looked mournfully at the blanket-shrouded body of their father. Above the old cabin where the slaughter had taken place there was a thin tendril of smoke. When it had grown to a cloud, the roof of the shack erupted in flames. Ten dismounted and they watched as the inferno grew, diminished, and finally died. They laid Brady Ward to rest on a knoll overlooking the Trinity.

Wes read a text from the Bible, and they rode away, none of them looking back.

Jesse Chisholm found the long steamboat rides to and from New Orleans tiresome, but he looked forward to this trip. When he had reached Fort Smith with his trade goods, there had been a hurried letter from Harvey Roberts. Once before boarding the boat for New Orleans, and a dozen times afterward, Chisholm had read Roberts's letter. It had given him his first real look at Priscilla LeBeau, the girl who had so smitten young Tenatse. She had so impressed Roberts that he had promised her a meeting with Chisholm, and from what Roberts had told him, Chisholm found himself anxious to meet Priscilla. She was beginning to emerge, not as a silly, infatuated young girl, but as a woman with character and courage. It said quite a lot for Tenatse Chisholm's judgment. Somehow, he no longer fitted Chisholm's recollection of a rebellious seventeen-year-old, kicked out of school for hell-raising and disobedience.

André LeBeau left Jason Brawn's office, his mind a maelstrom of anger, fear, revulsion, and desperation. His anger at Brawn was equaled only by his fear of the man. Brawn didn't make idle threats. Priscilla had called him a "lecherous old pig." LeBeau conceded he was that, and worse. The girl was more particular than he was, he admitted. He even admired her courage, but then, she didn't owe Jason Brawn a fortune in gambling debts. Going full circle, it brought him back to his own desperate situation. There was nothing left for him but to face the facts. Priscilla was not going to sacrifice herself to save him, and in all honesty, he didn't blame her. He was aware that she had done some investigating on her own, regarding Tenatse Chisholm, but so had he. Young Chisholm had escaped, and LeBeau didn't doubt he would be returning to New Orleans. For Priscilla? Slowly an idea began to grow in the fertility of LeBeau's desperation. He knew something of Jesse Chisholm, of his success as a government scout, and of his more than thirty years as an Indian trader. The man was wealthy. With that in mind, wouldn't it be worth *something* to young Tenatse, if he were able to take Priscilla with her father's blessing? Granted, when she was eighteen he'd probably take her anyway. Since she would be getting what she wanted, and Tenatse Chisholm would be getting what he wanted, why should LeBeau not get something in return?

LeBeau found Priscilla at the house, and she greeted him as usual, pretending he didn't exist. She mustn't suspect that this apparent change in him was the result of anything more than his own repentance. She must be convinced to the extent that she would arrange for him to meet with Tenatse Chisholm, so that he might bargain with the young fool in private.

"Priscilla," he began, "I need to talk to you."

"If it has anything to do with Jason Brawn, you can save your breath."

"It has nothing to do with Brawn," said LeBeau. "I'm through with him."

"Then what have we to talk about?" inquired Priscilla suspiciously.

"Do you know when Tenatse Chisholm is coming back to New Orleans?"

"No," said Priscilla, "and if I did, I wouldn't tell you. Why? Are you planning another ambush?"

LeBeau ignored the insult, fighting back his anger. He managed to calm himself before he spoke.

"I've had second thoughts about young Chisholm. He's part Indian, and so is his father, but Jesse Chisholm is one of the most respected men in the nation. When I was opposed to the boy, I didn't realize just who he was. I was wrong, and now I must admit I'm impressed with him. When he returns, I'd like to meet him."

He sounded so convincing, so sincere, Priscilla wanted to believe him. But she still had her doubts.

"I'd like to believe you," she said, "but how do I know this isn't just another scheme of Jason Brawn's?"

"I only want to talk to the Chisholm boy, to satisfy myself about some things. I don't blame you for having your doubts. To prove to you nothing is being planned, that no harm will come to him, let him decide where we'll meet. Make it some public place, like the lobby of the St. Charles Hotel. Wouldn't you rather go with him in peace, with my blessing?"

"You know I would," said Priscilla, "but I'm not sure you're being truthful with me."

"Leave it up to Chisholm, then," said LeBeau. "Let him decide whether or not he'll meet with me. When you hear from him, tell him what I've told you. Nobody is to know of our meeting. Make no mention of it, not even to your mother. I'm promising you he'll be safe with me, but I can't speak for Jason Brawn. He believes the boy is all that's standing between you and him. It was Brawn who set up the ambush and lured young Chisholm into it. Now, will you at least *ask* him if he'll meet with me?"

Priscilla was struck by the disturbing realization that she didn't know this man who was her father, and had never known him. Even now, when he seemed so sincere, she didn't trust him. Finally she answered him.

"Yes, I'll tell him what you've said, but it will be his decision as to whether or not he meets with you. Whatever he decides, just keep this in mind: in another six months, I'll be eighteen, and when he comes for me, I'm going with him. With or without your approval."

Priscilla still eyed him with well-founded suspicion. The expression on his florid face could only be described as one of relief.

18

*P*riscilla LeBeau paced the floor nervously. In Harvey Roberts's private office she awaited the arrival of Jesse Chisholm. When the door opened, she froze. She found it hard to believe the man who had stepped into the room was Ten's father. Except for the eyes, she saw little resemblance. Chisholm's once-sandy hair was mostly gray, as was his shaggy moustache. He wore a wrinkled suit, no tie, and beaded moccasins. His craggy face was burned brown as an old saddle, and his countenance seemed grim, until he smiled.

"You look a lot like Ten when you smile," she said.

It was the first thing that came to her mind, and she felt like a fool for having said it. But it was an honesty that Chisholm appreciated, and he laughed. It seemed to put him at ease. He studied her before he spoke, and when he did, there was a twinkle in his eyes.

"Now I understand why young Tenatse was bound to return to New Orleans."

She blushed, accepting the compliment, but her eyes never left his. "I begged him not to come," she said. "He was tricked into it."

"So Roberts told me. Have you any idea what all this is about? Who's after him? And why?"

Priscilla told him what she knew and what she suspected, including the possibility that her own father was involved. He listened gravely. She concluded with André LeBeau's request to meet with Ten, stressing her doubts.

"Perhaps he's being honest with you," said Chisholm.

"Oh, dear God, how I wish I could believe that! But I —I'm afraid."

"So was I," said Chisholm. "To be honest with you, I had my doubts about Tenatse, but after what's happened, I've changed my mind. He's young, but I'm convinced he can take care of himself. He has an agile mind, and he's lightning quick with knife and pistol. I once saw Ben Thompson draw, and Ten's faster than Thompson. Ten has a sense of responsibility that surprised me. Except for a borrowed stake, he refused help from me. Instead, he rode to every fort in Indian Territory and *sold* the herd he's gathering in Texas."

"He had to leave for Texas," said Priscilla, "not knowing where I was or what might have happened to me."

"I know that must have hurt," said Chisholm, "but like I told you, he's more of a man than I gave him credit for being. A man keeps his word, whatever it costs him, however painful it may be. Legally, his hands were tied. There was little he could do here, until you were eighteen. How do *you* feel, Priscilla? When Ten returns, may I ask what your plans are?"

"I'm going away with him," she said simply. "When I'm eighteen I will go wherever he wants me to go, whether my father likes it or not."

Chisholm liked the resolute set of her mouth, the color in her cheeks, and the fire in her gray eyes. She was the kind of woman the western frontier needed. Neither of them had bothered to sit, and he surprised her. He turned to her and took both her hands in his.

"Priscilla," he said, "in fairness to your father, I'm going to ask Ten to meet with him. Once Ten has finished this trail drive, he'll be coming here. Before he leaves Fort Smith, I'll have him telegraph Harvey Roberts. Once he's here, you can meet with him privately, here in Harvey's office. Ten should finish this trail drive in mid-April. By the week following, Harvey should

have a telegram from him. Thank you, Miss Priscilla
LeBeau, for seeing me. The West is going to be proud
of you. And so will I."

She choked on the words she wanted to say, and she
watched him out the door with a mist in her eyes.

On February 19, 1866, Ten began the drive with 1455
head, and they discovered that captivity had taught the
brutes nothing. Most of them had been roped downriver, and it was to these brakes they wanted to return.
That first incredible, hard-riding day, they had no point
rider and needed none. It was all they could do just to
keep the unruly longhorns moving in the same general
direction. Marty and Wes rode flank positions, fighting
the bunch-quitters constantly breaking away. Ten, Chris,
and Lou were at drag, swinging their doubled lariats at
dusty flanks, keeping them bunched. They covered less
than ten miles that first day, finally getting the herd bedded down only because the longhorns were exhausted.
But so were the riders. They all but fell out of their
saddles.

"I'm starved to death," said Marty, groaning, "but so
give out, I ain't got the strength to move my jaws."

"It's just as well," sighed Chris. "Who feels like cooking?"

"This is how it's goin' to be," said Ten, "until this
bunch settles down. We'll have to drive 'em until they're
ready to drop, and then sing 'em to sleep every night.
Skittish as they are, and with only five of us, the night-
hawking will be unhandy. Two of us will take it to midnight, and the other three until dawn. If there's goin' to
be trouble, I look for it after midnight, but it could come
any time. When you sleep, don't shuck anything but
your hats. If somethin' spooks this bunch of longhorned
jacks, they could be drinkin' out of the Gulf while you're
lookin' for your boots in the dark."

"I'll ride either watch," said Chris. "I can't think of
anything that could happen, including a Comanche at-

tack, that would be much worse than the terrible day we've just had."

"That goes just as strong for me," said Lou.

Ten took the girls at their word, waking them at midnight. They would join him in circling the herd the rest of the night. Mercifully, the longhorns were as exhausted as the riders, and except for an occasional restless lowing, the herd was quiet. For the first time Ten found himself alone with both the Ward girls. As the night wore on, and boredom set in, they became talkative. And curious.

"When we finish this drive to Indian Territory," said Chris, "Marty says you're going to New Orleans, to get married."

"Sometimes," said Ten, "Marty talks too much."

"I know it's none of my business, but in a way, it is. Perhaps a way you don't realize. Marty's going with you. To 'watch your back,' as he puts it."

"And you're going with Marty."

"If he'll have me," said Chris bluntly.

Ten chuckled. "You know better than that. You couldn't run him off with a double-barrel shotgun. Yes, I aim to go back to New Orleans."

"For Priscilla?"

"Who's Priscilla?" asked Lou, joining the discussion.

"The girl I aim to marry," said Ten, irked. "I'm surprised nobody's told you."

"Well, hell's bells," snapped Lou, "I didn't know it was a secret. Chris knows, Marty knows, and you're all gettin' ready to run off to New Orleans. What do you aim to do with me and Wes—drop us down a bog hole?"

Ten laughed in spite of himself. "Lou," he said, "Marty helped me shoot my way out of an ambush, and I don't feel like he owes me anything. I owe him, and I don't feel it's fair, leadin' him into what might well be *another* ambush."

"But we're an outfit," said Chris. "Marty went with you into the house, after Bodie Tomlin and his gang. So did Wes."

"I haven't forgotten that," said Ten, "and I won't. But this trouble—whatever I'm facing in New Orleans—is my personal problem. I have no right to expect the rest of you to side me."

"Tenatse Chisholm," said Lou, "you have *every* right. You took us in, knowing what our daddy was, knowing you'd have to fight Bodie Tomlin and his gang. You made us part of this outfit, and now you're stuck with us."

"I see it that way too," said Chris. "You're just going there for Priscilla, aren't you? You don't plan to live in New Orleans, do you?"

"My God, no!" said Ten. "I aim to take her far away from there."

"I know it's beating our tails into the ground," said Chris, "but this isn't a very big herd. Marty thinks we ought to come back to Texas and trail a much larger herd after you've rescued Priscilla. I know we'd need more riders, but why not *begin* with what we have?"

"I'd have to agree with Marty," said Ten, "and with you. To be honest, I haven't been thinking any further than Priscilla's next birthday and just getting her away from there. But I reckon it's time to think beyond that. Within a year the rails will reach eastern Kansas, and there'll be a *real* market for Texas longhorns. I'm having to split this herd among six forts, but the railroad can take four times this many longhorns. In the eastern markets, our prices will double. When we sell this herd, I'll owe the two of you twenty-four hundred dollars for your hundred and fifty cows. You'll each have six months' wages comin', for a total of four hundred and eighty dollars more. Suppose we came back to Texas, put all our money in the same pot, and *bought* as many longhorns as we could?"

"Lord," said Chris, "with Texans broke and half starved, we could buy thousands of longhorns. It would be so much quicker than having to rope them one at a time."

"There's Marty and Wes," said Lou. "What about them?"

"I reckon," said Ten, with a chuckle, "we could hire them easy, forty and found. Once we reach Indian Territory, I'll owe them two hundred and eighty dollars apiece in wages. Now, if they added that to what you girls will have, that would be almost thirty-five hundred dollars."

"It would," said Lou, "but then we'd be stuck with them forever. You reckon a pair of fiddle-foot cowboys with ragged drawers and holey socks is worth it?"

"I doubt it," said Ten.

They all laughed. A cow bawled, and another answered. The riders split up, circling the herd, as the night wore on.

Their second and third days on the trail were little better than the first. One old longhorn bull had been a constant source of trouble. Finally, Ten shot the brute, after it almost gored his horse. They were near the end of the third day, and within a mile or two of the little town of Crockett.

"We'll bed 'em down here," said Ten.

There was another hour of daylight, but they were exhausted. With the river an ever-present source of water, they need only look for good graze. While it was still light enough to see, Ten studied the rough map Jesse Chisholm had given him. Marty looked over his shoulder.

"If we didn't have to go to Fort Towson," said Marty, "we could follow the Trinity to Coffee's Post, on the Red. Once we was over the Red, Fort Washita and Fort Arbuckle would be right alongside that Chisholm Trail."

"We'll have to pick up Jess's wagon road after we go to Fort Towson," said Ten. "We'll go there first, so we'll have to leave the Trinity and drive northeast a ways. We'll cross the Red at Towson. When we've cut out their two hundred head, we'll follow the Red west to the Washita. From there, Fort Washita, Fort Arbuckle, and

Fort Cobb will be almost due north. When we're ready to leave for New Orleans, we'll take four hundred head with us. We'll leave half of them at Fort Gibson and follow the Arkansas on to Fort Smith. They'll get the last two hundred head, and from there we'll take a steamboat to New Orleans."

"Mighty slick plannin'," said Marty, "but that's only twelve hundred cows. Unless there's a stampede, or rustlers, we'll have better'n fourteen hundred longhorns when we get to Indian Territory."

"Whatever's left over," said Ten, "I aim for them to be cows. We'll just leave 'em to graze along the Canadian until we're ready for 'em. They'll be safe enough. Jess has half the Cherokee nation gathered around him."

They'd just finished supper when they saw the rider jogging toward them. He rode in from Crockett, but there was a dusty, trail-weary look about him that said he was a drifter. He forked a dun horse, and his old double-rigged saddle looked older than he was.

"Stopped at the store," he said, reining up. "Old woman said there was an outfit down here gatherin' cows. I reckon that'd be you."

"It would," said Ten. "Step down and have some coffee."

The stranger dismounted, and he proved to be a gangling youth, over six feet, his gauntness attesting to meals he'd missed. He wore rough-out, mule-ear boots, dirty Levi's, denim shirt, and a dusty, flat-crowned black hat. He carried a Colt on his right hip, thong-tied just above the knee. He had pale blue eyes, black hair, and a mouth that wasn't made for smiling. The fuzz on his upper lip said he hadn't begun to shave. He looked like what Ten suspected he was: a kid who had been too young to go to war, had found the aftereffects of it not to his liking, and was escaping the only way he could.

"I'm Bill Longley," said the stranger, "and wherever this herd's bound, I'd like to go with it. Who's trail boss?"

"I am," said Ten. "I'm Tenatse Chisholm. Can you handle longhorns?"

"I can handle this," he said, going for his gun.

He found himself looking into the muzzle of Ten's Colt, cocked and rock-steady. He released the butt of his own weapon, allowing it to slip back into the holster. He met Ten's eyes with no emotion in his own.

"Yeah," he said, "I can punch cows."

"Forty a month and found," said Ten, "from here to Indian Territory."

Longley nodded, and began unsaddling the dun. The rest of the outfit watched him lead the horse away, to picket it with the others.

"I ain't sure we need help *that* bad," said Wes.

"Me neither," said Marty. "That boy fancies himself a real gun thrower. Ten's chain lightning with a Colt, but that ain't worth a damn unless it's an even break. We'd best keep our eyes on this coyote."

Bill Longley seemed aware of their distrust, and did nothing to further aggravate it. He kept to himself, speaking only when spoken to. They night-hawked in pairs, Ten riding with Longley. But when trouble came, Tenatse Chisholm wasn't the cause of it.

While Longley said little or nothing, his eyes were constantly on Lou. He was doing nothing wrong, yet he began to haunt her, until she became frightened enough to talk to Wes.

"If he lays a hand on you," said Wes, "or even looks like he *wants* to, I'll kill him."

In the evening, after the herd was bedded down, Longley had taken to riding away for a while. Nobody knew where, or for what reason, until Marty trailed him. He returned in a somber mood.

"He's workin' with that Colt," said Marty. "Not firing it, just pullin' it fast as he can, time after time."

Sometimes Longley didn't return until after dark. They'd bedded down the herd a day's drive south of Fort Towson, and Longley had taken his usual evening ride. He would be gone at least an hour, and Lou had waited for him to ride out. Then, for obvious reasons, she had slipped into a scrub oak thicket. It was Wes who decided she had been gone too long.

"I'm goin' to see about Lou," he said.

Nobody laughed or ragged him. They understood his concern. Ten let him take the lead, then followed. They had scarcely entered the brush when they heard a scuffle, a half sob, and a savage blow. Lou was stripped to the waist and seemed in a faint. Longley flung the girl aside and went for his gun. But Wes was on him, twisting his arm, forcing him to drop the Colt. Wes brought up a knee, smashing the gunman in the groin. When his head came down, Wes again used the knee, catching Longley under the chin. He was thrown backward, and slammed head first into an oak. He tried to rise, but couldn't. Wes was on him in a fury, smashing his head against the tree when Ten dragged him off. Lou, covering herself with her ruined shirt, watched in horrified fascination. Wes was fighting and struggling to get back to the fallen Longley.

"Wes," said Ten, "that's enough. Take Lou back to camp. He'll be ridin' out if I have to tie him belly down across his saddle."

Wes still wasn't of a mind to go, but Lou saw the need and managed to get his attention. Longley finally sat up, his eyes glazed, fumbling at the empty holster for his Colt.

"When you're ready to ride out," said Ten, "I'll give you the gun. Now get up and get to your horse."

Longley stumbled to his feet, and Ten followed him to the dun horse. On his third attempt, Longley managed to get into the saddle. Ten handed him the empty Colt and two gold double eagles.

"A month's wages," said Ten. "Now ride, and don't come back. I just saved your worthless hide. I won't do it again."

Bill Longley rode away without a word. Ten had never seen such hate in a man's eyes. Longley had the instinct and temperament of a killer. He only needed a fast draw, and in time he would have that.

March 1, 1866, they forded the Red, bedding down the herd near Fort Towson. It was still early afternoon, and they had time to cut out the two hundred head Towson's quartermaster had agreed to take. Captain Mitchell greeted them, invited them to supper, and handed Ten a telegram. It was brief.

Priscilla is well and looking for you May first.

It was signed "Jess." He passed it around for the others to read.

"Sounds like it's all been settled," said Marty. "Maybe Jason Brawn roped an anvil to old LeBeau and dropped him in the Gulf."

Ten sighed. Chisholm was telling him he'd been to New Orleans and had met Priscilla. But why was she expecting him nearly three months before she would be able to leave? By some miracle, had LeBeau agreed to her leaving sooner?

"Oh, this is so exciting," said Lou. "The handsome prince rescues the beautiful girl from the terrible dragon."

"We'll have to do better than last time, then," said Marty. "There was six dragons, all with repeatin' rifles, and they near 'bout shot our tail feathers off."

They left Fort Towson at dawn, moving the longhorns west, following the Red River to the Washita.

"It's about seventy-five miles to Fort Washita," said Ten. "From there we follow the Washita north. We can reach Fort Arbuckle the same day, if nothing goes wrong, and then Fort Cobb a day later. That will reduce our herd by eight hundred head. Before we start for New Orleans, we'll spend a few days with Jess. I aim to cut out two hundred and fifty cows, which we'll leave at the trading post. That'll leave us two hundred head for Fort Gibson and two hundred head for Fort Smith. We'll trail to Gibson first, then follow the Arkansas to

Fort Smith. There, we'll board the steamboat for New Orleans."

In the evening, after supper, Ten told them of the plan he had already mentioned to Chris and Lou Ward. Marty and Wes were excited.

"If we got cash money to *buy* longhorns," said Marty, "then let's buy big steers, two years old and up. Draggin' 'em out of the brush one at a time, you got to take what you can get. I'm bettin' if we ride to Texas with a sackful of gold coin, we can buy longhorn steers for four or five dollars apiece. Suppose we get us a herd—maybe four thousand head—and have 'em waitin' when the rails reach Kansas?"

"You're looking at a hundred and twenty thousand dollars on the hoof," said Ten. "Maybe more."

"Dear God," cried Chris, "I don't believe there's that much money in the whole world."

March 15, 1866, they reached Jesse Chisholm's trading post on the Canadian River. By Marty's tally they still had 654 longhorns. They'd lost only the troublesome bull Ten had shot.

"It's a miracle," said Marty. "We'll catch hell on the next drive."

Jesse Chisholm hadn't expected them for another month. It was a feat worthy of a much older, much more experienced trail boss than young Tenatse Chisholm. Jesse made them all welcome and then, in private, told Ten of his meeting with Priscilla.

"She's dead right," said Ten. "LeBeau has something in mind, and it's got nothing to do with what's best for Priscilla and me. I'll listen to anything he's got to say, if only for Priscilla's sake."

"I thought you would," said Chisholm. "She's afraid for you, but I think you'll know, after talking to her father, if there's any danger. I'm sure he's learned that I'm not a poor man, and that I have considerable influence in Washington. Perhaps he's taken that into consideration."

Ten was sure of only one thing, insofar as LeBeau was concerned. He needed money, probably to buy his freedom from Jason Brawn. Since Priscilla wouldn't have Jason Brawn, how was André LeBeau going to cover his gambling debts? Tenatse Chisholm thought he knew.

19

*T*wo days after Ten's outfit reached Chisholm's trading post, a rider returned from Fort Smith with the
mail. He also brought newspapers from New Orleans
and St. Louis. Ten read the New Orleans paper without
finding a word about the LeBeaus or Jason Brawn. It
was Marty, reading the St. Louis paper, who discovered
something that drew their immediate attention.

"Ten," said Marty, "look at this."

The headline read: CATTLE PENS BEING BUILT AT ABILENE.
Marty had just spread the paper out on Chisholm's
huge dining room table when Wes came in. The three of
them were gathered around the newspaper when Jesse
Chisholm entered. Without a word he moved in close
enough to read with them. When the Cherokee cook
began setting the table for supper, Ten, Wes, and Marty
took their places. Chisholm folded the paper, seated
himself, and finished reading the story. Nobody said
anything, awaiting Chisholm's reaction.

"This is the start of something big," he said. "I've
heard of this Joe McCoy. He's a businessman from Illinois. Some people call him a dreamer, and maybe he
has been, but not this time. The railroad's still months
away, but we know it's coming. McCoy's gettin' the
jump on everybody, building cattle pens and calling for
trail drives to Abilene. Filling those pens with Texas
steers means an eastern market for Texas beef."

"There'll be a pile of gold for the first cattlemen fill-ing those pens," said Ten. "Why can't that be us?"

"It could be," said Chisholm. "There's a ready-made trail from the Red River all the way to Wichita, and Wichita's less than a day's drive south of Abilene."

"The Chisholm Trail," said Wes.

"Exactly," said Chisholm. "A smart outfit could trail a big herd of Texas longhorns into eastern Kansas, graze them along the Arkansas until McCoy's pens at Abilene are ready, and be first in line for shipment to the eastern markets."

"You control most of the land along the Arkansas," said Ten, "as part of your ranch. All the way to where the Wichita camp used to be. Any outfit grazing a herd along the Arkansas would need your permission."

"You have it," said Chisholm, "on two conditions. First, I want this herd to include twenty-five hundred steers for me, for which I'll pay you sixteen dollars a head. Second, I want you to take enough riders from here to make the drive. Take Charlie Two Hats and a dozen Cherokees. With the outfit you have, that'll give you nineteen riders."

"Jess," said Ten, "I don't need nineteen riders. Except for the thousand dollars I owe you, we'll put all we have into another herd, but I doubt that will be more than thirty-five hundred steers. That's all we can afford to buy. Besides, like I told you, I don't want you standin' behind me, proppin' me up."

"I'm not propping you up," said Chisholm, irritated. "I'm advancing you half the money for the twenty-five hundred steers you'll bring me. That will allow you enough, with what you already have, to buy another four thousand steers. All told, you'll be trailing ten thousand head. Now are you sure nineteen riders will be enough?"

"I don't know," said Ten. "Who's payin' Two Hats and the Cherokees?"

"You are," said Chisholm. "They can't work for me if

they're somewhere between here and Texas. I'm only paying you to bring me twenty-five hundred steers. All the trials, tribulations, and expense of getting them here belongs to you."

Marty hid a grin. Chris and Lou had arrived in time to learn that the discussion involved another trail drive from Texas.

"I reckon that kills our trip to New Orleans," said Lou. "But what about Priscilla?"

"I'm still going to see Priscilla," said Ten, "and talk to her daddy, but I won't be there for long. I'm comin' right back, and we're headin' for Texas. Not only are the rest of you giving up your trip to New Orleans, I need you to take care of things here while I'm gone. We still owe two hundred steers to Fort Gibson and two hundred to Fort Smith. I've written bills of sale to both quartermasters, and I want you to trail this last four hundred longhorns to the two forts. Jess says you can have a couple of Injun riders if you need them. When you've done that, get with Jess and begin gathering supplies from the store. Marty, get with Charlie Two Hats, find out who the riders are that we're taking and how they're fixed for horses. Figure on three good mounts for each of us, and at least three pack mules. The sooner I get started to New Orleans, the sooner I'll be back. When I return, we'll leave for Texas."

Preparing to leave for Fort Smith, Ten spent a few minutes with his outfit. They were concerned that he was going to New Orleans alone.

"I won't be alone while I'm there," he reassured them. "I'll be staying with Harvey Roberts, and I'll be meeting Priscilla at his office."

"I just wish you could bring Priscilla back with you," said Chris, "and be done with this."

"So do I," said Ten, "but I don't see how I can. I'd like to square things with old LeBeau, so I can take her away peacefully."

"I doubt you can," said Wes. "We all should be goin' with you."

"I aim to try," said Ten. "If I fail, I may need all of you next time."

Before Ten could ride away, Jesse Chisholm came out of the house. Ten trotted his horse over to the porch.

"When you get to Fort Smith," said Chisholm, "you ought to telegraph Harvey Roberts. You'll be arriving a month sooner than Priscilla's expecting you, and you'd ought to give Harvey some time to get a message to her. Having thought about it, I'm not sure we're being fair to Priscilla, planning this new drive to Texas so soon. You'll have to hustle, buying and branding that many long-horns, to get them to Abilene by September or early October. You may be until Christmas gettin' back to New Orleans. I believe you should tell Priscilla; don't leave her with false hopes."

Ten rode away without responding. They all watched him go, some of them with misgivings.

"It still bothers me," said Chris, "him going alone, since they've already tried to kill him."

"That's one Injun that'll take some killin'," said Marty.

"I'm not all that sure about this new drive either," said Wes. "I reckon Mr. Chisholm means well, but this bunch of smart-mouth Cherokees purely rub me the wrong way. They look at us and talk down to us like we're a bunch of tenderfeet."

"We'll change that," said Lou grimly, "once we're on the trail. We'll outrope and outride the lot of 'em."

After all Ten's haste in reaching Fort Smith, he had to wait a day and a night for the steamboat. He ignored Chisholm's advice, not bothering to telegraph Roberts. With or without Roberts's help, he intended to see the girl, even if he had to climb that magnolia tree and break into Priscilla's room after dark.

Ten waited impatiently while *The New Orleans* whis-tled for the landing at New Orleans. He was first ashore once the gangplank was down. Nobody expected him, yet he took his time, lest he be followed. He reached the Roberts and Company offices, only to find that Harvey Roberts was out. He waited more than an hour until the big man returned.

"You're more than a month early," said Roberts. "I'll have to send someone to the house with a message. If she isn't there, you may have a long wait."

"Where else would she be?"

"I don't know," said Roberts. "She said I could send her a message, but not to leave it if she wasn't there. I'll send a carriage and have it bring her here if she's at home."

Roberts had business in the warehouse, and returned there, leaving Ten alone in the office. He'd spent most of the day waiting, first for Roberts, and now for Priscilla. Just when he was convinced she wasn't coming, the door opened and there she was!

She was the same, yet different. She seemed even more beautiful than he remembered, yet older. There were dark circles around her eyes, and her shoulders seemed to sag under a great burden. But her eyes lighted at the sight of him and the years fell away. With a glad cry she came to him, and he met her halfway. For a long time she clung to him in silence, her tears soaking his shirt, her slender body trembling. Before she uttered a word, he was sure of one thing: if he had to steal her away in the dead of night and shoot his way out, he wasn't going to leave her at the mercy of André Le-Beau.

"The newspaper," she sobbed. "It said you'd been killed. Daddy sent me what they printed. He knew I'd come back, and he was right. I had to know. I couldn't stay in Louisville. I just couldn't. I talked to the wives of the men who had hunted you, and I went to the customs office. Then I came here, and Mr. Roberts was so kind. He—"

Her tears took control again, and he waited until she could continue.

"It's been hell at home," she said. "Mother swears she's leaving once I'm out and gone. She acts like she's a prisoner in the house and that it's all my fault. The newspaper prints a gossip column, and they've been hinting that Jason Brawn is courting me, that I'm secretly planning to marry him before the end of the year. People I don't even know are laughing at me, calling me 'Miss Moneybags.' One of the preachers preached a sermon about 'the greedy young girl taking advantage of an older man for his money.' I wasn't called by name, but everybody knew."

"Your daddy's been a busy man, hasn't he?"

"He swears it's not his doing," said Priscilla, "that it's Jason Brawn."

"But he gave Brawn the idea," said Ten, "so it's still his doing. You tell him I want to talk to him in the morning, and if he won't meet me here, then I'll come to the house."

"One word to Brawn," said Priscilla fearfully, "and they'll be after you again."

"That's a chance I'll have to take," said Ten. "Now, you listen to me." He drew away from her until he could look into her eyes. "In three months you'll be eighteen. But until then I don't want you here. Before I leave, I want you on a steamboat, bound for Louisville."

"But daddy won't let me go. He'll tell Jason Brawn—"

"He'll tell Brawn nothing," said Ten. "When I've talked to him, he'll let you go. Now you tell him he'd better be here at nine o'clock in the morning. You go home and pack anything you value, because you won't be comin' back here."

"But I—when will I see you again?"

"We'll talk after I've talked to your daddy. Give me an hour with him, and then we'll talk again. We have to make some plans."

"What shall I tell Mother?"

"Nothing, until I've talked to LeBeau. Suppose you tell her you're going to Louisville; will she object?"

"My God, no! She's all but turned against me, with the gossip that's going around. She'd be glad to see me go."

"Remember—say nothing to either of them until you talk to me again."

Harvey Roberts made himself scarce, allowing Ten the use of the office. LeBeau was there shortly before nine. He came in with the confidence that Ten suspected was the result of a couple of stiff drinks. He said nothing, waiting for Ten to speak.

"Sit down, LeBeau."

LeBeau sat in a ladderback chair facing the desk. Ten ignored the swivel chair and sat on a corner of the desk. When he spoke again, his voice was cold and hard.

"How much do you want, LeBeau?"

"How—much?" LeBeau didn't have to feign his surprise.

"How much money will it take to shut your mouth, to keep you away from Jason Brawn until Priscilla can get packed and aboard a steamboat for Louisville?"

"I owe Brawn fifty-five thousand dollars," said LeBeau, gaining confidence.

"Twenty-five thousand," said Ten. "No more."

"But that's—"

"That's all you're getting," said Ten. "Don't be a fool, LeBeau. Brawn won't settle for anything less than Priscilla. I'm offering you a stake, a way out, a chance to save your miserable hide."

"You mean—run out on my debt to Jason?"

"Do you have a choice? Once he knows he's lost Priscilla, you're dead."

"All right," LeBeau sighed. His flushed face had paled, and he studied the tips of his fingers.

"Here's what I want you to do," said Ten. "Get the word out that your wife's mother is very sick, and that Priscilla's going to take care of her for a few weeks."

"Jason won't believe that!"

"He will," said Ten, "if you tell him what he wants to

hear. Tell him Priscilla's changing her mind. Tell him Priscilla will be in Louisville only until mid-September. For once in your life you'll be telling the truth, because that's when I aim to take her away."

"But suppose I— What if I can't convince Jason?"

"You'd better," said Ten, "because it'll be September first before I'll have your money."

"September *first*?" bawled LeBeau. "But your father—"

"My father doesn't pay my debts, LeBeau. You wouldn't get the money now even if I had it, because I'm buying Priscilla some time. Double-crossing coyote that you are, you'd take the money and run. That would tell Brawn all he needs to know."

"You double-cross me," snarled LeBeau, "and I'll spill my guts to Brawn. Come September, you'll be three months dead once he learns of this."

"No deader than you'll be," said Ten. "Priscilla's not going to marry that old bastard, and when he finally realizes it, you'd better be gone."

"You want me to build up this lie to Jason so he won't stop Priscilla from leaving. Once she's gone, and you're gone, how do I know you'll pay up? How do I know you won't double-cross me, leaving me at Brawn's mercy?"

"You don't," said Ten. "That's what you'd do, given the chance. But I keep my word, LeBeau. Just remember this: once Priscilla's out of here, it's up to you to keep Brawn at bay until I can raise that twenty-five thousand."

LeBeau got up, and Ten thought he would leave without a word, but he paused at the door. He turned, and when he spoke, his hate was so strong that his voice trembled.

"I'll keep the lid on until September first. If you don't show, then I'll have to talk to Jason. I'll have to tell him Priscilla's not coming back, and why. I'll have to give him an address in Louisville so he can call on Priscilla and her poor old sick granny."

He stepped out, closing the door behind him. Ten

gripped the back of a chair. He would be safe enough this time, but when he returned in September, it might be a different story. Once LeBeau had the promised money in his hands, he might loose a band of back-shooting killers, with Tenatse Chisholm their prey.

Ten had to tell Priscilla the truth about his meeting with LeBeau. Nothing less would have satisfied her. Her response was about what he had expected.

"Dear God," she cried. "So much money! You're paying to get him out of a mess that's of his own making. Besides, I don't want to go to Louisville. I want to go with you."

"Priscilla, listen to me. I'm buying us some time, and I want you on that steamboat for Louisville in the morning. Be sure you understand what I am about to tell you."

He spoke to her earnestly for fifteen minutes, and when they parted, she was able to smile through her tears.

The following morning, Ten remained at the Roberts and Company offices until the steamboat had departed and Priscilla was safely away. He couldn't leave for Fort Smith until the next day. He had spent the previous night on a night watchman's bunk in the Roberts warehouse. He spent an hour with Harvey Roberts that afternoon.

"Nobody knows except you, Harvey," said Ten. "I couldn't leave her at their mercy any longer. I'll be leaving for Fort Smith in the morning, and I'll need that bunk for one more night."

Priscilla LeBeau stood at the stern of *The Saint Louis,* watching New Orleans fade into the hazy distance. Emily LeBeau had been visibly relieved when Priscilla had announced she was taking the steamboat for Louisville. André LeBeau had said nothing. They had given her not a penny more than the cost of her ticket. For the hundredth time she opened her purse and counted the money Ten had given her. Her heart pounded with excitement as she thought of what she was about to do with it. She would make her move in Natchez.

Ten was on deck when *The Talequah,* bound for Fort Smith, whistled for the stop at Natchez. It was a stop for fuel, freight, mail, and an occasional passenger. Before the gangplank was let down, Ten returned to his cabin in the first-class section. He cracked his door enough to see a deckhand wheel a luggage cart down the narrow corridor to a cabin two doors beyond his own. He waited until he heard the door close, and then watched the deckhand depart. Only then did he leave his own cabin and tap lightly on the door of the newly occupied one. The door opened and he stepped inside, into the arms of a laughing, crying Priscilla. They sat on her small bunk and he just stared at her in rapt silence until she spoke.

"Oh," she cried, "I've dreamed of this, prayed for it, but suppose they discover I—I'm with you? Am I to hide out like a—a fugitive?"

"Only until we get to Fort Smith," he said. "If nothing else, there'll be a post chaplain. We'll stand up before him and let him read the words from the Book. After that, anybody that comes lookin' for you will have to step over me."

Her eyes went wide, there was a new frenzy of tears, then a smile. But it was tempered with a frown.

"But . . . neither of us is eighteen. Won't somebody ask our ages?"

"No," he said. "If they do, it won't stop us. This is the frontier, Indian Territory. Men and women don't live by the calendar. When we leave Fort Smith, you'll belong to me, and nobody, short of God, will change that."

"It'll be the happiest day of my life!" she cried. "Now you'll never have to go to New Orleans again."

"Once more," he said, "after this next trail drive. I promised your daddy some money."

"No! You don't owe him anything. He'd just take the money and then have you killed!"

"He may try," said Ten, "but I'll have to go. I've given my word."

20

There were few women on the frontier, especially beautiful ones, and Priscilla's arrival at Fort Smith caused a sensation. The brash young Indian offspring of Jesse Chisholm's had already begun making a name for himself, having bossed a trail drive from Texas. Nobody seemed in the least surprised when Tenatse Chisholm showed up with Priscilla and announced they wished to be married. It was no less than any western man would have done. They were caught up in a whirlwind of excitement that virtually took Priscilla's breath away. Life on a frontier outpost was profoundly boring, and almost any event was seized upon to create some excitement. The officers' wives took Priscilla in tow, and when the ceremony took place, Ten could scarcely believe what they had accomplished in so short a time. The little chapel was knee deep in flowers from the surrounding woods. There were dogwoods, wild rose, violets, and boughs of pink, fluted honeysuckle. Even the post commander got into the spirit, insisting on being Ten's best man. He even doubled up a pair of bachelor officers, allowing Ten and Priscilla the use of a private cabin for the night. There was whiskey aplenty, and every man on the post partook, except Ten. Long after Ten and Priscilla had retired for the night, there was shouting and shooting outside the cabin.

"My God," said Priscilla, "what a racket. How do they expect us to sleep?"

"They don't expect us to," said Ten. "It'd be more peaceful out in the brush, with the bobcats and hoot owls."

"I never dreamed I'd be married like this." She sighed. "This is like another world. We got here at noon, were married the same day, and everybody seemed—well, to think it was the natural thing to do. Dear God, do you realize that in New Orleans society all this would have taken months, with stories in the newspaper, printed invitations, and fancy clothes created especially for the occasion?"

"Men on the frontier don't stand on ceremony," said Ten. "I've heard Jess talk of men who've ordered wives from back East. Mail-order brides from matrimonial bureaus in Chicago and New York. A woman would step off a train or stage in the morning, and by sundown she'd be married to a man she'd first met only a few hours ago. We've done a mite better than that."

She giggled. "Only a little. Six hours after we met, you left me nearly naked on the balcony, bawling because you were leaving."

"Then I reckon it's time to take up where we left off."

"I reckon," she said, mimicking him. "I've had this gown off ever since you put out the light. I thought western men were sudden."

"We are," said Ten. "I already got one boot off."

"I'm giving you until the count of five to get the other one off."

He stopped her at three.

Despite the excitement of the night before, and little sleep, Ten and Priscilla were awake early. Before getting up, they lingered awhile, talking.

"One thing I forgot to ask," said Ten. "Do you ride?"

"When Grandfather Edgerton was alive, he raised horses in Kentucky, and I spent my summers there. I love horses; I want a herd of them someday."

"We'll go to the store," said Ten, "and buy you some boots, Levi's pants, and denim shirts. From now on you'll be ridin' astraddle, like a cowboy."

"I always have," she said. "I like your father, but you're not leaving me with him and a bunch of Indians while you go galloping off to Texas. I can ride. It's been a while, and I'll have a sore behind for maybe a week, but after that I'll hold my own with anybody, including you."

While he wasn't used to the ways of a woman, her tone of voice warned him she fully expected him to disagree. He fooled her.

"I wasn't about to leave you behind," he said. "I aim to be a cattleman, so the sooner you 'learn cow,' the better. Besides, if old Jason Brawn gets suspicious and goes lookin' for you, he'll never find you in the dust. Who'd expect to find a proper lady ridin' astraddle and lookin' at the behinds of ten thousand wild Texas longhorns?"

Ten borrowed a saddle and a dun horse for Priscilla. They left all her town clothes at Fort Smith, taking only the range clothes Ten bought for her. Carrying enough food for three days, they rode out for Chisholm's trading post. Long before sundown, Priscilla began to lean in the saddle, favoring first one side and then the other. She didn't complain, but Ten took pity on her, reining up near a willow-lined creek.

"Good place to spend the night," he said. He dismounted and went to help her out of the saddle. For a moment she just stood there stiff-legged.

"You never get used to saddle sores, do you?"

"You've been out of the saddle too long," said Ten, "but I promise you, it won't happen again. You're a frontier woman now, and this three-day ride from Fort Smith to the trading post will be a help to you. Peel off your britches and take a dip in the creek. Then I'll doctor you with some sulfur salve. By morning you'll be able to ride again."

*   *   *

The second day was a marked improvement over the first. Priscilla smiled at him as he smeared her saddle sores with the healing salve.

"You're right," she said. "It's good we have this ride ahead of us. I want to dismount before your friends without disgracing myself."

"You'll be in good shape, saddlewise," said Ten, "by the time we get to Texas. The hardest part is the drive from Texas to Abilene."

They reached Chisholm's trading post at sundown of the third day. To her credit, Priscilla was able to dismount on her own, showing no evidence of her early misery. They caught Jesse Chisholm between the barn and the house. He showed no surprise, becoming flustered only when Priscilla threw her arms around him. No explanation was necessary. His sharp eyes hadn't missed the gold band on the third finger of her left hand. Marty and Wes came galloping in, following Charlie Two Hats. Marty, grinning, swung out of the saddle, followed by Wes. Chris and Lou had been at the other barn and were coming on the run. Ten waited for them and then performed all the introductions at once.

"I'm jealous," said Lou. "You went and put a ring on Priscilla's finger, while me and Chris has got to spend three months with a pair of cowboys, all with no protection."

Priscilla laughed. Ten had warned her of the situation that existed between his two cowboys and the Ward girls. Priscilla being near their own ages, Ten expected them to become friends. He got down to business.

"How close are we, Marty, to the start of this trip to Texas?"

"Just the decidin' on the supplies," said Marty, "and loadin' the pack mules. Charlie's boys are ready, and includin' the mounts we'll be ridin', we'll have a sixty-horse remuda. We'll need a couple of hoss wranglers. You want two extry men for that, or just use a couple of th' riders we already decided on?"

"We'll make do with what we've decided on," said Ten. "Jess, you keep a tally on everything we're takin' from the post, and I'll settle with you when we're done."

"I have a word of caution for you," said Chisholm. "You're going to be carrying almost forty-five thousand dollars in gold. There are bands of renegades and deserters, both Union and Confederate, roaming southern Kansas and holing up in Indian Territory. Every rider should be armed with a repeating rifle and plenty of ammunition. Once you have the longhorns, there'll be some danger on the trail drive, but not nearly as much as you're facing with all that gold."

"We'll need three pack saddles for the mules," said Ten.

"I have them," Chisholm replied.

"We'll secure the bags of gold to the frames of the pack saddles," said Ten. "Nobody can get to the gold, or even know it's there, without first unpacking the mules."

"Except for grub and supplies," said Marty, "we're ready to ride."

"Chris," said Ten, "you and Lou have a good feel for the needs of a cow camp. In the morning go to the store and begin laying out what we'll need. Priscilla, why don't you help them? Bear in mind, everything will be scarce in Texas, so don't short us."

Supper done, Ten and Priscilla retired to their room. Marty, Wes, Lou, and Chris watched them go. Enviously.

"Ten," said Priscilla, "you ought to send those four to Fort Smith. Wes and Marty ought to claim those two girls. When they look at me, I can see the hurt and envy in their eyes."

"I reckon I know how Chris and Lou feel," said Ten, "but your situation was different. They'll just have to wait until this next trail drive's done."

"I just . . . feel like I've gotten off on the wrong foot with them, like they resent me, because we . . . have what they don't."

Ten sighed. The last thing he needed was resentment within the outfit. He already had to contend with the Indians. Charlie Two Hats and his men were adept as cowboys, and to a man they were loyal to Chisholm. That was what bothered Ten. Whatever loyalty they felt for him was the result of his being Chisholm's son. They were full-bloods, while he was not, and as yet they had no respect for him as a man. He had to win their respect somewhere between Chisholm's trading post and Texas. With ten thousand longhorns on the trail to Abilene, there would be no time for anything else.

During breakfast, Chris and Lou seemed more friendly toward Priscilla. While nothing was said, Ten believed Marty and Wes had come to his aid. He needed all the help he could get. After breakfast he followed Marty and Wes to the Cherokee quarters. It was time to meet the Indian riders Charlie Two Hats had selected for the trip to Texas. Two Hats was the most personable of the Cherokees, and Ten liked him. The Indian came out to meet them.

"Adelantar," bawled Two Hats, "you no account *pelado* Injuns!"

He could get by with such irreverence. Doors opened and the riders stalked out of their shacks. They formed a ragged line, like indifferent, don't-give-a-damn troops. They all wore their hair shoulder length, and their attire mostly consisted of dirty Levi's pants and dirtier shirts, denim or flannel. Two or three wore boots, the others moccasins, and every man had a rawhide thong about his neck, evidence of an unseen Bowie. Each of them carried a Colt, either in a scuffed holster or muzzle down under his waistband. The man to the far left, at the very end of the line, was the most unusual. He was tall for an Indian and wore two tied-down Colts. It was with him that Charlie Two Hats began his introduction.

"Two-gun man," said Charlie, "is Buscadero. Next, that Sashavado, then Orejana, Maguey, an' Latigo. There Tejano; he git run outta Texas. Next, there Frijole, then Fiador. He tie damnedest hitch knots you ever see. Then ol' Crowspeak. He talk funny. Say somethin', Crow."

In a guttural, raspy voice, Crowspeak muttered something uncomplimentary and vulgar. The rest of them laughed, and Two Hats continued.

"There Man Who Ride Wild Horse an' we jus' call him 'Hoss.' Next hombre kill a Mex an' take his jingle bob spurs. He Jingle Bob. Jus' 'Bob' to his friends, when he got any. Las' hombre Kiaktiuz. Nobody say that; we jus' say 'Cactus.' "

Everybody seemed at a loss for words. Two Hats looked at Ten.

"Got anything say?"

"We ride tomorrow at first light," said Ten.

Without a word or backward look, they broke ranks and went their ways. Charlie Two Hats followed, and Marty grinned.

"Salty bunch," said Marty, "and I'd have to agree with Wes—they ain't partial to us. If your name wasn't Chisholm, I'd not be surprised if they scalped the lot of us somewhere between here and Texas."

"I get the same feeling," said Ten, "but we need them. I look for some of them to question my right to the Chisholm name before we're done. Don't provoke them, but don't let them crowd you too far. Somehow, somewhere, I'll be put to the test, and I'll have to convince them there's more Chisholm to me than just the name."

They rode out, heading due south, passing to the west of Fort Cobb. Ten estimated they were 125 miles north of the Red River and that they should cross it on the third day. But there was a feeling of unease among them that was almost tangible. While they rode together and took their meals together, it was as though they were two separate outfits. The Cherokee riders kept to themselves, and it wasn't until the morning of the third day that trouble erupted. Breakfast was over and the wranglers were bringing in the horse remuda. The Cherokee riders seemed more raucous than usual, and slow to mount. Ten swung out of his saddle and headed for the group just as Sashavado was tilting the bottle to drink. Ten drew and fired, and the bottle exploded in the Indian's face.

"You know the rules," said Ten grimly. "No whiskey. Who brought the bottle?"

Sashavado wiped his eyes on the grimy sleeve of his shirt before he spoke.

"Sashavado bring," he said, flashing a malevolent grin. "Who say no? You, mebbe, *hijo*?"

He came shambling toward Ten, fisting his big hands, his intentions obvious. His shirt was taut over his huge torso and brawny arms. His legs were like the trunks of oaks. He outweighed Ten, and none of it appeared anything less than solid muscle. Ten's outfit stood behind him, while the Cherokee riders had gathered behind Sashavado. Some of them grinned in anticipation. In contrast, Ten's few riders were grim, Priscilla near panic.

Sashavado clearly wanted to get his big hands on Ten, and Ten presented a tempting target. But just short of Sashavado grabbing him in a bear hug, Ten buried the toe of his right boot in the big Indian's groin. Not even Sashavado could withstand so brutal an attack. With a grunt of pure misery he folded in the middle, and when his chin came down, it met Ten's knee on the way up. Sashavado's feet left the ground and he came down on his broad back in a cloud of dust. He lay there heaving like a ruptured bellows, trying to recover his wind.

"Stomp the big bastard!" bawled a voice that sounded like Marty's.

It was what Sashavado expected, for it was what he'd have done. But he was hurt, and he had accomplished nothing. He grasped the rawhide thong about his neck and drew into his right hand the big Bowie, with its keen nine-inch blade. Ten had the throwing knife in his boot, but it was of no use, unless he killed Sashavado. Then there was a shout from one of the Cherokees. Charlie

Two Hats! The old Indian had drawn his own Bowie, and the big blade glinted in the morning sun as he flung it to Ten haft first. Ten caught the haft in his right hand and turned to face Sashavado. The big Cherokee was on his feet, advancing, the lust to kill in his eyes.

"Dear God," cried Priscilla, "let me have a gun!"

"No," said Marty. "This is Ten's fight. It's the only way."

Sashavado's first thrust nicked Ten's shirtsleeve. Ten passed the Bowie to his left hand and slammed the flat of the blade against Sashavado's head, just over his right eye. Sashavado stumbled, his eyes glazed. Wildly, Sashavado swung his own Bowie, and again Ten used the flat of his blade. It caught Sashavado in the bend of his right wrist. With a howl of pain he loosed his grip on the Bowie and it fell to the ground. He looked at the fallen weapon, and finally at Ten.

"Sashavado," said Ten grimly, "you have two choices. You can take orders from me and go on to Texas, or I'll cut your ornery gizzard out. Now what's it going to be?"

"Sashavado go to Texas," he said, managing a weak grin.

His comrades broke into a fit of laughter, and the crisis was over. Ten wiped the blade of the Bowie on the leg of his Levi's and handed it haft first to Charlie Two Hats. Charlie grinned.

"I personal stomp hell out of next *pelado* that call you half Injun," he said. Even Priscilla, pale and shaken, laughed at that.

Sashavado didn't ride well the rest of that day, kind of leaning back in his saddle. Ten heard the rest of the riders bullyragging him about it. But there was no more trouble from the Cherokee riders, and most of them became more sociable around the cook fires.

They crossed the Red River into Texas before making camp for the night. Ten and Priscilla took their bedrolls far enough from the others to afford themselves some privacy. Now that the danger was past, Priscilla was full of questions.

"They're your father's riders. Why did they put you through that—that awful fight?"

"You just answered that," said Ten. "They were my father's riders, but they weren't mine. Now they are. Who my relations are don't mean a damn thing here on the frontier. It's what I can do that counts. I had to prove myself."

"Would you have killed him—Sashavado—if he hadn't backed down?"

"Yes," said Ten. "I'd have had no choice. They all knew it, and they knew why. They resent me not being a full-blood, but I believe I've done a little toward changin' their minds. You heard what Charlie said."

"Tenatse Chisholm, I thought I knew you so well. Now I'm not sure I know myself. At first I was just scared to death. Then I—I wanted you to kill him! God help me, I'd have killed him myself if I could have gotten my hands on a gun! I was wild. Now I'm ashamed of myself."

"Nothin' to be ashamed of," said Ten. "You're learnin' the difference between society—what folks call 'civilization'—and reality."

"Where a man proves himself by killing another man."

"The most acceptable proof since the dawn of time," said Ten.

"But you didn't kill him," said Priscilla, "although you could have, and I'm proud of you for that. But won't he hate you and try to get even?"

"No," said Ten. "Among the Indians it's called 'counting coup,' and in a way, it counts for more bravery and honor than killing. It's one of the more sensible codes. I am not Sashavado's enemy, nor is he mine. While I am Jesse Chisholm's *hijo*, I was untried. Among the tribes, a man must prove himself before he is accepted as a leader of other men."

"These Indians seemed so peaceful," said Priscilla, "until we took them away from the trading post. I feel like I'm seeing them for the first time."

Ten laughed. "You are, and even now not in their true light. Fact is, they like to ride off to north Texas occasionally and fight the Comanches and Kiowa, purely for the hell of it."

"Everybody at Fort Smith made such a fuss over me," said Priscilla, "but these Indian men ignore me. Like I was a—a corral fence post."

"Don't let it bother you," said Ten. "It's their way. Indian men live for battle, the hunt, a good horse race, and gambling. Women come in a poor fifth, valued for their ability to do the heavy work."

"I'll count my blessings," said Priscilla. "I'm glad you're not a full-blood."

21

Ten's outfit pushed on into Texas, making camp just north of old Fort Worth. A town had sprung up around the old fort, and although the village had been chosen county seat before the war, there was still no courthouse. Union soldiers occupied the fort, and the stars and stripes flew above its battlements. Ten left the rest of the outfit half a mile away, rode to the sentry at the gate and stated his business. The officer in charge, Captain Fanning, eyed him skeptically. He listened while Ten talked.

"For what it's worth," said Fanning, "you have my permission to hunt all the cows you want. I must warn you, however, that you do so at your own risk. The Comanches have been raising billy hell along the Trinity and the Brazos, and we don't have the manpower to protect you. We're spread too thin as it is."

"We don't expect protection," said Ten. "We're nineteen strong, and we're armed. The Comanches come lookin' for a fight, they'll find one."

"Charles Goodnight's cow outfit is working along the Brazos, building a herd," said Fanning.

"Buying or gathering?"

"Gathering," said Fanning.

Ten said nothing. Once word got out that he was buying, anybody with the gumption of a horned toad would know he was carrying gold. He rode back to the outfit.

He got Marty, Wes, Chris, Lou, and Priscilla together for a talk.

"Startin' in the morning," said Ten, "we'll leave Two Hats and the Injun riders to look after our horses and supplies. The six of us will split up into teams of two and begin riding to every ranch in these parts. We have to spread the word we're buying steers, two-year-olds and up. For now, we just want a commitment. We'll take delivery of the longhorns later. We may have to travel as far south as San Antone, as many cows as we're lookin' for, and what we buy between here and there, we'll claim them on the way back."

Ten and Priscilla rode to Weatherford, and then to Mineral Wells. Wes and Lou rode to the town of Dallas and lesser villages east of there. Marty and Chris rode south, to Crockett and Nacogdoches. Their first day's ride netted them commitments of a little over fifteen hundred head, and a third of that number was cows.

"We got two things workin' against us," said Marty. "Texans are broke and can't afford a drive to market, and the damn Comanches are makin' things hot in the brakes. So why risk your hair gatherin' a herd you can't drive to market anyhow?"

"We may have to move farther south," said Ten, "maybe as far as Austin or San Antone. We need to find enough stock within a day's ride so we can have just one camp. I don't want us scattered all over Texas."

"Then we might as well go as far south as we need to," said Marty, "and not waste any time. Farther south we go, the longer the trail to Abilene. The sooner we get the steers, the sooner we can get 'em headed north."

They made camp just south of Bandera, several hours' ride north of San Antone. Ten called on some ten-cow outfits without finding longhorns for sale in anything even close to the numbers they needed. One tobacco-chewing old rancher sold them a hundred long-horn steers at four dollars a head. His eyes lighted at the sight of the gold coin, and in a moment of gratitude he passed along some invaluable information.

"They's an Injun camp a few miles south of San Antone," he said. "Lipan Apache. Somewheres on th' Medina River. They're peaceful folks, an' they purely hate th' Comanches. Lipans has always rounded up them wild longhorns, even back in th' forties. Back 'fore th' war, somebody was always buyin' a couple hunnert head an' drivin' 'em to Louisiana. Now, can't nobody afford to buy, an' couldn't afford a drive if'n he had th' cows. I reckon them Lipans ought t' have stock t' sell."

Ten made plans to ride to the Lipan camp the next day. While he had planned to take Priscilla with him, he saw no need for anyone else, unless or until they bought a herd from the Lipans. But Priscilla had other plans. They had already spread their blankets for the night when she made her request.

"Ten, won't we be going through San Antonio, or at least near it?"

"I reckon. Why?"

"I want Marty and Chris, Wes and Lou to go with us."

"Why?"

"There'll be a preacher in San Antonio, don't you think?"

"So that's how it is," he said. "Which one of them came up with this?"

"That's how it is," she said, "and none of them came up with it. It's my own idea. Why do they have to wait until the end of this trail drive?"

"Because they likely won't be worth a damn on the drive," said Ten. "I want them in their saddles, not in their blankets."

"You're not being fair to them," she said. "We certainly aren't spending any extra time in our blankets. What's wrong with me? Am I too sweaty and dirty for you?"

He'd never heard the like of it. First he was irritated, then angry, and finally he laughed. He kicked off his blankets and rolled over onto hers.

"All right, Miss Matchmaker," he said, "we'll take them to San Antone, and get Marty and Wes hog-tied forever. My God, a woman's never satisfied, as long as there's a free man anywhere in the world."

"You're crushing my chest with your elbow," she said. "If you have other plans for my sweaty, dirty carcass, rearrange yourself a little."

"If your carcass ain't sweaty and dirty, it will be," he said.

He rolled over, taking her blanket with him, and she followed.

They reached San Antonio just as the town was beginning its day. They found an old jeweler who had some wedding bands on display. They were far from gold, times being what they were, but the gold could come later. The best they could do, preacherwise, was an old priest in what was once a Spanish mission. The ceremony was brief, followed by tears from all the girls, led by Priscilla.

"Now," said Ten, "there must be someplace in this town with rooms for rent. Walls, a roof, and a bed. I reckon every man and woman's entitled to a bed on their marryin' day, and you'd better make the best of it. The next one may be somewhere beyond Abilene. Priscilla and me can call on the Lipans and see if they have longhorns for sale. We'll look for the four of you sometime tomorrow."

Chris and Lou smothered him with grateful kisses, while Priscilla, Wes, and Marty laughed at his embarrassment. When Ten and Priscilla rode out, she trotted her horse alongside his.

"I hope you're satisfied," he said, as sternly as he could.

"I am," she said. "Aren't you?"

"I reckon," he said.

Her laugh was infectious. He gave in and joined her.

* * *

The Lipan Apache village was as permanent as any Ten had ever seen. They lived in adobe mud-and-stick huts strung out along the Medina River. Ten judged there must be a hundred or more huts. There was a large horse corral, five rails high, cottonwood poles lashed with rawhide to upright cedar posts. But there wasn't a longhorn anywhere in sight. Their arrival drew a curious assortment of men, women, children, and dogs. Most of the men were bare from the waist up, wearing only buckskin breeches and beaded moccasins. The women wore drab, dark ankle-length dresses. The children were dressed much like the adults, except for the very young. They wore nothing. The spokesman for the tribe, likely the chief, stepped forward. Ten gave the peace sign, and it was returned. The first word the chief spoke, probably his name, Ten couldn't understand. The Lipan tried again.

"Flacco," he said. "Me *hijo. Flacco hijo."*

Ten nodded his understanding. He'd heard Jesse Chisholm speak of the Lipan chief. Since the Texas Rangers had been organized in 1835, there had been a continuing fight with the Comanches. The Lipan Apaches, forever the enemy of the Comanches, had served the Rangers well as scouts. One such Lipan, Flacco, had been commissioned a captain in the Rangers by Governor Sam Houston. When Flacco had been treacherously murdered by a Mexican, Ranger captain Jack Hayes had personally tracked down Flacco's killer. This Lipan, as he wanted Ten to understand, was Flacco's son.

Ten searched his memory. More than once Jesse Chisholm had traveled to Texas at the request of the Federal government, seeking to execute some workable peace treaty with the troublesome Comanche. Many chiefs had been present at these futile meetings. Had this Lipan Apache been one of them? Ten mentioned the names of other chiefs, the names of meeting grounds that he remembered, and finally the name of Jesse Chisholm.

"Chi-zoom?" said the Lipan. *"Chi-zoom?"* Again he made the peace sign.

The light of recognition came into his dark eyes. Chisholm had been the peace mediator for the government, and the Lipan knew who Chisholm was.

"Chisholm *hijo,*" said Ten, pointing to himself. "Chisholm *hijo.*"

The Lipan grinned and put out his hand. Ten took it. While neither knew the other's name, that didn't matter. Ten felt a bit guilty. The more he vowed not to live in Jesse Chisholm's shadow, the more dependent he became on the old man's reputation. He knelt, and with a stick, began to draw what he hoped could be recognized as a Texas longhorn.

"Vaca," he said, "cow."

Holding a thumb outward on each side of his head, he made the buffalo sign, the horn sign. The buffalo had short horns, and he swept his hands away to either side, indicating long, curving horns.

"Cow," said the Lipan. *"Malo vaca."*

Ten took a double eagle from his pocket and, on the palm of his hand, offered it to the Indian. He held up his other hand, open.

"Vaca," he said, indicating himself with the thumb of his open hand.

The Lipan looked puzzled. Ten knelt, and with his finger made five single marks in the dust. He pointed from the marks to the previous drawing of the longhorn. He then placed the twenty-dollar gold coin on the five marks. The Indian's eyes sparked with understanding. He held up his open hand, showing five fingers. With his other hand he pointed to the double eagle, then to Ten, then to himself. Ten nodded. The Indian spoke rapidly to a brave. A horse was brought and the chief made as if to mount. Ten was to follow him. He found Priscilla trying to make friends with a small, naked Indian boy. When the child saw Ten looking at him, he disappeared into the brush. Ten helped Priscilla into her saddle, then mounted his own horse, and they followed the Lipan along the riverbank.

They rode what Ten judged was five miles to the point where another river had once emptied into the Medina. The old riverbed, now dry, was deep enough, its walls steep enough, to prevent the escape of horse or cow. The mouth of the enormous ditch had been closed with a cottonwood rail and cedar post fence. By time or by hand, the earth had been taken away so that the water of the Medina River extended a few feet up the old riverbed. Their Lipan guide jogged his horse away from the Medina, following the old riverbed. It grew deeper, wider, leading to a grassy box canyon whose other end they couldn't see. There were longhorns by the hundreds. The Indian pointed to the grazing cattle and lifted one hand, his fingers spread. He thought they only wanted five cows! Ten raised both hands, spreading his fingers. He closed his hands into fists and opened them. He repeated the procedure many times. He then took all the double eagles he had in his pocket and made sign like he was removing still more.

"Mucho vaca," he said. *"Mucho, mucho vaca.* Much cow."

The Indian extended both his hands, opening and closing them many times. Then he pointed to Ten. He understood. Ten held up one finger, then two, then three, then four, and then five. He repeated the procedure and pointed to the grazing longhorns. How many of them? The Lipan nodded his understanding, and pointing to the sun, raised two fingers. He would have a tally in two days. Ten put five double eagles in his hand. The Indian lifted his eyebrows in question, pointing to the grazing longhorns. Ten shook his head, pointed to himself and then to the Lipan. It was a gift. He put out his hand and the Indian took it.

Priscilla didn't say anything until they were well away from the Indian camp. When she spoke, it was with some amusement.

"He remembered your father. Are you going to tell him?"

"I don't know," said Ten. "Just when I'm about convinced I'm my own man, I end up leanin' on something Jess has said or done."

"What's wrong with that? I think he'd be proud of the way you handled yourself. I was."

He looked at her, and the grim set of his lips softened.

"Maybe I am touchy," he said. "Trouble was, I didn't want to go away to St. Louis to school. I felt like I was just a troublesome little bastard that Jess wanted rid of. I didn't think he really cared a damn whether I got educated or not, so I didn't care either."

"So now you know he did care, and you feel guilty for letting him down. You feel even more guilty when you benefit from being his son, like you've taken something you haven't earned."

"That's it," he said. "That's how I feel." He looked at her wonderingly, relieved, yet a little afraid of having her understand him so well.

"Ten," she said, "tell him what you've told me. Tell him that you're proud of him. The time will come when you'll be glad you did."

Her eyes were on her saddle horn, and he looked at her with compassion. She envied him, and he knew why. She was right; he should be proud of Jesse. He never forgot her words, and the time would come when he'd bless her for saying them.

Ten and Priscilla reached San Antone and found a rooming house that had hot baths. Ten paid two dollars for a room, and another two dollars for hot water, towels, and lye soap.

"We ought to have learned where Marty, Wes, and the girls took rooms," said Ten. "We could go over there and rattle the doors, throw gravel at the windows and give 'em a real shivaree."

"I wouldn't let you," said Priscilla. "Let the poor girls

have a day and a night of peace and quiet. They've been nice to me, considering. I just hope Marty and Wes appreciate them. What do you know about Marty and Wes?"

"They're men with the bark on," said Ten. "What you really want to know is, have they been goin' to whorehouses."

"I'd never have asked you that. How would you know, unless you'd been going with them?"

"I can't say what they've done before they threw in with me," said Ten, "but as cowboys go, from what I've seen of 'em, they could go to church with a clear conscience. So could I, but for a deck of cards."

Marty, Wes, Chris, and Lou returned the following morning and were hoorawed by everybody except Priscilla. Ten told them of the large herd of longhorns in the box canyon and the willingness of the Lipans to sell them.

"There won't be ten thousand," though," said Marty. "That means we'll still be huntin' cows. Once we know how many's there, maybe we can just leave 'em in this canyon while we scout around for some more."

"I believe we can," said Ten. "I offered four dollars a head, and it was accepted. Even if there's only two or three thousand, that'll be a pile of money for a tribe of Indians."

The Lipan Apaches had 4400 longhorns in the box canyon. They also had an eye for beef; 3500 of the brutes were big Texas steers.

"No way out of it," said Marty. "We're goin' to end up trailin' a bunch of cows. They'll slow down the drive, but we'll need 'em if we're shootin' for ten thousand head."

"I promised Jess twenty-five hundred," said Ten. "We have the money to buy another seventy-five hundred, but that's no good if we can't find the cows. With what we've found between here and Fort Worth, we have only a little more than six thousand. Tomorrow will be May fifteenth, and I aim to have these brutes grazin' along the Arkansas, just south of Abilene, by September first."

For three more weeks they visited every outlying ranch within a day's ride of their camp. For all their riding, and paying in gold, they found only another 3100 head. That, with the herd bought from the Indians, plus what they would pick up near Fort Worth, would push their total to 9300 head, 3300 of them cows. The Lipan Apaches drove their 4400 longhorns as far north as Ten's camp near Bandera. This herd was left with Charlie Two Hats and the Cherokee riders. Ten took the rest of the outfit south, beyond San Antone, for the remainder of their last buy. With this 1600 head, they could begin the drive north. They were between San Antone and Bandera, Ten and Priscilla riding drag, when Ten spotted trouble ahead.

"Something's wrong at Bandera," said Ten. "Look at that dust."

"Dust?" cried Priscilla. "How can you see anything, with all the dust our own herd's stirring up?"

"Not a cloud in the sky," said Ten, "but look at that dirty gray against the blue, way up yonder on the horizon."

The cloud on the horizon came closer, and within minutes they could see a ragged line of longhorns half a mile wide, on a collision course with the herd they were driving north. Ten saw Marty dropping back, Wes, Chris, and Lou following. Their only hope was to push their own herd headlong into the oncoming longhorns and start the entire mass to milling. Failing in that, half the brutes might swing east, while the others went west, resulting in two stampedes.

"Push 'em hard," shouted Ten. "Keep 'em bunched!"

With the wind from the north, the dust cloud raised by the oncoming herd preceeded them. It blinded Ten's northbound herd until the southbound bunch was almost upon them. There was a bawling, horn-clacking panic as the lead steers from both herds collided. Ten drew his Colt and began firing until the weapon was empty. Even amid the dust, he could see steers from the southbound stampede going around both flanks of his own herd. At least they had only one stampede to contend with, he thought, and his own herd seemed to have slowed the panic-stricken rush of the other. Riders began appearing at right and left flank of the bawling, milling longhorns. Charlie Two Hats and his boys had arrived. Once they had the mixed herds under control, Two Hats trotted his lathered horse over to where Ten sat, reloading his Colt.

"Cow run like hell," said Two Hats. "Injun ride like hell, then ever't'ing jus' go to hell." Embarrassed, he expected a reprimand.

Ten surprised him. "We'll hold this bunch," he said. "Get your riders together and try to head that bunch that divided and flanked us."

Priscilla wiped her sweaty, dusty face on the sleeve of her shirt. Lou, Chris, Marty, and Wes had already begun to circle the newly formed remnants of the two herds.

"Is a stampede always this bad?" Priscilla asked wearily.

"Most of the time, it's worse," said Ten. "They run at night too."

22

Even with Charlie Two Hats and his riders striving to redeem themselves, Ten's outfit lost three days gathering the stampeded longhorns. They lost fifteen head, all a result of the herds colliding head-on. Three of the animals had broken necks. The rest had been gored, or had broken legs, and had to be shot. Rather than have the meat go to waste, Ten rode to the Indian village and offered the beef to the Lipan Apaches. The offer was accepted, and in return the Lipan chief sent a dozen mounted braves to help gather the stampeded longhorns.

"We learned one thing," said Priscilla. "All the Indians in Texas aren't bloodthirsty killers."

"The Lipan Apaches save all their hate for the Comanches," said Marty.

"If I understood their language," said Ten, "I'd be tempted to hire some Lipans for this drive and send Two Hats and his bunch home. They don't even know what started that stampede."

"Kinda unusual, in broad daylight," said Marty, "but with wild cows, you never know. I remember once, two old bulls got to hookin' at one another. They got bloodied up some, and the smell of the blood, as best we could figure, was what spooked the herd. Scattered 'em from hell to breakfast, with the sun not even noon high."

"That herd was fresh out of a box canyon," said Lou. "They're like our first herd was, there on the Trinity, except there's lots more of them."

"Until they become trailwise and settle down," said Ten, "we'll night-hawk in three watches, six riders at a time. There's no such thing as a good stampede, but if there's a choice, I'll take daylight over dark."

"Let's just hope this bunch settles down," said Chris, "before we add those cows waiting for us near Fort Worth. How many more do we have there?"

"I figure seventeen hundred and fifty between here and Fort Worth," said Ten. "Even with our loss, we'll still have 9375 head. Not quite the ten thousand we came after, but a blessed plenty, I think."

June 25, 1866, the first of the herd reached Fort Worth. The longhorns were strung out for nearly three miles, and everybody from the fort came out to watch the drive approach. Ten had Charlie Two Hats move up to point. Ten rode ahead to meet with Captain Fanning.

"Impressive," said the captain. "How many do you have?"

"At last tally," said Ten, "9375 head."

"Have any Indian trouble?"

"Not from the Comanches," said Ten.

"There's been some killing north of here," said Captain Fanning. "Along the Red. Had a pair of Rangers through here yesterday. Six of them were attacked in daylight by what they estimated was a hundred Comanches. Four Rangers died. The two who escaped had to ride for their lives."

It was disturbing news. Such a band of Comanches would outnumber Ten's riders more than five to one. He rode back to the outfit and passed the word to them. Everybody looked grim except Charlie Two Hats's Cherokees. They were practically jubilant over the possibility of a fight with the Comanches.

"Damn fools," snorted Marty. "I wish I could get that

excited over the possibility of gettin' my carcass shot full of Comanche arrows and my hair lifted."

"That many Comanches," said Ten, "and they could hit us in the daytime, when we're strung out for miles. They'll know we're expecting them at night. What better way to cut us down a few at a time than to attack us on the trail?"

They bedded down the huge herd a few miles north of the fort, and Ten called every rider to the supper fire to plan for a possible daytime attack.

"I'll be scouting far ahead of the herd," said Ten, "but not so far that you can't hear a rifle shot. I'll be looking for Indian sign. I look for them to stampede the herd, and in the confusion try to kill as many of us as they can. I doubt they'll come at us from the south, but I want five of you at drag. If they do circle around and hit us from behind, then one of you drag riders pull your rifle and fire a quick three shots. The rest of you keep your ears perked. If you hear three warning shots from the south, you'll know that's where you're needed. Pull your rifles and ride."

Nobody said anything, and he continued.

"Now, Charlie, this is for you, since you'll be at point. If they come at us from the north, I'll see them long before you do. If there's a hundred of 'em, like we've been told, here's what we're goin' to do. I'll fire three quick shots. Pull your own rifle, Charlie, and repeat my signal, so the rest of the outfit is sure to hear it. When you've done that, get out of the path of the herd. That's important, and here's why: this is where you drag riders figure in. When you hear those three warning shots somewhere ahead of you, I want you to pull your own guns and make all the noise you can. If we're goin' to have a stampede, then we'll start it ourselves, so we can control it. We'll see how scalp-hungry these Comanches are when they're out in front of nine thousand wild-runnin' Texas longhorns."

"Make cow run like hell," said Charlie Two Hats.

"That's it," said Ten, "and then you ride like hell

alongside the herd. Keep them moving north, and if you get close enough to the Comanches, shoot to kill. Just don't get sucked into the stampede and get yourself trampled, or your horse gored."

Ten still had the night divided into three watches, using six riders at a time. Ten, Marty, Wes, Priscilla, Chris, and Lou took the first watch, and Ten took that opportunity to talk to them.

"I want the five of you at drag," he said, "until this Comanche threat is past. I want Two Hats and his riders covering the flank and point positions, and I want them devoting all their attention to what's ahead of us. But those of you at drag will have to be twice as watchful. If I'm wrong, and Comanches hit the herd from behind, it will be up to you to warn the rest of us. But if an attack comes from the north, it'll be up to you to hear the warning shots and start the herd running."

The nights continued peaceful, leading Ten more and more to expect a daytime attack while they were on the trail. They were a few miles south of the Red River crossing when the Comanches struck. Ten was half a dozen miles ahead of the herd, and with the wind from the northwest, the dust warned him of approaching riders long before he saw them. He first sighted the Comanches as they emerged from a brushy draw. They rode in a column of twos, trotting their horses. Ten watched as long as he dared, not wishing to stampede the herd unless the odds were otherwise insurmountable. Clear of the draw, the mounted Comanches bunched, and Ten had his answer. He kicked his horse into a gallop, riding south toward the oncoming herd. He pulled his Henry and fired three quick shots. Even with the wind against them, the Comanches were close enough to hear his warning shots. They would be after him within seconds, but there was no help for it. It would take time for the drag riders to get the herd running. Against the wind, he heard Charlie Two Hats repeat his three shots. Almost immediately there was the distant thunder of rifles, and the drag riders began forcing the herd to run.

Ten slowed his horse, looking back. He must bait the trap, allowing the pursuing Comanches to see him. He rode one of the blacks they'd gotten from Maynard Herndon, and from here on his very life would depend on the valiant horse. He must lure the attackers into the very teeth of the stampede if the maneuver was to be successful. But he also must avoid being caught in the stampede himself. Once the herd began to run, they might overrun the flank riders, bearing down on him like a living avalanche of destruction. However they ran, his only chance lay in riding around the thundering herd at right or left flank.

When he saw the charging herd coming, it was even more massed, presenting an even wider front than he'd feared. Some of the longhorns from the middle and tag end of the herd had broken ranks, had swerved around, and were following the leaders. Coming at him on the run was an unbroken line of wild Texas longhorns a mile wide! It was time to get out of their path, if he could. He wheeled the black to the east, riding hard. But without warning the earth seemed to give away beneath them. The running horse screamed, stumbled, and Ten left the saddle. He rolled and barely escaped being crushed by the falling horse. Dazed, he got to his knees. The black had staggered to its feet just in time for a Comanche arrow to graze its flank. Nickering in fear, the black galloped away. Ten eyed the oncoming herd, and he saw no escape. Then, far to his left, from among the charging longhorns, came a buckskin-clad Indian rider. The task he had chosen was impossible, but on he came! Soon he was ahead of the herd, and he wheeled his horse directly across its path. But the attacking Comanches, seeking to escape the oncoming herd, had followed Ten. Now they found themselves within range of this oncoming rider, and loosed a barrage of arrows at him. Ten's would-be rescuer rode all the harder, and in response to the Comanche arrows, pulled his Henry and began firing. But the arrows were many, and one of them found its mark. Ten saw the rider flinch as the arrow caught him in the right side. But still he rode, and now he was close enough for Ten to recognize the grinning face of Sashavado!

The Cherokee circled Ten, wheeled his horse and gave Ten his hand. Ten pulled himself up behind Sashavado, and the Indian kicked the weary horse into a run. The animal's flanks were wet, and Ten could hear it blowing. There were no more arrows. Ten looked back, and the Comanches had given up everything except getting out of the path of the herd. Despite Sashavado's hard riding and the supreme efforts of his horse, they were caught up in part of the stampede. But they were near the outer edge, on the left flank, and Sashavado allowed the horse to lope along with the slowing longhorns. The stampede had lost its momentum.

Once free of the herd, Ten dropped off the weary horse. Sashavado reined up, but when he tried to dismount, he fell. Ten caught the Indian, easing him to the ground. The arrow had gone in just above his waistband, and he looked hard hit. Charlie Two Hats, Marty, and Priscilla reined up and quit their saddles on the run. Priscilla's face went white as she saw the arrow in Sashavado's side. Charlie Two Hats said nothing.

"Marty," said Ten, "bring me a horse, and a fresh one for Sashavado. You and me are takin' him back to Fort Worth. There'll be a doc at the fort, and they'll have medicine."

"Dear God," cried Priscilla, "he's hurt. How can he ride?"

"Sashavado ride," gritted the Indian.

Marty returned with a horse for Ten and a fresh one for Sashavado. Ten spoke to Charlie Two Hats.

"Charlie, the rest of you begin rounding up the herd. Move them to the nearest water and graze, and bed them down. Keep everybody on watch, just in case those Comanches have another go at us. Me and Marty will be back when Sashavado's been taken care of, and after I've reported this attack to Captain Fanning."

"There's nobody left with the herd," said Priscilla, "except Wes, Chris, and Lou. The Cherokees have gone after the Comanches."

Ten looked at Two Hats, and the Indian shrugged.

"Cow no run," said Two Hats. "Comanche run. Kill Comanche, catch cow."

It was Indian logic. Ten nodded. The herd was moving north and had slowed to barely a walk. Many of the longhorns had stopped to graze. Two Hats's riders wouldn't pursue the Comanches too far. The Cherokees were far outnumbered, and smart enough not to ride into an ambush. Ten turned to Priscilla.

"Find Wes, Chris, and Lou," he said, "and stay with them until I return."

Ten and Marty rode slowly, making it as easy on Sashavado as they could. The Indian rode between them, saying nothing. It was well past noon when they reached the fort. A sentry was sent, on the double, for Captain Fanning.

"Captain," said Ten, "we need a doctor for this man. When we've seen to him, I'll have some information for you about the attack."

Sashavado didn't trust the white "medicine man," and it was all Ten could do to convince the Indian he should allow the doctor to operate. They wasted half a bottle of laudanum before Sashavado finally swallowed enough for it to take effect.

"It's not as bad as it looks," said the doctor. "The barb hit a rib, and while it's cut deep, it spared his vitals. If you can keep him still for a couple of days, until the danger of infection has passed, he'll be all right."

Ten and Marty returned to Captain Fanning's office.

"Not much to report, Captain," said Ten, "except that what those Rangers told you was gospel. I'd say there's a good hundred Comanches in that bunch."

"But you didn't lose a man," said Fanning, "and had

only one wounded. If I may ask, how did you accomplish that, against so superior a force?"

"We let 'em come after us," said Ten, "and when they got close enough, we sent nine thousand wild Texas longhorns to meet 'em. That evened the odds some. Even Comanches can't fight a stampede."

Despite the doctor's warnings, Sashavado refused to remain at the fort. The Cherokee insisted on returning to the herd with Ten and Marty, so the doctor supplied them with alcohol, iodine, and fresh bandages for dressing the wound. It was near dark when they reached their camp, and Ten noted with approval that Two Hats had everybody with the herd except Priscilla. The cooking had been done, and the fire had been put out well before dark.

"I saved supper for you," said Priscilla, "although I didn't know when you'd be back. Sashavado, I'm so glad you're all right. How do you feel?"

"Sore lak hell," said Sashavado. "Much hungry."

Charlie Two Hats rode in, appearing unsurprised that Sashavado was there, eating as though he'd never seen food before in his life.

"No lose cow." Two Hats grinned. "Kill Comanche." He raised one hand, all his fingers extended.

Ten sighed with relief. Even with the stampede, they'd lost none of the herd. The Cherokees had managed to kill five of their attackers, and although Sashavado had been wounded, he would recover.

They spent part of the next day rounding up the rest of the herd.

"First stampede I ever seen," said Marty, "where the herd runs the way the drive's headed. Give 'em a choice, and they go skalleyhootin' down the backtrail fifteen or twenty miles."

"Mr. Chisholm," said Lou, trotting her horse alongside Ten's, "I owe you an apology. When we first throwed in with you, I wasn't sure you was a big enough

Injun to boss a trail drive, but that trick with the stampede convinced me. Those Comanches would have had us for breakfast."

"Wes," said Ten, "I ain't never heard a woman admit she was wrong before. Are you almighty sure this here person is a girl?"

"I'd swear to it on a stack of Bibles," said Wes.

"So could Marty," said Chris.

Marty winked at Lou, and the girl actually blushed. Ten only looked confused. Priscilla laughed. Someday she'd have to tell him what Marty and Wes never had.

Ten turned the drive slightly to the east, and they crossed the Red River just south of Fort Washita. It was July 10, 1866.

"This is one time the Red didn't live up to its reputation," said Marty.

"There's still the Canadian, the North Canadian, and the Arkansas," said Ten, "and any one of them could drown some of us."

"This has been kind of a dry year," said Wes. "Not that much rain."

"When it comes to river crossin'," said Marty, "high water ain't the only problem. Once you get the lead steers in the water, they got to head for the other bank. Let 'em get spooked, and they're just likely to take a notion to go back to the riverbank they've just left. Next thing you know, the herd's doubled back on itself, and you end up with steers drowned or gored. Been many a rider lost like that too."

But as it turned out, river crossings would be the least of their worries. Indian Territory was a haven for renegades and deserters, the dregs of the Union and Confederate armies. A day's drive north of the Red, they came upon a creek whose banks offered excellent graze for several miles, even for their large herd.

"We'll take a couple of days to rest," said Ten. "This is a good time and place to wash clothes and blankets."

"We can't be more'n five days' drive from the Canadian," said Marty. "You aim to stop at the trading post and leave the twenty-five hundred steers your pa wants?"

"We'll stop there," said Ten, "but I reckon he'll want us to trail his herd with ours and graze 'em on the Arkansas until McCoy's stock pens are ready."

"We won't actually be going to Abilene, then," said Priscilla.

"Not for a while," said Ten. "We'll spend a day or two with Jess, and after we leave his trading post, it's about 225 miles to his ranch on the Arkansas River. That's where we'll graze our herd. Abilene's maybe seventy-five miles north of there."

"It may be weeks before McCoy's cattle pens are ready," said Wes. "Who's goin' to stay with the herd? Us?"

"No," said Ten. "That's what I want to talk to Jess about. If it's all right with him, I aim to leave Charlie Two Hats and his riders there until we're ready to move the herd on to Abilene. Then I thought I'd take Priscilla to St. Louis for a few days. Marty, you and Wes are welcome to bring Chris and Lou. I have to track down Drago Herndon. I still owe him money, and I have to tell him about Hern."

"I wouldn't miss a trip to St. Louis," said Lou, "but what comes after that? Another trail drive?"

"Not immediately," said Ten. "I have some unfinished business in New Orleans."

There was an uncomfortable silence. As much as they wished to know the nature of his "business," they dared not ask. If he had wanted them to know, he'd have told them. Chris and Lou eyed Priscilla, and it was she who broke the prolonged silence.

"It's not something I'm proud of," she said, "but they're like family, and they might as well know."

With that, she turned to Chris and Lou.

"He promised my daddy some money," she said. "That's how he was able to get me away from there. Now he has to deliver the money."

"Why?" Wes wanted to know. "Ten's got you, you're past eighteen, and you're a married woman."

"Because I gave my word," said Ten, "and I aim to keep it."

"Even if he tries again to kill you," said Priscilla bitterly.

"He ain't goin' alone," said Marty.

"Alone," said Ten grimly. "I made the debt, and I'll pay it."

23

Three days into Indian Territory, Ten's outfit had just finished supper when their "visitors" rode in. There were twelve of them, a hardcase lot if Ten had ever seen one. The apparent leader wore a Confederate officer's coat and dirty Levi's pants. He was bearded, and his shaggy dark hair poked out through a hole in the crown of his old gray hat. He hooked one leg around his saddle horn, and with his left hand rolled a quirly. He popped a sulfur match with his thumbnail and lit the smoke. His companions reined up next to and behind him. They made no move to dismount, and Ten extended no invitation.

"Mighty big herd," said Black Hat. "Where you bound?"

"Mister," said Ten, "I don't consider that any of your business."

"Well, now," said the renegade leader, "I reckon it is our business. We're here to offer you our services. For, say, ten cents a head, we'll git you through th' territory. Otherwise, without our pertection, them cows might git stampeded, an' it'd take a right smart amount of work, roundin' 'em up."

Marty and Wes had moved up beside Ten, thumbs hooked in their pistol belts. Charlie Two Hats's riders had moved in, every man armed with a rifle or a Colt, some with both.

"I reckon," said the renegade, "you ain't int'rested."

The half-smoked quirly disappeared from his lips before any of them heard the sound of the shot. Ten holstered his Colt.

"You're right," he said. "We ain't interested. Now back out of here, the lot of you, and ride."

Without a word they turned and rode away, none of them looking back.

"They'll likely be back sometime tonight," said Marty.

"I doubt it," said Ten. "They rode in to take our measure, and didn't like what they saw. If their kind is goin' to be a problem, they usually just go ahead and stampede the herd. Then they'll round up as many as they can and demand payment for returning them. We'll be on our guard, but I don't think they liked the look of us."

But that wasn't the end of it. When a summer storm struck two nights later, so did the renegades. They waited until thunder and lightning became intense enough to stampede the herd. With the longhorns running toward the south, and the riders trying to head them, the band of outlaws rode in from the north. Slipping in behind the hard-riding cowboys, they began shooting. When Ten first heard the shots, he thought it was his own riders trying to head the herd. He changed his mind when a slug burned its way across his thigh and another ripped off his hat, which had been thonged down with rawhide. Ten reined up, drew his Henry and began firing at muzzle flashes. Some of his other riders had become aware of the danger, had abandoned the stampeding herd and were returning the fire. The longhorns could be rounded up later. The thunder and lightning diminished, along with the thunder of the running herd. The element of surprise gone, and their fire being returned, the attackers backed off. Slowly, Ten's outfit came together.

Of the Cherokee riders, only four were present. There was Buscadero, Sashavado, Hoss, and Jingle Bob. Ten could only hope the others were still in pursuit of the running longhorns, and not injured or dead. But his worst fears were realized when Wes, Chris, and Lou rode in. Wes led two horses. One of them had been ridden by Charlie Two Hats, the other by Priscilla.

"What about Marty?" Ten asked.

"Ain't seen him or his horse," said Wes. "We found these two trottin' along behind the herd."

As suddenly as the sky had clouded, it began to clear. By moon and starlight they backtrailed the stampede. They found Priscilla first, and Ten sighed with relief.

"They started shooting," she said, "and a bullet must have stung my horse. He just went crazy and threw me."

Ten gave her a hand up behind him, and they rode on. When they found Charlie Two Hats, he was afoot, the left sleeve of his shirt soaked with blood.

"Shoot Injun off hoss," said Charlie. "Mad like hell."

Using his good hand, Charlie hoisted himself up behind Buscadero. There was the thud of hooves from the south, and when the rest of the outfit reined up, Marty Brand wasn't with them. Chris was already far ahead, searching for Marty, and it was she who found him lying facedown in the mud. Hearing her frantic cry, the rest of the outfit went on the run. Even in the moonlight they could see the back of his shirt was bloody. But before any of them could make a move to help him, Marty rolled over and sat up, groaning. Ten could see the shine of blood as it oozed from a nasty wound above Marty's right ear.

"They nailed me in the shoulder," said Marty, "and the next one like to of took my head off. I feel like I been hit with a nine-pound sledge."

They got him mounted behind Chris and set off for their camp. There wasn't much of it left. Their pack mules were gone, their supplies had been ransacked, and a dozen horses were missing from their remuda.

"Maybe the horses and mules got caught up in the stampede," said Lou.

"The stampede wouldn't have taken twelve picketed horses and left the rest," said Ten. "Come daylight,

we're goin' after that bunch and show 'em the evil of
their ways."

It was a miserable four hours until dawn. Without
their supplies and medicines, they couldn't even see to
their wounded. Ten was ready to ride as soon as it was
light enough to see. He would take Wes and all of the
Cherokee riders except Charlie Two Hats.

"Priscilla," said Ten, "you, Chris, and Lou get a fire
going. Heat some water and do what you can for Charlie and Marty until we get back."

The worst of the storm had been over when the renegades had ridden out, so their trail leading north was
plain. Too plain. The outlaws didn't have that much of a
lead. Somewhere ahead they'd have to double back and
lay an ambush. Ten reined up and waited for the Cherokee riders to gather around him.

"Hombres," he said, "I reckon this bunch is goin' to
double back and lay for us. Buscadero, you take five
men, ride a couple of miles east, and then turn north.
Sashavado, you take five men, ride a ways to the west,
and then ride north. When you find where this bunch is
holed up, move in from east and west and get 'em in a
cross fire. Wes and me will ride on, like we're followin'
their trail. When we hear you shootin', we'll ride in from
the south. *Comprender?*"

Sashavado grinned. "Shoot lak hell. Kill all."

"Every one," said Ten. "Just don't get yourself shot in
the process."

They rode out, every man with his rifle cocked and
ready.

"We're givin' 'em the tough part," said Wes. "I feel
kind of guilty."

"Don't," said Ten. "When Buscadero and Sashavado
close the jaws of this trap, those coyotes are goin' to
run. Since they can only ride north or south, there's a
fifty-fifty chance it'll be just the two of us against any
who escape."

The fight, when it came, was short. When Ten and
Wes heard the crash of gunfire, they kicked their horses

into a run, drawing their Henrys as they rode. But it was over before they reached the scene. The Cherokees had indeed caught the renegades in a cross fire. Eleven of the outlaws had been killed. It looked like a battlefield. Ten and Wes reined up. Sashavado and Buscadero rode out to report.

Sashavado grinned. "Boss coyote run lak hell."

"Take gun, take shell, take hoss," said Buscadero.

The rest of the Cherokees were doing exactly that. Not only had they recovered Ten's stolen horses, pack mules, and supplies, they had taken the eleven renegades' horses and a loaded packhorse. Outlaw pistol belts hung from saddle horns, and the Indians were stripping the bodies of anything else of value, including fancy boots.

"My God," said Wes, "I know they were outlaws, but it's kind of gruesome, stripping the dead."

"Maybe," said Ten, "but they won't take anything the dead can use."

They spent the best part of three days rounding up the scattered herd, but Ten didn't begrudge the delay. While their wounds wouldn't have kept Marty and Charlie Two Hats from riding, a couple of days' rest might lessen the chance of infection. One night after supper, wanting some time to themselves, Ten and Priscilla walked down the creek a ways.

"I don't understand Indians," said Priscilla.

"I'm mostly Indian."

"Most of the time I don't understand you either."

He laughed. "What don't you understand, about Indians in general, and me in particular?"

"I can't forget how Sashavado looked when he fought with you," she said. "I saw death in his eyes, and if you hadn't disarmed him, he'd have killed you. Yet when your horse fell in front of that stampede, it was Sashavado who saved you."

"How do you feel about Sashavado now?"

"Although he seems limited to 'fight lak hell, ride lak

hell, and shoot lak hell,' " she laughed, "I like him. I suppose that's what's confusing me most of all. I don't think I understand myself any better than I understand the Indians."

"In the so-called civilized world," said Ten, "one man may like another without ever knowin' what kind of man he is. On the frontier, it's just the opposite. I couldn't like a man I didn't respect, and I can't fault another man for lookin' at me in the same light."

"So it's not so much the liking of one Indian for another, but a mutual respect."

He laughed. "Not entirely. Sashavado respects the Comanche, but there's not a shred of brotherly love between them. I'd say we have a liking for one another, and that he thinks more highly of me than he would a Comanche or a Kiowa."

"And I suppose you think better of him than you would a Comanche or a Kiowa, although you might still respect the Comanche and the Kiowa?"

"That's about the truth of it," he said.

"Ten, I've gotten used to Two Hats and his riders. When this trail drive is over, do we have to give them up? Couldn't they still be our outfit?"

"I'm goin' to talk to Jess about that. With his standing among the plains Indians, he won't be hurtin' for riders. I reckon if Two Hats and his boys are willin' to stay with us, Jess won't object. Now, Priscilla Chisholm, do you aim to talk all night, or will you drag me into the brush and have your way with me?"

July 15, 1866. They reached the Chisholm trading post on the banks of the Canadian River. With many families of Cherokees living in the area, it was friendly territory. With the graze good and water plentiful, the longhorns were left strung out along the river. The herd had become lean, mean, and trailwise. Ten found Jesse Chisholm had ridden to Fort Smith and wasn't expected back for another four days. Chisholm's Cherokee cook wasn't very talkative, and volunteered no information.

Chris sighed. "Four whole nights in an honest-to-goodness bed."

"This is goin' to be interestin'." Marty laughed. "These other Injuns are almighty envious of Charlie Two Hats and his riders. Here they are, back from Texas with a dozen extra hosses, and enough pistols, rifles, and shells to fight a war. When we do another trail drive, Mr. Chisholm won't have an Injun left. They'll all be goin' with us."

When Chisholm returned, he was surprised and pleased. He turned grim only when Ten told him of his plans to return to New Orleans, the result of his promise to André LeBeau.

"I gave my word," said Ten. "Are you suggesting I break it?"

"I suppose not," said Chisholm. "I just can't see the necessity of you having given it. You'd trust a man who would extort money from you under such circumstances?"

"Trust has nothing to do with it," said Ten angrily. "I wouldn't trust LeBeau as far as I could walk on water. I only bought his silence until Priscilla turned eighteen. I reckon you think I'm payin' for something I didn't need, but you don't know how vindictive and mean old LeBeau is. Like I told you, I don't aim to turn my back on him. Harvey Roberts promised I can use his office, and LeBeau will have to come to me. Once I've given him the money, why should he come after me?"

"You just said he's mean and vindictive. You turned Priscilla's head, and he'll blame you for his failure with her. If you're going to St. Louis, why don't you open an account with a bank there and send him a bank draft?"

"Because he's over his head in debt," said Ten, "and wants the money in gold. He'd have some trouble cashing a draft."

"But with gold," said Chisholm, "he can take it and run."

"That's exactly what I want him to do," said Ten. "If he's busy savin' his own hide, he won't be after mine."

"He may save himself and still double-cross you," said Chisholm. "I'm only suggesting that you expect betrayal. It could save your life."

Ten nodded somberly. It was good advice.

André LeBeau was furious. He had just learned, through Emily, that Priscilla never reached Louisville. Emily's mother, whom LeBeau despised, had written a very curt letter in response to Emily's. The LeBeaus hadn't bothered letting her know Priscilla was coming, so why should she have been disturbed when the girl hadn't arrived? From the tone of her letter, LeBeau believed that salty old woman was secretly pleased Priscilla had disappeared. Despite LeBeau's promise to Tenatse Chisholm, he still hadn't given up on the possibility he could collect the promised money from Chisholm, and still use Priscilla as a wild card in a high stakes game with Jason Brawn. Of course, Chisholm would have had to die. But now Priscilla was beyond LeBeau's reach, and where Brawn was concerned, all bets were off. LeBeau hadn't the slightest doubt the girl was somewhere in Indian Territory, sharing Tenatse Chisholm's bed. She was now old enough to marry, but would the empty-headed little fool even bother? It didn't matter; she was already ruined, as far as any bartering with Jason Brawn was concerned. He, André LeBeau, had trusted Tenatse Chisholm, and the damn Indian had double-crossed him. Chisholm had Priscilla, but he was going to pay plenty more for her than he expected. It made no difference when or where Chisholm delivered the money to him. It was only good sense for Chisholm to arrive by steamboat, meaning that he'd be stuck in New Orleans at least until the departure of the next packet. There would be time enough for a hired killer to stalk him, waiting for the right moment.

* * *

Jesse Chisholm had misgivings about Ten's proposed trip to New Orleans. When Priscilla came to him, he realized his doubts were well-justified. Ten, Marty, and Wes had ridden out to check on the herd. It was barely daylight, and Chris and Lou hadn't yet come to the kitchen. Priscilla found Chisholm there alone, and he could see the girl was afraid.

"He's going to be talking to you about a change in plans," Priscilla said. "He's changed his mind about grazing the herd on the Arkansas. Since McCoy's cattle pens won't be ready until November first, Ten says we'll hold the herd here on the Canadian. He says we can just take the longhorns from here on to Abilene, in maybe three weeks."

"That much makes sense," said Chisholm. "What else?"

"We're two months away from finishing the drive to Abilene. Ten plans on leaving the rest of us here while he goes to New Orleans. He's going to talk to you sometime today. He's going to ask for the rest of what you said you'd pay for bringing you twenty-five hundred longhorns. That will be exactly enough to pay what he promised my father."

"I promised him the money," said Chisholm, "and he's delivered the cows. What do you think I should do?"

"Don't pay him for them yet," begged Priscilla. "Tell him you need to wait until McCoy's pens are ready, until the herd's sold. He won't have the money to pay my father without your help."

"Priscilla," said Chisholm with a smile, "bless you for your intentions, but that won't work. He'd see through it in a second. He'd get a mad on, ride to every outpost in the territory and sell steers at ten dollars a head until he raised the money he needs."

"Oh, damn him and his foolish pride!"

Chisholm laughed.

"I'm sorry," she said, coloring. "What are we going to do? What can we do?"

"Get him to New Orleans," said Chisholm, "convince him to leave LeBeau's money with Harvey Roberts and then get out of town."

"But will he do that?"

"He will," said Chisholm, "after I talk to him. Just because he gave his word that he'll pay the money doesn't mean he has to hand it over in person. I'm going to suggest that he leave the money with Roberts, and that Harvey not send word to your father until Ten's safely out of New Orleans."

"Oh," cried Priscilla, "if he'll only listen to you."

"Thank you for coming to me, Priscilla. If he never makes another right decision in his life, he's made at least one."

Ten's decision to leave immediately for New Orleans didn't meet with anybody's approval.

"Cow ready," said Charlie Two Hats, "Injun ready. When ride?"

"You said we were going to St. Louis," Lou complained.

"Tenatse Chisholm," said Chris, "you're an Indian-giver. First you said we could go with you to New Orleans, then you left us behind. Now we lose out on a trip to St. Louis, and you're going back to New Orleans."

"But he ain't goin' alone," said Marty. "I'm takin' my Henry."

"Me too," said Wes.

"Cow ready," repeated Two Hats, "Injun ready. When ride?"

"Damn it," bawled Ten, "everybody back off!" Angrily, he turned to Priscilla. "You're almighty quiet. Why don't you make it unanimous?"

"Would it do any good?"

He knew she was afraid for him. They all were, and he was ashamed for having responded to their concern so rudely.

"Sorry," he said. "I'm obliged to all of you for your loyalty, but I've agreed to a plan Jess has. It'll get me there, get me out, and it'll end this obligation once and for all. When that's done, I promise you, we'll go to St. Louis."

"Injun ready," said Two Hats.

They needed to laugh, and they did.

The following morning at dawn, Tenatse Chisholm would ride to Fort Smith, where he would take a steam-boat for New Orleans. Alone.

$\mathcal{A}$ pair of bulging saddlebags held the gold Ten would deliver to André LeBeau. He had timed his arrival so that he would reach Fort Smith several hours before boarding the steamboat for New Orleans. He was in no mood for waiting. The journey itself would be torturous enough. As he rode, he had time to mull over the plan Jesse Chisholm had proposed and to which he had agreed. He would arrive in New Orleans as unobtrusively as possible, go to the Roberts and Company offices, and request the help of Harvey Roberts. He would entrust the gold to Roberts, who, once Ten was safely out of New Orleans, would get a message to André LeBeau. Roberts would deliver the gold when LeBeau called for it, and Ten's word would have been kept. The only ticklish part of Chisholm's plan lay in getting Ten out of New Orleans without waiting for the next steamboat bound for Fort Smith. Now that the war was over and some commerce had resumed, there were smaller packets on the river, most of them hauling freight, when they could get it. Harvey Roberts, being in the business of shipping and receiving trade goods, could logically hire one of the smaller boats for a freight run to Natchez. Nobody, including the packet's captain, would know the "freight" was Tenatse Chisholm; at least not until departure time.

There was just one possible flaw in the plan, Ten

thought. While he was arriving in early August, much sooner than LeBeau expected him, there was the possibility the sneaky old devil would have somebody watching the incoming steamboats. With arrivals from Fort Smith only twice a week, it wouldn't be all that difficult. Sneed knew him by sight, and it wouldn't take more than an hour of the little gunman's time, twice a week. While Ten had been aware of this potential danger, he hadn't mentioned it to Chisholm or Priscilla. Nothing they could devise would be foolproof, and it was up to him to cover his own backtrail as best he could. The Roberts and Company offices were near the river, so the distance he must travel to a hired packet wouldn't allow much time or opportunity for an ambush. But again, he hadn't dared tell Chisholm or Priscilla what he considered the real danger. While André LeBeau was capable of hiring a killer, and might, Jason Brawn seemed to have the law in the palm of his hand. Suppose LeBeau had learned of Priscilla's deception, and had made Brawn aware of it? LeBeau, the conniving old scutter, could safely collect the money he had been promised, and then turn Brawn's dogs loose. It would be the perfect double cross. The law could search even a rented packet and gun him down on some trumped-up charge.

When *The Talequah* whistled her departure and backed away from the landing, Ten was the only passenger aboard. There might be others at Natchez, but it wasn't likely. Ten wondered if Drago Herndon had been back to Natchez and received either of the written messages his nephew had left for him. While Ten thought the world of Marty Brand and Wes Fedavo, there would always be a special place in his memory for Maynard Herndon. He didn't relish the prospect of telling the old mountain man of Hern's fate, but it was a debt unpaid, the last thing he could ever do for Maynard Herndon.

Sneed's patience had worn thin. He was fed up with meeting the incoming steamboats twice a week, watching for that damn bothersome Indian that LeBeau be-

lieved would soon be returning. He hadn't forgotten
that failed ambush, when the Indian had not only escaped, but had gunned down two of the killers LeBeau
had hired. That money should have gone into his own
pocket, but every time LeBeau wanted some serious
gun work done, he hired somebody else. If he had a
stake, Sneed thought bitterly, he could leave New Orleans. Suppose Tenatse Chisholm did return? The half-
breed might pay handsomely for information he could
supply. Namely, that André LeBeau still wanted him
dead, and was making plans toward that end. Sneed had
no scruples against selling LeBeau out, and the more he
thought of it, the more the idea appealed to him.

While *The Talequah* took on fuel in Natchez, Ten
went ashore long enough to buy a St. Louis newspaper.
He found more news about Joseph McCoy's proposed
cattle pens at Abilene. McCoy had already begun negotiating with the railroad for favorable freight rates, and
there were unconfirmed reports that the rails might actually reach Abilene by Christmas. McCoy had managed
to resolve the tick fever dispute by going to Topeka and
appealing to Governor Crawford, who had signed the
original law against Texas longhorns being brought into
Kansas. McCoy had bought 250 acres of land adjoining
the town of Abilene. Besides the proposed cattle pens,
he was building a barn, an office building, a bank, a
fancy hotel and livery, and a set of livestock scales. A
messenger had been hired and sent to spread the word
of the new facilities, inviting Texas trail drivers to bring
their herds to Abilene. There was speculation that the
first herds of big Texas steers might bring as much as
thirty dollars a head! Ten became more anxious than
ever to be done with this foolishness in New Orleans, to
return to the Canadian and complete the trail drive to
Abilene. There were still millions of longhorns in Texas,
and the railroad was coming!

*   *   *

By the time *The Talequah* whistled for the landing at New Orleans, Ten was on deck. The sooner he met with Harvey Roberts, outlined his plan, and Roberts hired the private packet, the sooner he could leave New Orleans. He saw nobody on the dock that he recognized. He carried only a small satchel and the gold-laden saddlebags. He had buttoned his coat, concealing his pistol belt, but he could feel the reassuring weight of the Colt thonged to his right thigh. When the gangplank was down, he went ashore, making his way along the river toward the Roberts warehouses. He had gone but a few yards when directly ahead of him a man stepped out from between two buildings. Sneed! Ten had the saddlebags over his left shoulder. He shifted the satchel to his left hand, freeing his right. Carefully, he unbuttoned his coat. He waited, saying nothing. Sneed laughed.

"Always ready, ain't you?"

"What do you want, Sneed?"

"Money," said Sneed. "Make it worth my while, and I'll forget I ever saw you step offa that boat."

"And if I don't," said Ten, "you'll spill your guts to LeBeau."

Sneed chuckled. "You Injuns are quick. Figured it right out."

"Go ahead," said Ten. "Tell LeBeau. He's expecting me. After all, he's my daddy-in-law, and I'll be gettin' in touch with him before the day's out."

"Some daddy-in-law," sneered the little man. "He's goin' to stop your clock, and you ain't willin' to pay to shut me up."

"Sneed, if I wanted to shut you up, I could do it for the price of one slug. Now back off, or draw."

Sneed's thin face was twisted with hate as he back-stepped between the two buildings. Ten approached the alley cautiously, but found it deserted. He doubted LeBeau had taken Sneed into his confidence as to his plans, but the little gunman was no fool. LeBeau had something in mind beyond taking his gold and allowing bygones to be bygones. Jesse Chisholm's proposal, having Harvey Roberts hire a private boat, made more sense than ever. Ten hadn't wanted to risk the telegraph, so Roberts didn't know he was coming. He was crucial to the plan, and there was no one else to whom Ten could turn. He hurried on, hoping Roberts wouldn't be away. Sadly, Ten remembered John Mathewson. He had liked the man, and regretted there was nothing he could do to expose and punish the killer.

To Ten's relief, Roberts was there. Ten took a seat in an outer office until the big man could see him. When he was ushered into the private office, he took the chair Roberts offered and wasted no time outlining his plan.

"Old Jake Daimler's got a little stern-wheel packet," said Roberts. "I sometimes send him to Natchez, if I'm in a hurry. Fact is, I have a little bit of freight he could take this time, if I can get him. If I can't get him today, I can tomorrow. I can take you home with me tonight."

"No, you can't," said Ten. "LeBeau knows I'm here, and I don't want you gettin' in the way of a slug meant for me."

"He's not that big a damn fool," said Roberts. "You brought the gold; how's he going to get that if he has you gunned down?"

"I'm reasonably safe until he gets his hands on the gold, I reckon. As far as he knows, I'll be stuck here until there's another steamboat to Fort Smith. Jess wanted me to pull out for Natchez, leaving the gold with you. Once I'm gone, you're to send LeBeau word to come here. When he does, he gets the gold, and I'm finished with him. Me, I'm ashamed to be sucking you into this. Jess asks an almighty lot of his friends."

"I see no way it can harm me," said Roberts. "It's your gold. All I'll be doing is acting as a go-between. I'm ashamed that in a town the size of New Orleans the law is under the thumb of a man like Jason Brawn. I'll go see if I can find old Jake. If he's free today, I'll arrange for him to pull out after dark. You can wait here until then, and I'll wait until tomorrow before I send word to

LeBeau. With luck, you can be on your way to Natchez before he knows you're gone."

Ten didn't worry about LeBeau's killers stalking him, until LeBeau had the promised gold. But Sneed didn't know about the gold.

Roberts was gone nearly two hours, and Ten was restlessly pacing the floor when the big man returned.

"Jake's loading some of my freight now," said Roberts, "and he'll wait until dark before he pulls out. You know where those three lesser docks are, just below the steamboat landing?"

"I know," said Ten.

"Jake will be tied up at one of them. Not that many private packets on the river. He'll be dark; no running lights until he's safely away. I told him only enough about you and your situation to make him cautious."

Roberts brought in sandwiches and coffee for supper. After they had eaten, Roberts emptied the saddlebags of their gold, placing it in his big iron safe.

"It's a lot of money," said Roberts, "to waste on an old reprobate like André LeBeau."

"It's worth every penny," said Ten, "if it rids me of him."

Ten waited until it was good dark before leaving Roberts's office.

"Give my best to Jesse," said Roberts, "and good luck."

"Thanks," said Ten. "You've been a real friend; I won't forget."

He stepped out into the darkened street and, seeing nobody, began walking toward the river. Not wanting to be encumbered with the saddlebags, he had left them with Roberts. He carried the small satchel in his left hand, and with his right, he unbuttoned his coat. Everything had worked out too well. It was too pat. The night was deadly still, and sound traveled far. The sound, when it came, was faint, but one that no frontiersman ever forgot: the cocking of a pistol. Ten dropped to his knees, and a chest-high slug whanged into the brick wall

of a cotton warehouse behind him. Crouching in some
weeds, he tossed the satchel ahead of him, and another
shot sang off the bricks into the night. This time he fired
at the muzzle flash. There was a scuffling of feet as his
enemy retreated. It was a bad situation, a standoff in
which time was the enemy. There was no way Ten could
reach the waiting packet except straight ahead, and the
gunman was somewhere out there.

To Ten's right there was the river; to his left, a long,
seemingly endless brick wall of an old warehouse. He
suspected the other man didn't have adequate cover either. The man had probably been taken by surprise
when he'd suddenly left Roberts's office. Ten kept as far
away from the warehouse wall as he could, keeping to
the high weeds. He managed to get his satchel again,
and flung it ahead of him. It drew no response. He carried his gray Stetson in his left hand, lest it give him
away. He took a long, slender weed and used it to raise
the hat high enough to be seen. It drew a shot, and
again he fired at the muzzle flash. This time there was a
grunt of pain, and he fired again. Then there was only
silence. He crept forward, holding his breath. There was
an agonized groan, and Ten cocked his Colt.

"No . . . more. Don't shoot . . . no more. I'm . . .
finished."

"You're a damn fool, Sneed."

Ten waited for a long time. He didn't doubt the man
had been hit, but many a wounded man had played pos-
sum until the right moment, and then came out shooting. Ten put on his hat, and nothing happened. He got
to his feet and took a cautious step, only to have a slug
burn its way across his left side, just above his belt. He
drew his Colt and fired once. There was a grunt, and
then silence. He waited as long as he dared before taking another step, and when that movement drew no response, he moved ahead until he found Sneed's body.
Ten quickly reloaded his Colt from his shell belt. Then,
somewhere behind him, there were inquiring voices.
Somebody had heard the shots, and once they discov-

ered the dead man, the riverbank would be crawling with lawmen. He grabbed his satchel and his hat and began to run. He was already well past the steamboat landing, so the lesser docks couldn't be too much farther.

There was no moon, and he stumbled into the heavy wooden pilings of the first dock. But there was no waiting craft, and he ran on. Behind him there was more of a clamor than ever. Looking back, he could see the dim glow of a lantern. He reached the second dock, found it deserted, and kept going. He couldn't believe Harvey Roberts would have let him down. Jake Daimler's little packet had to be waiting at the third dock. But when he reached the third and last dock, there was nothing before him but the forbidding black water of the river, lapping softly against the pilings of the deserted dock. Behind him, coming ever closer, were many voices. There was no turning back. He ran on, knowing they had found Sneed's body, when there was a shot, and the excited babble of voices became more intense. And then he heard what he had been expecting. The ominous baying of hounds.

❦

25

*I*t wasn't the first time Harvey Roberts had heard gun-fire in the darkness along the river, but tonight it held a sinister meaning for him. He stepped out into the unlighted street, away from the building, until he was able to see the murky surface of the river in the star-light. Downriver, bobbing along like a firefly, was a light. There was a distant babble of voices, and finally a single gunshot. Roberts's eyes searched the river as far as he could see, knowing Jake Daimler's little packet had to be there. But he saw nothing. Hearing the clopping hoofs of an approaching horse, Harvey Roberts re-turned to his office building, climbed the steps, and waited just outside his door. The rider reined up, and in the light from his office window, Roberts recognized a policeman.

"That you, Mr. Roberts?" the officer inquired.

"It's me," said Roberts. "What was the shooting about?"

"Somebody done us a favor. Killed one of our local bad boys."

"What about the other man?" Roberts inquired cau-tiously. "Get him?"

"Naw, and I doubt we will. Took a couple of hounds down there, but they lost the scent at the water. Come daylight, we'll take another look, but I expect it'll be a waste of time."

With a sigh of relief, Roberts stepped into his office and closed the door. The river was deserted, so Daimler could hug the farthest bank and run without lights until New Orleans was far behind.

Ten continued along the river, unsure of any sanctuary, but knowing he must find one. He stopped to catch his breath, and for a moment he thought he saw something on the water. There it was again! The little packet, a dim hulk in the darkness, was running as near to the bank as it dared.

"Jake," Ten called cautiously, "Jake Daimler."

If it didn't happen to be Daimler's boat, he risked having the searchers hear his voice and send the dogs after him. Sound traveled far at night. Just when he had given up on a response, it came.

"Who be ye?" inquired a cautious voice. "Do I know ye?"

"No," replied Ten, equally cautious, "but you know Harvey Roberts."

"I haul some freight fer him," said the voice. "Where ye bound?"

"Natchez," said Ten.

"Ye'll have t' git wet some," said the voice. "I ain't comin' no closer t' th' bank. This ain't no time t' run aground."

Ten hung his pistol belt around his neck, held his satchel as high as he could, and waded in. When the big hawser was thrown to him, Ten slipped the loop over his head and under his arms. He was hoisted aboard, chilled and winded.

"Sorry," said Daimler. "I tied up at one of th' docks, like Harvey said, but he also said I was t' be almighty cautious. When guns started t' pop, I set us adrift an' floated downstream till things quieted some. We'll ease over along th' far bank an' run without lights fer a spell."

They were far from New Orleans when Daimler lighted his lanterns and hoisted his running lights.

* * *

While killings along the New Orleans waterfront didn't attract too much attention, Sneed's did. The man had been seen in the company of André LeBeau as a "bodyguard," and while nobody was quite sure why LeBeau needed a bodyguard, it was something that came to mind when Sneed ended up dead. LeBeau told the law nothing, except that he knew nothing. But he suspected plenty, and had it verified when a hack brought a message from Harvey Roberts. He cursed Sneed for a damn fool, and then himself for depending on the little gunman. Tenatse Chisholm had arrived, Sneed had pursued some fool plan of his own, and had been shot dead for his efforts. LeBeau's devious mind was in a turmoil when he entered Harvey Roberts's private office. Roberts glared at LeBeau like he was some hairy-legged varmint just out from under a rock, but LeBeau didn't notice. Roberts placed a single sheet of paper on the desk. It was a receipt for the gold, stating that André LeBeau had received, for services rendered, $25,000 from Tenatse Chisholm. Without a word LeBeau signed it, adding the day's date. Beneath his signature, Harvey Roberts signed as witness to the transaction, again adding the day's date. He took the paper, put it in his big iron safe, and removed the canvas bag in which he'd placed the gold. He hoisted the heavy bag to the desk. LeBeau took it, and without a word left the office. He went immediately to the bank where he had his account, often overdrawn. He left most of the gold in a rented safe deposit drawer, for which the bank had ungraciously demanded payment in advance.

Ten arrived in Natchez without incident, two days ahead of the next steamboat for Fort Smith. He avoided the several hotels, taking a room in an out-of-the-way boardinghouse. There was something Priscilla had asked him to do once he was safely away from New Orleans. From his satchel he took an oilskin pouch, and from it he removed an envelope. Unsealed, it was addressed to Prudence Edgerton, Priscilla's grandmother. Priscilla wanted him to read the letter, and he had promised to, before sealing and mailing it. He unfolded the single page. Despite her concern for Ten and her misgivings about his going to New Orleans, Priscilla had written a frank letter. Briefly, she told of her marriage, of the trail drive from Texas, and said she was happy. She mentioned LeBeau only to say that he had opposed the marriage and that she had deceived him only for that reason. In closing, she promised a future visit when Ten would accompany her. He was about to seal the envelope when he thought of something. It was a thing so ironic, it left him chuckling to himself. Where Le-Beau was concerned, it would be just the kind of knee in the groin Prudence Edgerton would appreciate. Ten took from his satchel a tablet and pencil and began to write. First he introduced himself and told her of his and Priscilla's plans. Then he repeated Priscilla's promise of a future visit, and closed with a suggestion. Since Priscilla was done with New Orleans, wouldn't it be appropriate for notice of her marriage to be sent to the newspapers there? Priscilla had given no details as to when and where the marriage had taken place, so Ten wrote down the information. Reading what he had written, he felt guilty. Not once had he mentioned Jesse Chisholm. He owed his successful cattle deal with the Lipan Apaches to their recognition of Chisholm, yet, as he had admitted to Priscilla, he resented being forever in the old plainsman's shadow.

"Ten," Priscilla had said in Chisholm's defense, "tell him you're proud of him."

Ten discarded what he had written. In the background on himself, he identified Chisholm as his father, giving him credit for his government service as scout and mediator with the plains Indians. He folded the page he had rewritten, along with the others, placed them with Priscilla's letter and sealed the envelope. Once news of Priscilla's marriage was made public, André LeBeau was going to be almighty glad he had taken his money and run out.

Ten hadn't underestimated Prudence Edgerton's hate for André LeBeau, and the information that letter contained would wreak more vengeance than the old woman had ever dreamed possible.

The police investigation of Sneed's death accomplished nothing except to stir up gossip involving Le-Beau. Somebody had remembered seeing him and Sneed in conversation in the St. Charles Hotel lobby less than a week prior to Sneed's death. While there was no proof, there was speculation that Sneed had undertaken some less-than-respectable mission for LeBeau, and had died when things went awry.

While LeBeau ignored the gossip and speculation, Emily didn't. A week after Sneed's death, she confronted LeBeau. Not with an argument, but with a trunk and three traveling cases.

"Where are you going?" LeBeau demanded.

"Home," said Emily. "For good."

"After twenty-one years you don't regard this as home?"

"No more," said Emily. "Your drinking, gambling, and carousing was bad enough. Now we're about to lose the house, the law is hounding not only us, but the neighbors, and I won't tolerate it another day. I'm leaving."

"Like hell you are!" snarled LeBeau. He moved like a striking rattler. She dodged, and his fist only grazed her head, but the force of the blow slammed her against the wall.

For a moment she leaned there, breathing hard, fumbling with the small handbag she still clung to. From it she extracted a pistol. It was a .41 caliber Remington double-barrel derringer. Her hands were steady as she cocked the lethal little weapon. She backed toward the door. Reaching it, she paused. LeBeau took a step toward her.

"Take one more step," she said, "and I'll kill you."

LeBeau didn't move. Hearing the commotion, the butler came to investigate the cause.

"Joseph," said Emily, "please take my trunk and bags to the front porch. When someone comes for them, see that all of them are taken."

The butler looked at Emily, at the gun, and finally at LeBeau. Then, without a word, he began removing the baggage. He took the trunk last. It was too heavy to carry, and he dragged it. Emily followed him out to the porch and, saying nothing, continued past him. LeBeau watched her walk away for as long as he could see her, a strange lump in his throat. He went to the dining room, and from a cabinet took a nearly full bottle of bourbon. He hooked his boot under the lower rung of a chair, dragged it out and sat down. He had neglected getting himself a glass, and drinking straight from the bottle, he contemplated his future.

He would lose the house, but what did it matter? Priscilla was gone, Emily was gone, Sneed was gone, and the neighbors, damn them, were looking down their noses at him. Well, he didn't need any of them. He had money, and he could leave too. But how long would $25,000 last? He needed a bigger stake, but how to get it? Then, in a moment of drunken inspiration, the answer came. He would double, maybe even triple his stake at the poker tables. Jason Brawn's wasn't the only game in town. There were other houses, likely more honest. He shoved the cork back into the bottle and returned it to the cupboard. When he judged himself sober enough, he left the house, went to the bank and took five thousand dollars in gold coin from his safe deposit drawer.

On its way to New Orleans, *The Saint Louis* made a fuel stop at Natchez, bringing the latest St. Louis newspapers. Ten bought one. He had time on his hands. He had another night in Natchez before there would be a steamboat from New Orleans to Fort Smith. He went carefully through the newspaper, and had no trouble finding an updated story on Joseph McCoy's efforts to build a cattle town at Abilene. McCoy had won the enthusiastic support of most Kansans, including that of the governor. There were some who still feared an outbreak of tick fever from the longhorns, but McCoy had an answer for that. He would guarantee payment for loss of any Kansas cattle infected by Texas longhorns. Tenatse Chisholm vowed to have his herd in Abilene first, if he had to arrive a month early and wait.

André LeBeau couldn't believe his unbroken streak of bad luck. He had lost ten thousand dollars in three days, none of it at Jason Brawn's tables. He couldn't afford such a loss, and promised himself that once he recovered it, he would take the $25,000 and go. He would visit the tables one more time. His luck simply had to change.

Ten reached Fort Smith on August 10, 1866, and rode out the following morning for the Chisholm trading post. He arrived in time for supper on the third day, and they rejoiced at his return. Priscilla laughed and cried by turns. He told them nothing of his fight with Sneed or of his narrow escape from New Orleans. Instead he got them excited over the success of Joseph McCoy's plan to make Abilene the first cattle town.

"We'll move out the herd on September ninth," said Ten. "We'll follow the Chisholm trail all the way to the Arkansas. From there it's seventy-five miles to Abilene."

"Then we're going to St. Louis," Lou said.

"Yes," said Ten, "but not from Abilene. First we'll return here with our riders and our horse remuda. Then we'll take a steamboat from Fort Smith to Natchez, and another from there to St. Louis."

"Whoa," said Jesse Chisholm. "What's wrong with going from Abilene to St. Louis? I've been meanin' to talk to you about that, and I reckon this is as good a time as any. Don't take it any farther until I get my maps."

He spread out his wrinkled map of Kansas, aligning it with that of Missouri. On both he had drawn laddered lines representing the completed portions of railroads. In blue ink he had drawn rough lines representing the rivers.

"Here's Abilene," said Chisholm, pointing to a tiny penciled dot, "and to the east of it, not more than a hundred fifty miles, is Kansas City. The Missouri River passes through Kansas City on its way to a confluence with the Mississippi, at St. Louis. Does that suggest anything to you?"

"It does," said Ten sheepishly. "A couple of things. First, I should have had a look at these maps before now. Second, when we get to Abilene, we're maybe three hundred miles from St. Louis, and from Kansas City we can make the rest of the trip by steamboat."

"Exactly," said Chisholm, a twinkle in his eyes. "Once you've sold the herd, it's no more than a three-day ride to Kansas City. Take Two Hats and his riders with you, because they'll be needin' grub to last them back to here. They'll bring your mounts, your horse remuda, and the pack mules with them, and you're free to take a steamboat on to St. Louis. Any questions?"

"No, sir," said Ten. "I was just thinkin' that before we head for Texas again, maybe you could figure out the best way there and back. You ought to be leadin' these trail drives instead of me."

The others laughed, but Chisholm only smiled. It was done humorously, but it was a concession. Tenatse Chisholm seemed more the son and less the hostile stranger Chisholm had met in St. Louis just a few months before.

"Now," said Chisholm, "I reckon you're planning another trip to Texas, when you return from St. Louis?"

"Yes, sir," said Ten. "Abilene ought to be wide open by then. I'd like to bring another drive or two up the Chisholm Trail before it gets crowded. Sooner or later those Texans will manage some drives of their own. More herds on the trail means lower prices, and less graze along the way. I aim for us to be in Texas the week after Christmas. Will I still have an Injun outfit?"

"You'll have them," said Chisholm. "They came back from Texas loaded like a Gypsy caravan. While you were gone to New Orleans, all they've done is sell or trade horses, saddles, and guns. I reckon you've spoiled them for any decent work."

"He's right," said Marty. "I ain't sure if that bunch of Injuns is goin' back to Texas to drive longhorns or to look for well-heeled outlaws."

André LeBeau was desperate. His stake had dwindled to five thousand dollars. He must win, and win big. If he lost again, he'd be broke. The bank had already served notice. He had ten days to vacate the house. He could take only his clothes. Even the furniture was to be sold at auction. There was a gambling house on Toulouse, in the Vieux Carré, where he wasn't well-known. He would take what money he had and go there. It was a long shot, but only the long shots paid. His was a do or die situation, and he didn't see how things could possibly get any worse. But they could and would. He didn't know the New Orleans papers had received word of Priscilla's marriage, and that the story would appear on the front page of the newspaper to be delivered that very afternoon.

The first of the month, Chisholm always sent a rider to Fort Smith for the mail and the newspapers. On September 7, two days before Ten and the outfit would depart for Abilene, the rider returned with the mail and the last three weekly editions of a New Orleans newspaper. The latest was dated August 31, and on the front page was news of Priscilla's marriage. Not only had they printed every last word, but in newspaper fashion, had printed related stories about the LeBeaus. The latest and most shocking, of course, was a rehashing of

Sneed's death and the possible implication of LeBeau. Using information from the story of Sneed's death, Priscilla made the connection.

"I just knew he'd send a killer after you," said Priscilla. "He did, didn't he?"

"No," said Ten, "he didn't. I left New Orleans without him knowing I'd been there, until Harvey Roberts sent him a message."

"But the newspaper says the law tracked Sneed's killer with dogs, and that they lost the trail at the river. They're saying whoever did the killing probably escaped by boat."

"Almighty smart of them," said Ten, "since the trail ended at the water. There's lots of boats on the river."

She said no more, but she knew.

André LeBeau was jubilant, convinced that his luck had finally changed. He now had $7500, and while it was a far cry from what he needed, it was a start. It was close to three A.M. when he left the gambling house on Toulouse. He walked along the river to Bienville, three blocks west, where he knew of a cheap rooming house. There he took a room. He would sleep most of the day, which was Saturday, and return to the gambling house sometime in the afternoon. The truth was, the empty house on St. Charles was getting to him. Priscilla was gone, Emily was gone, and Sunday would be Joseph the butler's last day. While all these realities clamored for his attention, LeBeau forced them from his mind, trying to prolong the excitement of his win. Finally he slept.

Jason Brawn was a vindictive man, but he had found it a waste of time to get mad. He got even. He was the kind who carried a grudge, allowing a sore to fester until there was no healing unless it had been lanced. Brawn had his suspicions about Sneed's death, believing it had resulted from the failure of some misguided scheme of LeBeau's, but having no proof. Now, as he read the newspaper account of Priscilla LeBeau's marriage, he made a decision. He allowed himself a grim smile at the irony of it. Tomorrow, the second of September, would be a year to the day since John Mathewson had been ambushed.

Priscilla had carefully clipped from the newspaper the story of their marriage so that she could save it. Ten had admitted adding a letter of his own to hers, and she was touched, finding that he had given not only his own background, but that of Jesse Chisholm. She had noted pride in Chisholm's eyes when he had read the story. All the rivalry and animosity between father and son had been Ten's doing. Now he had laid it to rest.

~~~<><~~~

$\mathcal{J}$ust after three o'clock Saturday afternoon, André LeBeau returned to the gambling house on Toulouse. He felt a certain camaraderie for even the house gamblers. They bought him drinks, laughed at most everything he said, and allowed him to win a few small pots. From there they encouraged him to raise his bets, and when he did, he lost. The more he lost, the more he bet, until there was no more. Five hours after his arrival, jubilant and hopeful, LeBeau was broke. The patrons and house gamblers no longer laughed with him, but at him. He begged for a loan of two hundred, one hundred, and finally, fifty dollars. But they knew him, knew his kind, and laughed all the more. Finally, when the drinks got to him and he was reduced to self-pitying sobs, they turned away in disgust. Then he became angry and belligerent, accusing the house of cheating, and was hustled to the door and thrown out. He lay there until he was able to struggle painfully, wearily, to his feet, and then limped away into the darkness.

September 9, 1866, Ten and the outfit moved the herd out at first light, heading them north. Rested and fat, the longhorns needed little urging. Charlie Two Hats and his riders were in high good humor. Two Hats led at point, while Ten ranged far ahead, scouting for graze and water. It had been an unusually dry year, and dust hung like smoke in the September sky. Chris, Lou, and Priscilla were riding drag.

"This bandanna over my mouth and nose is better than nothing," complained Priscilla, "but it's not enough. There's dust in my eyes, in my hair, in my ears, in my boots, and places I can't even talk about."

Her companions laughed delightedly.

"Just pray for a river that's deep enough and brushy enough that you can strip and jump in," said Lou.

"Wait'll we get to St. Louis," said Chris. "In one of the St. Louis papers Ten brought back, there was a piece about a hotel with bathtubs big enough for two people at the same time."

"Don't look at me," said Lou. "I can't think of any good reason for gettin' in a bathtub with you."

"I wasn't thinking of invitin' you," said Chris. "All you could do is scrub my back."

"That's all anybody could do in a tub of water," said Priscilla. "What I'd like to see is this two-story hotel in Virginia City, Montana, that's got a two-story outhouse. People on the second floor can go to the outhouse without going downstairs."

"If we ever go there," said Lou, "whichever floor I'm on, I'll still go to the upstairs outhouse. There's some things I won't put up with when there's somebody sittin' right over me."

André LeBeau walked along the river until he came to the trio of docks near where Sneed had died. LeBeau stood on the rough planks of the first dock, staring into the dark water of the river. Finally he backed away, shuddering. He knew what he ought to do, but he lacked the courage. But he had failed at everything else, he thought bitterly. Why not this as well? His hands, knees, and elbows were a mass of bruises, and he bled from numerous cuts, a result of having been thrown into the graveled yard of the gambling house. He put his hand in his pocket and brought out a single gold eagle, all the money he had in the world. He considered buying a bottle, but changed his mind. He would need food. Besides, there was most of a bottle of bourbon at the house. Anyway, he had to sleep somewhere, and with that and the bottle in mind, he started back to the house on St. Charles.

It was a long walk, and he was less than halfway there when he first heard the footsteps. Fearfully, he looked over his shoulder, but there were low-hanging magnolias and live oaks on both sides of the street, and he saw nothing. But the footsteps came on, relentlessly, maddeningly persistent. LeBeau stopped and turned, trembling, and did a very foolish thing.

"Stop following me!" he shouted. "I have no money."

But robbery wasn't what his pursuer had in mind. From across the street there was a roar and a muzzle flash, and the slug tore a burning gash along LeBeau's left side. With a cry, he stumbled back into some tall weeds and fell. He lay there panting and sweating, having the good sense not to move. He eased his right hand to his left side and felt the blood. He had been shot! He listened for some sound, for the footsteps, but heard nothing. He lay there for what seemed hours. Finally he got to his skinned and bleeding knees, and then to his feet. He must get to the house, see to his hurts, and find that bottle. When he came within sight of the house, there was a lamp burning in one of the parlors and another in the dining room. Ignoring his cuts, bruises, and the bleeding path of the slug, LeBeau went straight to the cabinet for the bottle. Everything else could wait. Kicking back a chair, he slumped into it, pulling the cork from the bottle with his teeth. But that was as far as he got. The newspaper lay on the table before him, with most of the front page devoted to Priscilla's marriage. Vividly, LeBeau recalled the haunting footsteps, the roar of the gun, the nearness of death, and he understood. He had drawn his last hand this night, in more ways than one, and his cards didn't measure up. He was startled when Joseph came in. He had forgotten the butler was still there. This would be his last day, when he left at ten.

"Will you be wanting anything, sir?" the butler inquired.

"Yes," said LeBeau, "I want you to mail a letter for me tomorrow, but I don't have it ready. What time is it?"

"Almost nine, sir."

"I'll have it ready before ten," said LeBeau, "and then you may leave."

When Joseph had left the room, LeBeau corked the bourbon, got up and went into his study. From a rolltop desk he took a pencil, a tablet, and an envelope. Forgetting his hurts, he returned to the dining room, sat down and began to write.

In the early afternoon of their second day on the trail, Ten and the outfit took the herd across the North Canadian River.

"Good crossing," said Marty. "I just hope we do as well crossin' the Cimarron and the Arkansas."

"No reason why we shouldn't," said Ten, "unless there's a gulley washer somewhere west of here. I can't imagine having trouble at a crossing, with the water this low."

Only one problem had begun to emerge. Of their three pack mules, one of them was a big white brute called Diablo. He belonged to Charlie Two Hats, and while Charlie swore by him, everybody else swore at him. Diablo had a fondness for biting people, sinking his big yellow teeth into them when they least expected it, and usually in a place that made riding difficult. Diablo also balked occasionally, usually at the worst possible time and place, for little reason or no reason at all.

"Ten," said Priscilla, "with all the pack mules we had to choose from, why did we have to bring *him*? That mule hates me."

Gathered around the supper fire, they all laughed.

The white mule had already nipped Priscilla, and she kept a wary eye on him.

"He belongs to Charlie," said Ten. "Jump on him."

"Him big," said Two Hats. "Work lak hell."

"Bite lak hell too," said Priscilla. "I've still got his teeth marks on my behind."

"It's all still there," said Chris. They laughed again, especially Charlie Two Hats.

"Yes," snapped Priscilla, glaring at Two Hats, "and it's all still sore."

"Just don't turn your back on him," said Ten. "We can avoid his teeth; it's his balking that could mean trouble."

The fiery path the slug had burned across LeBeau's ribs still hurt, but it wasn't that serious. He hadn't even bothered seeing to it, for soon it wouldn't matter. He folded the lengthy letter, a dozen pages written on both sides, and sealed it in the envelope. On the face of it, he wrote: *United States Customs Office, Washington, D. C.*

He found Joseph seated in the front parlor, waiting. He handed the old butler the letter, along with his last ten dollars.

"Whatever you do," said LeBeau, "don't forget to mail this. When you've paid the postage, the money that's left is yours."

"Thank you," said Joseph. Almost reluctantly he started down the hall, as though he hated to go.

"Joseph?"

The old man stopped, turned, waited.

"When you go out," said LeBeau, "fix the door so it will lock behind you."

Joseph knew what the neighbors were saying, and he knew the circumstances under which Emily had left. He had read the newspaper account of Priscilla's marriage, and while he didn't know why or when, he suspected the final chapter in LeBeau's life was about to be written. He paused at the front door and looked back. LeBeau still stood at the end of the hall.

"Good-bye, sir," said Joseph, "and good luck."

His mind strong on other things, the old man closed the door without remembering to set the lock.

Once more LeBeau went to the desk in the study. This time, from a bottom drawer, he took a revolver. It was a Remington .30 caliber, holding five shells, and it was fully loaded. He returned to the dining room, took the bottle of bourbon and went on to the front parlor. While he couldn't see directly down the hall, he could hear. They'd have to break in to get at him. He uncorked the bottle, took a long pull from it, then another. Vaguely, he remembered his hurts, but they no longer seemed to matter. He slept, awakening when the effects of the whiskey had worn off. The lamp had guttered out and the room was dark. The big grandfather clock struck three. Then, far down the darkened hall, came a sound that chilled him to the marrow of his bones. It was the slow, even cadence of footsteps.

When they reached the Cimarron, the water ran deeper and swifter than they'd expected. It was also muddy, proof of rain somewhere to the west.

"Been a while since anybody used this crossing," said Ten. "Jess says these riverbeds shift and what was safe last week might be quicksand today. I reckon we'd better test for it."

"How do you test for quicksand?" Priscilla asked.

"You ride in," said Marty, "and if it swallows you and your hoss, you know it's quicksand."

"Oh, stop teasing me!" cried Priscilla.

"That's mostly right," said Lou, "only it won't suck you under all that fast. A good cow horse knows quicksand, and he'll back out. Cows ain't that smart."

The crossing proved free of quicksand, and with two hours of daylight left, Ten gave the order to go ahead.

"If there's rain west of us, holdin' off till tomorrow won't help. Let's be done with it. Push 'em hard, keep 'em bunched, so's they got nowhere to go but the north bank!"

Cherokee riders Cactus and Latigo led two of the pack mules, while the unpredictable Diablo was led by Charlie Two Hats himself. The first two mules crossed without difficulty, but Diablo clearly didn't wish to cross the river. Two Hats was practically dragging the big mule, with the lead steers almost on his tail. Ten fought his way ahead of the herd. With his doubled lariat, he laid a stinging blow across Diablo's flank. It was a tactic that had worked since time began, but a blow that would have sent a normal mule surging to the opposite bank had exactly the reverse effect on Diablo. He reared, his sudden, violent action causing Two Hats's horse to stumble. Something went wrong, perhaps a bad dally around Two Hats's saddle horn, and Diablo's lead rope slipped loose. The big mule took that as an invitation to return the way he had come. He whirled and, undaunted by the oncoming herd, sunk his big teeth into the tender nose of one of the lead steers.

The steer let loose a bellow of pain and fury that spooked the other leaders. With the drag riders bunching the herd, there was no retreat for the leaders. They could go upriver, downriver, or straight ahead, but that crazy mule was out there ahead of them. Two Hats and Tejano had quickly dropped their loops over the head of the ornery Diablo, and he was being dragged to the farthest bank, where he should have gone in the first place. But it was too late to head the spooked lead steers. As one, they turned downriver. Marty, Wes, Buscadero, and Jingle Bob were on the downriver flank and rode for their lives, getting out of the way of the charging herd. The water, deep from the recent rain, was all that saved them. In places it was over the heads of the lead steers, and it slowed the stampede.

"Come on," shouted Ten, "we can get ahead of them!"

He galloped his horse along the north bank, some of the Cherokee riders right behind him. Marty, Wes, Jingle Bob, and Buscadero had gotten ahead of the herd and climbed out on the south bank. They galloped their horses downriver, following Ten's lead, and got ahead of the swimming longhorns.

"Ride into the river ahead of them," shouted Ten. "We'll rope the leaders and head them to the north bank."

He entered the water from the north bank, the other riders following. Marty, Wes, Buscadero, and Jingle Bob rode in from the south bank, and they had a solid line of riders across the river. Ten roped a lead steer, kneed his horse toward the north bank, and his cow-wise bronc did the rest. Other riders had followed Ten's lead, and when they had dragged half a dozen lead steers out on the north bank, the rest of the herd had calmed enough to follow. The drag riders had kept the steers bunched, and when it was all over, they had lost only a dozen steers, gored or drowned. Not a rider had been hurt.

The last cow emerged almost a mile downriver from where they had begun the crossing.

"Settle 'em down to graze," shouted Ten, "and we'll call it a day."

They were still an hour or more away from sundown, but they were wet, muddy, and exhausted. They needed hot coffee, a chance to dry out, and good food. Charlie Two Hats had removed the pack saddle from Diablo. The brute had a horn slash the length of his belly. Two Hats had some sulfur salve, and when he'd washed the bloody gash, began applying the medication. He was working from front to back, and with Two Hats on his knees and his back turned, Diablo showed his appreciation. He snaked his head around and sunk his big teeth into Charlie's backside.

When the mule let go, he looked at Charlie with such innocent eyes, everybody laughed, even Priscilla. Charlie Two Hats said nothing. He went to his horse, took his rifle from the boot, and headed for Diablo.

"No, Charlie," Marty shouted, "him big, work lak hell."

"Him *malo bastardo mulo*," growled Two Hats. "Kill him dead lak hell."

"No, Charlie," said Ten. "Leave him be. But when this drive's done and we get him back to the Canadian, let's leave him there. We got off easy this time, losin' a few steers and nobody hurt. No matter how big he is, how much a load he can handle, it's not worth gettin' one of us hurt or killed."

The truth of his words sobered them, but it didn't lessen their merriment at Two Hats's expense.

Priscilla laughed. "It's been worth it all, just to see that blessed mule take a bite out of Two Hats. I'd put up with the dust, the stampedes, the Comanches, the outlaws, all of it again, just to see Charlie get bit."

With trembling hands, LeBeau fumbled around in the dark, seeking the pistol. He found it, but knocked over the empty bourbon bottle. It fell, rolled across the floor, and bumped into the wall. LeBeau held his breath, and for a moment he heard nothing. Then it started again, the slow, rhythmic cadence down the hall. LeBeau weighed his options. They were few. While he was no gunman, suppose, on this last hand, his luck changed? If he shot his way out, what had he gained? What lay ahead? There was the letter he had written, soon to be mailed. Emily was gone, Priscilla was gone, he was broke, and the house was being taken from him.

He listened, but there was only silence. They were playing with him, like a cat with a doomed mouse. Then, seemingly louder, closer, there was a sound in the hall. LeBeau put the muzzle of the pistol to his temple, and it was cold against his sweating flesh. Did he have the guts to do it? He had no choice. The game was over, and it was time to fold. He pulled the trigger, and knew no more.

Following the roar of the pistol, there was a moment of silence. Then the maddening sound started again, like slow footsteps in the hall. There was a storm blowing in from the west. The rising wind rattled the leaves of the old magnolia tree against the balcony where Ten and Priscilla had parted just a few months before.

Downstairs, the front door stood open, old Joseph having forgotten to lock it. The night wind pushed the door to and fro, and on each backward swing, the brass knob bumped against the wall. When the wind paused, so did the door, but with each new gust of wind, the door again moved. The brass knob continued bumping the wall, a slow, rhythmic thump that sounded almighty like ghostly footsteps in the deserted hall. . . .

∿

27

*T*en continued scouting far ahead, finding an occasional blaze on a tree trunk that assured him they
were following the original Chisholm Trail. On a good
day, they made fifteen miles. He wasn't afraid to "short"
a day's drive, sacrificing distance for good graze and
water at hand. Chisholm's trail led due north. They were
roughly halfway between the Cimarron and the Arkansas when they came upon the trail of six horsemen riding east.

"Tracks maybe three days old," said Ten. "Shod
horses, so that rules out Indians."

"Mebbe outlaw," said Two Hats enthusiastically.
"Ride lak hell, go see."

"No," said Ten. "We don't know that they're outlaws,
and even if they are, they've given us no cause to go
after them. This is a trail drive, and our business is in
Abilene."

"We outnumber them three to one," said Wes. "Their
only chance would be to ambush us, and if they aimed
to do that, they wouldn't have left a trail for us to
cross."

"That's sound thinkin'," said Marty.

"I'd have to agree," said Ten. "We'll be watchful, but
I don't look for any trouble from this bunch. We're not
that far from the ranch on the Arkansas, and Jess keeps

twenty to thirty Injun riders there. This wouldn't be a healthy place for renegades and owlhoots to hang out."

"Since the Chisholm Trail leads right to the ranch," Priscilla asked, "are we going to stop there?"

"For a day or two," said Ten. "I think we'll leave Diablo there, and get him on the way back. We can get the loan of a less temperamental mule if we need a third one. That suit you, Charlie?"

Charlie Two Hats nodded. There were grins and chuckles from the other riders, as they recalled Two Hats being bitten by his own mule. He would be a while living that down.

September 25, 1866, they reached the Chisholm ranch on the Arkansas. Although Ten hadn't been there since he was eleven, some of the riders still remembered him. The little Cherokee in charge was named Bandywood, and was called "Bandy" for short. Bandy waved a greeting at Ten and then rode out to meet Charlie Two Hats. Charlie had lived and worked at the ranch until the summer of 1865, when he'd been one of the riders accompanying Chisholm and the tribe of Wichita Indians traveling south into Indian Territory. It would be a good time, Ten thought, for Two Hats to dispose of Diablo. The rest of the Cherokee riders were busy stringing the longhorns out along the Arkansas. As impressive as Chisholm's trading post was, the ranch was even more so. There were horses, mules, hogs, chickens, and a small herd of milk cows.

"I didn't know Indians milked cows," said Priscilla.

"The men don't," said Ten. "That's squaw work."

"That's disgraceful," said Priscilla.

"What, milking cows?"

"No," said Priscilla, "setting aside all the things men don't want to do and calling them 'squaw work.' I've never seen a cowboy milk a cow either."

"You won't," said Ten. "That's why we all drink our coffee black. When we get us a ranch, we'll skip the milk cows. You can scrape buffalo hides instead."

Everybody laughed at that; even the Indian riders.

"With a ranch like this," said Wes, "just seventy-five miles from the railroad, a man could run a million head of cows. How can your pa sit down yonder on the Canadian, in a tradin' post, with all this goin' to waste?"

"Back in 'thirty-six," said Ten, "somebody hired Jess to lead a party lookin' for gold. They didn't find the gold, but Jess liked the country, so he built his tradin' post there. I always reckoned Kansas was gettin' a mite too crowded for him, and maybe too tame. Besides, he didn't fancy himself a rancher, a cattleman. He's a trader, and he trades with the Indians. Bein' a government scout, he could see the time comin' when the tribes would be assigned lands in Indian Territory, and moved south, like the Wichitas were moved just last summer. For a man that trades with the Indians, I reckon Jess is where he wants and needs to be."

"If he likes it on the Canadian," said Priscilla, "and we're going to have a ranch, why don't we buy this one?"

"Because the railroad's coming," said Ten, "and it'll bring the farmers. They'll plow up the grass, fence the land, and the days of free range will be gone."

"I don't see how'n hell they're goin' to build that much fence," said Marty. "There ain't enough trees in Kansas for all the dogs to have one."

"They'll find a way," said Ten. "The Indians are bein' moved south, to assigned lands, lands nobody else wants. Yet. I believe there'll come a time when the tribes will have to fight for that land. Someday that land, Indian Territory, will be a state. Then the settlers, the sodbusters, and the politicians will decide it's too good for a bunch of Injuns."

"If that happens," said Marty, "where do you aim to settle?"

"West," said Ten. "Somewhere on the high plains, where there's room to grow. Where I can ride all day through the tall grass without seein' anybody's cows but mine."

None of them had thought beyond the next trail drive, and they listened to his words in some awe. Priscilla was the first to speak.

"Lord, you make it sound like an adventure, a quest. When are we going?"

"I'm thinking the spring of 'sixty-eight," said Ten. "I figure we can bring maybe two more drives up the Chisholm Trail before it gets crowded and prices began to fall. That last herd, then, will be a mix, some of it breeding stock. That's when I aim to move west."

"It's a dream," said Chris. "Is it just yours, or can we go with you?"

"You're welcome to come along," said Ten. "I don't aim to fight the outlaws, hostile Injuns, and catamounts by myself."

Toward late September, they left the Chisholm ranch on the Arkansas, pointing the longhorns north, toward Abilene. The troublesome Diablo had been left at the ranch, and a gray mule of gentler disposition had taken his place. Barring any unforeseen trouble, such as stampedes, they were five days from trail's end. But there was no trouble and there was no sign of the riders whose trail they'd crossed, south of the Arkansas. It was near sundown a few days later when they came within sight of the cluster of mud huts that was the "city" of Abilene.

"My God," said Marty, "a bunch of digger Injuns could have built a better-lookin' town. The whole damn place hung together without hammer or saw."

"None needed," said Ten, "for what they had to work with. But see the wagons beyond the huts? Joe McCoy has bought lumber and is havin' it hauled in from God knows where. Let's move the herd around the town and north a ways, until we find water and grass. We'll likely be here awhile."

They crossed a small river that ran just south of the town, and moved the herd west, and then north. They bedded down the herd on a stream they later learned was Mud Creek. Leaving Charlie Two Hats and his riders with the longhorns, Ten took Priscilla, Marty, Wes, Chris, and Lou with him. They rode back to the squalid collection of buildings that represented the town of Abilene. The crooked river they had crossed just south of town, they later learned, was the Smokey Hill, and the wagon track that followed the river to the southwest was a military road, bound for a distant intersection with the Santa Fe Trail. What concerned them was not the town itself, however, but what was taking place northeast of it. There were three wagons, their canvas a silver-gray in the October sun. An enormous tent was being erected, and half a dozen men with mallets were hammering stakes into the ground. Ten and his companions reined up, watching. One of the men, who looked like he might be in charge, turned to them, a question in his eyes.

"I'm Tenatse Chisholm," said Ten, "and this is part of my outfit. We got nine thousand Texas longhorns up the creek a ways. Is McCoy here?"

"McCoy's away on business. I'm Harlan Venters, and I'm in charge of all building that's to be done. We saw your dust as you come in. You're way too early. We ain't even got our tent up. The railroad's still three months away, and we're maybe two months away from havin' any accommodations ready, includin' cattle pens. Lumber, tools, ever' damn thing, has to be shipped by rail to end-of-track and wagoned in from there."

"We aim to be first," said Ten. "When do you look for McCoy to return?"

"About a week. There'll be more materials from end-of-track, and he'll ride one of the wagons."

They rode back through Abilene, and crude as the place appeared, they found it had a barbershop and bathhouse, a blacksmith shop, a store, a one-story "hotel," and a post office. The rest of the nondescript huts were dwellings in which a few settlers lived. They followed the Smokey Hill River to its confluence with Mud Creek, and turned north. While the area wasn't devoid of timber, it was concentrated mostly in the bottomland, along the streams. There was hackberry, elm, ash, burr oak, and walnut, but much more numerous were the prolific cottonwoods, their pale leaves whispering in the never-ending prairie wind. They discovered Mud Creek was aptly named, and three days later, moved the long-horns east of Abilene, to a clear-running stream called Chapman Creek.

"This is goin' to be an almighty long wait," said Marty. "Instead of us bein' in Texas the week after Christmas, we'll be settin' right here."

"Maybe not," said Ten. "McCoy and his two brothers are in the livestock business. They have connections in Chicago and New York. Suppose we sell them our herd, let them hold it here, and ship it east when the railroad gets here?"

"Suits me," said Wes, "if they don't beat our ears down on the price."

"They're sayin' the first herds may bring thirty dollars a head," said Ten. "If we sell for just twenty, we'll ride out of here with $187,000."

"All of that won't be ours," said Marty.

"No," said Ten, "fifty thousand of it will belong to Jess. But you and Wes, along with Chris and Lou, will have twenty thousand dollars among you. If we can get back to Texas before the price goes up, that'll buy you another five thousand head. Resell at twenty, and you'll come out of the next drive with a good hundred thousand dollars. You can stock some kind of ranch with that."

"Lord in heaven," said Lou, "just our part seems like a fortune. But you, you're a rich man, without ever making another trail drive."

"No," said Ten, "because I'm takin' the advice Jess gave me, and buying land. Remember what I said about farmers and fences? Jess told me that, and he says the high country will be safe for a while, but not forever. Legally, I can homestead a hundred sixty acres, a quar-ter section. So can Priscilla, but how many cows can you graze on three hundred twenty acres? Jess says a man can build an empire on the high plains, and when you buy and pay for the land, nobody can take it from you."

"Me and Wes ain't got the money to buy that kind of range," said Marty. "Not now, we ain't."

"You will after another trail drive," said Ten.

"You can share our range," said Priscilla. "If I'm going to be in the middle of millions of acres, with grass up to my chin, I want neighbors in there with me."

The seven days they waited for Joseph McCoy's return seemed like forever. When they finally saw the dust cloud to the east. Ten had to look twice to believe his eyes. When the whackers had drawn their teams to a halt, a lone passenger stepped down from the first wagon. Ten waited, allowing McCoy to converse with Harlan Venters. Venters said something to McCoy and nodded in Ten's direction. Ten dismounted and waited for McCoy to approach. He was much younger than Ten had expected, no more than thirty, if that. He was slender, wore range clothes under a short topcoat, had a black slouch hat on his head and heavy miner's boots on his feet. He had brown eyes, dark hair, and a goatee that partially concealed his receding chin. His grin and the enthusiastic sparkle in his eyes brought life to an otherwise bland face.

"I'm Joe McCoy," he said, putting out his hand. Ten took it.

Marty, Wes, Priscilla, Chris, and Lou were still mounted, and McCoy's eyes went to them. Ten introduced them.

"I'm sorry none of the facilities are ready," said McCoy. "As Venters told you, it will be a while. I'll have buyers coming, but not until there's a train. Nobody expected a herd so soon. How many do you have?"

"Ninety-three hundred," said Ten, "six thousand of them steers."

McCoy whistled long and low.

"We're not of a mind to wait for the railroad," said

Ten. "What kind of offer can you make me for this herd right now?"

McCoy was caught totally off guard. He swallowed a time or two, wiped his brow with the back of his hand and cleared his throat before he spoke.

"I really don't have the funds. I've bought land here, I'm having to haul materials from end-of-track—"

"You also have brothers in Chicago and New York," said Ten, "and all of you are in the livestock business. Successfully."

McCoy laughed, his eyes twinkling. "You're a bold young man, Chisholm. The truth is, I'd like to take you up on your offer, but I have no means of caring for a herd of this size until the railroad gets here. I'm sure you have adequate help, but I do not. My men aren't cowboys; they're here to build these facilities which we need right now but don't have. Besides, we're talking about a great deal of money, I'm sure, and all I have are travel funds and checks already consigned to specific debts."

"How far are we from end-of-track?"

"Between ninety and a hundred miles," said McCoy. "Why?"

"Make me a decent offer," said Ten, "and we'll trail this herd to end-of-track for you."

"That's generous of you," said McCoy, "but there's still the problem of money. I'd need time to raise it."

"There'll be a telegraph key at end-of-track," said Ten. "Telegraph your brothers and have them raise it. They can send it to you by train. I expect it'll take some time, but not as long as it'll take for the rails to reach here."

This time McCoy didn't laugh. He was thinking, tugging his goatee. "Suppose I was interested, contingent on your delivering the herd to end-of-track? How much?"

"Twenty-six."

"My God, no!"

"You know what prices are in Chicago and Kansas

City," said Ten, "and I don't. You know what you can sell for, what your freight costs are. Make me an offer."

"Sixteen," said McCoy.

"I can sell them to the military outposts for that," said Ten. "Twenty-five, delivered."

"Seventeen."

"Twenty-four," Ten countered.

"Eighteen."

"Twenty-three fifty," said Ten.

"Oh, confound it," said McCoy, "this is absurd. Twenty is my limit."

"Twenty-one," said Ten.

"Split the difference? Twenty dollars and fifty cents?"

"Sold," said Ten. "When can we start the drive?"

"Tomorrow," said McCoy. "These teamsters have to unload, and I owe them a night's rest before they start back. I must warn you, it may take several days to get the money. Will my check be acceptable, once it's covered?"

"No," said Ten, "we're goin' to Texas for another herd, and Texans won't take anything less than gold."

"Gold it is, then," said McCoy, "and I trust delivery includes loading into railroad cars?"

"It does," said Ten. "How long will it take the railroad to get the cars to end-of-track?"

"I really don't know," said McCoy. "We haven't gotten into that. I've just now gotten them to agree to a freight charge I can live with. I'll do all I can to get the cars quickly."

McCoy returned to his crew and began conferring with Venters. Ten mounted, kicked his horse into a lope, and the others followed.

"That was a good dicker," said Marty. "That extra fifty cents a head will cover us takin' the herd an extra hundred miles."

"We still don't know what he'll sell them for in Chicago," said Lou.

"Twenty-five or better," said Ten. "He was cold at

twenty-six, but when we dropped below twenty-four, he started to sweat. He'll make enough off of this herd that those brothers of his will kiss his feet. If they don't, they ought to. We may be a week gettin' to end-of-track, and have to wait when we get there, but it won't be like waitin' for the railroad to reach Abilene. We'll have St. Louis behind us, and be back on the Canadian by the middle of November."

28

October 4, 1866, they moved the herd out behind the three big freight wagons, heading east. The longhorns were trailwise, and easily kept up to the wagons. Rather than riding one of the wagons, Joe McCoy took a horse, riding with the herd. He seemed to be studying the longhorns he'd bought. Ten thought of something he should have considered sooner. Just as he was about to say what was on his mind, McCoy spoke to him.

"Longhorns is the proper name for them. I've never seen such horns. Are they all like this?"

"Mostly," said Ten, "and that reminds me of somethin' I should have asked before now. How many of the critters will a railroad car take?"

"With their horn spans," said McCoy, "I'd say thirty-five. Forty at the most."

"Even if we pack forty of 'em in there, we'll need twenty-five railroad cars to move a thousand head. How long is it goin' to take to get enough railroad cars to take them all?"

"Like I told you," said McCoy, "that's something I have yet to discuss with the railroad. I've suggested they make available two hundred specially-equipped, slat-sided cars for hauling cattle. I doubt they've taken my advice, at least not so soon. They're still several months away from Abilene, and they don't know if there'll be cattle waiting for them or not."

"I know I promised we'd load the cattle for you," said Ten, "but I purely don't aim to hang around end-of-track until the railroad builds the cattle cars. What are you goin' to do with all these cows?"

"I'll telegraph the Kansas City stockyards. Perhaps we can take them there, and the railroad can freight them out as the cattle cars become available."

"Kansas City! We only agreed to drive them to end-of-track."

"I know," said McCoy, "but when you reach end-of-track, you'll be less than fifty miles west of Kansas City. If the stockyards can handle them, you can just drive them there. Unless, of course, you'd rather wait at end-of-track for the railroad to supply cattle cars."

"Telegraph Kansas City," said Ten, "and if the stockyards can take them, then we'll drive them there."

"Even if the cattle pens are available, it's going to cost me for the use of them. Are you fair enough to make an adjustment in our agreed-upon price to defray some of the cost?"

"Maybe," said Ten, "if it's within reason."

"I figure it'll cost me at least a dollar a head," said McCoy. "Can we split that?"

"I reckon," sighed Ten. "Your price drops to twenty dollars a head. Just don't hand me any more surprises."

"We got nothin' to complain about," said Marty, "since we're goin' to Kansas City anyhow. It's better'n sittin' here on the prairie waitin' for railroad cars. This McCoy's run a sandy on us. Why, I'd bet a hoss and saddle this railroad ain't got enough freight cars to load this big a herd."

"You'd take the pot," said Ten. "I had a good deal goin', but I didn't finish it. This waltzin' around with cattle cars and payin' for the use of the stockyards should have been figured into the price. He took me, and I let him."

"So what?" said Chris. "We were counting on twenty dollars a head, and that's what we're getting. It's worth fifty cents a head not to be stuck here on the prairie, waiting to load cows onto railroad cars that may not have been built."

"That's right," said Wes. "We got here before anybody was ready for us, even the railroad, so we're havin' to pay for the extra arrangements. When we bring another herd, Abilene will have a railroad."

"Then let's get these brutes delivered," said Marty, "collect our money, and rattle our hocks back to Indian Territory. Let's buy another herd before the price goes up."

"Whoa, mule," said Lou. "Don't forget our trip to St. Louis."

"First we talked about New Orleans," said Wes, "and then we talked about St. Louis. All of us was goin' there, I reckon, to stand before a preacher. Well, we've done that. Why do we have to go anywhere, except back to Texas?"

"Because we want to spend this Christmas at the Chisholm trading post," said Lou, "and we want a few days in St. Louis to buy some things."

"It was my idea," said Priscilla. "Marty, Wes, Chris, and Lou have no kin, and but for my grandmother, I have none I want to claim. Ten's father is here, and I thought it would be wonderful if just this once we could all be together at Christmas, like a family."

Tenatse Chisholm had never celebrated Christmas, but Priscilla's words struck a chord within him, and he believed he understood her thinking. Jesse Chisholm was getting old. If they followed Ten's dream and headed for the high country, this might be the first and last Christmas they'd spend with the old man.

"There'll be time enough for going to Texas after Christmas," said Ten. "First, we'll go on to St. Louis, like we planned. Then, come Christmas, we'll make it the biggest and best that any of us ever had."

They came up on the grading crew first, about five miles west of end-of-track. Soon they heard the clang of steel on steel, as workmen swung nine-pound sledges, driving spikes into green ties. Paralleling the main line was a side track on which stood five boxcars that had been converted into living quarters for the grading and track-laying crews. Everybody else seemed to be head-quartered in a large tent, its dirty gray walls and top billowing in the eternal prairie wind. Ten had Charlie Two Hats turn the longhorns well away from the rail-road camp, moving them eastward. He and the Chero-kee riders would bed down the herd on the first decent grass, near water. McCoy dismounted and went into the tent. When Ten approached, he could hear the chatter of a telegraph key. Ten shouldered his way under the tent flap and went in. The telegrapher was taking down an incoming message. Joseph McCoy was seated at a table, writing on a long sheet of yellow paper. He looked up when Ten entered.

"I'll settle the money end of it first," said McCoy, "and when that's done, I'll check with the stockyards in Kansas City."

McCoy waited until the railroad business had been transacted, and then handed the operator the sheet on which his message was written. When the message had been sent, McCoy and Ten left the tent.

"Nothing to do now," said McCoy, "except wait. If they can raise the money, I'll have it sent to Kansas City, since you'll be going there anyway. Once we're sure the cattle pens are available, I'll take the work train in and make the necessary arrangements."

Within an hour, McCoy had his answer.

He grinned. "We got a deal. Now, let's just hope the stockyards can accommodate this many cows until the railroad comes up with some cattle cars."

The response from the Kansas City stockyards was favorable. They could take the longhorns. Did McCoy wish to sell?

Joseph McCoy laughed. With that kind of interest in Kansas City, just wait till he got that herd to Chicago! In the late afternoon, when the work train left end-of-track heading east, McCoy was aboard.

October 9, 1866, Ten and the outfit left end-of-track, following the rails east, toward Kansas City.

"Three days," said Ten, "if nothin' goes wrong, and we'll have this drive behind us."

"If we make this drive again," said Marty, "we could run up against the same problem. No railroad cars, or not enough. Did McCoy get around to tellin' you how many cows his pens at Abilene will hold, when they're done?"

"Close to fifteen thousand head," said Ten, "and he's bought enough land to build more pens if they're needed."

"But cows have to eat," said Wes. "Penned cattle can't graze."

"Once the Texas trail drivers discover Abilene," said Ten, "there won't *be* any graze for miles. That's why McCoy's buildin' that big barn. He'll freight in feed for the cattle in the pens, until he can get them sold and shipped east."

"So when we bring another herd," said Chris, "we could end up buying feed from McCoy until the herd's sold."

"Not me," said Ten. "Not when Jess has a ranch seventy-five miles south of Abilene. I'll ride ahead, make a deal with somebody to buy the herd, and then we'll deliver them. We'll let the buyer fight with McCoy over the price of corn and hay. Injun learn from mistakes."

They followed the newly laid rails eastward toward Kansas City, moving the herd well away from the tracks to avoid work trains bound for or departing from end-of-track. They took their time, reaching their destination by noon of the third day. Ten left the herd a few miles east of town, riding in to confirm McCoy's arrangements for use of the cattle pens and to assure himself that the terms of sale would be met. It couldn't have been more than a few weeks since the railroad had reached Kansas City, and already he could see the effects of it. Many of the buildings were new, warped green lumber a testimony to their hurried construction. There was a confectionery shop that sold ice cream, a crudely lettered sign proclaiming it the "only one in town." The stockyards, with its cattle pens, were east of town, and he had only to follow the railroad. He reached the barn first, finding it a long structure, strung out along the tracks. A wooden dock ran the length of it, while at intervals ropes and pulleys were mounted on beams that overhung the eaves. Baled hay could be hoisted from flat cars directly into the huge loft. Beyond the barn was a pair of corrals in which horses and mules wandered about. Next to that were the offices, and beyond, the cattle pens. Ten stepped through the first door he came to and found the room deserted. He opened another door and came face-to-face with a bald little man who wore spectacles and a questioning look.

"I'm Chisholm," said Ten, "and I got ninety-three hundred Texas longhorns. Joe McCoy should have made arrangements to bring 'em here. Has he?"

"Perhaps," said the little man. "He's at the Frontier House. You're to meet him there."

Ten rode back toward town, looking for the hotel. Despite Joseph McCoy's assurances, something hadn't worked out, moneywise.

Ten found McCoy stretched out on the bed, minus only his hat, newspapers, tablets, and pencils scattered about.

"I asked about leavin' the herd at the pens," said Ten, "and they said 'perhaps.' I hope you got a better answer."

"I hope I have too," said McCoy. "I promised to pay you in gold, but the truth is, I have only seventy-five thousand."

"I hope," said Ten, "you're not about to ask for another cut in price."

McCoy laughed. "No, you'll get all I promised you, but it will involve some inconvenience, I'm afraid.

"I was afraid of that too," said Ten. "What kind of inconvenience, and how much?"

"We're borrowing against the herd," said McCoy, "and the bank is in St. Louis. You'll have to go there."

"Why St. Louis, when you do business in Chicago and New York?"

"Because we've been dealing with the bank in St. Louis for many years, and they were more willing to loan us the money. We began dealing with them before the war, buying herds in Sedalia before tick fever closed the Shawnee Trail."

"I'm sure these folks in St. Louis think highly of you," said Ten, "but do you expect me to go there on nothing but a promise?"

"Of course not," said McCoy. "I told you this is a loan. I'll have to sign the papers. I'll be going with you, if you choose to go."

"I've gone with you this far, McCoy, so I'll play out the string. Make your deal with the stockyards, and I'll go get the herd."

Once the herd had been moved into the cattle pens, Ten and Charlie Two Hats took the three pack mules into town and bought supplies for the outfit's return to the Canadian.

"Back to the trading post, Charlie," said Ten. "Take our horses back to the Canadian. Defend yourselves if you must, but don't look for trouble. We'll all be goin' back to Texas after Christmas. *Hasta Luego.*"

Ten waved his hat at the rest of his Cherokee riders as Two Hats rode back to join them.

"It's a four-hundred-fifty mile ride," said Marty. "You reckon they'll go straight back to the Canadian, without fallin' into some mischief of their own or into that of somebody else's doing?"

"I doubt it," said Ten, "but unless they do something completely foolish, like picking a fight with the Union army, they'll be all right. They're all rough around the edges, but tame a man too much in a wild land and you kill him."

Ten took three rooms for them at the Frontier House. The hotel had its own dining room, and they joined Joseph McCoy there for supper.

"This trail drive is turning out a lot different than we planned," said Priscilla. "Mr. McCoy, if we bring another herd from Texas next spring, do you think things will be, well—more ready for us?"

"I'm going to do my best to see that they are," said McCoy. "Please be aware that all I've done and am trying to do at Abilene is based on nothing more than speculation. I didn't expect any herds at all until after the first of the year, and even then I believed they'd be small herds. I doubted that most Texans could raise more than a thousand head, if that many. You folks proved me wrong on both counts, by getting here three months early and by bringing a herd nine times bigger than I expected."

"If anybody's said for sure when the rails will reach Abilene," said Lou, "I must not have been listening. When will they?"

"Nobody's all that sure," said McCoy. "Until a few days ago I believed the tracks would reach Abilene before Christmas. Now I'd say sometime in February, if the weather holds. There's been some difficulty in getting rails. Production's still down, as a result of the war, and as you may already know, the Union Pacific is building westward from Omaha. This transcontinental railroad was President Lincoln's dream, and it's being given priority over lesser roads."

"I doubt we'll be here with another herd before March or April of next year," said Ten.

"We'll be ready for you at Abilene by then," said McCoy.

October 13, 1866, accompanied by McCoy, they took a steamboat to St. Louis. It was a first-time experience for Chris and Lou. It was a larger, more elegant boat than Ten had seen before, and compared to most of his journeys, it was short. By sundown, October 15, they were in St. Louis. It was late in the day, so their banking business would have to wait until tomorrow. They took rooms for the night, and the hotel they chose was a three-story brick structure. It was carpeted in burgundy, and every oval-topped window was graced with matching floor-to-ceiling drapes. The rooms, a trio of them, cost twelve dollars.

"They must think we're rich," said Marty. "That would of bought three Texas steers."

"We're lettin' this finery get to us," said Ten. "We could have brought our bedrolls and slept in the brush along the river."

"He is hoorawin' us, ain't he?" said Lou. "Much as we sleep in the brush, I'd swap three cows for a bed anytime."

The following morning, before they joined McCoy for breakfast, Ten gave each of them a hundred dollars.

"Hell's fire," groaned Marty in mock despair, "that'd buy 125 cows."

"Then save yours and buy cows with it," said Chris. "The rest of us are going to buy Christmas with ours."

"Is that goin' to be enough?" Ten asked.

"For today," said Priscilla. "When McCoy pays us, what are we going to do with all that gold?"

"I aim to leave most of it in the bank vault," said Ten, "until we're ready to leave St. Louis."

"Then you won't need us along to protect you," said Priscilla. "Why don't you go with McCoy to the bank, and turn us loose in town?"

"Maybe I'll do that," said Ten. "I need to track down the St. Louis Firearms Company and pay for the guns and ammunition Herndon ordered in his uncle Drago's name. Then I need to find out where Drago is, and send him the news about Hern."

Ten and McCoy were in the bank less than half an

hour. Except for a few hundred dollars, Ten left the money from the sale of the herd in the bank's vault. Their business finished, McCoy returned to the hotel, leaving Ten with an invitation to bring another herd in the spring. Ten found that he'd actually missed St. Louis, and taking advantage of the fact that he was alone, he walked past the St. Louis Academy, where he had spent three and a half years. Sixteen months since he'd left there, but so much had happened, it seemed like a lifetime. But one look was enough. He put aside the memories and returned to the business district. Reaching the boardwalk, he had no difficulty finding the firearms dealer from whom Herndon had ordered the guns and ammunition. When Ten told the clerk what he wanted, the man went and got the store manager. His name was Singleton, and he listened while Ten again explained what he wished to do.

"This is unusual," said Singleton, "but I see nothing wrong with it. You'll have to wait until I find the ledger."

When he returned with the ledger, there seemed to be only one current entry in it.

"It's $185 for the weapons," said Singleton, "and eighty-four for the ammunition. The price of the Henry rifles increased from forty-three to forty-five dollars, and the ammunition from ten dollars a thousand rounds to ten-fifty. It all comes to $275, including the freight. That leaves a balance of thirty-six dollars. Would you want to take care of that?"

"Why not?" said Ten. "Now, do you know how I can reach Drago Herndon? I have word about some kin of his."

"Haven't seen him for a year. He was on his way to Omaha, planning to shoot buffalo to feed the Union Pacific grading and track-laying crews. You could telegraph the Union Pacific office in Omaha and ask them to get a message to him. You're lucky I wasn't here the day your telegram came, ordering shells and guns in Drago's name. I knew he'd left Natchez."

Ten went to the telegraph office and sent a telegram to the Union Pacific office in Omaha, asking that Drago Herndon telegraph him in St. Louis. Since he wouldn't know when or if Herndon would receive his message, he'd have to give it a while, so he returned to the hotel. He wasn't surprised to find that none of his outfit had returned. Not wishing to sit idle in the plush hotel room, Ten returned to the lobby. There was a little shop that sold candy, fruit, and newspapers. Ten bought copies of Chicago, New Orleans, and St. Louis papers. Having had an early breakfast, he was hungry. He took the papers and went to the restaurant. It was too early for dinner, so he took a table of his choice. When he ordered his food, he spread out the papers. He began with the New Orleans paper, and immediately forgot the other two. It was dated October 5, almost two weeks old, and the entire front page had been devoted to the arrest of Jason Brawn by Federal agents. There were related stories on other pages that laid out the whole grim scenario, from LeBeau's death to the arrest of Brawn. Leaving his papers on the table, Ten returned to the lobby. He rang the bell at the desk until he got the desk clerk's attention.

"I need three or four back issues of the New Orleans paper," said Ten. "Got any idea where I might find 'em?"

"We may have them," said the clerk. "They didn't send us any papers last week, but of what we've received, we may have a copy or two, if they haven't been thrown out."

He returned with two back issues, one for August 31 and one for September 7.

"You may have them," he said.

Ten returned to the restaurant, shoved the other papers aside, and went immediately to the September 7 issue. It was an enlarged edition, eight pages, devoted almost entirely to LeBeau's death and events leading up to it. Typically, the newspaper had pieced together the last days of LeBeau's life, attempting to justify his final act. It wasn't difficult. They had reprinted the story of Sneed's death, embellishing it with reports of discord within the LeBeau house and the departure of Emily. Following that was news of the impending auction of the LeBeau estate, the sale of everything, down to and including the silverware. The writer speculated that it wouldn't cover the outstanding debts. Finally, there was a story covering the last hours of André LeBeau's life. It was told mostly in the words of those who had witnessed LeBeau's devestating loss at the poker tables. The writer had closed with LeBeau's writing and mailing of a letter, as told by old Joseph, the butler. The old man recalled to whom the letter had been addressed, and it was the beginning of the end for Jason Brawn. Ten went back to the paper of October 5 and again read the account of Brawn's arrest. There were few actual facts. The government had admitted only to having received a letter from an "informant," but the newspaper had quickly tied this back to the letter written by André Le-Beau. It was an ugly, depressing story, the kind dear to the hearts of newspaper editors. For Ten, the worst was yet to come. Priscilla had to be told.

Ten's food had gotten cold, but it didn't matter. He wasn't hungry anymore. He gathered up the papers, paid for his meal, and returned to the hotel room. Finally he slept, and was awakened by a thumping at the door. He opened it to find Priscilla, so loaded with parcels and bundles, she hadn't been able to let herself in.

"We'll have to leave all this at Fort Smith," he said, "and send a wagon for it. I reckon the others bought this much or more."

"More," she said, her eyes twinkling. "I don't think Chris and Lou have ever been to town before, and Marty and Wes forgot all about going back to Texas and buying cows."

He hated to diminish her joy, to destroy the mood, but there was no way to lessen the blow. He wanted to be done with it. He led her to the bed and sat her down on it. Wordlessly he spread out the New Orleans paper that detailed LeBeau's death. She read only the head-lines. She paled, the light went out of her eyes, and she buried her face in her hands. Ten held her while she wept. There was a lump in his throat, not for LeBeau, but for her.

Finally she looked at him, her eyes still brimming and her throat so tight she could scarcely talk.

"I know what he was," she said, "but it still hurts. Why didn't he take the money and go? Why?"

"Maybe because he'd failed at everything else, and he felt the need to win. It's something that drives a man, whether he realizes it or not, but it don't always hit us at the same level. It sent a half-breed Injun, kicked out of school, to Texas to hunt longhorn cows."

"I know he was a loser," she said, "but he did win, didn't he, at the last?"

"Yes," said Ten, "he took the last pot, the big one. He mailed the letter to the customs people in Washington a year to the day after Mathewson was ambushed."

"It was John Mathewson who sent you to the house that first time, wasn't it? He used that foolish party to get you in."

"Yes," said Ten, "he did, but not to get at your daddy through you. John Mathewson was a better man than that. He was afraid Jason Brawn might do something to get back at your daddy, and that you and your mother might be hurt. He wanted me to become friends with you, so he could help. He had some strong feelings for your mother. But the moment I laid eyes on you, I for-got everybody and everything else. I wouldn't have cared if your daddy had been the devil himself, with horns and spike tail."

She smiled. "I believe you. I always have. Now I'll tell you something that fits what you've just told me. Mother and Daddy had been married about six years when I was born. As far back as I can remember, I've heard talk that there was another man in Mother's life, someone from her past. It was gossip, of course, but I believed it. I found a note once, in Mother's dresser. It was signed only with a man's first name, and it was John. Now I think I know who he was."

"It's all water under the bridge," said Ten. "Let's put it behind us. I'll get rid of these papers."

"No," said Priscilla, "save them. Later, when I've accepted it, learned to live with it, I'll read them. But not now."

29

*D*espite her heartbreaking news of the day before, Priscilla arose in a better mood than Ten expected. He encouraged her to spend another day in the shops and stores. Ten waited until the afternoon before returning to the telegraph office. He had a reply, but not from Herndon. It was signed by someone in the Union Pacific division office, and read:

Herndon departing Omaha for St. Louis and requests you wait.

To reach St. Louis by rail, Herndon would have to go all the way to Chicago and double back, which didn't make sense. The shortest, quickest route was by steamboat, through Kansas City. The next steamboat from Kansas City was three days away, and Ten planned to be at the landing for its arrival. He believed he would recognize Drago Herndon on sight, and he found himself anxious to meet the old mountain man. Ten made the rounds of the shops with Priscilla, buying a few things on his own.

"Our first day here," said Lou, "I never thought I'd get tired of all this, but I'm startin' to. I'll be glad when Hern's uncle Drago gets here, so we can go."

When Drago Herndon arrived, they had no trouble recognizing him. He wore moccasins and was dressed entirely in buckskin. He wore an old flop hat whose wide brim sagged all the way around, like he'd just come in out of a hard rain. With his hat, he was nearly seven feet tall, and thin as a rail. He had a sweeping moustache that flared out like the horns of a Texas longhorn. His eyes were pale blue, and his craggy face had been burned the deep brown of an old saddle. He had brought his buffalo gun, a .50-90 Sharps Special.

Ten introduced himself and his friends to Herndon and then told him the purpose of the telegram.

"I knowed somethin' important had took place," said Herndon. "It was th' first telegram I ever got."

"You came a long ways, just to get bad news," said Ten.

"Wasn't just that," said Herndon. "I was in Omaha when I got th' message. Me an' Bill Cody's been slaughterin' buffalo for th' railroad, and we about had enough. I was ready to come back here for a spell, so I just had 'em send you a message askin' you to wait. Hope I ain't put you out too much."

"Not a bit," said Ten. "Maynard Herndon spoke of you often. I needed rifles and ammunition for the trail drive from Texas. We couldn't find 'em anywhere, so Hern telegraphed the firearms people here, using your name. They shipped the guns and shells to us at Natchez. I've already been to the gun dealer and paid the bill."

"Glad to of been some help to you," said Herndon. "Now tell me about the boy."

Ten told him all there was to tell, starting with his and Herndon's first meeting.

"I'm obliged to you for takin' him with you," said the mountain man. "He'd just kinda drifted from pillar to post all his life. His daddy—my only brother—was killed when his hoss fell an' rolled on him. Maynard—God, how he hated that name—was just a young'un when his mama died. She was always a sickly woman, an' I don't think she ever got over birthin' th' boy. I just took him in, doin' th' best I could for him. When he joined th' Confederacy, I never expected to see him agin. Not alive, anyhow. But he come back, sick in his lungs, spittin' his life away. I almost wished he'd died in th' war; would of been easier on him. He had his daddy's grit an' spirit, but his mama's sickly nature. He seemed like he was scared I was goin' to be ashamed of him."

"Remember him with pride," said Ten. "He was sick, but he was a man who pulled his weight, and more. He died with his boots on and a gun in his hand, fighting for the outfit."

"It helps, knowin' that," said Herndon. "I'll always be obliged to you for trackin' me down an' tellin' me."

Herndon took a room in their hotel and joined them for supper.

"This ain't where I stay usually," said the old man. "Too highfalutin, but I reckon I can stand it for a night."

"Tell us about you and Buffalo Bill Cody shooting buffalo," said Lou.

"Ain't much to tell, ma'am. You find you a herd an' get downwind from 'em. You drive a forked stick in th' ground, lettin' it support th' barrel of your gun, takin' th' strain off'n your arms an' shoulders. Then you just start shootin', killin' poor brutes that's too dumb to know what's happenin' to 'em."

"It sounds like a shameful thing to do," said Priscilla. "It's so sad."

"It is, ma'am," said Herndon. "Whatever th' eastern writers say, there ain't nothin' brave or romantic about it. Me an' Cody saw it for what it was an' give it up. Th' railroad's got money; let 'em buy beef to feed their men."

"We're thinkin' of buying some Texas longhorns," said Marty, "and startin' us a ranch somewhere on the high plains. Tell us somethin' about the country."

"It's a land where a man with some seed cattle an' some money can build an empire," said Herndon. "Still some trouble with Injuns. Mostly th' Arapaho an' th' Sioux, but I hear there's a treaty in th' works. Was I lookin' for land, I'd grab me a piece of th' Sweetwater Valley, in southern Wyoming Territory. Heard talk there's folks stakin' claims there already, mostly along th' Sweetwater River. Th' Sweetwater Valley's a good hundred fifty miles long, stretchin' from th' Platte River in th' east to th' green in th' west. But there may be a fight brewin'. Bill Cody says there's a land grab takin' place, an' somebody with th' Union Pacific is involved in it."*

"We took the four broncs you left at Natchez," said Ten. "I was to pay for them when our first herd was sold. I promised Hern two hundred dollars."

"I can't hold you to that," said Herndon. "I didn't make th' deal."

"But they were your horses," said Ten.

"No," said Herndon, "your deal was with th' boy, an' it died with him. How'd th' broncs work out?"

"The best cow horses we've got," said Ten. "Is it true they're running wild in Montana Territory?"

"They are," said Herndon. "I got them four from th' Crow Indians. I'm tempted to go there, hire me some Crows, an' trap enough to start me a hoss ranch."

"I wish we could go with you," said Priscilla.

"Maybe you can," said Herndon. "The Union Pacific is buildin' a town in southern Wyoming, an' it'll be a division point for th' railroad. There's gonna be a land office, an' you can find me through that, if I decide to go back an' settle there."

October 25, 1866. There would be a steamboat departing for Natchez at two o'clock in the afternoon. It was time to visit the bank for an accounting and division of money from the sale of the herd. On Ten's first visit to the bank, he'd been accompanied only by Joseph McCoy. This time, he took Marty, Wes, Chris, Lou, and Priscilla with him. The bank officer's name was Miller, and his little office was barely large enough to accommodate them.

* Trail Drive Series 2, *The Western Trail*

"Don't mean to crowd you," said Ten, "but we're all partners."

"It's going to take all of you to carry this money," said Miller, "if you insist on taking it in gold. We're talking about $186,000, and that's ninety-three hundred double eagles. This day and time, carrying this much money could be the death of all of you."

"I know," said Ten, "but fifty thousand of this belongs to my father, and he does his banking in New Orleans. We're goin' back to Texas for another herd, and depending on prices, we may need another fifty thousand ourselves."

"Then let me suggest this," said Miller. "Deposit your father's share in his name, and if he chooses not to leave it here, we can transfer it to his bank in New Orleans. Take with you only the fifty thousand in gold that you'll need for buying more cattle. Let me hold the balance on deposit for you here. If you have further dealings with Mr. McCoy, we can transfer funds from his accounts in Chicago and New York to your account here."

"Miller," said Ten, "you're a convincing man. Set it up like that, but go ahead and get our fifty thousand in gold. There's a steamboat leavin' at two, and we aim to be on it."

When Miller had left the office to get the gold, Ten turned to Marty and Wes.

"Your share gets you twenty thousand of what he's bringing us. Unless prices have gone up, that'll buy you five thousand longhorns. I aim to buy another five thousand, if we can find that many."

"Two Hats and his boys have to be paid," said Marty, "and what about grub and supplies? We oughta be payin' our share."

"You'll need what you have," said Ten. "I have extra money for whatever we'll need. We'll settle up at the end of the next trail drive. You'll be better able to do it then."

* * *

They departed St. Louis, reached Natchez, and boarded a steamboat bound for Fort Smith. They found that Chisholm's riders had delivered a herd of mules to Fort Smith, and that Chisholm had thoughtfully sent along their horses and saddles.

"Well," said Ten, "we know Two Hats and his boys got back alive, or the horses wouldn't be here waiting for us."

30

Ten arranged for two packhorses needed to carry their goods from Fort Smith, and they arrived at the Chisholm trading post on November 11. Ten greeted Jesse Chisholm, and then went looking for Charlie Two Hats. He found Two Hats and several of his riders at one of the corrals, working with some unfamiliar horses. Horses Ten hadn't seen before.

"Charlie, where'd you get the horses?"

Charlie took off his hat and ran his fingers through his shoulder-length hair.

"Swap *mulo*," he said. "Him *malo bastardo*."

It was suppertime, so Ten returned to the house. He found Chisholm at the table, with a cup of coffee.

"Jess, Two Hats and his boys brought back some extra horses. When I asked Charlie where he got 'em, he said he traded the mule. That's some kind of trade, seven horses for one cantankerous, bitin' mule. Where you reckon they got the horses?"

"I don't know," said Chisholm, "and don't want to know. You figure it out." He grinned. "They're your riders."

It was more than a month until Christmas, and they used it in different ways. Taking a trio of riders with him, Jesse Chisholm rode to his ranch on the Arkansas. Priscilla allowed him to go, only upon his assurance that he would return in time for Christmas. Ten, Marty, and

Wes went hunting for deer and wild turkey. Priscilla, Chris, and Lou found a suitable fir, took it to the dining room, and covered it with the decorations they'd bought in St. Louis.

"That's done," said Lou. "Now what're we goin' to do until Christmas?"

"There's something you can do for me," said Priscilla, "if you will."

"Of course we will," said Chris. "What is it?"

"Teach me to use a rope, to rope cows."

"Why don't you have Ten teach you?" Lou asked.

"He says we have riders enough without me, that I'd end up with hands and arms like a brush-popping cowboy."

"Like us," said Chris. "But that doesn't seem to bother Marty and Wes."

"I don't care," said Priscilla. "If I'm going to be part of this, I want to live it. What else is there to do?"

"You could get Ten to build you a fancy house, with a highfalutin cookstove and china globe lamps," said Lou with a wicked laugh. "Then you could stay home and have young'uns."

"Is that what you aim to do," Priscilla asked, "after we settle in the high country?"

"My God, no!" said Lou. "I ain't havin' young'uns until I'm too old for anything else. I'll wait till I'm thirty, an old woman."

"Priscilla," said Chris, "me and the old woman, here, will show you all we know about building and throwing a loop. And we won't say anything to Ten."

After the trip to Texas and the trail drive to Kansas City, Priscilla rode as though born to the saddle. The three girls took to riding every day, getting far enough from the trading post for Priscilla's early efforts at roping to go unobserved.

"You're gettin' the hang of it," said Lou after the first few days. "You're goin' to purely surprise old Ten somethin' terrible."

* * *

Christmas was an event none of them would ever forget. Chris, Lou, and Priscilla had managed to buy a gift for everybody. Even the Indians, from the youngest child to the oldest adult, had been remembered. For Christmas dinner there was fried chicken, ham, fish, roast wild turkey, and venison. There were dried apple cakes, dried apple pies, rice pudding, and bear sign.*

"Lord," said Jesse Chisholm, surveying the loaded tables, "we could have invited the whole Cherokee nation."

The day after Christmas, the weather changed from mild and dry to chill and wet. For three straight days there was a drizzle, not a sign of the sun, and a cold wind out of the northwest.

"Let's give it another day or two," said Ten, "and maybe it'll change."

On January 2, 1867, Ten and the outfit rode out, heading south. The rain had ceased, but the northwesterly wind was still with them, and still cold. Ten and Priscilla took the lead, followed by Marty and Chris, then Wes and Lou. Charlie Two Hats and his riders brought up the rear, three of the Cherokees leading pack mules. Again they followed Chisholm's road, already being referred to as the "Chisholm Trail." Nobody noticed Priscilla now carried a coiled lariat on her saddle. They traveled at a steady trot, and Ten estimated they made fifty miles the first day. They saw nobody, and crossed no trails of shod or unshod horses.

"We goin' all the way to San Antone this time," Marty asked, "or do you aim to look for some cows a mite closer?"

"We'll put out the word," said Ten, "soon as we cross the Red, but I got a feelin' we'll have to ride south a ways. The brakes get deeper and wilder, Jess says, the farther south we go. I reckon that accounts for there bein' more wild longhorns in South Texas. I just hope

* Doughnuts

somebody's been catchin' some of 'em and is willin' to sell."

"Well," said Priscilla, "if we can't find enough cows to buy a herd, why don't we just catch them ourselves?"

Ten, Marty, and Wes laughed. Priscilla colored, but her response wasn't quick enough. Lou spoke up.

"She's right. Why don't we catch them ourselves? There's nineteen of us. On our first drive, six of us caught 1450 longhorns. So what if it takes longer? We could work the brakes till June and still have the herd to Abilene by September. Just because we've got money, are we too good to work?"

This time, nobody laughed.

"I don't often agree with her," said Chris, "but this time I'll have to. Ten, you wanted to get this trail drive done in time to make another one this year. Why don't we let this one drive be it, as far as Abilene's concerned? If you meant what you said, about going to Colorado, Wyoming or Montana, why not take one more drive to Abilene, and let our next trail drive be to the high country?"

Ten looked at Marty, then at Wes. He saw no disagreement.

"Let me think on it some," he said. "Goin' at it like that does take some of the hurry out of it. One thing we can't afford to forget, though, if we go into the brakes to rope our own cows. The Comanches are likely to be there with bells on. We got off easy last time. I believe in luck at the poker table, but not when it comes to Comanches."

"There's enough of us to put up a good fight," said Marty. "Wasn't but six of us there on the Trinity, if you don't count Tomlin and his gang."

"Let's see how things look when we get there," said Ten.

They crossed the Red and rode into Texas. Three or four miles south of the river, they came up on a macabre scene that told a grim story. There was the charred remains of an army wagon, the unburned parts of its box bristling with the shafts of Comanche arrows. There was the rotted carcass of a mule, and six grassed-over mounds that could only be graves. But that wasn't all. There were the splintered dregs of what had once been weapons and ammunition cases. Enough of the wood was intact for them to read the famous name of Winchester, which had been burned into the flat lid of every case.

"My God," said Marty, "it's plain enough for a New York tenderfoot to figure out. Somewhere on these plains there's ten dozen Comanches armed with seventeen shot-repeatin' rifles, and likely enough shells to wipe out every white man in Texas."

"It's bad news," said Ten. "We'll stop at the fort and let Captain Fanning fill in the details."

Fanning supplied the details, and they were grim.

"Ten cases of new Winchester rifles," he said, "with ammunition. These were arms intended for the soldiers in North Texas. I'm afraid it's going to be hell with the lid off until we either whip this bunch or finally sign a treaty with them."

"You can't count on either," said Ten. "How many in the party?"

"Fifty or more," said Fanning. "They split seven ways from Sunday, and trailing them was impossible. Washington's ready to declare war."

"It's likely to take one," said Ten. "We're goin' to South Texas for another herd. If we can't buy them, we'll rope them ourselves."

"Charles Goodnight's outfit's been working the brakes along the Brazos," said Fanning. "Last spring, just south of old Fort Belknap, the Comanches stampeded his gather, and they never did get 'em back. Goodnight started over, built another herd, and I hear he's blazing a new trail. He's headed for the Pecos, planning to drive through eastern New Mexico, to Colorado."*

* Trail Drive Series #1, *The Goodnight Trail*

"I wish him luck," said Ten. "Any other herds bein'
gathered, that you know of?"

"No," said Fanning, "but since you were last through
here, there was a rider who brought word that Texas
herds are welcome at Abilene, Kansas. He said the railroad was coming."

"It is," said Ten. "That's where we'll be taking our
herd."

"That's a fine-looking horse remuda," said Fanning.
"If I were you, I'd double my guard."

They spent one night at the fort, riding out the following morning under heavy gray clouds. The wind grew
chill and shifted to the northwest, a bad sign. By noon
they'd donned their slickers and had tied down their
hats with leather thongs against the rising wind. The
storm grew in intensity, and by early afternoon they
rode through gathering darkness.

"Soon as we find enough shelter for a fire," said Ten,
"we'll make camp."

The best they found was a windblown cottonwood, its
mass of roots a small bulwark against the storm. Using a
tarp from one of the pack mules, they extended the
shelter until there was room to cook and eat.

"Three-hour watches," said Ten, "four riders at a
time. If we crowd it some, that'll make room for us all to
sleep dry."

"Comanches would have to want hosses mighty bad,"
said Marty, "to be out in this. Hell of it is, this is just the
kind of night they'd choose."

Since they had enough men for all the watches, Ten
suggested the three women remain in the shelter. They
refused, taking the last watch with Ten, Wes, Marty, and
Charlie Two Hats.

"You can't have too many riders on the last watch,"
said Lou. "If they come after us, it'll likely be just an
hour or two before dawn."

They hadn't bothered picketing the remuda. Picket
pins or not, a band of shrieking Comanches would send

the horses rattling their hocks for parts unknown. If the Comanches struck, it would all depend on the defenders and the horses they rode. Despite their precautions, the attack caught them by surprise. There was only the moan of the wind and the slap of rain against their slickers, when a second later all hell broke loose. There were shrieks that drowned out the storm, and a thunder of rifles. It was too dark for accurate shooting, but the slugs had an effect. Ten snatched his Henry from the boot, but before he could cock it, lead stung his horse and the animal tore off into the night. The rest of the outfit rolled out of their blankets to find most of the horse remuda off and running. A horse screamed and fell. A rider was shot from the saddle and lay still.

Ten calmed his terrified horse and rode back to camp. As far as the stampeded horses were concerned, there was nothing they could do in darkness. But he was concerned about his riders. He hadn't expected the Comanches to cut down on them with rifles. The rain had begun to slack, and clouds had parted, revealing a pale quarter moon. Ten swung out of his saddle, his heart in his throat. At first he thought it was only the whimpering of the dying horse, but it was more than that. Lou was on her knees, sobbing over the girl who lay facedown. Her hat had been torn away, and he could see only her dark hair. Was it Chris? He fell on his knees beside her, and Lou threw her arms around him.

"It's Priscilla," she cried. "Priscilla's dead!"

Ten had to tear himself loose. Gently as he could, he rolled Priscilla over. Lou's frantic words ringing in his ears, he took Priscilla's wrist, seeking a pulse. It was weak, but it was there. She was alive! He took hold of her shoulders, and Charlie Two Hats took her feet. They carried her back to the shelter and built up the fire.

"She's alive," said Ten, "but not by much. Lou, while I hold her up, take off her slicker."

Out of respect for Priscilla, they all backed away, except for Chris and Lou. Ten unbuttoned Priscilla's shirt and Levi's pants, confirming what he had feared. She had been shot in the back, and there was no exit wound. Slowly, he rolled her on her stomach. There was hardly any bleeding, but the wound was low down, dangerous. The slug was still in there, near her spine.

"I'm taking her back to the fort," said Ten, "and I need a pair of poles to make a travois. Some of you fire a pine knot, whatever you can burn to make some light."

They made enough light to cut the poles he needed, and he set about making a crude travois. Using Priscilla's slicker and some blankets, he made a narrow bed. With rawhide thongs, he bound each side of it to one of the poles. The long ends of the poles, one lashed to each side of the saddle, would create a "drag" behind the horse. But the horse had never pulled such a rig before, and kept nervously turning his head to look at the unfamiliar thing behind him. Marty steadied the animal, while Ten and Wes carefully lifted Priscilla onto the narrow bed suspended between the slender poles.

"Marty," said Ten, "you're in charge while I'm gone. I don't know when I'll be back. Soon as it's light enough to see, take the horses that didn't run and find as many of the others as you can."

"I aim to find 'em all," said Marty. "Me and the rest of the outfit is goin' huntin', and it ain't got nothin' to do with longhorn cows."

"Ten," said Wes, "maybe Lou and Chris ought to go with you. We'll all want to know if she—how she is."

It could have been Lou instead of Priscilla, and Marty intended to go after that band of Comanches. It was bad enough Priscilla had been hurt. Why not keep Chris and Lou out of it?

"Maybe you're right, Wes," said Ten. "Lou, why don't you and Chris ride back to the fort with me? Marty and Wes can always meet you there and ride back with you."

It was a slow ride back to Fort Worth. Once Priscilla had been placed on the travois, they had wrapped more blankets around her, tying them in place. Chris and Lou trotted their horses behind Ten, watchful lest some of the rawhide should tear loose. They stopped occasionally to rest the horses, especially Ten's horse. Priscilla was wrapped in blankets, so he was unable to get to her wrists; instead, Ten checked the big artery at her throat. It was first light, and she opened her eyes. He was startled when she spoke.

"What . . . happened to me?"

"You were shot," he said gently. "We're taking you back to the fort, to the doctor. Are you hurting?"

"No," she said, "I don't feel . . . anything. My body seems . . . dead. Ten, I—I can't feel my legs—my feet."

A tear smudged the dirt on her cheek. Chris and Lou turned quickly away, so she couldn't see their faces. Ten calmed Priscilla, and they rode on. It seemed forever before they saw the welcome log walls of Fort Worth. The post doctor was a young man, but seemed competent enough. Priscilla was made comfortable. Ten, Chris, and Lou waited impatiently while the doctor made his examination. When he returned, he looked grim, and for a moment he didn't say anything. He sighed and spoke.

"She's paralyzed from the waist down."

But for swift intakes of breath, Chris and Lou were shocked into silence.

"There must be something you can do!" Ten almost shouted.

"I'm no surgeon. I can pull teeth, set broken bones, give you laudanum if you're hurting, but I'm not trained beyond that. That slug needs to come out, but I'm not qualified to remove it."

"If it's removed, will she—"

"I don't know," said the doctor. "The damage may have been done, and if it has, removal of the bullet won't change anything. We don't know anything about the spine, except that it controls the nervous system. Given time, with the lead removed, the condition might heal itself, but we don't know if it will, and if it does, why."

"But there is a chance?"

"Yes, but you'd need to get her to a surgeon in New Orleans or St. Louis."

"I'll get her to New Orleans," said Ten. "It'll be closer."

Ten went immediately to see Captain Fanning.

"You're welcome to use the ambulance," said Fanning, "and I'll provide a driver and an escort, if you're sure you can get a steamboat as far as Doan's Crossing, on the Red."

"I can get a private packet out of New Orleans," said Ten, "but I'll need to use the telegraph."

Granted the use of the telegraph, he quickly wrote a message to Harvey Roberts, in New Orleans. If he ever needed old Jake Daimler and his little packet, it was now. He breathed a silent prayer that Roberts wouldn't be away, as he took occasional trips to Natchez or St. Louis.

"I'm torn between wanting to go with you and wanting to stay with the outfit," said Lou. "I don't think I could stand it in the brakes without knowing if—"

"I'll send a telegram to you here," said Ten, "as soon as I know anything. I'll want to leave twenty thousand dollars with you, in case Marty and Wes want to go ahead with the trail drive. I'll come back and be part of it, if I can, but if I can't, and you decide to rope your own longhorns, maybe you can buy another five thousand for me. Remember to tell Marty and Wes that if you go ahead and buy or gather another herd, take them back to Indian Territory and wait for me. I'll be there as soon as Priscilla can travel."

Roberts answered Ten's telegram, promising another as soon as he had rented a packet willing to navigate the Red. Captain Fanning shook his head.

"The Red's a treacherous piece of water," he said. "There's been times when the water's low, we've been without supplies for weeks. But maybe that won't be a problem; there's been a mighty lot of rain."

Harvey Roberts's telegram, when it came, said:

JAKE KNOWS RED AND ON HIS WAY STOP FEE IS THOUSAND DOLLARS.

"I don't know when he'll be here," said Ten.

"I have a map with nautical miles," said Fanning. "You can estimate it."

Captain Fanning detailed four privates to escort the army ambulance to Doan's Crossing, where steamboats docked to unload military supplies. The soldiers were to wait there until Daimler's boat arrived. Chris and Lou had remained at the fort, having promised to wait until Marty and Wes came for them. Priscilla had said little. The post doctor had given Ten a bottle of laudanum, should there be pain. There was no pain, and while Ten was thankful for that, he feared it was the result of the lack of feeling in her legs and feet. The doctor had thoroughly cleansed the wound, had used all the antiseptics he had, and it didn't seem infected. They had to wait a night and most of another day at the Red before Jake Daimler's little steamboat arrived. Ten thanked the ambulance driver and the soldier escort. Daimler got his packet tied up at the dock and, taking one end of the blankets on which Priscilla lay, helped Ten take her aboard. Jake asked no questions. They placed Priscilla on a small bunk in the captain's quarters. There were cracks in the floor, and Ten could see a muscular Negro in the boiler room below. Few steamboats traveled the Red, except government packets, hauling supplies for frontier outposts, and Ten wondered what Jake planned to do about fuel. He soon found out. Just before sundown, Jake tied up his little stern-wheeler at a crude dock, and with the help of his Negro fireman, took on wood from what obviously was the government supply. Jake caught Ten watching.

"Guv'mint's got time t' cut wood," said Jake. "We ain't."

From the talk Ten had heard, the Red was treacherous during dry years, dropping the water level and raising sandbars that made river travel all but impossible. Ten blessed the rainy December. He examined Priscilla's wound often, praying he wouldn't see the dread discoloration that might indicate gangrene. The night before they reached New Orleans, Priscilla's fever began to rise. Long before they tied up, Ten paid old Jake his money, lest any time be lost at the dock. Leaving Priscilla on board, Ten hailed a hack and sent it on the run to fetch an ambulance. It arrived with a driver and an attendant, and they carried Priscilla to the ambulance on a stretcher. Ten climbed into the back with her, and for the first time she seemed afraid.

"Ten, what are they going to do? What can they do?"

"First, they'll have to remove the bullet."

"Suppose I still—can't move? Suppose I'm crippled for the rest of my life? For your sake, that bullet should have killed me."

"Don't you ever say that again," he all but shouted.

Startled, the driver and his attendant looked around. Ashamed of his outburst, Ten took Priscilla's hand and spoke more gently.

"You're going to beat this," he said. "We're going to the high country, and when we do, you'll be riding beside me. Remember that night I had to leave you, when I promised I'd return for you?"

"I'll never forget," she said, almost in a whisper.

"Just as surely as I kept that promise," he said, "I'll keep this one. Whatever it takes, regardless of how long it takes, I'll see you through this. I'll be with you every step of the way."

"I believe you," she said, and for the first time since the shooting, she smiled.

31

When it was light enough to see, Marty, Wes, Charlie Two Hats, and the Cherokee riders went looking for their stampeded horse remuda. Fortunately, the same darkness that had protected the Comanches had prevented them from rounding up the stampeded herd. Many of the horses, once the screeching and shooting had stopped, had begun drifting back toward camp. The riders quickly found thirty of the horses and the three pack mules.

"The bastards still got more'n half our remuda," said Wes.

"Maybe not," said Marty. "Just 'cause we ain't got 'em don't mean they have. When a herd stampedes— hosses, mules, or cows—some of 'em will run lots farther than others. Injuns reckon we'll gather the closest ones first, and while we're doin' that, they can make off with the others. They can't see in the dark any better'n we can, but they know they got some time once it's light."

"They ain't too worried about us," said Wes. "With all that rain last night, they left tracks an old granny could follow, without her spectacles."

"It's them tracks they're countin' on," said Marty. "They outnumber us maybe four to one, and they look for that to scare hell out of us, keep us off their trail."

"Since they ain't expectin' us," said Wes, "that'll cut

down the odds some. Let's give 'em a taste of what it's like on the receivin' end of a middle-of-the-night ambush."

"Pardner," said Marty, with a grim laugh, "you done spent so much time in Texas, it's startin' to rub off on you. We'll find out where that bunch of war whoops aims to spend the night, and we'll pay 'em a visit."

"Kill Comanche dead lak hell," said Charlie Two Hats.

"That's the idea," said Marty, "but after dark, without them knowing we're comin'. Charlie, send two of your best scouts after these Comanches, find out where they bed down for the night, and we'll want our Injuns to lead us there after dark. *Comprender?*"

"Comprender," said Two Hats, and went galloping off.

The surgeon's name was Bannister, and he made no promises, except that he would perform the surgery. Beyond that, they'd simply have to wait and see. The doctor, one of the nurses told Ten, had seen service with the Union army. Ten heard that with mixed emotions. From what Marty and Wes had told him, most battlefield "surgery" had consisted of cutting off arms and legs before gangrene set in. Ten had gone virtually without sleep the four days and nights he'd spent on the deck of Jake Daimler's boat. Concerned as he was for Priscilla, he was dozing when Dr. Bannister came looking for him.

"She's asleep," said Bannister. "I can only tell you that, although the slug had come in contact with the spine, there was no visible damage. I had a few words with her before the surgery, before the laudanum took her out. She has no feeling in her feet and legs, and she doesn't believe she'll ever walk again. That's not a good sign."

"You mean if she doesn't believe . . . ?"

"If she doesn't believe she can," said Bannister, "I seriously doubt she will. When the mind surrenders, the body follows suit. There's a cure for this kind of thing, but it takes determination and will. It may take weeks, or even months."

"I don't care how long it takes," said Ten, "or what it takes. She's goin' to walk again. You tell me what I can do to help her, and I'll do it."

For the first time, Bannister smiled.

"That's what I wanted to hear," he said. "Given time, she has a chance."

Charlie Two Hats chose himself as one of the scouts, and, taking Sashavado with him, they rode out. The trail led south, toward the headwaters of the Trinity. Marty and Wes joined the remaining riders in rounding up as many of the scattered horses as they could find. Just when Marty had begun to wonder if the pair would return before dark, they rode in. Two Hats was brief.

"Much hoss, much gun, much Comanche."

"Find 'em in the dark?" Marty asked. He then held up one finger, then two, and finally three.

Two Hats nodded. Yes, he could find the camp in the dark. He held up both hands, fingers spread. He dropped his hands, raising only the right one. He extended one, two, three, and finally four fingers.

"Only fourteen Comanches?" Wes asked.

"Fifty," said Marty. "He's sayin' ten, plus four times again that many."

"Coulee," said Sashavado, speaking for the first time. "Ambush lak hell."

It was a good plan. The two scouts had tracked the Comanches more than twenty-five miles. Believing there was safety in their greater number, they had driven their stolen horses into a shallow coulee through which ran a creek. The Cherokees were in their glory, and Marty wisely allowed Two Hats and Sashavado to split the outfit into two attacking forces. Sashavado took eight men, including Marty and Wes, while Charlie Two Hats took the remaining seven. They had ridden out at midnight, and picketing their horses far from the Comanche camp, had advanced on foot. Charlie Two Hats

had taken his men in a wide circle, coming on the coulee from the east. Sashavado and his force moved in
from the west. Each man carried a rifle cocked and
ready. Sashavado and Two Hats would take the lead, the
signal for the others to begin firing. No other signal was
needed. They had allowed themselves enough time to
get into position. There was no order given. Marty and
Wes were amazed at the Indian sense of timing. Two
Hats and Sashavado opened fire at exactly the same
instant, the others joining in. Their targets were blanket-wrapped blobs in the pale moonlight, and it was
slaughter. Those who escaped were able to only by
clinging to one of the stampeding horses. The thunder
of rifles sent the horses galloping madly from both ends
of the coulee. Within seconds it was over. Lacking
targets, the attackers ceased firing. They waited for so
long, Marty was about to speak, when Sashavado made
a move. He raised his hand, palm out, a command to
stay. Rifle in hand, he advanced toward the rim of the
coulee, and they lost sight of him until he descended the
wall. Beyond the creek, down the farthest wall, came a
shadowy Charlie Two Hats. As silently as he had departed, Sashavado returned, and at his silent command,
they followed. When they reached their picketed horses,
Two Hats and his men were waiting. Marty held up one
hand, fingers extended. Two Hats held up both hands,
all fingers extended. He lowered his hands and repeated
the gesture, lowered them again, then raised two fingers. Twenty-two dead. Come daylight, they'd go looking for the rest of their horses.

    January 15, 1867, Marty and Wes rode to the fort. Not
only had they recovered their horse remuda, but Two
Hats and his riders had gleefully captured more than a
dozen Comanche broncs. Reaching Fort Worth, Marty
and Wes were escorted by Captain Fanning's first sergeant to the little room that had been assigned to Chris
and Lou. The girls were relieved to see them alive and
well.

"We got the horses back, with interest," said Marty. "Any word from Ten about Priscilla?"

"Only that the lead was removed," said Chris, "and that she can't walk. Ten's not sure how long they'll be in New Orleans. We can telegraph in care of Harvey Roberts, if you want to get a message to him."

"Before we leave, I'll send one," said Marty. "Me and Wes has decided we're goin' ahead with this trail drive. We're goin' to buy or gather that big herd, and take it up the Chisholm Trail for him, and for Priscilla."

"I'm glad!" cried Lou. "Where do we start?"

"We're ridin' to San Antone," said Marty. "We won't waste any time tryin' to buy cows between here and there. We're ridin' back to that Lipan village. Somehow, maybe with the help of Two Hats, I'm goin' to make them Lipans an offer. If they've caught any more longhorns, we'll buy 'em. If they don't have any, then we'll buy as many as they can catch. There's just fifteen of us, but there must be two hundred of them that can rope and ride. I want every one that can set a saddle and swing a loop workin' for us."

"We'll be getting more than just their help hunting longhorns," said Chris. "With that many Comanche-hating Lipans in the brakes with us, we'll be safer than if we had the Union army."

"It's a slick move," said Wes with a laugh. "If we wasn't imposing on the government telegraph, I'd like to tell ol' Ten about it. He'd really be in high cotton, knowin' we're going ahead with the gather and the trail drive."

"Let's save that for a better time," said Lou. "If Priscilla never walks again, he won't care if we've hog-tied and branded every longhorn in Texas."

It was a sobering thought. Marty made the telegram brief, telling Ten only that they were going ahead with the gather. When Marty, Wes, Chris, and Lou reached their camp, Marty had Two Hats and the Cherokee riders round up the horses and ready the pack mules. Soon they were riding south, toward San Antone.

* * *

Ten read Priscilla the telegram from Marty, and she showed no feeling one way or the other. It seemed to hold no excitement for her, as though she was no longer a part of it. Two weeks following her surgery, the wound had virtually healed, but there was no evidence that any life had returned, or would ever return, to her feet and legs. She had no real enthusiasm for anything, except leaving the hospital, and it was the one thing Ten refused her. The only hope was the therapy the doctor had in mind, but without her cooperation, it was impossible. Day after day he sat beside her bed while she lay silent, her face to the wall. Harvey Roberts came to see her a time or two, but she received him with a wan smile and had nothing to say. She ate only a little, and without supervision, nothing. There were dark circles around her eyes, and in their gray depths, a misery that brought a lump to Ten's throat. His meetings with Dr. Bannister accomplished nothing.

"She's willing herself to die," said Bannister. "I've seen it happen before. The mind kills the body. She needs a jolt, a challenge, something to live for. Otherwise, she'll be dead in three months."

Ten walked along the river, his mind in a turmoil. He needed help, but from whom? Praying hadn't helped; maybe God had given up on him. Without knowing why, he ended up at the telegraph office. He went in, took a sheet of paper and began to write. Finished, he had the message sent to Louisville.

32

On their previous trail drive, when Ten had bought longhorns from the Lipan Apaches, he hadn't brought them in contact with Charlie Two Hats and the Cherokee riders. For sure, Ten had known the Lipans hated the Comanches, but he hadn't been sure where they stood with other tribes. They might have accepted the Cherokees as friends, or there might have been war. Marty was faced with the same decision, and decided to take the risk. He needed the help of Charlie Two Hats in establishing communication with the Lipan chief. As it turned out, his decision was good and, mostly by sign, Two Hats was able to talk to the Lipans. They remembered Marty, Wes, Chris, and Lou from the last drive, and it wasn't difficult to convince them Two Hats and his riders were part of the outfit. In a moment of inspiration, Two Hats gave the Lipan chief three of the horses taken from the Comanches. The animals still had their war paint, symbols applied by their Comanche owners. Two Hats, with hand signs and drawings in the dust, managed to tell the Lipans of the ambush. The chief slapped his buckskinned thigh and laughed. As it turned out, any foe of the Comanches was a friend to the Lipans. Marty's respect for Charlie Two Hats rose considerably. Marty, Wes, Chris, Lou, and Charlie Two Hats followed the Lipan chief to the holding area Priscilla and Ten had been taken to before. While there weren't as many longhorns this time, there was a substantial herd. Two Hats made sign with the Lipan chief, then turned to Marty.

"Two Hats stay," he said. "Count cow."

They'd made their own camp a mile or two north of the Lipan village, on the Medina River. They returned there, believing they had made a good move. Even if they had to gather most of the longhorns from the brakes, they had the enthusiastic cooperation of the Lipans.

"Marty," said Wes, "if you don't ever have another good idea in your life, this one will make up for it. With all them Injuns workin' for us and with us, why can't we maybe take Sundays off and ride into San Antone?"

"Why?" Marty asked. "You aim to go to church?"

"I like a town-cooked meal once in a while," said Wes, "and a bath once a week. January ain't a good time to go swimmin'."

"Wait'll Charlie takes a count on them longhorns," said Marty. "If they got a bunch, and we're gettin' a pretty good start on this trail drive, then maybe we'll take ourselves a day of rest."

It was a decision they almost regretted. As valuable as Charlie Two Hats had been in gaining the trust and cooperation of the Lipan Apaches, and as great an asset the Cherokee riders were on the trail, their presence in town would prove disastrous.

So great was Tenatse Chisholm's mental anguish following his and Priscilla's arrival in New Orleans, he completely forgot to send a telegram to Jesse Chisholm. But Harvey Roberts remembered. Chisholm arrived on the twenty-fifth of January, and Roberts directed him to the private hospital. Priscilla had a private room, and Ten was paying extra for an adjoining room with a connecting door. Ten was surprised and pleased that Chisholm had come. Priscilla was asleep, or pretending to be, and Chisholm waited patiently.

"Priscilla," said Ten, "you have company."

Grasping the iron headboard, she rolled over to face them. There was only the ghost of her old smile, and Chisholm was shocked at how frail and wasted she had become. After the first few words of greeting, there wasn't any conversation. Ten wrung his hands, and Chisholm ended the visit by giving Priscilla the gift he had brought her. She unwrapped the small parcel, and for a moment there was color in her cheeks. But when she removed the lid from the box, she dropped it as though it was hot. It contained a pair of fancy silver spurs. Priscilla covered her haggard face with her hands and wept. Wordlessly, Chisholm left the room, and Ten followed him into the hall.

"I'd hoped they might have a positive effect on her," said Chisholm.

"Nothing helps," said Ten. "She's convinced she'll never walk again, and the doc says she won't, unless she changes her thinking. I've sent for Prudence Edgerton, her grandmother. She answered my telegram and promised to come. I'm expecting her tomorrow."

Jesse Chisholm remained in New Orleans for several days, accompanying Ten to meet the steamboat on which Prudence Edgerton arrived. She surprised them both. While she was elderly, probably past sixty, she was far from feeble. She came ashore carrying her own bag. She was trim, smartly dressed, with silver-gray hair curling to her shoulders. Ten introduced himself and Chisholm, and took her bag.

"I reckon you're tired," said Ten. "I'll find a hack and get you to a hotel."

"Don't bother with the hack, young man, unless you need one. I'm not that far gone. We'll go see Priscilla first, and we'll walk. That'll give you time to tell me what's happened."

She smiled, lessening the severity of her abrupt speech, and she had all her own teeth, Ten decided. She also had Priscilla's gray eyes. A bit more at ease, he told her the story. When he had finished, she spoke.

"This doesn't sound like the Priscilla I know. When

she was little, she spent her summers at our horse ranch in Kentucky. The child was always being thrown, and I feared she was going to kill herself. But she never gave up."

"This is different," said Ten. "She's not thinkin' of herself, but of me. We'd planned to ride to the high country, to start us a ranch, and she feels like she's let me down."

Charlie Two Hats's tally revealed the Lipan Apaches had fifteen hundred longhorns in their canyon holding pen. They would sell what they had and join the gather, riding the brakes and roping as many more cows as they could find.

"Catch cow," said Two Hats, "all same pen."

"Good," said Marty. "Put our cows in the canyon with their gather?"

Charlie Two Hats nodded. It would take an enormous burden off Marty and the outfit, allowing them the freedom to rope wild longhorns without fear of Comanches or outlaws stampeding what they'd already gathered.

"This may be easier than we thought," said Marty. "With the Lipans out there in the brakes with us, and our gather goin' in their canyon, I reckon we can spend a day in town."

Following his return from St. Louis, Ten had paid Charlie Two Hats and his riders for the first trail drive. Marty had no idea what Indians might do in town, with money in their pockets, so he laid a warning on Two Hats.

"No whiskey, Charlie. *Comprender?* No firewater."

"Comprender," said Two Hats. *"Malo."*

It was good advice, as far as it went. Marty, as he was to discover, should had prohibited gambling along with the whiskey.

When Ten, Jesse Chisholm, and Prudence Edgerton reached the hospital, they found Priscilla distraught and angry.

"A man from the newspaper was here," she cried. "They're going to print something about me!"

"Let them," said Ten. "If we don't tell them anything, what can they say, except that you're in the hospital? The doctor won't talk to them."

While the arrival of Prudence Edgerton had some positive effect, there was no real change in Priscilla. The New Orleans papers speculated in print as to the reason for her continued stay in the hospital, and Ten finally pulled his Colt on a reporter who persisted in hounding him. But there was much interest in Priscilla because of André LeBeau's confessed ties to Jason Brawn. While Brawn had been arrested, he had hired the nation's best attorneys and had posted bond. He would soon be going to trial.

Jesse Chisholm left for Indian Territory on the first of February. His last visit to Priscilla accomplished no more than had the first. Prudence Edgerton took a hotel room, while Ten remained in the private room adjoining Priscilla's room at the hospital. It seemed the grandmother's presence had accomplished little.

"Ma'am," said Ten, "I'm sorry I brought you all this way for nothing, but I thought—"

"You thought it would help her," said Prudence Edgerton, "and I'd never have forgiven you if you hadn't sent me that telegram. Now stop calling me ma'am. I'm Prudence."

"All right," he said, "Prudence it is." Despite their predicament, he grinned at the peppery woman.

"I've run the doctors ragged," said Prudence, "and I'm satisfied there's nothing more they can do. Dr. Bannister says she needs something strong, a shock, to jolt her out of that state she's in. He says she'll walk again only if something cuts her to the quick, touching her heart and mind in such a way that she forgets this affliction."

"But what?" Ten cried. "What's it going to take?"

"Give her another week," said Prudence, "until Jason Brawn's trial ends. Priscilla's in for the shock of her life, and perhaps you will be too."

It was near sundown Saturday evening when Marty led the outfit into San Antone. They rode past the ruins of the Alamo, the famed old mission where 180 valiant men had stood off Santa Ana and the Mexican army for thirteen days. They reined up before the little hotel where Marty, Wes, Chris, and Lou had stayed before.

"Charlie," said Marty, "this is where we'll be if you need us. Now the rest of you can stay where you like, or sleep in the brush. We're goin' in and have ourselves a bath before we do anything else."

Two Hats and his riders went clattering away. The little hotel had but one bathtub, and it took a while for each of them to have a turn at it. Afterward, they found a restaurant and had supper.

"This bein' Saturday night," said Marty, "the barbershop ought to still be open. Me and Wes is needin' our ears lowered."

"Then walk us back to the hotel," said Chris.

They had to wait their turn, and were an hour getting out of the barbershop. Marty eyed the Mexican barber with misgivings, but didn't say anything until they'd left the shop.

"Makes me almighty nervous, havin' a Mex standin' over me with a straight razor, after the whippin' we give 'em at San Jacinto."

They passed the Alamo Saloon, and found four of their horses tied at the hitch rail.

"Them damn Injuns," said Marty. "I'd better not find 'em bellied up to the bar. Come on, let's see what they're doin' in there."

Cactus, Crowspeak, Sashavado, and Tejano would have been far safer at the bar. Instead, they sat around a poker table whose fifth occupant had the look of a professional gambler and killer. He wore a solid black coat, a white boiled shirt, and a flowing black string tie. His face was thin, his ears large, and his brushy black moustache curled up on the ends. A high silk hat was perched on his head, tilted rakishly over his left eye. He might have been an undertaker, and as Marty and Wes were to learn, it was a look that suited his reputation. Smoke shrouded the room like a fog, and the lamps that hung from the ceiling were barely visible. Marty and Wes moved closer. Tejano was shuffling the cards when the little man in the silk hat twisted around in his chair and spoke to a young man standing behind him. His voice was cold, deadly.

"Friend, I don't take kindly to strangers comin' up behind me, puttin' their hands on me. Now, vamoose."

"I'm with the newspaper," said the young man persistently. "Is it true that you're Ben Thompson, that you're going to Mexico to join the army of Emperor Maximilian?"

Before the unfortunate newspaperman knew what was happening, he found himself hoisted up on his toes, a fistful of his shirt in Thompson's left hand. The Colt in Thompson's right was cocked and ready, its muzzle under the very nose of the inquisitive young man.

"I *said* vamoose," Thompson snarled. With a violent shove, he sent the unfortunate young man sprawling to the sawdust floor. Thompson turned back to the poker table, the Colt disappeared, and the gambler took his seat. He ignored the cards Tejano had dealt him, and when he spoke, it was loud enough for everybody to hear.

"I don't like the way you deal, chief."

When Thompson kicked back his chair, Marty shot out the lamp that hung almost directly over the poker table. His second and third shots took out two more lamps, with a shower of oil and a tinkle of glass. Somebody in the rear of the saloon got into the spirit of things and shot out the rest of the lamps. Marty and Wes began fighting their way toward the door. There was the sodden thud of fists, shouts, curses, the tinkling of breaking glass, and a resounding, jangling crash that could only be the big mirror behind the bar. Being afoot, Marty and Wes lost themselves in the shadows. Looking back, they saw riders galloping away into the night.

"My God," breathed Wes, "just who is Ben Thompson, anyhow?"

"There's not a colder-blooded killer west of the Mississippi," said Marty. "In New Orleans he once challenged another man to a knife fight. They fought in a darkened room, with the door locked."

February 1, 1867. Ten sat in a chair next to Priscilla's bed while she stared at the ceiling, saying nothing. It was Sunday night, and the lamp had been lighted on the nightstand. Rain rattled against the small window next to Priscilla's bed. Jason Brawn's trial would begin in the morning, and the newspapers continued to print gossip, going so far as to resurrect old stories wherein Brawn had courted Priscilla. Ten kept the papers from her; things were bad enough. He wondered at Prudence Edgerton's keen interest in the trial of Jason Brawn. She had delayed her return to Louisville for a week, and Ten had agreed to accompany her to the courthouse until the trial was over. He had a sickening feeling Jason Brawn would wriggle off the hook and go free. The defense attorneys had been talking to the press, making no secret of their strategy. André LeBeau had been into Jason Brawn for more than fifty thousand dollars in gambling debts, and when he had tried to collect, LeBeau hadn't been able to pay. LeBeau had been a vindictive man, and before taking his own life, had framed Jason Brawn with a bogus confession. There wasn't a single witness against Brawn, the defense lawyers crowed. LeBeau was to be branded as the culprit behind the smuggling and black-marketing activities the government was attempting to pin on Jason Brawn.

* * *

Ten and Prudence reached the Federal courthouse an hour before Brawn's trial was to begin, and then almost didn't get a seat. When Brawn entered the courtroom with his attorneys, he was smiling as though he hadn't a care in the world.

"Look at him," Ten growled. "He's got it all bought and paid for."

"Maybe not," said Prudence. "It's not over yet."

For three days the prosecution dragged through the dismal reading of John Mathewson's files and LeBeau's final twelve-page letter. On the fourth day, the judge cleared his throat.

"Will there be any witnesses for the prosecution?"

"Yes, Your Honor," said the Federal prosecutor. "The prosecution calls John Mathewson to the stand."

To Marty's surprise, there was no trouble as a result of the saloon brawl. Union troops occupied San Antonio, of course, but he suspected they wouldn't become unduly upset, as long as Texans were fighting Texans. If the soldiers involved themselves in every Saturday night saloon fight, they'd soon have time for little else. When the four Indian riders showed up Sunday afternoon, they were the envy of their comrades. Sashavado's left eye was swollen shut, and their cut and bruised faces were ample proof of the conflict. They knew they were in for it, and Marty didn't disappoint them.

"Pay attention, you slick-dealin' jaybirds," he said sternly. "From now on, when you sit in a poker game, keep it honest. I don't care how much you cheat one another, but next time you cold-deck a snake-mean killer like Ben Thompson, I'll back off and let him shoot your gizzards full of lead."

Their gather, even with the help of the Lipan Apaches, went more slowly than expected. Each day they rode farther south, and the herd grew not nearly as rapidly as they had hoped.

* * *

There was pandemonium in the courtroom when John Mathewson stepped out of the judge's chambers to the left of the bench.

"Order!" the judge shouted. "Order, or I'll clear the courtroom!"

Mathewson had brought with him additional evidence against Jason Brawn, but it soon became obvious the Federal prosecutor had something more serious in mind.

"Mr. Mathewson," said the prosecutor, "last September second, you were ambushed on the docks by several armed men. Did you recognize those men?"

"I did," said Mathewson. "A pair of Jason Brawn's hired killers."

"I object," Brawn's lawyer shouted.

"Mr. Prosecutor," the judge cut in, "are you prepared to prove that accusation?"

"We are, Your Honor," said the prosecuting attorney. "These men should already be in custody."

"Objection overruled," said the judge. "Let us dispense with this one question at a time by the prosecution. Mr. Mathewson, please explain to the court how and why this took place, and your role in it."

"This is highly irregular," shouted Brawn's lawyer. "I object."

"Objection overruled," said the judge. "Go ahead, Mr. Mathewson."

"Black-marketing and smuggling ran rampant during the recent war," said Mathewson, "and Jason Brawn was the only man powerful enough and rich enough to handle it. He played on LeBeau's weakness for gambling because he needed somebody to take a fall. Trouble was, I saw LeBeau for the puppet he was, and began using him to get to Brawn. That's when Brawn decided to get rid of me. When I found his killers were stalking me, awaiting their chance, I gave it to them. When I returned from a trip to Washington, I made known the time of my arrival, and purposely took a boat that arrived after dark. There were government agents trailing the would-be killers who trailed me. I purposely let them make their play on the docks, so I could disappear into the river. I was picked up by an unmarked, unlighted government packet, and I've been under cover in St. Louis until now."

"Phenomenal story," said the judge. "Mr. Prosecutor, have you anything to add?"

"Yes, Your Honor," said the prosecutor. "I expect these two would-be killers will sing like mockingbirds. In view of that, the prosecution will be filing charges of attempted murder against Mr. Brawn."

"Your Honor," bawled Brawn's lawyer, "we request a recess until nine o'clock tomorrow morning, to study this, ah . . . new development."

"Does the prosecution have any objection?" the judge asked.

"None, Your Honor," said the prosecutor.

"Under the circumstances," said the judge, "bailiff will take the defendent into custody. Court is recessed until nine o'clock in the morning."

Newspapermen and friends literally mobbed John Mathewson.

"Come on," said Prudence. "We'll have our turn with him. First, we're going to see someone else."

Emily, Priscilla's mother, had stepped out of the judge's chambers and stood there uncertainly. She wore a long dark dress, and her hair, even with some gray, reminded Ten of Priscilla's. Ten was uncomfortable, not knowing how to greet her. She ignored his outstretched hand and threw her arms around him. When she backed away, there were tears on her cheeks, and her first words were almost a whisper.

"How . . . is she? How is Priscilla?"

"Not good, ma'am," said Ten. "She doesn't believe she can walk, and she won't try."

"Oh, I've wanted to go to her," cried Emily, "but I wanted John with me, and he couldn't reveal himself until after his testimony."

Ten felt a hand on his shoulder, and he turned to face a grinning John Mathewson.

"I've blessed the day I sent you to save Priscilla," he said, "and cursed myself a thousand times for leaving you to face all the dragons alone. But we had to convince Brawn he was rid of me, and give LeBeau time to break."

"You did what you had to do," Ten said, "and I don't think anything less would have worked. I'd go through it all again for Priscilla, but now she's needin' help beyond what I can give."

"We have a surprise for her," said Mathewson. "The day after Emily became a widow, she and I were married in St. Louis."

"I'm glad for both of you," Ten said, "but I doubt it will be enough of a shock to help Priscilla."

"There's more," said Prudence. "Let's go shock that girl out of her sickbed."

When they reached the hospital, Ten, Mathewson, and Prudence remained in the hall, allowing Emily to enter the room alone. She paused in the doorway, and at first Priscilla could say nothing. When she spoke, it was with a sob.

"Mother?"

Emily dropped to her knees beside the bed, and there were no words, only tears. Finally Emily got to her feet, drying her eyes on a white linen handkerchief.

"Priscilla," she said, "I—There's someone I . . . want you to meet."

She went to the door and John Mathewson accompanied her into the room. Priscilla looked at him uncertainly, never having met him.

"Priscilla," said Emily, "this is John. John Mathewson. He and I were married in St. Louis."

Priscilla's face went white. She almost fell out of the bed, using the bed post to pull herself shakily to her feet. John Mathewson had backed away, leaving Emily and Priscilla face-to-face.

"All these years," cried Priscilla, "you've lived a lie,

taking a lover but keeping the LeBeau name. He was no good, but he *was* my father."

"Priscilla," Emily cried, "André LeBeau was no more a father to you than he was husband to me. Your real father is John Mathewson!"

33

For the next week, John Mathewson spent at least an hour a day with Priscilla. Nobody knew what they talked about, but Priscilla's cheeks began to fill out, her appetite improved, and she began to walk. The day Priscilla left the hospital, they celebrated with a gala supper in one of the fanciest hotel dining rooms. Priscilla sat between John and Emily, while Prudence and Ten sat on the other side of the table.

"It's time I was going home," said Prudence. "Is there any reason the four of you can't go with me? Ten and Priscilla already owe me a visit, so why don't we just make it a family affair?"

"I'd like that," Priscilla said. "The rest of our outfit is in Texas, gathering another herd of longhorns. I think I'm going to write them a letter, in care of Captain Fanning, at Fort Worth. I'm going to ask them to finish this gather and take the herd on to Abilene. Me and Ten can meet them there. We can take a steamboat from Louisville to St. Louis, and from there to Kansas City, and ride the train on to Abilene."

"Why is it so important you be in Abilene?" Prudence asked. Her eyes were on Ten, but he nodded to Priscilla, and she continued.

"Because we're going from there back to Texas," said Priscilla, "and this time, we'll be buying mostly breeding stock. Ten and I are looking forward to that. I'll never forget those first few days in New Orleans, when he promised I'd ride alongside him into the high country, when I was convinced I'd never walk again. He believed in me when I didn't believe in myself, and if I never do anything else, I'm riding with him to the high plains."

"You have the spirit of a pioneer," said Prudence. "Your grandfather would be proud of you, just as I am. When must you be in Abilene?"

"It depends on how long it takes our outfit to gather a herd and drive it there," said Priscilla. "If they're able to buy the cows, they can trail-brand them and probably reach Abilene sometime in August or early September. But if they're having to rope them out of the brush, it'll take them longer to get the herd together."

"Well, let them manage without you as far as Abilene," said Prudence, "and the two of you go home with me. John and Emily, is there any reason the two of you can't come along?"

"No," said Mathewson, "but I'll have to return to New Orleans sometime in October, for Brawn's trial for attempted murder. The first of the year, I'm taking a government job in St. Louis, and Emily and I will be living there."

The day before the five of them were to depart for Louisville, there was a letter from Marty. It was five pages long, and Priscilla read it aloud. It was dated February 1, 1867, and went into some detail. Marty had overlooked nothing.

"Thank God he didn't send a telegram," said Priscilla. "We'd be broke. At least we know we can send them a letter to San Antonio."

"That was a smart move," Ten said, "getting the help of the Lipan Apaches. I've been some worried about our bunch, there in the brakes, especially when I think of what that last Comanche raid almost cost us. I reckon we got us a *muy bueno* outfit, and I'm goin' to let them finish the gather and take the herd on to Abilene. Send Marty an answer, give him the Louisville address, and have him telegraph us when the herd reaches Fort Worth. From that, we can figure and know just about when they'll be in Abilene."

The letter Marty received from Priscilla was as long as the one he had written Ten. Marty gathered them all around the supper fire and read them the letter. They could feel her pride as she told them her natural father, John Mathewson, was alive and well.

"I'm so happy for her," said Chris. "When she would look at Ten's daddy, I could see the hurt in her eyes. Now she has a father of her own that she can be proud of."

"She deserves a man like Ten," Marty said, "because she's got as much sand as he has. They're trustin' us to make this gather and finish the trail drive, and I aim for us to show up in Abilene with bells on."

"They're not pushing us," said Lou, "and since the time is being left up to us, let's hang on here until we get at least as big a herd as last time."

"I aim to," said Marty. "We couldn't ask for better, with these Lipans working the gather. All we have to worry about is the Comanches on the drive north, and maybe a bunch of outlaws."

"Kill dead lak hell," said Charlie Two Hats.

It was the happiest, most restful time of Ten's life, taking the long steamboat ride to Louisville. John and Emily were delightful companions, and so was Prudence Edgerton. Ten was at ease where the outfit was concerned, thankful for partners like Wes and Marty. The bad times in New Orleans were behind them, he had Priscilla well and happy, and the days ahead would be a time to remember. They had just left Cairo, Illinois, when Ten remembered something.

"When you were hurt," he told Priscilla, "I was so rattled, I forgot to write or telegraph Jess. He was there only because Harvey Roberts remembered to send him a telegram. Once we get to Louisville, will you send him

about the same kind of letter you sent Marty? He's goin'
to think I forgot how to write."

"No," said Priscilla, a twinkle in her gray eyes, "he's
going to be impressed with how thoughtful you are. I
mailed him a letter the day I sent Marty's, telling him all
that's happened, and I gave him the Louisville address."

"All that," said Ten admiringly, "and you're beautiful
too."

By July 1, 1867, Marty did a rough tally and found
they had 7500 longhorns, including what the Indians
had captured before Marty and the outfit had arrived.

"We'll be here until September, at least," said Marty,
"if we shoot for ten thousand head."

"Let's get 'em," said Wes.

Already they were twenty-five miles south of the
Lipan village. There were few longhorns any closer.
They were in the saddle sixteen hours a day, often drag-
ging their day's gather to a holding pen in darkness.

It was a wonderful visit for Ten, Priscilla, John, and
Emily. Prudence was an excellent hostess, and despite
the death of her husband, she still kept a decent stable
of horses. Ten and Priscilla took to riding every day,
keeping in shape for the long ride to the high country.

"But for you," Ten told Priscilla, "I probably wouldn't
have come here. Now I'm going to hate to leave."

"I'll remember that," said Priscilla. "However much I
like the high plains, I'll still want to come here. Grandmother thinks she's going to live forever, but one day
she'll be gone, and so will this."

September 3, 1867, Marty gave the order.

"Move 'em out!"

The long drive to Abilene had begun, and as usual,
the first few days were a cattleman's idea of Hell. Hard
as they tried, it was impossible to keep the herd
bunched, and they were strung out for miles. Every
longhorn in the herd seemed obsessed with but one de-

sire: to return to the chaparral from which they'd been unwillingly taken. Their final tally had been 10,013 head. By the end of the third day on the trail, Lou expressed an opinion they all shared.

"Thirteen is an unlucky number. We should have caught one more cow, or turned one loose."

Four days out of San Antone they were hit by an afternoon storm, and despite all their efforts, the longhorns stampeded, running south. They lost two days, rounding them up, and were still shy twenty-five of the brutes.

"We'll count them as lost," said Marty, "and move on."

There were two more time-consuming stampedes before they reached Fort Worth. From there Marty sent the telegram Ten had requested, and on September 27, 1867, they left the fort, heading north. Without incident or delay, they crossed the Red, taking the Chisholm Trail and moving into Indian Territory.

Ten and Priscilla left Louisville on October 15. They left the Ohio at Cairo, Illinois, taking a steamboat north to St. Louis. From there they went by steamboat to Kansas City and took the train to Abilene. They were thoroughly shocked at the way the little town had mushroomed. There was the big, new hotel Joe McCoy had promised, a railroad depot, and a seemingly endless string of cattle pens that stretched out along the railroad track. In the office building McCoy had built, there were numerous little offices that had been assigned to various cattle buyers.

"Twenty-one dollars a head," one of the buyers quoted Ten.

Despite McCoy's widespread advertising, Abilene's first year promised to be a lean one. So far there had been only three or four herds.

October 17, 1867. Ten saw the dust far to the south. Abilene had added a livery to its blacksmith shop, and

Ten got a horse for himself and one for Priscilla. The first rider they saw was Charlie Two Hats, at point, and Two Hats cut loose with a whoop that startled some of the longhorns in the front ranks. Then Marty, Wes, Chris, and Lou discovered them, and there was a glad reunion.

With buyers on hand, they moved the longhorns directly into the cattle pens. McCoy's barn stood ready, abundantly stocked to accommodate the expected herds. They sold at $21.50, splitting the herd among three buyers. Their final tally was 9875 head.

"Dear God," shouted Chris, "we're rich!"

"Let's go to St. Louis again," said Lou, "and buy for Christmas. We have the time, if we're not going to Texas again until the spring."

Jubilant over their success, Ten agreed. He paid Charlie Two Hats and his riders, giving every man a fifty-dollar bonus. He then instructed them to take the horse remuda and the pack mules and return to the Chisholm trading post.

When they reached St. Louis, they checked into the same hotel in which they'd stayed before. Ten, Marty, and Wes went immediately to the bank and deposited their money. Despite their eagerness to reach St. Louis, they were soon tired of it. On the first of December they took a steamboat to Natchez, and there boarded another for Fort Smith.

Reaching the Chisholm trading post, Ten and his friends found Jesse Chisholm weak and sick. From the Cherokees attending him, Ten found the old man had been seriously ill during the summer.

"Jess," Ten said, "why didn't you send me word? You knew where I was."

"It wouldn't have served any good purpose," said Chisholm. "You've had your troubles, and I wanted you and Priscilla to have some time together, without any worry hanging over your heads."

Despite the gifts, the good food, and that they were

all together, it was a gloomy Christmas, nothing like the one of the year before. Chisholm just couldn't seem to regain his strength.

By late February, warm spring winds were caressing the cottonwoods, elm, and blackjack, and new leaves were beginning to bud. The greening meadows along the North Canadian were dotted with Indian lodges, as the plains tribes came together for tribal rituals and to trade for the white man's goods. It had become an annual event, and despite Jesse Chisholm's poor health, he insisted on being there. How else could he get the best of the season's furs and robes? It was a balmy day, April 4, and a friendly Indian woman offered Chisholm a meal of bear grease and honey. It was an Indian favorite, and Chisholm ate directly from a small brass kettle. But the metal pot had poisoned the grease, and it was Jesse Chisholm's final meal.

When word came, they were stunned. The Cherokee women began to wail, and when the shock wore off, Priscilla, Chris, and Lou joined them. But there was much to be done. Chisholm was to be buried beside the North Canadian, with all tribal honors. Burial would take place on the morning of the fifth of April.

There was only the creaking of the wagon that bore the blanket-wrapped body of Jesse Chisholm. That, and the mournful death song of old Ten Bears, a Comanche chief and longtime friend of Chisholm. The funeral procession stretched for more than a mile, as the plains tribes came to pay their respects to the only white man many of them had ever trusted. When the procession halted, some of Chisholm's Cherokees carried the blanket-wrapped body to the open grave. The body was unwrapped, and the mourners walked slowly past, taking their last look. Ten Bears sat at the head of the grave until everybody else had gone. The old chief had been given a gold peace medal by Abraham Lincoln. Ten

Bears wore the medal around his neck, on a leather thong. Now he removed the medal and, kneeling beside the body, slipped the leather thong over Chisholm's head. He then placed the medal on Chisholm's chest. When he stepped back, the body was again wrapped with the blanket, and then with a buffalo hide. When it had been lowered into the ground, dirt was shoveled into the hole and mounded. The grave was then covered with rocks. Finally a headboard was put in place, with Jesse's name and date of death.

Ten waited until all the Indian mourners had departed. Marty, Wes, Lou, and Chris stood a respectable distance from the grave, waiting. They sensed Ten's reluctance to leave. While he had shed no tears, they knew he was hurting. Priscilla stood beside him, tears streaking her cheeks. Ten took her hand, and she followed him to the grave. For a long time he said not a word, and when he finally spoke, his voice trembled.

"I was proud of you, Jess. I hope you knew. *Vaya con dios, muy bueno companero.*"

Their last day at the Chisholm trading post was a sad one.

"He's a man that won't be replaced," said Marty. "What's going to happen to all this, now that he's gone?"

"I don't know," said Ten.

"Maybe there's a will," said Chris. "Perhaps he left it to you."

"No," said Ten, "he wouldn't have done that. There are some who would have expected me to fill his shoes, or try to, and I couldn't. He always allowed me to be my own man, to sink or swim. He never tried to force me to live in his shadow while he was alive, so he wouldn't do it in death."

"Then we're still going to Texas for breeding stock," said Wes.

"We are," said Ten, "and from there to the high plains."

*   *   *

April 7, 1868, they rode away from the Chisholm
trading post for the last time. Ten and Priscilla led out,
followed by Marty and Chris, and Wes and Lou. Charlie
Two Hats and his Cherokee riders followed, leading the
pack mules. From Texas they would ride to the high
country, to the mountains of Colorado, Wyoming, Montana, and perhaps beyond. To whatever destiny awaited
them.

EPILOGUE

*J*esse Chisholm's grave is on the north bank of the North Canadian River, near the present-day town of Geary, Oklahoma.

The old "LeBeau" mansion was built in the mid nineteenth century, in the Garden District of New Orleans, and is still in existence.

The Lipan Apaches take their name from Chief Lipan, who defied the Comanches, establishing a village on the Medina River, south of San Antonio. The Texas Rangers found the Lipans invaluable as scouts, and they are due some of the credit for Texas' eventual conquering of the Comanches.

William Preston ("Wild Bill") Longley, was born in Austin County, Texas, on October 6, 1851. He killed his first man at sixteen, and by the time he was seventeen, he was riding with the infamous Cullen Baker. At the time of his death, Longley had killed thirty-two men. He was hanged at Giddings, Texas, on October 11, 1878.

Ben Thompson was born in 1843, of English parents. When he was only thirteen, he shot and wounded a friend. In New Orleans he killed a Frenchman in a knife duel, the two of them fighting in a locked, darkened icehouse. Thompson joined the Confederate army, and later went to Mexico to join the Mexican army, under Emperor Maximilian. When Maximilian was executed in June 1867, Thompson returned to Texas, where he continued gambling and killing. When sober, Thompson was a kindly, soft-spoken gentleman. When drunk, he was arrogant, poison-mean, and deadly. He killed twenty-five men, and was himself shot to death in an ambush in San Antonio, Texas, March 10, 1884.

Abilene was the first of the cattle towns, and its success was due almost exclusively to the efforts of Joseph McCoy. In 1867 only 35,000 Texas longhorns were trailed to Abilene; in 1869 there were 300,000; and in 1871 there were 700,000.

Lorenzo Esteban Valverde rode south, his thin lips
set in a grim line. He was a small man in every sense,
standing but an inch over five feet. His high-heeled riding boots didn't add enough to his short stature to make
any difference. He was barely forty years old, yet his
hair had begun to thin on top, and he rarely removed
his hat unless circumstances demanded it. He had the
thin face and the furtive eyes of a weasel. His mother
had died while he was young, leaving him at the mercy
of a less-than-tolerant father. When the elder Valverde
had died, his only son had felt no remorse. Finally, if
only by inheritance, he had become the *patrono*.

Suddenly, Esteban Valverde was jolted back to reality
by the nicker of a horse. He reined up. Angelina Ruiz
trotted her horse out of a stand of scrub oak. She wore
pants and faded shirt, riding astraddle, like a man. She
reined up, hooked one leg around her saddle horn, staring at him silently. He could read nothing in her dark
eyes, unless it was contempt. He rode on, thinking of
Angelina. She was a good ten years younger than her
sister, possessing an innocence that Victoria would
never see again. If, indeed, she ever had. Angelina was
but a snip of a girl, but there were times when she
seemed older, wiser, and more the woman than Victoria. When Clay Duval had disappeared, it had been Angelina who had gone looking for him. When it suited his

purpose, he decided, he would tell the girl what had become of the foolish Tejano. Drawing near the ranch, he put Angelina out of his mind. He had little choice. Victoria waited for him on the porch, and there was no welcome in her eyes. When he was close enough to hear, she spoke.

"Turn that horse around, Señor Valverde, and get off my range. You are not welcome here."

"I was welcome enough," he sneered, "when your sainted Antonio was haunting the bordellos of Mexico City."

"You were not man enough to steal me from him, so you had him shot in the back. You're a treacherous little beast."

"You are far short of the Blessed Virgin yourself," he snapped. "Your husband was not dead a month, and you were sleeping with a gringo, a Tejano."

"He was more a man than you and Antonio combined," she said, "because I am expecting his child. You killed Clay Duval, didn't you?"

"Would it matter, if I said I did not?"

"It wouldn't to me," she said bitterly. "I wouldn't believe you as far as I could walk on water. But it might make a difference to his friends. They are here to gather cattle, and if you had anything to do with the murder of their friend Clay Duval, I pity you."

"That's why I am here," he said. "Because of Duval's Tejano friends. Through your dealing with them, you are risking the ire of the Mexican government, and the gringos are risking their lives. They must leave Mexico while they can. If they can."

"I'll let you convince them of that," said Victoria. "They're coming."

Gil and Van trotted their horses into the yard. They only nodded to Victoria. Their eyes were on Valverde. It was Victoria who spoke.

"Gil and Van, this is Señor Lorenzo Esteban Valverde. Señor Valverde, this is Gil and Van Austin. The Señor Valverde brought a message, and since it concerns you Tejanos, I will allow him to deliver it himself."

The Texans eyed Valverde in silence. His saddle was silver-studded, as was his pistol belt. He wore a dark suit, white shirt, a flaming red tie, and highly polished riding boots. Ill at ease, he back-stepped his horse until he faced the Texans. Then he spoke.

"I am suggesting that you leave Mexico immediately, for Victoria's sake, and for your own. The Mexican authorities will be harsh on her, if she is caught harboring Tejanos."

Gil kneed his horse uncomfortably close, and as he spoke, looked the Mexican in the eye.

"You're hidin' behind a woman's skirts, Valverde, and threatening us with the Mexican army. Why don't you stand up on your hind legs and say what you really mean? That any man gettin' too close to Victoria risks bein' shot in the back by you, or one of your hired gun hawks?"

It was the kind of deliberate insult a man couldn't ignore. Esteban Valverde went for his gun, but the weapon never left his holster. He hadn't seen Gil Austin's hand move, yet he found himself looking into the black bore of the Texan's Colt. Cold sweat beaded Valverde's brow, and he moved his hand carefully away from the butt of his gun. He seethed with shame and fury, for he owed Gil Austin his life. The Texan could have shot him dead. Briefly his eyes touched Victoria's, and he could see the laughter in them. Damn her, she knew what this was costing him! It was Gil Austin who broke the silence.

"You came here with a warning for us, Valverde. Now I'm going to send you home with one of your own. We came to Mexico, lookin' for Clay Duval. Whether we find him or not, we aim to get somethin' out of the trip. We'll be taking a herd of longhorns back to Texas, and our business here is no business of yours. We're not in the line of march for Santa Anna's troop movements, so the Mexican army shouldn't be a problem until we're near the border. If soldiers show up here, we'll know who sent them: *you*, Valverde—and before I leave Mexico, I'll personally gut-shoot you."

"You are dead men," said Valverde, with as much comtempt as he could muster. "Driving a herd of longhorn cows through the wilds of Mexico is the work of a dozen good riders."

"I have promised them the loan of my riders as far as the border," said Victoria.

"You are *still* dead men," said Valverde, with obvious relish. . . .

The Bandera Trail—Look for it soon from St. Martin's Paperbacks!